I0763270

LAST RIDE
AT ELYSIAN PARK

JONATHAN MURNANE

Copyright © 2026 Jonathan Murnane
All rights reserved. No part of this book may be reproduced or used in any manner without the prior written permission of the copyright owner, except for the use of brief quotations in a book review.

To request permissions, contact the publisher at info@excellentawkward.com

Hardcover: 979-8-9947427-0-9
Paperback: 979-8-9947427-1-6
Audiobook: 979-8-9947427-2-3
Ebook: 979-8-9947427-3-0

First paperback edition: February 2026

This is a work of fiction. Names, characters, businesses, places, events, and incidents are either the products of the author's imagination or used in a fictitious manner. Any resemblance to actual persons, living or dead, or actual events is purely coincidental.

Content Warning: While the story and characters are a product of the author's imagination, the book explores themes of abuse, trauma, suicidal ideation, emotional manipulation, drug abuse, violence and other difficult subjects. These themes may be triggering for some readers. Reader discretion is advised. If you or someone you know is affected by similar issues, please seek support from a trusted professional or helpline.

Cover art by CJ Whitlock

Printed by Ingram Global

excellentawkward.com jonathanmurnane.com

For Brianna, Mandy, Linda

and all those gone too soon.

Halloween 1992 (well, technically the first morning of November)

"There's a body," the voice said nervously, rushed and spastic. "At the party. Elysian Park. One of the kids, from the party, they fell. Or jumped. I don't fucking know. I think they're dead. Oh god, they're dead. What the hell, man, you know?"

"Just take a deep breath. And can I get your name?

"What do you need my name for? I don't know them. I don't know anything. I just… I saw it. I saw the body."

"We just need your name for documentation."

"Jesus H. Tapdancing Christ, I'm telling you, I have nothing to do with this. Just get someone out there. They're dead. I know they're dead."

They hung up.

The dispatch operator had already sent emergency services to the area, but it was too late before the call was even made.

1. ABBY

Abby always thought she'd get used to the cold. That eye-drying, snot-freezing cold that Omaha winters delivered was one of her least favorite things about growing up in Nebraska. And she didn't like anything about growing up in Nebraska. It wasn't even winter yet, not officially. It wasn't even Halloween. The week before she had been wearing shorts outside, but now the wind was harsh and piercing and her car was covered in thick frost. The first snow of the season hadn't hit yet but the windchill was already nearing zero. She blasted the heat in her car, and used the large plastic scraper to make a decent-sized hole for her to see through.

It was seven in the morning, and she had to get to school. For some stupid reason.

As the engine chugged, she had a flash. It was that day, the dark day. It was a different car entirely but the engine whirred just the same. She shook it from her mind and turned the radio up. Noise made it easier to put it out of her mind. She could just zone out.

She dressed in layers. The uniform for St. Dymphna (the kids just called it "Dymps") required a blue plaid skirt for freshman and sophomores (upper classmen wore gray plaid), and as she was technically a sophomore (her second time), she was stuck with the blue, but she wore thick leggings underneath. She had the requisite white, collared shirt and gray uniform sweater. Only uniform sweaters were allowed. Nothing could possibly be in style or look flattering in any way. For most of the students this was a source of frustration, but Abby could at least appreciate the ability to fade in the background. Being noticed was way overrated.

Over her sweater she had a hooded sweatshirt she stole from her stepbrother and her winter coat that went down to her knees. A stocking hat was pulled tight against her frizzy, wavy, brown hair and made her glasses tight on her head.

And still she was shivering.

Boyz II Men were crooning through the speakers, but she was tired of "End of the Road," so she flipped to another station, which was playing another Boyz II Men song. She turned the radio off and tried to remember the equations that were going to be on her math test, but her brain wouldn't let her. Instead, it told her she was an idiot for not remembering, she was sure to fail, and she probably deserved to fail, because she clearly wasn't as smart as the other kids in her class.

It was like this every morning. Not so much the Boyz II Men part, but the self-doubt and defeatist attitude was pretty common. She hated going to that school. She hated the uniforms. She hated the other students. She hated the teachers. And yet, it was better than the alternative. Her freshman year (and the first time she was a sophomore) she was at Aksarben Central High, AC High for short (lots of things were called Aksarben in Omaha, which was just Nebraska spelled backwards. It was stupid. Abby wondered if

Miami had a lot of Adirolf named things.).

It was so close, AC High, she could still see it every morning, as it loomed on the hill on the other side of Dymps' football field. That was a whole other circle of hell and after the, um, incident, she was happy to put her AC career behind her.

Dymps was supposed to offer her a chance to reinvent herself. New school, new friends. But the student body was not welcoming of a new sophomore, especially not when they heard about what happened at AC. And it didn't take long for rumors to spread. The schools were too close to each other, and teenagers have an extensive and exhaustive network. Abby had only been at her new school two weeks before she heard the whispers in the bathroom, felt the snotty looks as she walked down the hall, if anyone bothered to look in her direction at all. It was only October and she wanted to try again, maybe something a little further away this time, but didn't want to have that conversation with her mom once more.

Abby made it to school in less than ten minutes, thanks to some well-timed lights and a complete lack of enthusiasm for suggested speed limits. She parked in the first spot she could find. She slung her backpack over her shoulder, but it wasn't big enough to carry all of the books she took home, so she clutched Biology Companion Labs and a notebook in her hands as she darted off to homeroom. As she neared the front steps, she didn't notice a small patch of ice and slipped, completely tumbling forward on the ground. Her knee smashed into the curb and her books went flying forward. She winced in pain, even shouted "fuck" to alert anyone that hadn't seen it, but when she heard laughter of other students nearby, she quickly got back on her feet. Her leggings were torn and she could feel the blood dribbling down her leg, but she grabbed her backpack and looked for the books she dropped.

"You all right? This yours?" she heard a voice say as she looked up and saw a boy standing there with her math book.

It was Percy Van Allen. A senior.

And he spoke directly to her.

He had sensitive eyes and a soft smile. His perfect blond hair was parted on the left and swooped just above his eyes. He exuded charm and class, which wasn't surprising since he had been born into one of the richest families in town, much less the school. Percy's father was the infamous Harlan Van Allen, a local businessman who seemed to have stakes in every big venture around the city. There was going to be a building named after him. Or a bridge, something like that. Abby couldn't remember exactly what, in that moment that his son was smiling at her with his perfect teeth. He probably made it to the dentist every six months like you were supposed to.

Abby was flummoxed. The whole scenario was too fresh, too ludicrous, and too risky, as if everyone was waiting for her to fall on her face again. She wanted to say something, something pithy, full of wit, something to make a senior boy laugh and maybe fall for her, just a little. She wanted to say something that would change the entire conversation about her at St. Dymphna's.

"Like you didn't just fuckin' see me eat shit in front of everyone," she snarled.

That wasn't what she hoped for.

"Did you hit your head?" he asked.

"Just the…um… back of the ego part. Can I have my book?"

She grabbed her book back, offered a quick "thanks" and bounded up the steps away from the scene as quickly as possible. She didn't look back at Percy but heard him mutter "...I don't know, some girl" to someone.

Good. He didn't know her name.

* * * * *

Abby made it through three periods without having to say a word. Sitting in the back of the class and doodling in her notebook generally made her appear busy enough and even slightly engaged. She was rarely called on. Even teachers had their crowd. And it's not like anyone talked to her if they didn't have to.

She had lunch early, which was fine with her as it wasn't as busy as the later periods. Munching on a sandwich at 10:55am didn't feel completely ridiculous.

Dymps didn't have a cafeteria. They had a snacketeria. Rows of machines with microwave-ready meals-burritos, pizza, and the like-and about six microwaves for hundreds of students. Abby just brought her lunch rather than deal with the social circles around the microwaves. The upper-class girls would swarm around, flirting with the boys or judging the younger girls for eating anything with carbs. And waiting for a bean burrito that was always still frozen in the middle no matter how many minutes it was blasted was rather pointless.

She sat by the window. There was a good view of the entire room but she was semi-obstructed by a large column so avoiding detection was easy. She could observe the students in their natural habitat while picking at the skin of her knee, which was now scabbing over. Percy Van Allen was across the room with the other senior jocks. Abby hadn't noticed him in her lunch period before but that was prior to having a face-to-face conversation with him (such as it was). Percy was laughing, a boisterous guttural laugh that echoed throughout the din of the massive lunchroom. He looked so comfortable, and happy. Abby had no idea how to begin to even imagine such a thing.

On the other side of the column from her, and a few meters down, were the large glass doors leading outside. Some students would eat on the porch. Others would take advantage of the free period to go to the Burger King up the street. Only seniors were allowed to leave campus, but it wasn't policed very well. Abby debated on eating lunch in her car but it was way too cold for that.

As she looked over she saw Jake. He was a senior, and one of the biggest assholes she knew. He was tall and lanky, and his St. Dymphna's-issued sweater clung to his chest a little too tightly. He hadn't noticed her, but he went out of his way not to at school. He was alone and moved surreptitiously out the door. Abby knew that Jake didn't have a free period, but it's not like he was a stickler for the rules. She looked back to find Percy but he was no longer with the friends he was just laughing with. Her eyes darted around the room trying to lock onto him again, but when she came up blank she returned to her notebook, annoyed that she had devoted so much time to boys anyway.

* * * * *

Abby always chose the computer in the back left for her study hall. Again, it was the perfect place to hide out and still keep a decent eye on the rest of the room. She hadn't really set out to be the constant observer, but it was a better use of her time and energy than wallowing and internalizing everything. Unfortunately, on this particular day, Bridget Kent was entirely too close to her. Bridget was loud and gregarious. She was popular, effortlessly so, but while she was the envy of the rest of the student body, some of the faculty never quite warmed to her. Abby wondered if it was because Bridget was black (one of only two students in the St. Dymphna junior class, six overall), or was it because they knew what Abby knew: Bridget was a bitch. There really was no other word for it. Bridget thought she was above everybody and she expected everyone to cater to her every whim. Boys would fawn over her for whatever reason. Abby just couldn't stand that fake smile and how everything Bridget said was just dripping with disdain.

Bridget leaned back in her chair and bumped into Abby.

"Watch it, nerd," Bridget spat. Bridget's friends laughed, but Abby just rolled her eyes and returned to her screen. She had been accused of being a lot of things, but a nerd was hardly one of them. Bridget made some comment under her breath to her friends, and it rankled Abby enough to say something.

"You bumped into me," Abby returned.

"Excuse me?"

"You leaned back and-"

"Oh, I'm sorry, I don't give a shit," Bridget smirked, let out a quick laugh and shifted her focus entirely to her friends.

Abby took a deep breath and let it go. It wasn't worth it. She couldn't win. Bridget was friends with everyone, including a large number of seniors. And Abby had no one in her corner. She had her paper on "A Tale of Two Cities" to finish anyway.

"Oh, and nice leggings," Bridget said when she got up to talk to someone at the front of the class. Bridget was a cheerleader and in the requisite garb. She had leggings (not torn, of course) and a turtleneck under her uniform, but her midriff was still exposed, and her flat stomach and innie bellybutton was just out there, winking at all the boys. This was the longest conversation she'd ever had with Bridget, so she wasn't sure why it was so hostile, but Abby had gotten used to that by now.

She glared at Bridget as she leaned on one of the desks, obviously flirting with one of the other boys in class. God, she hated her. Bridget had everything Abby wanted: ample friends, perfect breasts, flawless skin. There was no reason for her to be so mean.

Abby shook her head and looked down. Bridget's backpack was sitting by her chair, completely open and practically spilling out onto the floor. There were a number of books, covered with paper sacks judiciously taped along the edges. In front, she could see a smaller pink notebook.

Abby recognized the journal. Bridget spent a lot of time writing in it during study hall. Page after page of what she imagined were the dumbest thoughts on boys and fashion. Abby looked up and Bridget was still leaning over the desk, her tits at eye level with Timmy O'Neill, surely not an accident. There was no one else in her row so Abby quickly reached down and pulled out the notebook and relocated it into her own bag, all the while keeping her eye on Bridget. She never looked back.

There was no earthly reason why she did it. If she got caught she knew she could even get suspended. Probably a violation of the student code of conduct. But it was right there. And Bridget made Abby's already shitty day just slightly worse. Abby wanted a victory. Even this small one.

Abby kept her eyes on Bridget. Mr. Sutton was grading papers at the front of the class and only occasionally would glance up to keep an eye on things. Abby wanted to tell Mr. Sutton that Bridget was taunting her but he was a young teacher, and even though he was married, he always seemed a little too chummy with the popular girls, and didn't seem to have the same disdain for Bridget the other teachers did. There was no recourse there.

The bell rang and Bridget ran back and grabbed her bag. She zipped it up without even checking the contents. Abby kept an eye on her the whole time.

Bridget caught her looking and cocked her head to one side.

"The bell rang, Abby. Don't kill yourself getting to your next class."

Bridget slung her backpack over her shoulder and walked out while Abby suppressed the urge to leap over the desk and smash her face into the glass window of the door. Though imagining it was comforting.

* * * * *

"She knew what she was saying. Of course, she did," Abby was pacing around the office. It was more comfortable than sitting on the couch.

"And how did that make you feel?" Dr. Gant asked.

"Man, that is really all they teach you in psych school isn't it?"

"I'm going to guess…angry."

"Yes, it made me feel angry. What kind of person throws that in someone's face? That's the reason I didn't go back to AC. I didn't want to deal with everyone being dicks about it, or worse, feeling sorry for me. I just want it to go away."

"But it happened. You can't change that."

"Yeah, I get that. But does it really have to be the only thing people know about me?"

"Have you given anyone a chance to know anything else?"

"And how am I supposed to do that, doc?"

Dr. Gant tried to offer a sympathetic smile.

"No, I'm actually asking," Abby continues. "I don't know how to talk to people. In the best of situations. How am I supposed to make friends now? Especially when everyone has already made up their mind about me."

"Have you thought about joining a club? Or a sport? Those are good ways to meet people and get your mind off of things."

"I'm not really the joining kind."

"Well, I think you need to find something. You need a hobby. A goal. Something to keep you focused and moving in a more positive direction."

"I do have this new book I'm dying to read," Abby scoffed.

She couldn't bring herself to open the journal while she was in school. She didn't want to risk someone seeing her with it. Abby had seen Bridget after last period, while she was heading to practice. She didn't stop and yell at Abby and accuse her of stealing so Abby assumed she hadn't even realized it was gone, which would make denying she had it a bit easier. After school, Abby had rushed over to her mandated psychologist appointment where she usually struggled to think of anything to say, but today she was a bit more chatty.

Abby liked Dr. Gant. He was younger, early thirties maybe. Abby wasn't great with ages. Even though a lot of psychologists act like they understood how shitty it was being a teenager, he actually seemed to get it. But he wasn't skeevy like some of the others. He was the fifth doctor she went to, but the first one she felt comfortable going back to. He was decent looking, not so hot she fantasized about him or anything, but nice enough that she could look at him for an hour while talking about things she never told anyone else.

The hour went by faster than usual.

* * * * *

Abby walked in the door and her mother was sitting at the kitchen table. There was a plate in front of her with some chicken concoction. It was untouched. There was a glass of wine, practically empty next to that.

"I thought you were coming home right after therapy?" Olivia sort of asked. There was a hint of judgement, but there was in most things she said.

"Sorry," Abby said. She couldn't tell her mom that she went for a drive and that she stopped in the parking lot of the Blockbuster video and read a few pages of Bridget's journal before she lost track of time. The journal actually wasn't even that interesting. Typical teenage bullshit. But Abby felt powerful reading it. Abby left the journal in the glove box of her car, worried if she brought it in the house it would somehow make itself known, beating in her backpack like the Tell-tale Heart.

There were two other plates made around the table.

"Are you hungry?"

"Sure," Abby said and she dropped her bags on the floor and walked to the table.

"That's not where those go." It was an order.

Abby turned back around and put her things in the corner of the living room before returning to the kitchen. She sat down quietly, and began to pick at her food.

"How was your day?" Olivia asked, as she poured herself another glass of wine. Every word she uttered was weary. There was nothing about her demeanor that suggested she really cared about the answer to that question.

"Fine. Nothing special."

"Do you know where your brother is?"

"He's not my brother."

"Step-brother. You know what I meant."

"No idea."

Abby hated being asked about him. Her mom should know better. It's not like they were exactly close. They sat in silence for a few minutes before the door finally flung open.

Jake came stomping in and up the stairs to the kitchen.

"Hey," he offered.

"There's dinner," Olivia said.

Jake looked down at the plate, stuck his finger in the sauce and licked it off.

"I'm good," he said. "Ate with the guys after practice."

Olivia took another sip of wine.

"Okay, then," Jake said and went upstairs to his room where the door shut behind him.

Olivia grabbed his plate and her own dumped the remnants into the garbage. Abby took another bite of chicken. It wasn't that bad.

Jake was just a jerk. His dad married her mom about three years ago. They had met in a grief group, which Abby always thought was a bit ridiculous, but they both had lost their spouses. He, to cancer. Abby's dad, car accident. It was about two years ago when Jake's dad had a heart attack. Jake lived with his aunt for a few months, but it was too difficult with school and he eventually moved back in with Olivia and Abby, and it was just the three of them. All of them counting the days until he went off to college and they could stop pretending they were any sort of family.

Abby knew that Jake wanted to be there even less than she did, and if he wasn't such a prick she might feel sorry for him. Even though her mom was cold and overbearing, she still had a mom. Jake had no one.

Olivia started to do the dishes while Jake's music reverberated from his room. Abby threw the rest of her dinner out and grabbed her bags without saying another word to her mom.

* * * * *

It was past midnight and Abby couldn't sleep. This wasn't uncommon, but usually there was something swirling through her head. Her thoughts tonight were surprisingly empty. School wasn't weighing on her any worse than usual, despite the day she had. Sure, she imagined dropkicking Bridget in the face, but that was more comforting than anything. Abby turned back to her clock to watch the numbers tick when she heard the door behind her creak open.

It was dark but she could make out Jake's figure. This wasn't the first time. Abby rolled back over and didn't say anything as he closed the door softly behind him and took a few steps toward her and quietly climbed into her bed. He lifted up her comforter and slid next to her. His body was warm, but his hand was cold as it touched her shoulder. It gave her a jolt.

Abby always thought she'd get used to the cold.

She rolled over to face him and without a word his tongue was in her mouth. Abby grabbed the back of his neck and pulled him closer.

2. KIRA

The whole family was sitting in the living room. Kira and her little brother Timmy were squeezed together on the big chair, while their father, Randall, sat on the couch with Georgina, his girlfriend. Randall was squeezing Georgina's hand while struggling to start the conversation.

"I talked to your mom. She knows and she's supportive, so I don't want you guys to think that this is some kind of fight or argument we're going to be having. Everyone is happy and excited and I hope that you two will be as well."

Kira had some idea what was coming. Randall had been dating Georgina for nearly two years now, a full eight months after the divorce was finalized. Kira knew that Randall wasn't getting back together with her mom, but she wasn't quite sure that she was ready for Georgina to be a permanent fixture.

"What are you trying to say, dad?" Kira asked stubbornly. She didn't mean it to come out so aggressively, but that's just how she sounded some of the time. Timmy writhed next to her. He was only ten and really didn't care about any of this.

"Georgina and I are going to get married."

"I'm not calling her mom," Kira said reflexively. "I mean…"

"Oh, darling, I'm not trying to be your mother. You already have one and nothing we do will change that."

Georgina spoke with her syrupy British accent that made everything sound so regal, charming, polite, and smarter than everyone else. Kira wanted to like her, but she just couldn't. She sat there and looked at them, all gooey-eyed and in love and Kira wanted to barf and run from the room. She didn't hate her. She just couldn't bring herself to like her.

Kira idolized her father. It wasn't easy being one of the few black families in their neighborhood, or even in the city, but people looked up to Randall Hudson. They respected him. He was a boss. Wore suits nearly every day. Carried a briefcase. Kira didn't quite know what his actual job was. Something about underwriting, but she was clueless as to what that actually meant. All that mattered was that he was important. And then Georgina comes in, all pale and poised. She was half-British and half-Asian, Chinese, she thought, but she wasn't sure. She couldn't figure out a way to ask. Looking at them on the couch, ebony and ivory and smiles and hand holding. It was all just a little much.

"Cool, can I go play Nintendo?" Timmy asked, mostly out of boredom.

"Sure, kid," Randall said. "We can continue this later."

"Honey..." Georgina whispered, but Timmy had burst out of his chair and ran off before anyone could stop him. Kira wished she could've been fast enough to join him.

"What?" Kira asked. "Is there more?"

Randall sighed.

"Yes, there is one more thing."

Kira looked into his eyes waiting for him to say something other than the nightmare scenario her brain immediately went to.

* * * * *

Kira clutched her pillow tight and stared forward. Bridget had her arm around her and rubbed her neck.

"I can't believe they're going to have a fucking kid," Kira vented. "That's the last thing I need, a little Oreo baby asking me what's on the god damn telly."

Bridget chuckled.

"I don't think it will be all that bad."

"What do you know? You're lucky enough to not have any little brats at home."

"Yeah, so lucky my dad left before I was out of diapers and my mom hasn't been able to meet anyone that wants to deal with her bull-shit since."

Kira turned to face her. "Sorry. Didn't mean anything like that, but …can we just do my thing right now?"

Bridget smiled and pulled Kira closer. "Sure. What are BFFs for?"

"Actually, girlfriend, you're right. Talk more about you. How's school? How's the boyfriend?"

"Oh, no. My life is boring. Everything is whatever. This is your time."

"Will you help me stop the wedding?"

"Oh, sure. Maybe we could start a fire?"

"With her wedding dress? While she's in it?"

"Damn, girl. Remind me never to get on your bad side. Anyway, I thought you liked Lady Turtledove Devonshire?"

"George is fine if my dad wants to date someone, but now he's putting babies in her? Come on."

A knock at the door interrupts them.

"What?" Kira snaps.

The door creaks open and Breck pops her head in.

"This a bad time?"

"Oh god, sorry, I thought you were my dad or wicked soon-to-be stepmonster."

"They said I could come up."

Kira and Breck shared a welcome embrace, and Breck waved softly to Bridget.

"Hey, Bridget."

"Hey," Bridget said jumping off the bed. "It's a good thing you're here, we were definitely needing some reinforcements and I should probably be heading back."

"Oh, you don't have to leave just because I got here."

"No, my mom's been up my ass all week, and I don't want to set her off any more than I need to. I'll call you tomorrow to make sure everything is still…not on fire."

Bridget gave a comforting hug to Kira and a rushed one to Breck and pulled the door behind her when she left.

"She's always doing that when I'm around."

"What?"

"Leaving. What did I ever do to her?"

"I'm sure you're making a big deal out of nothing."

"You saw it, I walk in and she walks out. Does she hate me? You can be honest with me."

"Bridget doesn't hate you, swear to Christ."

"Oh, I don't think you're supposed to do that. Be careful or they'll try and ship you off to Dymps too."

"Who is "they"? And ship where? It's a block away from our school. And maybe making fun of her school is what is making her all weird."

"Do you think so?"

"No, because she's not weird. Now, can we please pay attention to me right now?"

"Sorry, sorry," Breck said as they both sat down on her bed. "You've got the floor, tell me everything. Go."

* * * * *

Thankfully, Breck stayed through dinner to make it easier to avoid any further conversation. Randall offered small talk over spaghetti, while Georgina continued to be overly nice.

It's not like Kira didn't like Georgina. She did. There was something so exotic about the way she spoke, and how she would talk about all the different places she'd been. The furthest out of Omaha Kira had been was North Carolina on a ridiculously long road trip the summer before her parents split up.

Georgina took Kira shopping once and they had a reasonably good time as they damaged Randall's credit cards for hours at Oakview Mall. Georgina paid for Kira to get her hair done and marveled at how different it was working with a black girl's hair. It didn't make her feel weird though. It made her feel special. But marriage was forever. Supposedly. And the kid meant that Georgina was always going to be there. But the new kid was going to be the golden child, naturally.

God, she thought, what if it's another boy? Kira already had trouble figuring out one little brother, but with two they could gang up on her. Shit, what if it's a girl, and suddenly she had competition for her father's attention. It was obvious Randall favored her and she knew she could take advantage of that sometimes, but that would all come to an end. Neither scenario appealed to her. And she was pretty sure there wasn't a third option out there.

It's not like she harbored any illusions about her parents getting back together. Kira's mom, Yvonne, was difficult to say the least. Kira was actually a lot happier that she didn't have to see her every day. Even at twelve years old, Kira knew they weren't happy. They couldn't keep their fights from ringing throughout the whole house. And the things they would say to each other were so mean.

Kira called her mom first after her conversation with her dad and Georgina, but Yvonne didn't answer. It would likely be days before she would return the message, even with Kira's voice quivering on the answer machine. It no longer stung any more. Kira was actually pretty happy with her home with Randall and Timmy, and it was really losing that which hurt the most.

Kira tried to put it all out of her head and cracked open The Great Gatsby again. She had to keep reading chapters over and over because her brain wouldn't let her retain any of it. She thought it was a bunch of white nonsense and the issues of party-going flappers from more than half a century ago wasn't anything she found particularly relatable.

* * * * *

Kira had fallen asleep reading. Again. She would try the chapter in study hall tomorrow. Her clock was shining "2:14am" in bright blue hashmarks. She wondered if her dad had knocked on her door and offered a "good night" and thought she was ignoring him. There would be plenty of time to deal with the whole marriage and half-baby situation though. Kira wanted ten minutes to stop obsessing about it, but of course it was the first thing she thought about when she drifted awake.

Kira was still wearing her clothes. Her desk light was still on. Last night felt like days ago and like only minutes had passed. She stood up and stretched. She pulled off her jeans, took off her bra and found her favorite shirt to sleep in. It was an old concert t-shirt from the Bell Biv Devoe show she saw a couple years back. She purposely got an XL so it would hang off of her. Even though it shrunk in the wash, it was still almost to her knees. Bridget's mom drove the two of them to Kansas City and waited in the parking lot for the show to finish. Kira couldn't imagine her mom ever doing such a thing.

They used to be so inseparable, her and Bridget. Kira was so excited when another little black girl moved in right across the street. They were about the same age (Bridget was a year older, but that didn't make a difference back then), and nearly every day they would play at each other's houses, or ride bikes in the neighborhood. Kira expected to follow Bridget to High School, but Bridget's mom put her in St. Dymphna's, while Kira was stuck at AC. They shared stories and would talk about how different their schools were, but that was the beginning of things being different. Bridget started hanging out with her new friends and suddenly their everyday hangouts turned into maybe once a week. Then every other week. It wasn't Breck that made Bridget make a hasty exit. It was just who Bridget was these days.

Kira turned off her light and peered out her window. Bridget's house was diagonally across from Kira's. The street lights seemed positioned to create a direct path. Kira could still see them, drawing in chalk all over the small slope of the cement or running through the sprinkler in her front yard. Kira probably spent as much time at Bridget's house as her own. And now, she was lucky that she even came over when Kira called to tell her the news.

Kira told herself she was being silly. There was nothing wrong with her and Bridget. This is what happened as you got older. Bridget probably got annoyed that Kira and Breck were always hanging out.

From her vantage point, Kira could see Bridget's bedroom window. They used to wave good night to each other, but now the lights were off, and Kira was just standing there alone, feeling sorry for herself.

Kira went to close her blinds, but then she noticed someone outside of Bridget's house. She gasped at first, until she realized it was Bridget. She was quickly walking towards her car, parked in the street. Kira took a step aside to keep watching but not wanting Bridget to look up and see her. As she opened her car door, Kira could see Bridget's breath in the cold, illuminated by the streetlights.

Bridget sat down in her car and turned it on. The motor grumbled, and Kira was surprised she wasn't worried about waking up her mother. Bridget looked in her rear view and put on…was that lipstick? None of this made sense to Kira. Where was Bridget going at this hour? And why the lipstick? Was she sneaking off to see someone? Wasn't Bridget still seeing Javi? Why would she be seeing him this late?

Kira watched as Bridget's car rolled off in the night. They definitely had something to talk about the next time they saw each other.

3. SCOTT

As he walked down the hallways of AC High, Scott Jetter had a wink or smile for anyone that met his eyes. It was like he was running for mayor, although Homecoming King was way more prestigious in his mind. He had his letterman jacket on, hoping to add three more patches in this, his senior year.

Scott wasn't traditionally handsome. He had a boyish face, dimples when he smiled, broad shouldered, but he was somewhat gangly. He could never put on weight no matter how hard he tried. His brown hair was always in some state of messiness, but not the forced messiness other kids worked hours to perfect. Acne had set up permanent residence on his face, though the address changed regularly. Even so, he was able to snag a decent girlfriend, a junior, but that didn't preclude Scott from keeping an eye on every woman that crossed his path. His hormones were at peak functionality.

He slammed his locker door shut after putting everything except his calculus book and notebook inside, but Scott still had one free hand to hi-five Javi as he walked up to him. They had already seen each other that day, three periods before in Honors English, but smacking palms was their most common form of communication.

"How'd your physics test go?" Javi asked.

"B-plus, but I think my average is still an A," Scott smirked confidently. The B+ actually frustrated him. It was only the second one he had ever gotten on an exam his entire scholastic career, but he didn't want to let on. It had been suggested to him more than once that not getting an A wasn't the end of the world. Especially from his friends that struggled to maintain B's.

"I forgot to ask but can you drop me off at Dymps after practice?"

It was just down the street from AC High, but with all the fences and the small creek that ran in between, St. Dymphna's was about a mile and a half walk. In this cold, that was just unnecessary. Scott and Javi continued walking through the halls, Scott smiling and nodding at nearly everyone he passed by. Javi just trying to keep up with him.

"Oh yeah, got a special meeting planned?"

"Just going to dinner after her cheerleading practice."

"Uh huh," Scott elbowed him in the ribs. "I know those Catholic school girls like to wait, but this is getting ridiculous."

"It's cool," Javi said. "Believe me, if anything more happens, I will let you know. You just worry about your own girl."

"I know. We're seniors now, we should really be having a lot more sex."

Scott towered over Javi; a full head taller after hitting a growth spurt sophomore year. Even though they looked mismatched, they had been best friends since Javi was born (Scott was older by three months), because their parents had been friends. All the kids of both families played together (Scott had a little sister, Javi was one of seven kids), but Scott and Javi were the closest, same age, same grade. They bonded over action figures, then video games, comics, and eventually sports.

They worked together in the summers at Elysian Park, a local amusement park in the middle of Omaha that was filled with small rollercoasters and other rides, carnival games, and a large swimming pool that was like a small lake, with a large tower in the middle. Everything had Greek names, as if there was some connection to the absolute middle of America and the ancient civilization. Scott was a lifeguard in Poseidon's Pool, high up on the hierarchy of employees. Javi worked concessions, just a notch above janitorial staff, but they didn't let the perceived difference in status make a difference in their friendship.

Scott could see Javi bristle at the mention of sex. While Scott had been sexually active, excepting his current girlfriend, Javi had yet to mention any sort of action. Scott chalked it up to his religious upbringing, Javi's family was a church every Sunday kind of religious, something Scott never quite understood. Javi probably should've gone to St. Dymphna's, but with seven kids, private school was really out of the question for them.

Scott always had a lot on his mind. He was maintaining an A-plus average with all of his advanced placement classes, was one of the student council representatives, and had already made the varsity teams in football, basketball, and lacrosse. He hardly slept, between studying, working out, and his favorite pastime: girls.

Choosing Breck Hartman was the easy part. Breck was a junior. Scott had crossed paths with her several times before actually working closely with her on student council. Breck was the junior class representative and never missed a meeting. She also was dedicated to her studies.

In the fall she was on the volleyball team, but the rest of the school year she eschewed sports for being a part of every club she could squeeze into. Though Scott's friends would chide him for dating someone younger, Scott didn't care. When Leo Perditti called Breck fat though, Scott shoved his head so hard into his locker that it left a permanent scar.

Scott thought Breck was beautiful. She had a sweet smile, and carried herself with such a confidence that he thought it was easy to overlook that she wasn't a size zero like so many other girls in school, but he couldn't believe anyone would call her fat. She was curvy. And he loved her curves. They had been dating since April, and even after a full summer of making out (which included stuff with their hands at least), he still hadn't convinced her to go all the way with him. He wasn't a virgin, but she was, and she wanted to wait. He tried to respect that, but it didn't keep him from asking her every time they were together if she was ready yet.

As Javi and Scott rounded the corner towards their class, Breck was outside the door, clutching her books to her chest. Scott couldn't help but smile when he saw her.

"See you after class," Javi said and walked on, while giving a quick nod to Breck.

"Hey there," Breck said as Scott approached.

"Hey," Scott said, leaning down to give Breck a quick peck. Giving the other kids the impression you were having sex was almost as important as having it. Almost.

"I can't study tonight," Breck said. "My dad is being a dick."

"That's okay, I've got a lot to do anyway.'

"Okay, well call me like at nine or so. I think he'll chill out by then."

“Okay,” Scott said and reached down for another kiss, this one with a bit more enthusiasm. It went on for a moment until the bell rang. Scott broke away and smiled as he backed into his classroom waving “bye” to Breck, ignoring the other students that were pushing to get through the door.

* * * * *

As they drove to St. Dymphna’s, Scott and Javi mostly complained about the football practice they just endured. It was a lot of drills, and the whole time Scott tried to work through the equations he needed to decipher for his calculus homework so that when he put pencil to paper later, it would hopefully come easy to him. Scott pulled his used Honda into the parking lot marveling at the disparity in the cars of the private school. Some cars were brand new, bright red or shiny black, and clearly purchased by parents. Other cars were beat up clunkers that he couldn’t imagine getting up the hill.

As he rounded the lot to the entrance of the school he saw Bridget standing there. He rolled the window down as he came to a stop.

“I’ve got the package, you got the money?” He joked.

Bridget rolled her eyes. Javi was already out of the car and grabbing his bags. Javi greeted Bridget with an awkward peck. Scott really couldn’t figure out how they ended up together.

“Bye, Scott,” Bridget yelled sweetly as he pulled away. Scott waved bye to both of them as he continued to watch them in his rear-view mirror. Bridget continued to watch him, while Javi had already started yammering about something Bridget seemed wholly uninterested in. Scott smirked but quickly tried to hide it, even though he was the only one in the car.

* * * * *

"So, what did you learn in School today?" Eric directed his question to 13-year-old Bernie. Scott chuckled and rolled his eyes. Nearly every Jetter family dinner started this way. Dad would ask what you learned and the kids would respond. In the early school years, it was met with enthusiasm, factoids about rocks or planets or the Revolutionary War would be dropped joyfully. But by the time they were teenagers, Scott and his little sister, Bernie, would usually respond with sarcasm and annoyance.

"I learned that Michelle Beckham can't keep a secret," Bernie snarled.

"Well, that's something, I guess," Robbie interjected. Scott's mom was amiable and appeared playfully annoyed with her husband. Scott appreciated that his parents seemed to genuinely still like each other when so many of his friends were dealing with divorces, step and half siblings, and multiple holidays.

"I learned that my car can go at least two miles past empty," Scott offered.

"And that, my son, is knowledge that will serve you well in life."

Not all family dinners were as light and jovial, but it wasn't uncommon. Robbie and Eric didn't have many rules for the kids, but they tried to adhere to half an hour every night to just be a family. Scott didn't understand kids that complained about their parents. He was lucky that his parents were so easy going, for the most part. Other kids were afraid of their parents. Scott was only ever afraid of disappointing them.

Eric helped himself to more mashed potatoes, while Bernie openly discussed the backstabbing seventh graders she had to suffer.

* * * * *

Scott had spent over an hour on the phone with Breck, only hanging up when Robbie demanded he take out the trash. He finally rolled the bins out some time after eleven. The neighborhood was dark and quiet, the cold air was brisk and biting. Scott looked up and saw the lights out in his parent's bedroom.

He quietly crept back up to their room and listened from the outside. He could hear his dad snoring from the other side of the door. Eric usually waited until Robbie fell asleep before he tried so that his snoring wouldn't keep her up, so the proverbial coast was clear.

Scott went back to his room, grabbed his shoes and his jacket but waited until he was downstairs to put them on. He didn't want to risk waking his parents by starting his car, so he tucked his jeans into his socks and grabbed his bike from the garage.

He picked up the phone and dialed. After one ring he quickly hung up. He counted to one hundred and then dialed again.

"Hey," the voice on the other end said.

"Hey. Give me an hour. Just have to make a quick stop first," Scott whispered before hanging up again.

He listened again for any noise from upstairs and when he was sure it was still quiet, he sneaked out the backdoor and hopped on his bike.

* * * * *

Scott stopped at the house and left his bike by the bushes in front. He bounded the fence on the side, careful not to be seen by the motion light. He stuck close to the house as he made his way around to the back. The light was on in the window so he tapped three times. The curtains opened and Scott nodded. A finger pointed him to the back door.

The door opened and Percy was standing there in nothing but

gym shorts.

“It’s kind of cold, you know, you could put on something.”

“You look retarded,” Percy snapped.

“I don’t think you’re supposed to say that anymore.”

“No, I mean actual special needs,” Percy motioned.

Scott realized he was still wearing his helmet, so he unsnapped it as Percy let him in. Scott pulled the door shut and he clanged loudly.

“Shit, sorry.”

“It’s cool,” Percy responded. “My parents are, you know, elsewhere.”

Scott followed Percy into his bedroom.

“Come into my office, Mister Jetter. What can I get for you?”

“I need more of those things, you know, to stay awake. Beanies?”

“Don’t try to use the words, it doesn’t work for a dork like you.”

Scott agreed with him. He wasn’t this guy. He wasn’t some druggie. He just needed the speed to stay awake, to study, to practice, to work, to keep his world in balance. He got used to not sleeping some nights but he wasn’t willing to do anything to risk his status, whether it was his grades, his team, or anything else he crammed into his life.

“I’ve got this test coming up that I really need to study for and it’s right after the homecoming game and…”

“Yeah, yeah, yeah, I don’t care. I don’t need your life story or whatever, I’m just here to help you out.”

Percy pulled a lock box from beneath his bed and rolled the numbers to their rightful position and opened it up. He pulled a bag of pills out and held them up.

“How many?”

“How much?”

"Same as last time."

"I have two hundred."

Percy counted out the pills.

"Tell you what, because you're such a good customer, I'll throw in a few extra."

Percy smiled and threw the bag to Scott.

* * * * *

The parking lot was empty when Scott rode in. He hopped off his bike over by the tree near the entrance gate and walked around to the other side. There was one part of fence that did not have any spikes at top. Most of the kids that worked at Elysian Park knew where this fence break was and how to hop over it thanks to a conveniently placed picnic table.

When the park was empty it was creepy. None of the lights were on and while the tracks of the train shuttle and the other rides were still around, the cars that manned them were nowhere to be seen. With all the lights out, the large creature images around the carnival games were straight out of an 80s horror flick.

Scott rounded the corner by the ballroom and made his way under the waterslides over to the bathhouse, which was at the edge of the now empty pool. He still had a key for the chain lock on the front door, but it was already open. He made it through the employee area where he would take his breaks and up the stairs to the second floor. There was an apartment on the second level, but no one was living there now. He didn't have a key for that, unfortunate as that would have made it so much easier, but on the other side of the door there was a ladder that made it up to the flat rooftop.

He swung his foot over the top and stepped onto the roof. It overlooked the whole park and even though it was only a couple stories up, you could also make out quite a view of Omaha, at least to the south and east. She was waiting for him.

"Hey, Bridget," Scott said.

"You're late."

"It took me a little longer than I thought to bike over here."

"I suppose I'll forgive you."

"Come on, there has to be some way I can make it up to you."

Scott moved towards her and put his arms over her shoulders and pulled her closer. They started to kiss, awkward and aggressive, like teenagers do. He knew it was wrong. Every time they would get together he would feel guilty afterwards. Guilty for betraying Breck. Guilty for betraying Javi. Guilty for sneaking out. But in that moment, that moment before all the shame came rushing in, he felt glorious.

"I brought a blanket," Bridget said. "But it's cold so we should hurry."

"That's not a problem at all," Scott said with a chuckle. He rubbed her shoulders and began to kiss her neck, letting out a soft moan when her hand found his jeans.

4. TJ

He never had the gene that every other kid his age seemed to have. TJ wasn't a joiner. And he never truly felt a part of anything. Not his family, not his school, his city, his state, his country. On Saturdays when the Nebraska Cornhuskers would take the field, and seemingly everyone else in town was glued to their televisions, TJ would walk the quiet streets, or play video games at the Dragon's Lair, which was mostly a comic book store. He could never get on his favorite game (incidentally also called Dragon's Lair) during the week, after school when he would pass by on his walk home. The comic book store was the opposite direction of his house, but no one was waiting for him anyway. There was always someone else hogging the machine. And another someone else who had next. It was a waste of quarters, but on game days he would spend hours in front of the stand-up machine, with its vibrant animations of death whenever he made the wrong choice. He was actually starting to get good.

During the week, on days he would actually go to school that is, he spent most of time trying to avoid any sort of human interaction. He could spend hours, sometimes days without speaking in class. Teachers seldom called on him. His stringy, greasy brown hair, perma-slouch, and consistent wardrobe of oversized flannel and baggy jeans, even in the hot summer months, gave the impression he didn't want to participate. It was valid, he didn't. Not with the teachers, not with the other students at AC that didn't know what to do with him. The jocks thought he was just another burnout, but the burnouts wouldn't claim him as one of their own. The nerds were afraid of him, like all the other creepy quiet kids, but he never did anything to them. One of the bullies had shoved TJ into a locker when he was a freshman and the following day he followed the kid home after school and took a baseball bat to his knee. No one bothered him after that.

TJ was good at avoiding confrontation, beating bullies with bats aside. Whenever he could, he took seats in the middle, towards the back of any given classroom, where the kids in all directions could turn their backs to him. He dreaded forced partnerships, and failed out of biology, mostly by not going. During lunch breaks and study halls, he would put headphones and sunglasses on, and zone out. He had the reputation for being a stoner before he ever took a puff of anything, including cigarettes, though that eventually changed. These days a pack would hardly last him a week.

It's not like anyone was looking out for him. He figured this out when he went four days without speaking a word. Not at school, not at home or anywhere else.

TJ's family was a mess. His mom had died suddenly a few years back. Car wreck. And his father just wasn't the same. His older sister and brother were off at school, and they would chat when they would come home for holidays, but after a disastrous Christmas the year before, neither of them opted to come home during the summer.

TJ was a junior now, despite his solid D average threatening to hold him back each year. Somehow he managed to push through. He knew graduating was unlikely at this pace, but he really couldn't think beyond the next week. Senior year, college, that shit felt so far away, and neither really held any interest for him. He would eavesdrop on other kids in his class, talking about college visits with their parents. TJ would count the seconds until he was through with school, if he had the energy.

It was cold when he walked home, but he didn't have a car so it was really his only option. He tucked his hair into a stocking hat, pulled his jean jacket tight and hoped the wind was at his back. His sporadic facial hair hid out amidst his freckles and gave the illusion that he was older than he was. It let him buy cigarettes without hassle, but he was seldom successful in purchasing alcohol. Didn't keep him from trying though. Although at the 7-Eleven down the street from his house, he could just as easily slip a bottle of whiskey in his pants without getting caught.

He took the long way home. He wasn't in a hurry to get anywhere even though it was pretty cold out. He lit a cigarette as he cut through Elmwood Park, and caught a couple kissing on one of the large rocks near the overpass. He darted across the street before they saw him, but they were pretty oblivious. He ducked behind a parked car and looked over at them.

It was Scott Jetter and Breck Hartman. He had been friends with Scott years ago. Their parents knew each other, but they grew apart when Scott got more into sports and TJ got more into nothing. He would nod at Scott every so often if they caught each other's eyes walking through the hallways, but TJ was pretty sure they hadn't shared a word since they got to high school.

Breck was another story. She was one of the few girls, few anyone really, that was nice to him. They had been in the same small group in English class sophomore year and she wasn't afraid to include him in the conversation as she (naturally) took charge. He thought she had a nice smile and appreciated her bold demeanor. He was a little annoyed she was dating him. Scott used to be a nice guy but he became a tool somewhere around when he made that three-point shot to win some stupid basketball game freshman year. TJ put out his cigarette so the smoke wouldn't be noticeable and continued to watch them laughing, softly touching each other, and Scott sneaking in for a kiss every other word. It was sickening.

A car whizzing by broke their attention and TJ ducked back, sure they caught him staring, but when he looked up again they had already started walking on, seemingly clueless that anyone was in their vicinity.

TJ re-lit the cigarette he had and continued along the same path they were on, but at a much greater distance. He lamented that Breck would spend any time with that douchebag, even as he remembered playing hide and seek with Scott and their siblings the summer after fourth grade.

TJ followed them through the park and out the other side. When they crossed Pacific Street, he followed suit, sure now that they were going to his house a few blocks up. TJ was now walking in the opposite direction of his own house, but who would even notice.

He passed Pierce Street, expecting to turn on Woolworth Ave, but noticed that they had moved up the street. Maybe they weren't going to Scott's. TJ moved to the other side of the street and ducked behind a tree so he could continue to watch. The couple walked to a small brick house, and Breck opened the gate and pulled Scott through the backyard. This was her house, he realized, impressed at his own detective skills. He never realized how close she lived to his neighborhood.

His spying nearly over, TJ started back up the sidewalk, face forward, but eyes focused on the house. As he neared it, there was nothing indicating anyone was even home. Unless he got closer, and risked getting caught, he was probably done. He memorized her address and continued forward, trying to imagine what they were doing now that no one could see them. Then he tried unimagining that.

* * * * *

TJ heard the door slam. His father was home from work. It was early, which meant one of two things. He quit (again) or was sent home (more likely). Adam Griffin used to be a decent dad, a solid husband, and marquee employee. He was regional manager for some insurance company, but when his wife, Maureen, TJ's mom, died, he had to stay closer to home with the kids. That car wreck killed both of TJ's parents. Adam was just a husk left behind. Now, he worked in a video store and blew most of his paycheck on alcohol.

TJ waited about half an hour for Adam to settle in before he made his way downstairs. He kept his fingers crossed there might be something in the kitchen to eat besides Hot Pockets. TJ opened the fridge and saw nothing but the mustard and expired grapes that were there when he got home from school.

TJ let out a small grunt.

"Something the matter, Ace?" Adam asked from behind him. TJ thought he was in the living room otherwise he would've been a little more quiet.

"Just looking for some food."

"What happened to all the crap I got last week?"

"I ate it. I tend to do that almost every day."

With one quick motion, Adam grabbed TJ's head in his large hands and slammed it into the wall. The light switch immediately jabbed into his skin, but Adam just held TJ's head firm. Some days he would struggle or fight back, but this was not one of those days.

"Do not disrespect me," Adam said, almost with a whisper.

TJ started to wince in pain, the light switch felt like it was poking his brain, but he didn't say anything, just took a deep breath. Finally, Adam relented.

TJ grabbed the side of his head and felt the stickiness where blood had started to leak out. He looked at the red on his hand and looked at his dad. He wanted to say something, to scream what an asshole he was, and that he hated him, but he knew that would only make things worse. He simply turned around and went back to his room.

"Oh, don't be baby," Adam shouted after him. "You're fine."

TJ locked the door behind him and plopped down on his bed.

One day, he thought. One day, Adam would be sorry.

* * * * *

TJ lit another cigarette. Rather than go home, he'd been spending the past few nights outside Breck's house, chain smoking Marlboro Lights, and sitting in front of the parked car across the street in case anyone wandered by. A lady walking her dog asked him if he lived in the neighborhood and he said he was a block over and that seemed to appease her. He didn't accomplish much with his surveillance, only figuring out that her room was on the side of the house, and that her father worked nights. He didn't see anyone else around the house, not even Scott.

He knew this was creepy, and if she ever saw him lurking outside it would be hard to come up with an excuse good enough to make her okay with him, but he didn't care. What were the chances they would ever speak again anyway?

He had a large bruise on the side of his face, and a scar where the gash had been, but he just let his long hair hang down on the right side and, thankfully, no one really looked at him long enough to notice. TJ avoided everyone, more so than usual.

The light flipped off in the room that he was still pretty sure was Breck's. He took another drag off of his cigarette and then started the trek back to his house.

* * * * *

As he neared home, TJ saw the Chevy truck his father drove swerve right in front of him, moving the other direction. TJ looked in the window and saw Adam, but there was no recognition. Adam looked away, but not as if he was seen, or caught, but as if the person that he passed was inconsequential. Adam was clearly in the middle of a pretty extensive bender, and driving no less. TJ felt the rage inside him swell. It was weird hating the car wreck that took his mom and praying for one to take his dad.

When he made it home, he wasted no time in grabbing his book bag and another large backpack. He shoved in as many t-shirts, socks, and underwear as he could. On his desk was a GI Joe toy, a small action-figure of Scarlett, the redheaded special ops agent. Her red hair and pony tail always reminded him of his mother. He shoved the toy in his pocket.

In the kitchen, he found some Girl Scout cookies in the freezer and bag of pretzels that he snatched. He didn't want to be home if the cops came. He didn't want to be home for any reason. So, he left.

* * * * *

He didn't know where to go at first. He didn't have any friends really. His brother and sister were both out of state and he didn't even know where their phone numbers were. He walked through Elmwood Park, it was different at night: quiet, scary. There were a couple cars parked at the pool (which was closed this time of year), but he took the street up towards Dodge Rd.

Then, he had an idea.

Last summer he had gotten a job at Elysian Park as a ride operator. He mostly did Hermes' Ferris Wheel, but could also sub in for Persephone's Pendulum. That was a lot busier, and thus, a lot less of a pain in the ass. He worked fewer hours this summer but still knew how to get into the park after hours. Everyone knew how to get in.

There was an old apartment above the bathhouse. No one lived there, at least not the last he heard, and he doubted anyone would be there this time of year. It wasn't going to be nice, but it had walls, and that's really all he needed. It had warmed up the last couple days, but it was the Midwest and the weather would shift on a daily basis so he wouldn't be surprised with sun or snow, and neither would be good on the streets.

It was maybe a couple miles to the park. TJ thought about dropping his big bag in the trees here, but he would have to get it at some point, so he decided to brave it. At least it was a bit warmer this evening.

Sure enough, getting into the park was as easy as he thought it would be. After he threw his bags over the fence, he climbed up and jumped over himself. He sat on the ground for a few minutes, catching his breath and making sure that he was alone. Kids were always sneaking in, looking for a place to drink and party. It was quiet tonight.

TJ climbed up to the apartment and knocked on the front door, just in case someone was actually living there (or like his plan-squatting). No one came to the door. He went around to the side and thought about breaking the window, but with the wood cross pattern, it didn't look like it would be easy. Luckily, it was unlocked. It just took a little bit of strength to lift the window and climb in.

It was dark. TJ looked for a light, but when he flipped the switch nothing happened. Not sure why he expected something to, why would anyone pay to keep the lights on in a place no one lived? As his eyes adjusted, he felt around, using his lighter as a small flashlight.

It was a small studio. A small kitchenette with a counter separated the room in two. On the other side, there was a queen-sized mattress directly on the ground-teens were always sneaking off to the apartment to get together. Many virginities were lost on the mattress, if the stories were to be believed. It was gross, but TJ didn't have any other option. The water was off in the bathroom, but for some reason the toilet still flushed. Small miracles. TJ stayed bundled and curled up on the old mattress. Across the room it looked like the ground was moving, but it was just a cockroach.

TJ closed his eyes and tried to imagine that he was in a nice hotel, with down blankets, and fluffy pillows, and not in some poor man's amusement park, in an apartment by the pool, with what felt like a roach crawling all over him.

5. BRIDGET

She loved crossing things off a list. It gave Bridget a feeling of accomplishment, even if the first thing on every to-do list was "make to-do list." She just crossed off "withdraw money," "note," "gas," and "costume." Now, all that was left was a bunch of names. Progress. It was such a simple pleasure, but it was one of the few things that made her legitimately happy.

She had to make a few more stops before going to the football game. She was a cheerleader, and this was part of the deal. She didn't want to go. She didn't give a shit about the school or the team and trying to keep that fake smile on her face was exhausting. Also, she had a lot on her mind, what with tomorrow being the party.

It was a Halloween party, well, really it was the closing party for anyone that worked at Elysian Park over the summer, but the first two that were planned were canceled over weather. First, there was the tornado. It didn't actually blow through Omaha, but the warning was active, and the winds were severe enough that it didn't make sense to try to get together. Then, two weeks later, there was an early frost that was causing accidents all over the city and the streets became emergency only. The final employee party is usually right after Labor Day when the main park closed for the winter, but as it got pushed towards the end of October it was now doubling as a Halloween party. The rides around the park weren't supposed to be open, as everything was already closed for the season, but the ballroom would be the central hub and a make-shift haunted house, sure to be lame, was set up around the picnic area.

Bridget knew she could sneak away if she needed to. The bigger problem would be how many other people would have the same idea. Security was never a big priority at the park. At least not for the employees.

Bridget had her hair plastered back and pulled into a tight ponytail. Underneath her uniform she had a turtleneck and thick leggings. It wouldn't keep her completely warm but she could put on her coat in between performances. She got her big coat too. The one that would completely hide her uniform. As she pulled it tight and sinched the belt, only her turtleneck was visible beneath. With all the makeup she had on, she looked like an adult.

Well, almost.

* * * * *

Her car was parked across the street from the small, brick house on Poppleton Ave. She had found the address in the phone book. One of the few on her list still. There was only one car in the driveway, which was his, but Bridget couldn't be sure if his wife parked in the garage or just wasn't home yet. She decided not to ring the doorbell. She grabbed the card from her purse and walked across the street.

She peered into the windows. There was no sign of anyone. She walked to the front of the car, a small, white Honda Civic hatchback. It was a few years older than the car Bridget herself drove, but that's what happens on a teacher's salary. She lifted up the windshield wiper when she heard a voice from behind her.

"Bridget?"

She turned to see Mr. Sutton standing there. He was in a sweater and jeans, casual, completely unlike the shirt and tie he wore every day at St. Dymphna's.

"Hi."

"What are you doing here? You shouldn't be here."

"It's nothing, I was just dropping off this," she waved the card. He wasn't smiling. "Can we talk?"

"It's cold out."

"I've got a coat."

Mr. Sutton shook his head and then motioned for Bridget to get in the car. He turned the heat on.

"You really shouldn't be here."

"It's nothing. It's just a card."

"This is inappropriate."

"I know. I just…I wanted to thank you. You didn't have to let me retake that test and my whole GPA could've been blown because of the ones I missed and…"

"Bridget, we've talked about this."

"Danny, come on, there's nothing weird about this. It's a thank-you card. It says thank you. I appreciate you. You're a great teacher. That's it."

"Are you okay?"

She didn't look at him when she answered.

"I'm fine."

"My wife is on her way home. You shouldn't be here when she gets here. Do you need me to call one of your friends?"

"Look, Danny…"

"Mr. Sutton."

"There's something I need to tell you."

Bridget took a deep breath and turned back to face him. She had the conversation in her head many times already, but it didn't make it easier, like she thought it would.

* * * * *

Bridget made the drive downtown in only fifteen minutes. She was worried it would take longer with Danny, Mr. Sutton, but he couldn't get her out of his car fast enough. She should be hurt, but she wasn't even surprised. Besides, it would make this next stop a lot easier.

Bridget parked outside the First National Bank Building, one of the oldest buildings in downtown. It was only fourteen floors, but Omaha's skyline wasn't full of skyscrapers. Bridget waited near the parking lot. She had figured out what car was his. It was easy really, and she was glad that it was still in the lot when she made it downtown. She kept her fingers crossed he was working late and hadn't jaunted out of town for some reason. These rich fuckers, you could easily lose track of them.

It was dark out when he finally left the building, but he looked exactly like his picture: silver-speckled hair, perma-smirk, a face in his fifties (which he was) but his suit hung off a body that would make men half his age jealous. Bridget watched him as he walked to his car, the one with the parking spot labeled just for him: Harlan Van Allen.

Percy's father was well known throughout town. His name was a fixture in several businesses. He had a small financial firm that operated out of this building. He owned several apartment complexes, a few bars, was majority shareholder in one of the local radio stations. It was not uncommon for news stations to seek out his opinions on whatever new development was happening in town. The Van Allens could be traced back to the Mayflower, but somewhere along the line one unlucky cousin settled in the Midwest. Harlan's father was HP Van Allen, a cantankerous old millionaire who was so popular in town that his funeral was televised. Cotton Van Allen, Harlan's great-grandfather, was one of the first prosecutors in Omaha, and there was still a law practice boasting the Van Allen name in their TV ads. The Van Allens were inescapable.

Bridget got out of her car and walked over to Harlan before he could get into his car.

"Excuse me," Bridget said, but Harlan didn't even register her when she was only ten feet from him. "Mister Van Allen?"

"Yes?" Harlan said as he turned to see Bridget. She felt his eyes look her up down, probably assessing some threat level. It was night, he was white, she was black, although she was only sixteen. She did look older.

"Can I help you?" He snarled when Bridget paused for a moment, psyching herself up.

"I was wondering if I could talk to you…" she stammered. She was nervous, justifiably so.

"I'm running late, call my office if you need to make an appointment," Harlan said, continuing for his car and pulling the door open.

"It's about your son. Percy." Harlan stopped and let out a heavy sigh.

"What's he done now?"

"That's why I'd like to talk to you."

* * * * *

Bridget was late to the game and got a lecture from the cheer advisor, but she really didn't care. It was her last game. She knew that, even if no one else did. The next afternoon, as she got ready for the Halloween party, things felt so much easier, especially after the big conversations she had the night before.

Javi was supposed to pick her up for the party, but she convinced him to meet her there. She needed a little extra time to get ready. And she wanted to have her own car. As she looked at herself in the mirror, she was almost ready.

The bright white dress-half-turtleneck, sleeveless-was pretty faithful to Basic Instinct, the movie where she took her inspiration. The giant, gold, hoop earrings she wore were her own touch. She was already black, no one was going to confuse her for Sharon Stone. She also was wearing underwear (and leggings, it was still cold out) but she was fully prepared for the number of boys that would ask her if she had anything on underneath. Teenage boys were nothing if not predictable.

"Is that what you're wearing?"

Bridget was putting on lipstick when she turned to see her mother in the doorway.

"I thought you were still at work?" Bridget asked, ignoring the obvious and condescending question.

"I took a half day. Seriously, what is it with you girls today? This is who you want to be emulating? A murderous slut? I guess I shouldn't be surprised."

"Well, I'm just impressed you've seen a movie this year."

"I don't suppose it's worth asking you be home at a decent hour?"

"It's a work thing, Mom, nothing's gonna happen."

"That's not what I asked."

"You didn't actually ask anything."

"Do you always have to be such an ungrateful brat?"

Bridget inhaled loudly and returned to putting her lipstick. As arguments with her mom went, this was actually pretty tame. But Bridget knew something her mom didn't. She knew that this might be the last time she would have to listen to one of her tirades.

Vanessa Kent was the only parent Bridget ever knew. Her dad was a mystery. Some name her mother shared once and he never made an appearance her life. Mother and daughter were close when Bridget was growing up, but the past few years, Vanessa changed. She grew more aggressive. More personal in her insults. More physical in her disagreements. She wasn't regularly abusive but Bridget had received a slap more than twice. Maybe she was asking for it, she knew how to push her mom's buttons, and even somewhat enjoyed baiting her.

Bridget had no idea what would set her mother off. Some days, Vanessa would be overly sweet and clingy, laughing and bouncing off the walls. Other days, she wouldn't even say "hi" when Bridget walked in the room, and any words she could muster were generally insults. Sure, she apologized, mostly, eventually, but apologies were only good if they were sincere, and they could only be sincere if the actual behavior she was apologizing for would ever stop.

Bridget made the decision months ago. She knew she was done that night. She had come home late and Vanessa was still up. Vanessa berated her, called her names, and Bridget knew then that she was no longer going to put up with this. It made things easier. The insults and derision rolled off of her. And the hope of escaping gave her something to look forward to.

Bridget focused on her image in the mirror and stopped listening to her mother altogether. She picked up a couple words, but there was no point. None of it mattered any more. Bridget only felt one thing: resolve.

* * * * *

The party was in full swing when Bridget showed up, which in this case meant that En Vogue was blaring from the loudspeakers, the ballroom had been decorated with bales of hay and skeletons, and kids in costumes were dancing awkwardly while sneaking sips from flasks.

Bridget walked to the bar where she talked a bartender she knew into adding whiskey to her cup of soda. She needed to calm down, but it had already been a long day. She took a sip. It helped but she was still a bit shaken.

Across the room she saw Kira, big baggy pants, bright purple shirt and red suspenders. Bridget made her way over.

"Oh, girl, you looking fly," Bridget said, plastering a smile across her face. She knew Kira was dressed like some R&B star, but thought the condom in her glasses was a little much, albeit accurate. Kira told her about her inspiration regardless. After some small talk about their outfits, Bridget thought she would take the moment to get sincere.

"Kira, look, I need to say something," she started.

"What? Is everything okay?"

"No, it's not okay. I miss you. And I know we haven't really hung out in a while and I'm sorry for that and you have everything going on with your dad and I'm just across the street and I never see you and I'm so sorry."

"It's okay, Bridge, you don't have to be sorry. And what's this about anyway? You ain't ever been sorry for anything ever," Kira chuckled.

"That's not true. There was one time, back in the 80s."

"Oh, that one time."

Bridget hugged Kira and held on tightly. It was a relief. She wanted to tell Kira everything, but she couldn't. Not yet. Bridget almost started crying but she knew that might require an actual explanation. Instead, she rocked Kira back and forth along with the music. The two separated, but Bridget held Kira's hand for a moment.

"You been a really great friend," Bridget said, sincerely.

"What is with you being so nice? It's freaking me out."

"Sorry. Period sweetness I guess."

"Actually, there's something I've been meaning to ask you…"

Bridget was distracted by Javi on the dance floor that she cut Kira off. "Oh, there's my boyfriend that I haven't actually seen at all today, can you give me a sec?"

Bridget was off before Kira could even respond. Javi was wearing his clothes backwards (another pop group reference) and pretending he could dance with a group of concession girls when Bridget pulled him away.

"Hey, babe," he said and gave her a peck on the cheek.

"Hi."

"I called your house but your mom said you already left."

"That's why I said I'd meet you here." With her heels on she was now taller than Javi and the idea that they were mismatched was even more obvious. But he was sweet.

"Did you get everything taken care of that you needed to?"

"Mostly," Bridget said.

"Then we should dance."

"Who'd you come with?" Bridget said, somewhat shouting over the music.

"Scott and Breck. You should see their costumes. They're great."

"Oh, Scott and Breck are here?" Bridget asked as she pulled Javi off the side.

"Somewhere."

"Hey, do you think you could find Doyle? I hear he stashed some vodka by the back hall and I'm totally jonesing for a drink."

"Yeah, sure."

"Thanks, hon."

Javi started to walk off on what Bridget hoped was a decent snipe hunt, but after a few steps he turned around.

"Oh, and you look nice," he said.

"Thanks." She knew the only end for them was Javi getting his heart broken one way or another and the thought upset her, but she couldn't dwell on that now. She had to stay on task.

* * * * *

Bridget found Scott outside with the smokers, even though he wasn't partaking. She grabbed his Han Solo vest and pulled him to a quiet corner outside where no one was around.

"Hey, not now, Breck is around here somewhere," Scott said.

"No, idiot, we need to talk."

Bridget gave Scott a look demonstrated how serious she was. And then she began the speech that she had been practicing in the mirror.

"Scott, I took a pregnancy test today and it was positive. Now, I don't want to freak you out, but we both know that Javi and I haven't…you know. And don't worry, I don't have any intention of having this baby, but I need a little help, you know, paying for…it. The thing us good Catholic girls aren't supposed to know about."

"Woah. This is a lot. Are you sure?" Scott asked so innocently. Even in his Star Wars getup, plastic gun in a holster on his hip, she thought he was handsome. In another life, maybe they could've been something other than two troubled kids dating virgins that enjoyed sharing their bad decisions.

"Yes. I'm sure."

Bridget thought Scott was about to fall over but he looked at her with those warm eyes.

"Are you okay?"

She looked down. She couldn't look at him.

"Well, not especially. But I don't think either of us needs this fucking everything up."

"I wore a rubber."

"Not every time. Look, what's done is done. I'm not blaming you for anything, but can you help me out?"

"I've got some savings. How much does it cost?"

"I don't really know. Five hundred dollars?"

"Shit. Really? Okay. Wow. Um, yeah, sure, I got you. It'll be okay. I don't know how much I can take out though."

"Look, if you hit the ATM before midnight you can make another withdrawal five minutes later. So, why don't we meet in our place around one?"

"Tonight? Won't the party still be going on?"

"They're supposed to kick everyone out at midnight."

"Okay, yeah, sure."

* * * * *

"Where were you? I've been looking everywhere." Breck asked Scott, with a slight twinge of accusation.

Bridget and Scott had walked around the other side of the ballroom and came back in through the front.

"Oh my god, I love your costume," Bridget said, perhaps a bit over-effusively. Breck had her hair in side buns, and was wearing a re-formatted sheet with a belt that gave a pretty good homage to Princess Leia. She practically shoved Scott into Breck.

"You guys are so cute together."

"Scott's idea, of course," she said. "He's such a nerd at heart."

"I had no idea."

"Come on," Scott said. "I look cool."

"Sure thing."

Soon, Javi had returned, and even managed to find some alcohol for the group. Bridget sipped hers, and kept a smile plastered on her face while they talked, mostly about the party being late this year and their memories of the park. They were laughing hard enough Bridget didn't even notice when someone joined their circle. He made a quick comment that she couldn't hear but she turned and was surprised to see some stranger standing with them.

"Hello?" she asked, pointedly.

The boy was scruffy, and wearing normal clothes-t-shirt, flannel, ripped jeans-and his hair hung in his face.

"Breck, right?" The boy asked Breck, not even acknowledging Bridget. "We had English last year."

"TJ?" Breck responded.

"Yeah."

"Oh, yeah, I remember. This is Bridget and Javi," Breck said politely. "And this is my boyfriend, Scott."

"Yeah," Scott said, obviously uncomfortable. "We've actually met before. Our parents…used to be friends, I guess."

"Something like that."

"Who are you supposed to be?" Bridget asked. "Kurt Cobain?"

"No, I'm a cereal killer," TJ responded, producing a box of Cheerios with a large, kitchen knife through it, and blood drawn on in red marker.

"Is that supposed to be funny?"

"Well, it's more punny," TJ said with a smirk.

Bridget rolled her eyes. She didn't have the energy for this.

"Oh, I think I see my old manager. I better say something if I want to get asked back next year. Back in a sec," and she excused herself, leaving the rest of them behind.

As she walked towards the dance floor, she looked back to make sure no one was paying attention and then darted towards the side exit. The smoking area was filled with people so Bridget took the stairs up to deck on the second level. She swung her legs over the chains and a big sign that read NO ENTRY.

Nice idea, but Bridget wasn't the only one to have this thought as she saw smoke wafting from one of the tables. She walked over to the sole person sitting there, a girl with a nun costume, taking a deep drag on a cigarette. As Bridget neared, she could see that it was actually a pregnant nun costume, at least she hoped so. No one should smoke when they're pregnant.

"Can I bum one of those?" Bridget asked.

"Are you fucking kidding me?"

Bridget was taken aback until she saw the girl turn and that it was Abby Williams.

"Of course, why wouldn't it be you?" Bridget said mostly to herself, before turning on her attitude. "Hanging out with all your friends?"

"That's a nice dress you're almost wearing. But isn't the psycho bitch thing a little on the nose? And the hoop earrings are gauche."

Bridget chuckled. "Okay, that was pretty good. Look, I don't really have the energy for this, so can I bum one or not?"

Abby slid a pack of cigarettes across the table. Bridget sat down and pulled one out.

"Light?"

Abby reached over and cupped her hand around the lighter as she lit Bridget's cigarette.

"Thanks."

Abby nodded.

They sat in silence for a moment, puffing on their cigarettes before Bridget finally relented.

"I thought you had to work here to make the invite list?"

"Came with someone. And I wasn't having any fun, despite my hilarious costume, so I came up here."

"Yeah, these things are really just collections of 'remember when?' Completely exhausting for anyone not in the club. Or with half a brain."

"I thought this type of thing would be just your scene."

"Well, what you don't know about me is pretty fucking extensive."

"I'm sure."

"Abby, look, I should apologize for the other day."

"Oh yeah, what's that?"

"You know, in class. Bringing up…well, it wasn't cool. I had my own shit going on and sometimes it's just easier being mean."

"Whatever, it's fine. I don't need your apology. Or your pity."

"This isn't pity. Believe me. I really don't have the energy for that. I wish I did. Honestly. Sometimes I hear the things coming out of my mouth and it's like I'm hearing 'em for the first time. My brain really can't keep up. There's too much other stuff rattling around up there."

"You ever talk to someone?"

"Like a counselor? No, thank you."

"I know, I fucking hate it. But I think it's helped me. Standing up for myself. Last year, I don't think I would've been able to call you a bitch to your face."

"Well, hooray for progress."

The two girls laughed and continued to talk, the cold air showing their breath long after they put their smokes out. Bridget still wasn't sure she even liked Abby, but she liked that for a brief moment she forgot about everything else going on.

* * * * *

It was three a.m.

The ballroom was empty of people, though plastic cups and paper plates were overflowing in the trash cans. The floor was sticky with booze, a problem for another day.

Beyond the ballroom, past the fence, and in front of the large swimming pool that had been drained for winter, there was a lump of white and red.

It was Bridget.

In front of the bathhouse, below the apartment and rooftop overlook, her body was splayed, arms and legs mangled in positions they shouldn't be in. Blood pooled around her. Her white dress was barely recognizable.

Now, she was just a body.

6. PERCY

Hazy. And cold. He was cold. Breathing was hard.

It was dark. Percy couldn't quite make out where he was other than outside. There was a breeze.

His side. Pain. He reached down and saw that he was bleeding from his side. His hand was wet and sticky. Nothing was making sense. Was he dreaming? No. This was real. The pain was real. He felt high, but when had he smoked? He couldn't remember.

Percy staggered to his feet and tried to focus. There were tracks on one side. Red tracks. Curving out. Trees on the other side. He saw the wires for the sky car. Elysian Park. The bathhouse. Rooftop. That's where he was. He held his hand to his side and realized he had to solve one problem at a time.

The rooftop was mostly flat with turreted edges, which made no sense as no one had ever waged war on the amusement park, and felt out of place with the whole Greek theme. It looked like it had become a repository for crap from the park. There was an old bumper car, metal rods that may have been used on one of the rides, rusted tools and old equipment.

Percy stumbled over to the junk in one corner and found a roll of duct tape. He taped the open wound on his side, pretty sure he was giving himself an infection as he was doing it, but it stopped the bleeding. It was still dark and as his eyes adjusted, he saw the pool of blood that he had left behind. On the other wall were cleaning buckets filled with water. Dirty rain water likely. He dumped it on the pool of blood, directing it towards the drain nearby.

Some old deflated pool toys were crumpled off to one side. Percy pulled them over by his blood, making them cover the space from which he arose. That would have to do it. He was starting to feel light headed and really didn't want to pass out here. Who would find him? The park was closed for the winter. He would freeze to death before anyone would notice he was gone.

He had parked on the street when he arrived because the first lot was full and it was closer, but it felt miles away now. How long ago was the night before? It was a blur. It was still dark. Middle of the night dark. Regardless, he was pretty confident he wanted to be as far away from the park as soon as humanly feasible. Especially given the wound in his side, which was big enough, and painful enough to be deeper than he realized.

What was he doing on the roof? He had flashes of memory. Like a dream he was trying to recall the details of. Bridget had paged him. Was she there? He can't place her. The party was still going when he got there but it was on the other side of the park. Did he see anyone else? How did he cut his side?

Percy raced home, not bothering to stop for lights. He didn't see any other cars on the road. Thankfully, his neighborhood was only about a mile away. He had an old sweatshirt in his car he tied around his side to keep the blood from getting everywhere.

Fairacres was one of the few rich neighborhoods in Omaha. The city's elite either lived in the old brick mansions there or the newer homes over in Regency. Fairacres was a more isolated area, which housed the church to St. Dymphna's. The school was just on the other side of the Fairacres park, where the houses had less floors, less bedrooms, and were less elite. The Van Allen house had a long driveway behind an easily navigable gate that they only really closed when they were out of town. Though he normally parked in the garage, he didn't want to risk waking his parents (though their room was in the other wing of the house and most nights they never noticed him coming and going).

Percy hobbled down around to the back of the house. God, why did it have to be so huge. The large, white bricks seemed to go on forever. He could feel his brain starting to fog up again. He needed help.

Percy struggled with his keys and only barely managed to close the door behind him. He went into the family room, there was a phone on the bar. He picked up and dialed 9-1-1. He thought he would have to try to sound wounded, but when he heard himself speak, there was no need for a performance.

"I…need an ambulance. I fell. Cut myself. Losing blood. 6616 Underwood. I'm… in the basement. Please hurry."

He hung up the phone. He hoped the paramedics or whomever showed up would beeline for the basement. The upstairs was mansion-like and it could take them forever to make their way down. He grabbed a bottle of whiskey from the bar.

The family room was pristine. The housekeepers must've come that day. Percy stood above the large glass coffee table in front of the leather sectional couch. Boy, white was a bad color choice. He left a large, bloody handprint on the top edge. His mom was going to go batshit bonkers when she saw it. Percy hoped he would live long enough to see that.

He took a swig of the whiskey, as much as he could stomach. Then, he let the bottle drop to the floor, spilling on to the, surely, priceless Persian rug. Percy had one more step left. No guts, no glory, right? He mustered up all the strength he had left and took a step up to the couch and then jumped right into the middle of the coffee table, smashing clean through and sending glass shooting everywhere.

"Ouch," he muttered aloud, even though no one was around.

There was now more blood. He couldn't manage to stand again, so he pulled himself across the floor back towards the bar. He didn't quite make it before he passed out completely.

* * * * *

Percy's eyes fluttered open. He wasn't in pain, at least not in the same way. It was more of an ache all over his entire body. The room was bright, and mostly plain white. This was not home.

He looked around as his eyes adjusted. There was a TV on a raised shelf that was turned off. A window had curtains closed, but light was still bleeding through. The overhead light was round and fluorescent. Sitting by the window was his mother, Donna. She was curled up in a chair and her always perfectly straightened hair was wavy and hanging in front of her face.

Percy reached for her which was when he noticed his hands were strapped to the bars of the bed and tubes were running out of him.

He was in a hospital, but why the straps? His arms were all scratched up. The coffee table. It started coming back to him. And then he remembered the rooftop. What happened? The whole night was hazy.

"Mom," Percy eked out, but his voice was scratchy and soft.

Donna quickly awoke and moved to his side. She grabbed his hand and squeezed, but it was colder than he expected. Was that him or her? She squeezed too tightly.

"Ow," he muttered, and Donna let go.

"Percy, honey, how are you doing?"

"I…" not only could he not think of how to answer that question, his voice wouldn't let him. His mouth was dry and swollen.

"Dad?"

"He was here, but he had to go into the office."

"What… why… here?"

"There was an accident. I think you tripped and fell. There was alcohol."

"Sorry."

"Don't worry about that now. I'm just happy you're awake. Was a little worried after the surgery."

"Surgery?"

"It looked like you had a deeper cut on your side and they had to go in and repair some of the stuff inside. But you're going to be fine."

"Why…straps?"

"The doctors couldn't be sure that, well, that you did this to yourself. And I swore to them you couldn't have, but I guess it's procedure."

"I didn't. I swear."

"I know you didn't, honey. I believe you. But there was another accident that night and I think they are just trying to be careful."

"Another?"

"Yes, another student. She was at Elysian Park. So sad."

"The park?"

"I know you weren't there, your friend, what's his name, that always wears the leather coat? He said you were at his house for Halloween. They had some party at the park for all those, summer workers I guess you call them. It's so sad, the girl died. Poor thing killed herself."

"Died?"

"When I heard the sirens and the ruckus in the house and I went down and saw the paramedics tending to you, I screamed and I was so worried and then when the news about the girl broke the next day and you were in surgery, I was just so scared that we might lose you too."

"Who?"

"Oh, some girl named Bridget Kent, I think. It's been on the news all day, although they aren't saying her name. Jordan's mother called and told me who it was. It's just so unreal. You kids have so much going on, don't you? I told the police I didn't think you knew her."

Hearing her name sent shivers through Percy. He knew Bridget. They weren't close or anything, but he had sold to her before. At Tina Moreno's back to school party they took some pills and wait… the park. He went to talk to her, but when was that? Did she page him? Everything was hazy.

Donna grabbed the remote control and turned on the television. It was the afternoon news.

The last thing Percy was clear about was hearing that the Elysian Park end of season party was going to be crazy and he should bring some stuff. It wasn't his scene though. He skipped it. Went to his friend's house. Then Bridget paged him. 911. She had to talk. He had only had a few beers when he drove over. He might've been buzzed, but he wasn't drunk. Then, he woke up bleeding, on the rooftop. He remembered the coffee table. Pieces were coming back to him, but not everything.

And why was the afternoon news on Sunday?

"How long have I been here?"

"Oh, honey, you've been out for a bit. You had surgery on Sunday and we thought you were coming to yesterday. They took that oxygen mask off thankfully, but they said it was possible you could be out of it for another few days."

"What day is it?"

"It's Tuesday, sweetie."

Three days. He almost lost three whole days. Did the police know he was there? Did they know that he knew Bridget? Oh, shit. Did they search his house and find his stash? Where was his pager? His parents didn't even know he had one. Did he hide it before he fell? His mom would be acting completely differently if she knew exactly what his extracurricular activities were for the past couple years.

"I should get the doctor."

Donna brushed her fingers through her hair and gave Percy a reassuring smile before she left the room. He was her favorite, he knew. His older sister would have aggressive fights with their mom, and everyone knew she was Dad's favorite. His little brother was spoiled, but that's just what happens to the youngest. He seemed more like a nuisance than anything. But he was his mom's special boy. And he could get her to do anything he ever needed. He knew that would all be gone if she actually knew what a prolific and successful drug dealer to the high school students of Omaha he really was.

7. JAVI

Sunlight poked through the small window that was in the corner of the basement room that Javi shared with two of his brothers. He was the only one still sleeping. His brother Diego slept on the pullout couch and it wasn't even set up, which meant that he probably never came in from the night before. No matter, Diego was twenty and no longer under the same scrutiny as the rest of the family. Antonio also had the same freedom. Antonio graduated from AC the year before and was taking some classes at the community college, but still slept on the lower bunk he shared with Javi. As Javi rolled over to the ladder, he could see Antonio's bed was made.

Javi and his older brothers made up the first wave of the Marquez family. They were rowdy boys growing up, constantly getting in trouble, mostly because of Diego and his ability to manipulate all of his younger siblings that worshipped him. Diego dropped out of high school when he was seventeen and went to work at the auto shop of one of their uncles. Antonio also worked there some nights, and they both pulled shifts at Hermanos, the Mexican restaurant that their father, Julio, ran. When

Javi was six, he finally got a sister, Claudia. And a couple years later his mother, Lucinda, gave birth to twin boys, Jeremy and Justin. Dario, the baby was now three.

Claudia was the only kid with her own room. The younger boys were squeezed into the room across the hall from their parents. Javi used to be with the twins, but he moved to the basement with his brothers when the baby was born. The Marquez house was almost never clean, and the basement room never was clear of some aromatic mix of feet and wet laundry. On the other side of his bunk bed was the old washer and dryer that seemed to always be running.

Javi knew they were poor, but it was all he knew so it never really bothered him. If he needed something his parents would scrape together the money somehow. Both of his parents worked more than normal hours. Lucinda was a nurse at Methodist Hospital, and would run shifts at Hermanos on her days (or hours) off. Julio spent most of his nights at the restaurant, taking care of the youngest in the morning, when Lucinda was at the hospital. With Antonio and Diego mostly out of the house, and Claudia not yet old enough to be trusted, Javi spent a lot of time taking care of his younger siblings, which is why it was so uncommon for him to sleep in so late.

The digital clock on the large dresser that the three older brothers shared read "10:17am." It was Sunday, the night after the end of season party at the park, and Javi was starting to feel the effects of how much he drank the night before. Normally, he had no trouble holding his alcohol-his brothers first got him drunk when he was thirteen-but the night before he mixed the cheap beers that his managers were sneaking him, with the pills and weed that he got from Bridget. She normally wasn't into such things, neither was he really, but something seemed off about her and he didn't want to fight.

He threw up behind Zeus' Tilt-a-Whirl and walked through the off-limits area of the park to clear his head. When he returned to the party proper, he couldn't find Bridget, and Scott and Breck were elsewhere as well. He didn't want to tell Scott he had gotten so faded. Scott was such a goody-goody and would be all weird about it. Especially with football.

Javi hated football. He never told anyone that. It's not like he was great at it, but he was a decent running back because of his size and speed. It was what he was supposed to do. His brother Diego was a wide receiver on the varsity team before he dropped out and Antonio was first quarterback his senior year. Javi couldn't avoid being on the team, especially with his best friend being such a jock. Scott wouldn't understand, he lived for football. And basketball. And baseball. Javi couldn't stomach more than one team sport. The rest of the guys were a bunch of douchebags.

Getting a girlfriend was also what he was supposed to do. He met Bridget at the park over the summer and they quickly hit it off. They made out at one of the after parties and declared themselves boyfriend and girlfriend before school started, but the whole thing was kind of foreign to Javi. Bridget was probably the first real girlfriend he'd had, and he really wasn't sure what he was supposed to do. He brought her flowers, held her hand when they saw a movie, but when she went for his belt at one of the parties they got together at, he admitted he was a virgin and not quite ready. He was pretty much terrified of having a kid, after so much time spent with his younger siblings. And his parents were staunchly Catholic, and he didn't want the weight of letting God down.

Even though he and Bridget talked on the phone almost every day, it wasn't ever about anything. They were expected to go out at least one weekend night, but in football season it was mostly about meeting up after the games. Bridget was a cheerleader for her school and they were hardly ever available at the same times.

He liked her though. She was nice. And he liked that she wasn't afraid to stand up for herself when the guy at the movie theater short-changed her, or when one of the girls at school would pick on her. He still hadn't met her mom, Bridget always said she was super strict, but he was fine with that. She had been to the restaurant for dinner and met his parents, but he didn't tell them they were actually calling themselves "boyfriend" and "girlfriend." He wasn't sure if they would care that she was black and he didn't want to make a big deal about it until he knew she was going to be sticking around.

And was she going to stick around?

She had been weird the night before, and if he thought about it, she'd been acting weird more often lately. Nothing crazy, just everything seemed to bother her. She hated her school, hated her mom, hated Omaha, and if he pressed her she didn't want to talk about it. Javi liked having a girlfriend. He liked saying he had a girlfriend, but he wasn't sure if Bridget made sense. Wasn't he supposed to feel something every time he saw her? Wasn't there supposed to be butterflies or some shit like that?

Nothing like that ever happened with Bridget.

* * * * *

By the time he finally rolled out of bed and went upstairs, the house was fairly quiet. Javi had heard the phone ring a couple times and so he stayed in his room until he felt like it was safe. He didn't want to get stuck talking to his grandpa. He didn't want to form words right now. Besides, Grandpa couldn't hear anyway.

When Javi didn't hear voices, he walked upstairs.

In the kitchen, his mom was drinking coffee and facing out the window.

"Good morning," she said.

"Morning," Javi said through a yawn. "Where is everyone? It's so quiet."

"Your father is at the restaurant. And Antonio took Claudia and the boys to the park."

"I didn't mean to sleep so late. Can't believe it's past ten already."

"Well, it's just past nine. The clocks turned back last night."

Javi opened the fridge and pulled out the milk. It was almost gone so he drank directly from the jug.

He didn't realize anything was amiss until his mom turned around. Her eyes were watery, like she'd been crying, and she offered him an awkward smile.

"Can you sit down, Javi. We need to talk."

* * * * *

Javi was in shock. His mother offered him a hug but he didn't want to talk about it. He still didn't know what to think. Dead? She was really dead? He knew she'd been acting weird and clearly had something on her mind, but he didn't realize their awkward kiss on the dance floor, when she said she'd be back in a bit, that it would be the last time he would see her.

Ever.

Javi threw some clothes on and started walking. It was a hazy morning, and it wasn't quite raining, but there was a light mist spitting all over. He knew the phone calls would continue. Scott had already called, but as the news spread, everyone was going to reach out. He didn't want to talk to anyone. What was he supposed to say anyway? Was he supposed to have some great insight? His girlfriend was dead and he had been having doubts about even liking her. He was the worst person in the world.

His mom was pulling an overnight at the hospital when Bridget was brought in. They found her ID in her purse on the rooftop. All signs seemed to indicate she jumped. It was only about thirty feet from the top of the roof of the bathhouse, but on the front side there was a small section that opened to the storage areas below, which made it more like forty. Javi didn't want to listen to any more details. He was picturing it. Picturing Bridget lying on the ground like that, her body smashed, and it was making him ill.

She jumped. That's what the police thought. Javi couldn't believe that. Why would she jump? He knew she was off. Something was going on, but what could push her so far over the edge that she would end it all? It made zero sense. And after everything he was thinking about that morning. How there weren't any butterflies, he started to feel guilty. Did he have something to do with this? Did she sense that he wasn't really into her? Was that something that would damage her so much? Was this his fault?

Frankly, she didn't seem that into him. Javi never had a real girlfriend before so he had nothing to compare it to. When he was supposed to go out with Trina Alvarez in ninth grade she called him like fifty times every night and he felt smothered even before they made it to the movie theater for their date. Bridget didn't smother him. She held his hand. She called him. She wanted to have sex. He was the one that stopped it.

It just didn't make any sense. They got the wrong girl. Bridget traded costumes with someone and someone else was brought in. That was more plausible than her jumping. Bridget was too strong to just jump and end it all.

Without fully realizing it, Javi had walked over two miles. The houses on the other side of 55th street were starting to get nicer and the yards bigger. He wasn't anywhere near Fairacres, but the majority of kids at AC high were around Westbrook. Nearing Center Road, he was close to Scott's house so he turned up the hill and continued towards it.

Scott was sitting on the front porch, his elbows on his long legs that dangled down the steps. When Javi approached Scott immediately got to his feet, but seemed trepidatious about coming any closer.

"Hey," Scott offered.

"Hey."

"I tried calling."

"Yeah, I heard."

"You walk here?"

"Yeah, I was thinking, I guess."

"How are you?"

"I have no fucking clue."

"Yeah."

Javi could tell that Scott had been crying or something. His face looked different. Javi didn't cry. If he cried it would somehow make it feel more real. And he wasn't ready for that. It didn't make sense that

Scott would be crying, he didn't know her that well. But Bridget was friends with Breck, he supposed, so maybe that had something to do with it.

"Can I do anything?"

"No, thanks. I really don't know what I should be doing."

"You don't need to be doing anything," Scott said and he motioned for Javi to join him on the porch. They sat on the old, wooden swing, and slowly rocked. It was mostly quiet. Javi didn't know what to say but it felt good to feel like he didn't have to say anything.

They sat for a bit (hours?) until Javi worked up the strength to return home. There would be phone calls and his mom might start worrying. Scott offered to give him a ride, but Javi wanted to walk some more. It seemed right.

* * * * *

Javi spent the rest of the day talking to friends and family. They all said the same thing. They were sorry. It didn't make any sense. She was such a sweet girl. Many said that she loved him but that just made him feel guilty. He didn't love her. Didn't even know what love really felt like. All he felt was sad. And confused.

After a few minutes, though, no one really knew what to say and they would find an excuse to get off the phone. But if you need anything, they would say, anything at all. Javi didn't need anything. Every phone call meant to offer him comfort only made him feel worse.

"Maybe it was an accident," someone said. "Maybe she just fell."

Maybe.

The next day the sun was shining. Typical Omaha weather-no relation to the day before. Javi went to school like normal, but after he skipped practice and borrowed his brother's car and drove out to Lake Zorinsky. It was about ten miles down the road in West Omaha, and had an eight-mile path around the water. Javi liked to run around the lake. It felt like being in the woods, even with the neighborhood just a few blocks away. New houses were being built on the south side of the lake, but there was still a chance to see turkeys, deer and other wildlife wandering around.

Javi found the whole thing incredibly calming, even as he pushed himself to run faster and farther.

He was sweating through his jacket when he was in the middle of his second lap. He took a seat on a bench overlooking the lake, as the sun shimmered in the water's reflection. He prayed a little, asking God to take care of Bridget and to forgive her if she did in fact jump.

"Javi?" a voice asked.

Javi turned and saw Trevor Rhodes. He had worked with Trevor over the summer, but hadn't seen him since the park closed. Trevor was at the party, Javi saw him across the room, but they didn't talk. They never talked if Javi was with Bridget.

"Hi," Javi said as Trevor sat next to him on the bench.

"I… heard."

"Were you looking for me?"

"Kind of. Is that weird? I knew you liked to come out here whenever you were stressed. I called and your mom said you were out and I took a guess. Well, I was going to drive out to the park where you liked to go biking, but that is like another forty-five minutes so I've been walking around here hoping you would come by. And here you are."

"That was really unnecessary."

Trevor's mom was black and his dad was white so his skin was a soft brown color, not unlike Javi's Mexican hue. Trevor was tall though, not quite as tall as Scott, but he had thick, fuzzy hair that stuck up high enough to make him seem taller. Javi's hair was jet black and long enough to hang in his eyes if he wasn't constantly brushing it back.

"I wanted to see if you were okay."

"I'm fine."

"How can you be fine?"

It was a fair question. Javi didn't answer. He simply smiled and said "thanks for finding me."

They were the only ones on this part of the path. Despite how nice it was out, the lake wasn't crowded like it could get in the summer. Javi had seen some people on the north side, where the picnic tables were, but here it felt like they were the only two people in the world. Trevor must have felt that way as well because he reached his hand down to Javi's thigh and gave it a reassuring squeeze.

"Trevor, come on."

"I'm always here for you."

And that's when Javi felt it: butterflies. But it was more than that. He felt safe. He knew he should push Trevor's hand away. Someone could see them. But he didn't want to. And then everything came at him like a wave: the generosity of the gesture, how well Trevor knew him, better than his best friends, and how comfortable all of this felt. But also, Bridget was gone. His girlfriend had died and Javi had this fleeting moment of comfort, something Bridget would never feel again. It was wrong.

Javi felt guilty and sad and crazy and uncomfortable and it was all too much and finally, for the first time since he heard about Bridget, he started to cry. It came out soft at first, but soon became a full, body-shaking sob. Trevor held him and Javi continued to cry into his shoulder for what seemed like hours, but was only like two minutes.

Then, he pulled back.

Javi thought he heard someone nearby, but he looked around and it was still just the two of them.

"I gotta go," he said and he quickly stood up and started to run back to the car. He couldn't say anything else. He just had to keep running.

8. THE PERFECT GIRL

THEN

Bridget stared at the symbols on the chalk board, numbers and symbols in long equations that Mr. Sutton was writing. When he turned to look at her, he saw her eyes grow wide.

"So, tell me how you solve this equation?" Danny asked.

"Honestly, I'm looking at this and I have no clue where to begin," she said.

"Come here, let me show you."

Bridget stood up, straightened her blue, uniform skirt that was probably too short according to the specific wording of the dress code, but Danny wasn't going to be the one to give her a demerit.

The student went to the board, and pressed the chalk to the board, but nothing followed.

"Come on, it's order of operations, what's first?"

"This?" Bridget asked, pointing to the (X-4) on the board.

"Right, parentheses first. Good job."

Danny held out his hand and Bridget gave him a solid high five, perhaps a little overzealous. Danny recoiled.

"Ouch. Solid arm."

"Sorry, Da- Mister Sutton."

They looked at each other for a moment. Bridget smiled. Her big, brown eyes locked into his for a moment, as they held each other's gaze.

Danny turned her attention back to the board.

"What's next?"

NOW

Danny sat in the pew at St. Dymphna's Church, an old, vast brick building with bold stained-glass images of religious torture high above the congregation. He looked forward at the coffin in the center of the altar and Bridget's large school picture from the year before. He gritted his teeth hard, forcing himself not to betray any emotion deeper than the inherent sadness of a student's young life lost too soon.

His wife, Eli (short for Elizabeth), squeezed his hand. She knew this was hard on Danny, but she wouldn't have a clue how difficult.

Father O'Leary was blathering on, some platitude how there was a reason for this, but did anyone really think there was some master plan in the gruesome death of a seventeen-year-old girl?

The Omaha World Herald, the only newspaper that really mattered in town, lead with the story on Monday. They had quotes from police about how the case was still being investigated, and from friends that were just "so shocked" this happened. When the police floated the idea that this was likely a suicide, Bridget Kent was relegated to page 8 at best. City news. A small blurb. The investigation was ongoing, it said, but no one had the sense that it was going to be a case that would garner a lot of follow up.

Father O'Leary motioned for everyone to rise and Danny stood, looking across the aisle. Students were crying and leaning on each other.

All this posturing was stupid. Danny liked teaching, but teaching at a Catholic school was not his first choice. He hated all the masses and other services that he was expected to attend. He wanted to work with students. Everything about this felt like a waste of time.

And then he wondered if anyone saw her in his driveway that afternoon. The afternoon the day before she died.

THEN

"Thanks for the ride," Bridget said as Scott pulled into her driveway.

"Yeah, Javi was a little bombed tonight," he said, putting the car in park. "But seriously, you ever need anything, I'm here."

"You're such a nice guy," Bridget said, demurely.

"Well, I wouldn't go that far. You know, Javi's my best friend."

"Yeah, you would do anything for Javi."

"Well, yeah."

"I hope someone cares that much about me one day," Bridget said, and Scott detected a hint of sadness in her voice.

"I'm sure someone already does. You know, Javi is really into you."

"Is he? We've been going together for a couple months and… I don't know. I can tell he likes me, but I don't think he's the Edward to my Vivian."

"Is that like a royal family thing? I'm out after Charles and Di."

"No, it's…never mind. You boys never know anything. But hey, thanks for the ride."

Bridget leaned over and kisses Scott, on the lips, and it lingered, just for a moment. Scott is taken aback.

"Any time," he said, as she quickly got out of the car and bounded up to her door. She turned around and looked over her shoulder, waving her fingers back at him.

NOW

Scott pulled the large vacuum through the backseat of his car. He watched as every crumb and bit of fuzz was swooped up into the machine. When the suction stopped, again, he dug in his pockets for more quarters and plugged them into the slot and waited for the whir of the vac to start up again.

His car was going to be spotless.

When it was finally done to his satisfaction, he closed the doors and shoved his stuff back in the back – his gym bag, book bag, and other equipment. There was a paper bag filled with garbage: candy bar wrappers, condom wrappers, old homework. He found a card in the glove box. It was innocuous enough. It had a cartoon banana on front with some pun on "a-peeling" and inside there was a note scribbled. "Miss you – B."

Scott tore the card into dozens of pieces and dropped it into the bag of trash. When he was finished with the rest of his car, he grabbed the bag and clutched it in the front seat while he drove away.

He didn't see any other cars at the grocery store on 84th street, quite a few miles from his neighborhood, so he pulled around to the back. He jumped out of his car and lifted up the lid to the large dumpster and threw the garbage bag in, looking around to make sure no one was watching him.

THEN

Trevor filled the customer's slushie and handed it to them with a smile and "thank you." It was hot, pushing a hundred degrees, and humid. He was sweating through his undershirt, but the blue polo he had over it hid any sign.

Misters were spitting water over the customer side, but the workers had no such reprieve.

"Where are those cups?" Trevor shouted to the back of the concession stand.

Javi returned with a large box.

"Here," Javi said. "Was just soaking in a little of the sweet fan action in back."

"Oh no, if I have to suffer through this, we all do."

"I'm suffering. It's like a swamp in my pants," Javi said without any hint of entendre. He set the box down and Trevor watched the way Javi's shorts gripped his butt when he squatted.

"I can only imagine," Trevor said softly.

"Hey, can I get a diet?" a voice asked behind them. Trevor turned to see a young, black girl, hair in a pony tail and wearing the same blue polo.

"Oh, hey," Javi said when he saw Bridget. Trevor watched Javi lean over the counter and give Bridget a kiss hello. Instantly, they both seemed to forget he was there.

"I'm on break and my manager is being a total d-bag so I thought I would take a walk around. What about you?"

"Just trying not to bake."

"Can you walk with me?" Bridget asked with a flirtatious smile.

"Trev, can I take my break now?"

"You want to take your three o'clock break at 2:07?"

"That cool? Oh, this is my girlfriend, Bridget."

"Hey, Trev."

"It's Trevor. And fine. Just be back in fifteen?"

"Sure."

With one quick action, Javi vaulted over the counter and joined Bridget.

"And use the door, next time," Trevor shouted but Javi was already off.

NOW

Trevor parked his car on the street behind a tree. He had been driving down Dodge, when he saw Javi out walking around. He wanted to stop and talk to him, but Javi had been acting weird the past few days. Trevor knew it was normal, he didn't judge him for it, but he thought it was probably better if he kept his distance for a bit. Still, he was curious what he was up to.

He shouldn't have been surprised when he saw Javi walking into the cemetery. Bridget didn't have a headstone yet, but Trevor watched Javi stop a bit up the hill and pull some flowers out from inside his coat. It was a modest bouquet. Probably bought at the grocery store up the road, but it was the thought, right?

Everything about Javi's actions seemed perfunctory. This is what he should be doing. He wasn't crying or anything, and he (hopefully) had no idea anyone was watching him, but it felt to Trevor like he was checking some item off a list. He stood over the grave, gave the sign of the cross and bowed his head. After a few minutes he started walking back towards the exit.

Trevor slunk down in his car, praying to himself that Javi wouldn't notice him or his car. Thankfully, Javi rounded the corner once he left the cemetery and continued walking the other direction. Trevor debated on continuing to follow him or leave him be. He started the car, still not sure which direction he was going to go.

THEN

Vanessa stared at the clock. The numbers were blurry but she could tell it was past 7am. She was laying on her side, the covers wrapped tightly up to her neck. Sunlight was peering through the blinds.

"Come on, get up," Bridget called from the hallway.

"I will," Vanessa said. "It's fine. Go to school."

"You are going to be late for work. And we can't afford you getting laid off again."

"I will," she responded, but she knew nothing was going to happen. She had been trying to will herself to move for over an hour now and it wasn't happening.

Vanessa heard Bridget's footsteps walking away. She closed her eyes again, but then what felt like immediately after, the covers pulled her to one side. Vanessa wanted to let out a startled scream, but nothing came.

Bridget was standing at the edge of the bed with the blankets in her hands. Vanessa looked at the clock. It was after 8.

"You're still wearing your clothes from yesterday."

Vanessa looked down and saw the skirt and blouse she had spent the day before in. Even her stockings were on.

"Get up," Bridget spat. "I'm not your fucking mother."

NOW

Vanessa stood in the doorway to Bridget's room. It was clean. The bed was made. Everything looked in place. On the desk in the corner was a cheerleading trophy she had been awarded the year before.

Vanessa closed the door. She couldn't do this today.

Downstairs in the kitchen, there were baked goods all over the counter. People had been bringing casseroles, cakes, and muffins all week. Vanessa still wasn't hungry.

It was so quiet. Even if they weren't speaking, Bridget's mere presence was audible. Now, there was nothing. Vanessa turned on the TV in the living room and turned the volume up. Anything to drown out the silence. It was a soap opera. Someone was blackmailing someone else about their affair. She turned the volume up as loud as it could go. Anything to fill the house with noise.

Vanessa returned to kitchen. She dug her fingers into one of the cakes-this one a chocolate bundt cake with creamy white frosting-and slowly chewed. Her jaw was sore with every bite, probably after eating very little all week. It was too much. She spat the cake into the sink and sat down at the kitchen table. She poured herself a glass of water and stared out the window while the sounds of divas catfighting echoed through the house.

THEN

Harlan returned to his office. It was late, most everyone was gone, so he felt free to yell "Dammit!" at the top of his lungs as he threw his briefcase against the wall.

"It's about your son," she said, and the words continued to play on a loop in his head.

Harlan sat down behind his desk, a large, ornate, cherry wood number with a glass top. He rubbed his hands through his hair. He thought about calling Percy, but he didn't want to know what he would say. No answer could satisfy him.

"It's about your son," she had said. This young kid, with that smug face and standing there like she didn't have a damn clue who he was.

Harlan pulled his keys out from his pocket and unlocked his desk drawer. He pulled out one of the ledgers and opened it. There was a full page of checks. He made one out for ten thousand dollars and signed it. He left the name blank. He tore out the check, and put it in an envelope, then folded it and put it in his suit pocket.

This was a problem. But it was a problem that offered more than one solution.

NOW

Harlan flipped through the newspaper. There was nothing on the front page. He went to the local news section. Nothing. It was no longer a story, thank Christ. The last thing he read was that the police suspected it was a suicide, though they noted the investigation was still ongoing. He folded the paper back up.

Harlan sipped his coffee. This was all going to blow over soon enough.

He heard the clack of heels behind him and turned to see Donna walk in. She was wearing a suit, her hair and makeup impeccable.

“Where are you off to?” he asked.

“There’s a planning meeting for the ball, over lunch of course.”

“Didn’t we already have that?”

“Next year, dear.”

“And what about Rip Van Winkle downstairs?”

“Percy is staying home today.”

“The doctors said he was fine to go back to school.”

“Doesn’t mean he has to go to that one.”

“What does that mean?”

“It means there are students there that actually think he had something to do with that poor girl’s death. There have been phone calls. He’s not feeling up to it.”

“Police are saying suicide.”

“Since when does that matter? People still talk. You know what it’s like in this town. Everyone has an opinion on everything.”

“Are you sure he didn’t have anything to do with it?”

“Harlan, how dare you. He’s our son.”

“A son that has kept a lot of things from us.”

“I don’t have time for this now. Percy is staying home. If you have an issue with that we can discuss it later. Now, tell me I look beautiful so I can go into this meeting confidently.”

“You look wonderful, dear.”

“Imagine how great I would feel if you actually meant that.”

THEN

TJ listened to the sounds of the party going on in the ballroom, while he sat on the cement outside, puffing on a cigarette. He doesn't want to be here, but he knew Breck would be here, and this was the best time to connect with her without all the bullshit of school around. Still, he couldn't watch her fawn over Scott another second. Although it's not like he had anywhere else to go. He was squatting not too far from there and didn't know how to get back to the apartment without anyone seeing.

He put out his cigarette on the ground and stood up to go back to the party. He looked around for his cereal box, and realized he must've put it down somewhere.

Great.

Walking in the door, he bumped into Bridget, literally. Her head was down and it barreled right into his shoulder. She quickly looked up and scoffed when she made eye contact.

"Watch where you're going. Creep."

Bridget pushed past him.

"Why are you such a bitch to me?"

"Excuse me," she said, turning around to face him.

"What did I do to you?"

"I don't know. Existed?"

"You walk around like everyone works for you or something. I am not doing anything wrong by breathing the same air as you. Sorry, sister, you're not that special. You may have everyone else fooled like you're this perfect student, perfect girlfriend, perfect daughter. But I know you. You're nothing."

"Okay, one, don't call me sister. Don't think I don't know what you're doing. And two, you want to talk fooling everybody, why don't you tell me how you got that black eye?"

The marks around TJ's eye had mostly cleared up, and his long hair was hanging over it, but there were still some purple and black bruises. No one, not even any of his teachers had noticed it, or ever said anything. He figured he was in the clear.

"That's what I thought," Bridget said, as she turned around and walked away.

TJ reached out and grabbed her arm, but she jerked away from him instantly.

"Don't ever touch me."

NOW

It was getting cold again. Over the weekend, it had started to warm up but now it was back to frost on the grass every morning, and seeing everyone's breath.

TJ couldn't stay at the apartment at the park anymore, he knew that. Luckily, he was able to get his stuff out of there before the police took it over and, hopefully, left no indication that he ever was there.

He blasted the heat in the car. He couldn't leave it on all night, but if he got it warm enough, it would usually not get to freezing by morning. At least the frost on the windows would give him some semblance of privacy.

There was a parking lot at St. Gabriel's Church, miles away in South Omaha, that was well hidden, behind the church, off the street, and wouldn't alert attention if someone was parked there overnight.

He had changed the plates, stolen off an old lady's car from his old neighborhood that wasn't likely to be out much. He doubted she would even notice.

It wasn't the safest bet, but it was probably good for a few nights. He had to find somewhere else. Soon.

He couldn't keep sleeping in a dead girl's car.

9. ABBY

"I mean, I didn't even know her that well, you know. Or at all, really."

Abby sat on Dr. Gant's couch, slouched, with her hands fumbling around in her lap. There was a window on the other side of the therapist that Abby always focused on. She had told him many times about her issues with eye contact.

Bridget's death was old news. There was a funeral. There was crying in classrooms, and workshops on suicide, and even a press conference with the police chief. Given the trajectory of the fall, interviews with family and friends and other indicators, it was likely that her death was a suicide. There had been signs. She was giving stuff away, things that could be construed as cries for help. Her mother had tremendous guilt and could not make it through one TV interview without sobbing. In others, she looked like a zombie. Still, Abby couldn't shake one thought.

"I just don't think she did it. I don't buy it."

Abby had talked to the police herself. They interviewed as many kids as they could that were at the party, and Abby was one of the last ones to see her, but she wasn't as open with her theory. She didn't want to admit that she was smoking, in case her mom found out, or that she knew who was drinking, that she had even had a couple. Abby went to the party with her step-brother. He had friends that had worked there, but he promptly ditched her upon arrival and she didn't see him until later that night when he sneaked into her room, like usual. Only that time they actually did sleep together. He big spooned her until morning, their clothes remaining on the whole time.

Abby didn't tell anyone about that. She never brought up her relationship with Jake to anyone. It's not like they had grown up as step-siblings. Her mom married his dad like three years ago. She had only met him a few times before they were living across the hall from each other. Then, barely six months after the marriage, John Davenport had a heart attack while on his boat, and being on the lake, was too far from a hospital to get there in time to save him. Jake was upset. He had already lost his mother. Abby's dad had died as well, and part of the reason that Olivia and John had met and married was their shared grief over losing spouses.

There was a custody thing, Jake's aunt offered to take him, but Jake wanted to finish school with his friends and Olivia fought for him. Abby felt sorry for him, it seemed like no one wanted him. He could be aggressive and mean, but Abby knew that was just masking the hurt little boy that had been left behind by everyone he had ever known. Abby had gotten drunk and ended up kissing Jake. Jake was the one who pushed further, and Abby didn't relent but one of her friends, Breck Hartman, had caught them. Breck and Abby's friendship didn't survive that and Abby continued to find solace with Jake. She didn't have a crush on him or anything like that, really she didn't even like him that much, but there was something about him that made her feel seen in a way she never had before.

But none of that could she tell Dr. Gant.

"What is it about Bridget's death that seems to affect you so much?" he asked. "Is it bringing up thoughts of your own suicide attempt?"

"Wow, you really just throw that out there like it's nothing, don't you?"

Abby and Dr. Gant had discussed her suicide attempt ad naseum. It was the reason she was sent to see him in the first place. Even Abby wasn't sure if she really intended to go through with it. She had taken a bottle of pain killers that her mother had in the medicine cabinet and for good measure had sat in the garage with the car on. She had passed out from the pills before anything else could happen, and with the gap at the bottom of the garage door that never quite closed, she was found before the carbon monoxide could take effect. She woke up in the hospital the next day. Word had gotten around the school and everyone looked at her differently. She convinced her mom to let her transfer to St. Dymphna's even though it was only on the other side of the public high school, and they hadn't gone to church a day in their lives, save for the funerals and weddings.

"I'm not trying to make light of your past," Dr. Gant said. "I think it may be possible that this is bringing stuff up for you."

"Well, kind of. Like how everyone treated me like a leper with AIDS and everyone is ready to make Bridget a saint. Believe me, she wasn't a saint."

"You said yourself you didn't know her that well."

"Well enough. Besides it wasn't like she had this dark cloud over her.

I know what it's like when you're under that cloud. When you want to scream 'notice me' at the top of your lungs in the middle of the entire world, while pushing everyone away because how could they possibly understand. Bridget had a light in her eyes. She had plans. And not plans like this. She was going someplace."

"Where do you think she was going?"

"I don't know. But she had friends. Everyone seemed to love her. She had options."

"I think you and I both know that it's impossible to know what someone is actually thinking or feeling."

"Maybe. But I talked to her just a couple hours before she died. And if she was really thinking about this she hid it so well. Or something else happened after that to really bring her down. So to speak."

Abby didn't mean to make the pun, and would've laughed if she didn't get stuck on something Dr. Gant said: you could never know what someone was actually thinking.

But what if you could?

Abby had forgotten about Bridget's journal, the one she stole and shoved in her glove box weeks ago. She had only read a few passages and was unimpressed and mostly uninterested in Bridget's inner thoughts.

Things were a little different now.

* * * * *

Abby sat in her car in the parking lot of Dr. Gant's office and started to pore over the journal. It took a completely different tone now that Bridget was gone. The first entry was from January. The middle of Bridget's sophomore year. She complained about her classes and other little things but nothing that seemed to indicate deeper issues. At first there was an entry every day, but by the time March rolled around, she was down to two or three times a week. That was good, Abby could only stomach so many whines about her classes and her overbearing mom. Honestly, Bridget's mom didn't seem any worse than Abby's.

By April things started to get interesting.

Bridget mentioned a crush on a teacher. She didn't name him, instead using a code name (Mr. Darcy, barf). It wouldn't be too difficult to figure out though. All Abby had to do was cross reference Bridget's class schedule from last year to get the teachers in her orbit. There were mostly slim pickings at Dymp's anyway. A lot of the teachers were in the clergy or mean nuns left over from a more stern era. Abby could really only think of four teachers that were even crush eligible.

Still, Bridget became a much more whole individual the more Abby read. At first, she was just that bitch in her study hall. Abby resented Bridget and her popularity, and also her connection to Abby's friends from her old school. AC High felt inescapable, and part of the reason for that was Bridget. She lived across the street from Kira, and Kira and Breck were close so there was plenty of overlap from there, especially once Bridget started dating Javi.

Abby made it to the end of the school year in the journal before she put it down and had to focus on her actual homework, but as she went to essays and equations, her mind kept drifting back to Bridget, and thinking of her on that rooftop. Was she really alone? Did she jump or was she pushed? Were there ever going to be any real answers?

* * * * *

"Did you have any classes with her?" Abby asked.

Jake was smashing buttons on his Nintendo, watching Ryu take down Chun-Li, and only seemed to be tangentially listening to Abby. Talking wasn't really their thing anyway. So, she asked again.

"Bridget? Did you have classes or hang out with her?"

"I don't think so. Who knows? Not that I remember."

"She's one of like four black girls in the school. I think you'd notice."

"Why are you asking about her?"

"I'm just curious. It's kind of weird, right?"

"What's weird? Isn't she like the fourth person to off themselves in the last two years?"

Abby bristled at Jake's nonchalance. He must've caught it, because he paused his game and actually turned around to face her.

"Hey, I didn't mean…"

"I know. Whatever. It's fine. Sorry if I'm being nosy. Someone was saying that they don't think she jumped. That she might've been pushed. And I was just wondering if you knew her."

"Maybe you should ask Percy Van Allen."

"I don't… really know Percy. Why? What does he have to do with anything?"

Jake returned to his game.

"He hasn't been back to school since that whole thing. Supposedly he got hurt or something, but I heard he was questioned by the cops."

"Why would they question him?"

"I don't know anything, man, that's just what I heard."

Abby thought of Percy from the morning at school when she dropped her books. She still thought of his smile and generous spirit when everyone else was laughing at her. Honestly, she thought about him a lot since then. At no point, did she think of him as capable of anything like this.

But did she really know him at all? And if she thought about it, could she really imagine anyone she knew pushing Bridget off a building? There was something in her that simply wanted to believe that Bridget wasn't the type of person who would jump, who could jump.

Nothing about the whole situation made any sense to her. Maybe she was too far removed from it. Maybe her borderline obsession on this student she barely talked to spoke more about her own feelings toward suicide and how everyone reacted to her attempt. Maybe that was where she needed to start.

* * * * *

"Thanks for meeting me," Abby said as Breck sat down on the other side of the booth from her. Abby chose the diner that lived roughly half-way between their houses. It was the first restaurant (with waiters, at least) Abby went to without a parent. She and Breck used to walk out of their way after school, just to sit for hours, eat hamburgers and go over their homework.

"I wasn't sure if you were actually going to show."

"Why wouldn't I?" Breck asked, somewhat defensively. She crossed her arms and leaned back in the booth. Her dark hair was in pig tails, and her overalls made her look like she was still a kid.

"Come on, it's not like we've actually talked in forever."

"And that's my fault?"

"Hey, I didn't call you to fight."

"Why did you call?"

"I wanted to say I was sorry. About Bridget. I know you guys were kind of friends."

"Thanks."

"Kind of weird, huh?"

"Yeah, I still can't believe it. I mean, we were hanging out that night at the party. And then she's, you know, gone."

Breck let her arms fall to her side. Abby could tell she was softening towards her.

"Did you think that… anything like this could've happened?"

"You mean, did I know she was thinking about jumping off a building? That's a big fat 'no.' I still can't figure it out. Kira said she was talking all weird and saying how great their friendship was and then gave her this necklace thing. They say that's one of the signs, giving stuff away."

"Well, there's not just one way to do these things," Abby said.

Breck looked down for a moment, as if she was just now putting together that Abby had her own history.

"Abby, I just… can I say that, you know, the whole thing last year. I was mad and I had no idea that-"

Before she could continue, Abby held her hand out.

"I don't want to talk about me. I'm fine. This is about Bridget. She was your friend and I wanted to see how you were, not to rehash anything."

Abby stared at Breck for a moment, not sure if what she had just said was true or not. She was only sure that she didn't want to talk about it in the middle of the diner on a Tuesday afternoon.

The college-aged waiter interrupted them to take their order and Abby was grateful for the distraction. She ordered the hamburger combo and told Breck she could share if she wanted, but Breck just ordered her own side of fries and a pop.

When their conversation resumed, it took on a more small talk vibe.

They talked about classes. Breck gushed over Scott. Abby decided not to pepper her with too many questions. She got stuck hanging out like when they were younger, and she enjoyed the comfortability of it. It felt so far from where they were usually.

* * * * *

Abby had asked around Dymps about Bridget. A simple lie that she was working for the school paper and people talked openly about Bridget, what classes they shared, what they heard, what she was like, everything. Abby drew up a grid and easily captured Bridget's class schedule not only from that year, but both semesters the year before. There were only a few teachers that seemed plausible for Mr. Darcy before she narrowed down her classes. After, only one name fit.

Abby continued to take notes in study hall, she had sat at a closer desk, right by Mr. Sutton.

Danny Sutton was a "cool" teacher. He wasn't yet thirty, and joked with the students like they were peers, not subordinates. He was constantly fighting against the system of the Catholic school, which made him feel even more like he was on the students' side. He was handsome, in a plain sort of way, Abby could admit that. He wore his button-down shirts a little too tight, and they seemed to cling to his muscles. He rolled his sleeves up and his forearms had veins like he worked out a lot. He had light brown hair that was parted, but always looked like he needed a haircut. His jokes were sometimes too familiar. Abby always thought he buddied up to the jocks and popular kids. He might've been a coach. Abby made a note to get her hands on last year's yearbook from someone.

Mr. Sutton was married, but Abby didn't really know anything about his wife. She made a note to ask around about that as well. Maybe he got married too young and they were having trouble. Maybe his wife had passed away but he still wore the ring. No, she probably would've heard something about that. In any case, Abby now had Mr. Sutton plainly in her sights.

She wanted to learn everything she could about this man. She was going to learn everything about him, especially as it pertained to Bridget.

10. KIRA

Fuck Bridget Kent!

It took eleven days, most filled with tears, before Kira let herself express this thought so directly. She wanted to shout it at the top of her lungs, with a megaphone in the middle of the busiest intersection in town (72nd and Dodge was what she imagined, but she could be flexible on this point). Kira had spent so much time being sad about Bridget's death that it took her eleven days to reach anger. Bridget did this to herself. Bridget left without giving her so much as a reason why.

Kira was pissed, which only made her more sad, which only made her more pissed. She didn't know how to get out of this circle, but she also didn't want to ask for help. Her mother tried to be supportive, but when Kira talked to her about her dad having a baby with and getting married to his new girlfriend, she wasn't exactly thrilled. Dishes were broken. Names were called. Kira didn't want to pile on. And her dad was so focused on Georgina and the baby that Kira didn't want to burden them either. She tried to talk to Breck about it, but Breck seemed to be extra sensitive and sad about Bridget's death, even though they weren't that close. Kira wanted to talk to Bridget, to run across the street, toss a pebble at her window and see the light flip on, the blinds stretch open, and Bridget motion for her to come in the back door. But that stopped happening a few years ago, and now it wouldn't happen again. Ever.

Kira laid in bed with her music playing too loud. It was the only way she could stop thinking. Zoning out felt so much better. It just kept gnawing at her that Bridget was feeling so alone that she couldn't talk to her, talk to anyone, and resorted to this drastic step. Kira wanted an answer, something, that would put this in the right context, but there was nothing. So, she blasted her music, kept her smile up, and continued to tell everyone she was fine.

Bridget's death cast a pall over everything. School had this morose air, even though Bridget didn't even go to AC High. There were several suicides over the past few years there, so it brought a lot of stuff up for a lot of people. And Bridget was still a known figure. The schools were so close together, Bridget lived in the neighborhood, and she worked with a lot of the same kids that Kira saw in her classes. And even though it wasn't a big deal, Bridget and Kira were two of the handful of black kids that were around. Bridget's school had few black students. There were more at AC because of the bussing laws, but the Hudson and Kent houses were two of the few in the neighborhood that had black families.

Omaha had a history of segregation and racism that wasn't relegated to the distant past. In the fall of 1919, there were riots in South Omaha. Fifteen thousand white men crowded the courthouse where Willy Brown, a black man accused of the rape of a white woman, was being held. Though the police tried to maintain order, they lost control of the mob and the courthouse was under siege, windows broken, shots fired. The mob attacked any black men and women they saw. Blacks were dragged from their cars and beaten. When the (white) mayor tried to restore order, he was hanged, though he was rescued before he passed. The mob had set fire to the courthouse, and were eventually successful in getting custody of Brown. Brown was hanged at 18th and Harney, though he was likely killed before then. Still, as he hung there, he was shot dozens of times, then dragged through the streets before his body was eventually burned. Pictures were taken of Brown's crisp, black body, with dozens of white men and women posing and smiling around it.

Kira was twelve when her father told her the story of Willy Brown. This was not something she was ever taught in school. Randall Hudson told his daughter how she had to be extra vigilant, and wary of her surroundings at all time. He told her how the rules were different for them because of the color of their skin. How it would always be different.

There were other incidents besides Willy Brown. In 1969, Vivian Strong was a 14-year-old girl shot in the head by a white police officer with no warning. The cop was acquitted by an all-white jury and eventually returned to the police force. There were riots then too, but of course, not the same kind. Kira felt all of these incidents in her bones every time they taught slavery in schools and the white boys (it was almost always the boys) made jokes at her expense. She felt it when she tried to get a job over the summer but was continually denied for a lack of experience and then would see younger, and equally inexperienced white girls, working at the same place soon after. She didn't think Omaha was as overtly racist as its (fairly) recent history, but it was always there.

She tried to bring up the Willy Brown case in her Social Studies class in seventh grade but was shot down by her (white) teacher, who simply said it wasn't part of the lesson. She continued to research race relations in Omaha on her own. While reviewing old newspaper articles on the Brown story on microfiche at the downtown library, she could look out the window and see where he was murdered just three blocks away.

Every time she drove down Harney she got a pang in the pit of her stomach. After the riot that ended with Brown's burned body, government intervention followed. Omaha became even more segregated and the black community was predominantly located in North Omaha. It wasn't that rare for black families to be peppered throughout other parts of town, but it also wasn't uncommon to get strange looks when Kira would sit on her front lawn from a neighbor walking by, or to be followed when she went to a store.

Bridget was more confrontational than she was. Kira never forgot her father's warnings and always worked to remove herself from any situation that could turn ugly quickly, but Bridget almost seemed to enjoy getting in someone's face. There was that time the two of them went shopping at the mall and, naturally, as soon as they stepped foot into The Limited, they were followed by the fat, white security guard with the child molester mustache. He didn't make any attempt to be subtle and after a few minutes of this, Bridget turned and faced him, shouting "Can I help you, sir?"

The security guard said he was only doing his job, but when Bridget asked if his job was "sweating through a two sizes too small shirt, and making the place smell like baked bean farts," he forced them out of the store. They were both laughing too much to care about the racism on full display.

Kira's mom lived in North Omaha, which is one of the reasons why she lived with her father full time. When Yvonne and Randall Hudson split, they thought it was safer and better for Kira to stay in the house she grew up in and with her friends then to move to North O with Yvonne. Because of this, the North Omaha kids that got bussed into AC High viewed her as an "other" almost as much as the white kids did. Bridget was one of the few people that could understand this feeling of being caught in the middle, and now she was gone.

And Kira was all alone.

And she couldn't forgive Bridget for doing that to her.

* * * * *

"You should come by though, really, it's good to talk to other kids that feel the same way you do," Breck said, a little too emphatically.

"How do you know how I'm feeling?" Kira asked, somewhat softer than it came out.

"Well, I don't but that's why you should come."

Breck had started a support group for those that had been affected by suicide at AC High. Kira thought it a little ridiculous, since, again, Breck wasn't that close to Bridget, but you wouldn't know that by all her actions. Kira thought she was acting like it was her own sister or something. It made talking to her really difficult.

Kira started walking home on her own, trudging through the muddy puddles left from the rain the night before. She stomped her dark boots through every one just to hear that "squish" sound. Something about that was comforting. Breck had caught up to her and was fluttering around trying to get Kira to join her group, which only made her more withdrawn.

"You've been a little distant lately, you know?" Breck said.

"Yeah, it's been a rough couple of weeks."

"But you can talk to me, you know that. We are going through the same thing."

That was it. Kira's fuse was already short, and that burnt it to the end. Kira stopped to face her.

"How are we going through the same thing? You barely knew her. I grew up with her and I barely knew her. I lived across the street from her for most of my life. We shared clothes. Her mom babysat me. This is not the same for you and me."

Breck stood there, mouth agape. Kira was just as surprised at her own outburst, but it didn't feel wrong. Kira turned and kept walking, and Breck kept pace next to her though she didn't say anything for about a block.

"I'm sorry, I didn't mean to act like it was the same. I just know that when I heard about Abby, you know and the pills, I was mad and angry and everything."

"This is not the same thing as that."

"I know. Because that was my fault."

"I'm sure it wasn't your fault."

"No, it for real was."

"What do you mean?"

"Because I'm the one that talked."

"About what?"

Kira was confused. It was bad enough that Breck was being weird about Bridget's death, but the Abby "situation" was before her time. Breck and Kira had gotten close the year before because of some shared classes and their close proximity. Kira knew that Breck and Abby had been friends and that Abby was abruptly no longer in school. She heard that she OD'd on pills, but she had no idea why. Frankly, she didn't give it much thought. She hadn't shared any classes with Abby, and could barely even remember what she looked like. Breck didn't talk about her, and Kira had other things to worry about.

"Never mind," Breck responded.

"Are you saying that Abby didn't OD?"

"I'm saying that she purposely OD'd. She tried to kill herself. And that it was my fault. We used to be friends, and then I wasn't there for her when she needed me. I dropped her because, well, it doesn't matter. I felt so badly. And after, when she was okay, she switched schools and stopped taking my calls. And I felt like such shit."

Kira still wasn't sure why they were talking about this. This wasn't about Abby; this wasn't even about Breck. This was about Bridget. Kira felt many things, but she hadn't quite landed on guilt. Bridget had friends. Bridget knew that Kira was there if she needed her. Bridget was the one keeping secrets. She was the one sneaking out. She was the one avoiding conversations. Sure, Kira could've pushed more but would that have done any good.

There weren't any answers. Breck and Kira kept walking quietly until it came time to split and go down their respective streets. They hugged and Kira apologized for snapping. Kira wasn't sure she had any better grasp of the situation around Bridget but she was suddenly wondering if there might actually be someone she could talk to about this.

* * * * *

Kira had been going over to Bridget's house after school to help her mother out. It wasn't an everyday thing, but often enough that it wasn't weird if she let herself in. Kira shouted out for Vanessa, but heard no response, so she took off her boots and left them on the front mat, and put her coat in the front closet. There was a large portrait of Bridget and Vanessa in the hallway, one of those things they took at the mall with the two inexplicably sitting on a bale of hay. Kira stared at the picture, looking at Bridget's eyes, trying to imagine what she was thinking, feeling. She felt sad that this was the last mother/daughter photo they would ever take, and this is how Bridget was going to forever remembered: a teenager, big smile, ugly jean jacket, on a fucking bale of hay.

In the living room, Kira saw (what she hoped were) the remnants of takeout from the night before. Barely eaten orange chicken that had attracted a couple of flies. She picked up the cold Chinese and threw it in the trash in the kitchen. There were dirty dishes in the sink so Kira started a water and splattered soap over the plates and bowls.

Vanessa hadn't gone back to work since Bridget's death. She had spent most days in the house, creating a mess, and with a little prompting from her father, Kira offered to help clean up. For someone that didn't seem to be eating, she certainly left a decent mess. Kira started to scrub the dishes. She zoned out a bit replaying her conversation with Breck, as she scrubbed caked on food from each plate. Even though it was cold out, Kira cracked a window to help the smell dissipate.

"I knew you were faking. This is just fucking like you," a voice snarled behind her.

Kira gasped. She thought she was alone. She turned to see Vanessa, in a ratty blue robe. The robe was undone, showing a dirty white t-shirt below. It wasn't clear if she was wearing anything else, but it was clear by the hair on Vanessa's legs that she wasn't shaving.

"Oh, hi, Miss Kent. I didn't know you were home."

"So formal. What's that about?"

Vanessa was kind of swaying and her hand was shaking, but she still managed to pull out a chair from the kitchen table and sit down. Vanessa looked around.

"This place is a shit hole."

Kira returned to the dishes. She turned the water off, careful not to move too suddenly. She had seen Vanessa a lot over the past few weeks. Some days she wouldn't leave her bed. Others, she was bright eyed and effusively grateful. She'd never been like this though. Kira wasn't sure if she had been drinking. Bridget mentioned that sometimes she could be out of it, but Kira never imagined it was like this. She put the dirty dishes in the dishwasher.

"Kira, when did you get here?" Vanessa asked as if she hadn't been talking to her already.

"Just walked in, Miss Kent."

"Oh, call me Vanessa."

"Sure, Vanessa."

Vanessa smiled. "You're so sweet to help me out."

"I need to use the restroom," Kira said before excusing herself. She didn't want to be there. It felt wrong. Invasive. Like she was seeing behind the scenes of a movie she wasn't supposed to watch. She washed her hands in the bathroom sink and sat on the edge of the bathtub for a few minutes. Maybe if she waited it out, Vanessa would return to the bedroom.

It was starting to feel too long so Kira got up and walked out.

Bridget's room was across the hall from the bathroom and Kira could see the door was slightly ajar. She tiptoed over and peeked in. Kira let out a soft gasp when she saw the room.

It looked like someone had broken in. The mattress was hanging off the bed frame. Every drawer of Bridget's desk and dresser had been opened and the contents, apparently, thrown all over the room. Clothes, books, cassette tapes, and numerous other items littered the floor. Shelves that held Bridget's trophies had been knocked down, and pieces of little gold cheerleaders sat amidst the other rubble. Before she could take much more in, the doorbell rang. Kira went to the window and saw a police car in the driveway.

Downstairs, she could hear Vanessa move to get the door. Kira crept to the hallway to listen better.

"May we come in," she heard someone say.

"No, you may not," Vanessa spat back. Kira was reminded of Bridget's rebellious attitude and where it came from.

There were two officers from what Kira could make out. They said they had been calling, left messages, but hadn't heard anything. Vanessa asked what they wanted. She was cold and harsh. They apologized, saying there was no advancement in the case. They had been investigating, but all signs pointed to Bridget choosing to jump.

"My daughter did not kill herself," Vanessa said firmly.

"We are not closing the case. We are going to keep looking, but frankly right now there aren't any substantial leads."

"Is this because she's black?"

"I don't know what you mean."

"I mean that if she were a young white girl who was found dead her face would be plastered all over this town, but because she's not, you're quick to wrap it up."

"That's not what's happening here."

"I don't care what's happening. You do your job and find who killed my baby girl."

There were more apologies that Kira could make out. It wasn't as easy to hear the police because they were talking normally, but Vanessa kept shouting. They had only been at the door a few minutes when Vanessa slammed the door shut. Kira jumped back into the bathroom and flushed the toilet.

She made as much noise as she could walking back down the stairs and found Vanessa staring at a game show on the TV.

"Everything okay?" Kira asked.

There was no response.

"I'm really not feeling well. I can come back tomorrow to finish up. Sorry."

Kira pulled her boots on as fast as she could. Thankfully, the police had pulled away and she made her way back across the street into her own home.

* * * * *

It wasn't difficult to get the address. Kira wondered if she should call first, but she still hadn't figured out what she was supposed to say. Something just compelled her to go.

It was a nice enough house. Bigger than hers. It was on the border of the rich neighborhood and the more middle-class area, so it could be construed as being a part of either. Two cars were in the driveway, a souped-up BMW and junkier Honda. It didn't look like they belonged in the same household.

The door swung open and she stood there. Hair in a pony tail, hiding behind big glasses.

"Yeah?" the girl asked.

"Abby?"

"Yeah."

"I'm Kira. Breck's friend. And Bridget's. Can we talk?"

11. PERCY

Thankfully, he had a full prescription of Vicodin, because everything about him hurt. Part of it, sure the bulk of it, was the numerous gashes and cuts and, now, stitches that were all over his body. The rest was mostly due to his mother's pacing. And the yelling.

"Are you even listening to me?" Donna said, as Percy looked down and hoped she didn't have any specific follow-up questions.

Percy had hobbled up the stairs, pulled out stuff to make a sandwich from the fridge and, when he sat down at the kitchen island to eat it, his mother came in and started berating him. It felt like a worn tirade. He picked up small things like "lazy," "wasting your potential," and how his actions "reflect on your parents." He tried hard not to roll his eyes, so instead he focused at a point on the wall and tried to play back Metallica lyrics in his head. Donna seemed to enjoy yelling at her son, well, her oldest son. Percy's little brother, Simon, could do no wrong. Oh yeah, and there was something about "setting a bad example" in there.

"What do want me to do?" Percy asked.

"I want you to go back to school."

"Fuck that."

"Do not speak to me like that."

"I'm not going back there. I'm taking the GED. And then I'm going far away to college."

"Oh, you think colleges love to accept GED students with a criminal record?"

"I don't have a criminal record. I wasn't even charged with a crime. They could've given me an MIP and they didn't even do that."

"I still don't think it's going to be easy."

"Well, maybe Dad can add a wing on to a library or something."

"That is our money. Not your money."

"Is this about me or is this because you got kicked off your planning committee?"

"I did not get 'kicked off.' I took a step back because the rumors were distracting."

"For you or for them?"

Donna grunted and walked over to the fridge and pulled out a pop. Percy had never even seen his mom drink a soda, so this was particularly interesting. He watched her open the can and pour it into a glass. Clearly, she was unable to put her lips to something so pedestrian as aluminum.

"I've talked to your father. If you're not going back to school then you are going to work."

"No school will accept me, but you think getting a job will be easy? Who is going to hire me?"

"You are going to go into the office with your father. You can make copies or whatever he tells you to do. It can keep you out of trouble."

"I'm not getting into trouble. I didn't do anything, Mom."

"Were you at this party?"

Percy paused and shook his head. "I wasn't there. I told you. I was at a friend's house. I did drive by on my way home, but the parking lot was mostly empty. So, I came home and had something to drink here."

"I wish you weren't so good at lying. You always were. When you got caught shoplifting that comic book at Target you looked me straight in the eye and said you didn't do it as they opened your jacket and it was right there. I honestly don't know what to believe."

"Mom, that happened when I was ten years old. Are you ever going to let it go? It has nothing to do with this."

"I was mortified."

Percy acted offended and shuffled out of the kitchen, but really his mom wasn't wrong. He did lie. He was lying. And, yeah, he was pretty good at it. It was one of the few things he actively worked at. He wasn't proud of it, not really, but mostly because it wasn't something he could really ever share with anyone. Telling someone you are a great liar doesn't exactly endear them to you. It's not so much a trust builder.

But also, Percy wasn't exactly sure what he was lying about. He wasn't at the party. Not technically. He wasn't really at a friend's house either though. He had made a few rounds to some clients. Saturday was a busy time for him. Halloween even more so. He got a page from Bridget and when he called her back, she asked him to meet her at the park. That's what he thinks, at least. He kind of remembers that but it's a little foggy. He only recalled the page when he saw it on his bill. Thankfully, he has that sent to a PO Box that wasn't even in his name, so the police weren't likely to connect it to him.

Percy had been on the roof before, another night that was a little foggy for him. The whole thing was a mess and until he understood it better, he couldn't tell anyone. How was he supposed to explain his innocence, when even he wasn't sure? He was a good liar, but that good?

And how sure was he? Did he push her? Could he have pushed her?

No.

He couldn't have. He wasn't like that. He was a good person. He knew that. Sure, he was a liar and a drug dealer, but he was a good person.

Right?

* * * * *

Percy wore the shirt and tie he would normally wear to school to the office with Harlan. The office was officially HVA2 (Harlan Van Allen and Associates, though Percy thought it should be HVA3, if you want to get technical). Percy evaded most of Harlan's questions on the ride downtown to the First National Bank Building that housed Harlan's company. They had the entire 10th floor and a few offices on the 12th that were mostly used for storage.

Percy got out of his car and grabbed his backpack. He noticed the "Reserved for President/CEO" sign that was in front of Harlan's car. It had been a long time since Percy had been to the office, made even more noticeable as they walked inside and nearly everyone commented about how he'd grown. A few mentioned how handsome he was and Carol in accounting even touched his face which felt really weird, but he smiled anyway.

He assumed he would be in his father's office, but instead he was given a desk in a poorly lit cubicle, covered by a couple plastic and fabric half-walls. There was a stack of files and Harlan gave some quick instructions on how to organize. Percy sat down in the office chair and went to work. After maybe three minutes, when he was decidedly bored, he pulled his Walkman out of his backpack, and his wallet of CDs. He settled on the Beastie Boys, and played the disc too loudly while he continued to sort.

When the CD finished, Percy found the bathroom. He repeated this pattern three times. Twice to take a dump, once to masturbate. He noticed one of the customer service ladies whose name he didn't catch giving him a look after leaving the bathroom for the third time, but then he remembered he didn't care and that he was the boss' son, so he was fairly confident no one was going to say anything. Besides, he would just say he wasn't feeling great and maybe he might even be able to leave early.

But no such luck.

Harlan came by the cube around lunchtime to check Percy's progress. Harlan nodded some half-hearted approval, handed him a hundred-dollar bill and told him to grab some lunch, that he had a meeting.

Percy roamed the streets of downtown Omaha, until he found a sandwich shop. He got a combo meal for about nine dollars and then went around the corner to a record store and spent the rest of the money on CDs. If he was going to make it the rest of the day he was going to need some new tunes.

Back at the office, he shoved his haul into his backpack just in case his father asked for change and he would have to make up something. He returned to filing and his music, rocking out to Rage Against the Machine while trying to force the clock to move faster. If he was at school now, he would be in English class. He also tried to make the clock move faster there.

How did everything get so fucked?

Percy hadn't been back to school since everything went down. He was in the hospital for nearly a week. He apparently lost a not insignificant amount of blood, but after that, aside from the bruises, scratches and scars, he was on the road to recovery. He could walk normally, though sometimes if he turned his body a certain way, he would get a shooting pain throughout his lower back. Luckily the most noticeable scars weren't on his face.

He had a few guys call. More than a few clients. But Percy definitely became more aware of how expendable he was to those he thought were friends. He didn't want to go back to school mostly because he was pissed he wasn't getting more attention. Yeah, he knew there were rumors that he was connected somehow to Bridget's death, but no one actually saw him (right?). There was no actual proof he had been there at all that night. And people just liked to make shit up sometimes.

Percy tried to think of something else and focused more on the filing (ugh) until he actually fell asleep for a solid forty-five minutes. He took two pills at lunch, not that he needed to, but they made it difficult to stay awake. He woke up with a post-it note stuck to his face and saw that it was nearing five o'clock. Percy stretched and went to find his father's office.

Harlan had a corner office, naturally, with views of the river from one side, just on the other side of the smaller downtown buildings. To the north, it was just the parking lot and boring streets. His desk was a large cherry wood with a thin glass plate on top. The round table on one side of the room, bookshelves on the other, all matched. The couch and chairs were all leather.

Percy knocked on the door. His dad was on the phone but waved for Percy to come in. Percy looked at the pictures on the wall, one a large family photo they took three years ago. It looked like a completely different family. Mom and Dad were in the center, smiling and holding hands. Harlan had on a nice, pale pink sweater and jeans. Donna had her hair up. Her blouse matched Harlan's sweater, but she had a dark jacket over it. On one side of them was Bailey, Percy's older sister. She was away at school now, but that was probably her junior year of high school. She had the teased bangs and wavy curls she had back then. Percy was on the other side, scrawny, before he hit his growth spurt. His lips pursed in more of a smirk. He and Bailey both had outfits that complemented their parents. In front, Simon, Percy's baby brother, only three or four at the time, had overalls and a toothy grin. They looked like the family you would find on the brochure of the photo place, or any place really. They looked happy. Connected.

They were nothing of the sort.

"Your mother wants to get another one," Harlan said once he hung up the phone.

"Why? It'll never be as good as this one. And good luck getting Si back into overalls."

Harlan let out a soft chuckle. For a quick second, it almost felt like they were that family. But then that second was over.

"You finish with the files?"

"Pretty much. Do I have to do that every day?"

"I'm sure we can find plenty of things for you to do."

"How long do I have to keep doing this?"

"You can always go back to school."

Percy shook his head. Harlan stood up and started to gather his stuff. He put some folders into his briefcase and snapped it shut. Then he crossed in front of Percy, but as Percy followed, Harlan stopped and shut the door.

"Look, I know we've talked about this before, but I've got to ask you, honestly, father to son, did you know that girl?"

"Who, Bridget?"

"You know damn well who and why I'm asking."

"I never said I didn't know her. We had a couple classes together. I'm sure she was at some parties I went to, not that night, but we weren't like friends or anything."

"Come on, Percy. You can tell me anything and I can protect you, but only if I know the truth."

"There is no other truth."

Harlan exhaled aggressively and opened the door back up.

"Let's go."

* * * * *

For a minute there, Percy actually thought about telling his dad the truth. Well, more of the truth. What he said wasn't exactly false. He barely knew Bridget. But she was a client, and how was he supposed to admit that without opening up too many other doors? Percy had gotten rid of most of his stash. He thought the police might want to search the house, but they never did. Donna, however, didn't need a warrant. When Percy got home from the hospital there were things pulled out of hiding places -Playboys, condoms, and cigarettes- but none of the drugs. Normal mom snooping wouldn't have turned those up.

Percy had gotten the page from Bridget that night. But that wasn't the first time she had paged him. Over the summer, she had paged him and invited him over to Tanya Gibbs' party. Percy was only planning on delivering her some weed, but Bridget talked him into smoking a joint with her, and then sticking around to play some drinking games.

Percy got trashed. He normally could hold his liquor pretty well, but that night it hit him hard. Bridget led him into the spare bedroom in Tanya's basement, and they tumbled onto the bed and started kissing before Percy blacked out. In the morning, Percy rolled out of bed to vomit and couldn't find the bathroom so he puked in the closet. It was then that he realized he was completely naked. Bridget was asleep on the other side of the bed. He quickly found his clothes on the floor and got dressed before sneaking out to his car.

It's not like it was that odd. Percy couldn't really think of a time he had hooked up with a girl when he wasn't drunk.

They never talked about it. The next time Bridget paged him, she just asked if he had any LSD. It wasn't his specialty, but he was able to get some and pass it along. She paid him, they joked about how she had to clean up the vomit he left in the closet, and he feigned innocence. It was a perfectly normal exchange. There was probably one other time she reached out to him before the night of the Halloween party, which is why he thought nothing of it when he did get her page.

He remembers the roof. Cleaning it up. But that was after he woke up. He feels like he saw her, but he can't even remember if she was wearing a costume or not. There was nothing about that in the newspaper. In his head, he pictures her in her school uniform, but that can't be right at all.

The doctors did say that with the drugs and alcohol in his system, it's not surprising that he couldn't quite remember everything, but they didn't know that a lot of the alcohol was consumed after he woke up. He was a little drunk the night of the party. He had a beer at every one of his stops, and he was no stranger to blacking out when he drank too much, but this was different. Percy hated having holes in his memory, especially given the circumstances. He can't think of any reason he would be mad at Bridget, certainly nothing to be mad enough to push her off a fucking building. His parents, sure, he could knock them down, but the most violent thought he'd had about anyone his age was punching a wall when he found out that Dean Hendricks had asked Gloria Wallace to junior prom.

If he asked anyone about trying to piece together that night, he'd have to admit far more than he was willing to about what he was doing there in the first place. It's not like he was the main guy. He got his drugs from dangerous men that the police would most definitely give more attention to. How could he open the door to his dealing without making himself vulnerable to the hierarchy?

It was all just too much. Percy laid in his bed and put his headphones on. Maybe the music could lull him to sleep.

* * * * *

Working with his father wasn't working for Percy. He found himself rolling out of bed and getting dressed minutes before he was supposed to leave. Every night he sequestered himself in the basement: watching TV, working out, playing video games. He would stay up until 2 or 3 in the morning, before crashing and then would be dragging ass all day at a job for which he was barely getting paid. The cycle felt never ending.

It was after midnight, and he knew he should be in bed, but after rotating through hundreds of push-ups and sit-ups, Percy figured he needed a shower. As he was drying off, he caught a glimpse of himself in the mirror. He hadn't paid much attention to his wounds in a few days, but seeing the scars all over his body was a bit jarring. A slash across his chest was red and jagged. Down his right leg was a thick welt. The bruising around his side was still odd shades of purple and green. Percy turned a bit to see his back and the deep scar where the knife went in. He still had stitches there. And the scar would be there for the rest of his life. He ran his finger across the stitches and it still felt tender. He figured he should take a couple pills before bed and that maybe he would fall asleep a little better.

But then he heard a tapping at his window. He threw on some clothes before he went to the blinds and peeked out.

Shit.

He motioned towards the back door. He walked over to the back door and, quietly as he could, opened the door to see Scott Jetter standing there. He didn't look great.

"Thanks, it's kind of cold out."

"What are you doing here?" Percy asked, though it was obvious. It's not like he and Scott were friends.

"I tried paging but I guess that's out."

"Yeah, no shit. What do you think I meant by 'laying low'?"

"Come on, man, you gotta have something." Scott's voice was shaky, and a little louder than Percy cared for.

"Keep your voice down. My parents are right upstairs. And the last thing I need is for them to know about this whole thing."

"So, then help me out."

"I don't have anything for you."

"Come on."

"No, you come on. I can't be doing this."

"I just need a little bit. I have two tests next week and then we've got the Homecoming game…"

"I don't need to hear the reasons. I don't have anything. For real. I got rid of it."

"What am I supposed to do?"

"I don't know. And I don't care. There are plenty of other kids working, just ask around."

"I can't risk it getting out, either. If someone finds out I'm doing speed I could get kicked off the team."

"Or kicked out of school."

"Exactly."

"I'm sorry, man. I can't help you."

"Well, maybe you need to help me figure something out, or I might have to share how helpful you've been, you know, historically."

"Jesus Christ, Scott. You trying to blackmail me? Get the fuck out of here. And don't come back. If you think you can make things any worse than they already are, you have no fucking clue what's going on."

"What am I supposed to do?"

"Fuck off. After that, I don't really care."

Percy opened the door and glared at Scott until he walked out. Percy shut and locked the door behind him, and softly said a prayer that Scott wouldn't do anything rash.

* * * * *

Percy had been entering numbers into a database on the computer. It was mind numbing how dull a task this was and once his eyes started to feel heavy, he figured it was time for his afternoon wank. He saved his progress and then walked towards the bathroom. He found the men's room on the west side of the building near the accounting team was less busy than the other one and he could usually hide out in there for half an hour or more without anyone else coming in.

The only downside was it took him longer to get there because he'd inevitably be stopped by various co-workers of his father who hadn't seen Percy in forever and had to comment about how much he'd grown. He'd been at the office over a week now, but the novelty had not been worn down.

Percy kept his eyes down, hoping that avoiding eye contact might help him make it through. But then he noticed her. The school uniform was one he was quite used to. The plaid. The bulky sweater. She had her hair pulled back into a pony tail, and she was wearing glasses, which he was pretty sure she didn't usually, but otherwise he was almost certain it was Abby Williams.

She was standing near an empty reception desk, her backpack on the ground beside her. She was hurriedly writing on a piece of paper.

"How's your knee?" He asked. Wondering if she would even remember that meeting in front of school that morning.

"What?" Abby said as she turned to see him. He smiled. She didn't. She just turned and kind of looked him up and down.

"Oh...how's your...everything?"

"Fine, thanks for asking. Abby, right?"

"Yeah."

"What are you doing here?"

"Oh, my mom works here. I was just leaving her a note."

"No shit. Small world."

"Totally."

She finally let out a small smile. Just the quick upturn of the corner of her lips. But it was enough. Percy was smitten. There was something so fierce about her. She was more sure of herself than other girls his age. It seemed like she didn't care what anybody thought of her, something that made Percy completely envious. He was also completely attracted to her. She had perfect pert breasts, and nice legs, despite how much the uniform tried to hide it. And he loved her dark fingernail polish, something that felt subtle and aggressive at the same time.

"My dad, uh, works here too."

"Yeah, his name's on the door. Not hard to figure out."

"Yeah, I guess."

"How's school? I, you know, haven't been back in a bit. Helping out here."

"You're not missing much."

"Well, it was good to see you, Abby. Hope it's not a rare occasion."

Percy smiled as he walked on.

"Good to see you too, Percy."

He wanted to turn around, see if she was looking his way, but he knew he had a better chance if he was a little more aloof. He wasn't particularly great with women. Mostly, because it came so easy to him. His family had money and he was decently attractive. He never had to work to get a girl to make out with him. But it had been a while since he was actually interested in a specific girl.

This might take a little effort.

12. ROBBIE

Was the outfit too much? Her meeting was important, but she didn't want to go overboard. She spent more time looking in the mirror today than in the past week collectively. Robbie wore a patterned vest which fit a little too snugly. The blue suit jacket was long, but roomy enough that she wasn't even self-conscious about her butt. Her skirt went past her knees, but the rolled-up sleeves on the suit coat made the whole look work both professionally and casually. She clipped her hair back so the fact it was a richer red than usual wouldn't be quite so obvious.

It was a small presentation, but one of the few times that she would be invited to speak to the board of directors and she wanted to make a good impression, especially if she would be looking for a promotion in the next year. Robbie worked in the financial offices of a large shipping company. And if her boss retired in the new year, he was seventy for Christ's sake, she would be in a good position to succeed him. Even though her presentation today was a small and unexciting segment of the day's itinerary, it was easily one of the best opportunities she had to make a good impression.

Her husband, Eric, had left for work an hour ago. It took him ten minutes to shower, part his hair just right, and put on the suit and tie she laid out for him. She hated men. This was the fourth outfit she chose, and her hair alone took thirty-seven minutes to perfect.

Robbie took one last look in the mirror, confident that she couldn't have chosen any better. She smiled. She might even put on some lipstick.

Her good mood faded when she walked into the kitchen. Dirty dishes were thrown into the sink, Cheerios still swimming around in faded milk. The coffee pot was empty. Scott, dressed only in his boxers, was sipping from a still-smoking cup.

"I know you own pants. I've bought you plenty."

"What?"

"Why aren't you dressed?" She asked.

"I don't have to leave for half an hour."

"No, you have to take your sister to school in seven minutes."

"Oh, shit. That's today?"

"You know, you're not too old for me to wash your mouth out with soap."

"Sorry, I completely spaced."

"Come on, Scott, I need this. I have to get to the office early. And you took the last cup of coffee. I should ground you for that alone. And you shouldn't be drinking coffee. It'll stunt your growth."

If only. Scott already towered over the rest of the family; a full five inches taller than her six-foot husband.

"It's okay. Here, drink the rest of this," he said, offering her the cup. "I can throw on my clothes in two seconds. No big. I got it."

Scott kissed the side of her cheek and jumped out of the room. She wanted to be mad at him, but he was such a good kid. He brought home good grades, was always respectful, never missed curfew. Aside from the swearing, which she didn't even have a real issue with, Scott was practically an angel.

"Bernie?" she shouted, hoping her daughter got up the last time she yelled into her room.

"What?" Bernie said as she walked in the room. "I'm ready."

Robbie looked at her thirteen-year-old daughter, with t-shirt cut off above her belly button and had to decide if she was ready for an argument.

"It's going to be cold today. You might want another shirt."

"Relax, I'm putting a flannel on over it."

"I am relaxed. And your brother is taking you to school today."

"Why? His car is so gross and smells like feet."

"I know, but Mommy has a meeting."

"Don't say 'mommy,' that's weird."

"Did you get breakfast?"

"I'll get something at school."

"I don't like you eating that vending machine crap."

"But you'll live with it, right?"

Robbie took a quiet breath. Teenagers are assholes. Even the good ones. She poured the coffee Scott left her into a cup she could take in the car. She made sure she had lipstick in her purse and began to say "wish me luck," but the room was empty when she turned around.

Teenagers.

* * * * *

Robbie was slamming groceries into the cart. It's not that the meeting went bad, not exactly. She just didn't feel like she blew the board away. By the time she got up to talk they had been lulled into a strong boredom from all the boring men that spoke before she did. Her dream of that Working Girl moment where she wows the higher-ups with her worth and gets plucked from obscurity into a cushy corporate gig would have to wait another few years. And she was taking it out on the frozen entrees.

It's not that Robbie didn't like her life. She loved it. Mostly. She had a great husband that never forgot an anniversary. Her kids could be annoying but they had good hearts and were good students, well liked, and she knew that they would someday make the world better. She just wanted something more. Something her own. She didn't want to be only a wife and mother, as proud of that as she was. She turned forty-two years old this year, and still felt like her life was just waiting to start. She got married, graduated law school, and gave birth, all within the span of a year. And has been treading water ever since.

She came to Omaha for college: an accelerated program of pre-law and school in six years at Creighton University. Robbie never intended to stay. But she met and fell in love with Eric in college and never looked back.

Her job was fine, but nothing special. Her career was put on the back burner in order to get the kids situated and to try and go back to it felt daunting. She hadn't practiced law in a number of years, although being a lawyer helped the resume. Wasn't she too old now to start a practice? To cultivate clients? She was probably better off figuring out how to vicariously live through her children. Surely one of them could get into law school.

As Robbie rounded the corner into the liquor aisle she ran cart first into her past, something all too common in Omaha. It was more rare to go the store and not run into someone you know, or used to know.

She was lost in thought when her cart tapped into the man in front of her.

“Oh, I’m so sorry…Adam?”

Adam turned and looked at Robbie for a moment before registering her.

“Wow. Of all the gin joints, huh?”

“You live like a mile away from me, Adam. And it really hasn’t been that long has it?”

“At least a year.”

“No, weren’t you at that open house thing for the boys?”

“Yeah, but that was two years ago.”

“Wow. Time flies, huh? How is TJ?”

Adam paused for a second and made a face that Robbie couldn’t really decipher.

“He’s fine, I guess. Teenagers, you know.”

“Oh, yeah. Believe me.”

Something was off about him. He wasn’t looking her in the eye. He seemed agitated, or maybe just distracted, even if he was being cordial. It was three o’clock on a Tuesday. She left work early once the board meeting was over, but what was Adam doing here?

It was really none of her business. When Adam’s wife died, he pulled away from both her and Eric. Given their history, she didn’t push too hard. She figured he had his hands full with three kids and that he would reach out if he needed anything. He never did, and this man that she spent summer holidays with became someone she barely recognized in a grocery store.

“How are you?” Adam asked.

“Oh, great. Eric too. You should come by for dinner sometime. We miss you.”

“Yeah, same.” There was something about the way he said it. It was almost a scoff, or completely sarcastic. Robbie didn’t know how to take it.

“TJ too. I’m sure he and Scott could catch up on-”

“Look, I gotta run. I’ll call you, though. Promise.”

And with that, he pulled a twelve-pack of Budweiser off the shelf and walked away.

“Good seeing you,” Robbie said halfheartedly as he walked away.

* * * * *

“There was something so off about him,” Robbie said.

Eric was already in bed, his reading glasses on as he flipped through some book on World War II. She could tell he wasn’t fully paying attention to her. Robbie was busying herself in the closet trying to sort a less-impressive outfit for tomorrow.

“Uh huh,” Eric muttered.

“I think he might’ve been drunk. Or drinking.”

“Robbie, you haven’t seen the guy in years. He was probably just uncomfortable.”

“He was buying beer in the afternoon. Isn’t he working?”

“Maybe he’s back on nights.”

“You should call him.”

“I don’t want to call him.”

“You used to be such good friends.”

“I used to be friends with a lot of people. We probably would’ve grown apart long ago if you didn't get along so well with his wife."

"It was such a tragedy. She was so young."

"What's really bothering you?" Eric put his book down so Robbie knew he was really asking.

"I don't know. Work was shitty today."

"You're not turning him into another cause, are you?"

"Excuse me?"

"You have this need to fix things. Even when they aren't broken."

"I don't do that."

"You most certainly do that."

"Well, I'm not doing that here."

"Just be grateful that your date never worked out. Otherwise, you might be married to him and he really would be your problem."

"Are you pretending to be jealous?"

"Not at all. I'm just lucky it wasn't more."

"You're damn straight. Did I ever tell you why I didn't go out with him again?"

"Obviously you fell for his handsome friend from high school."

"Well, before that. We were down in the Old Market going to dinner and someone bumped into him and he lost it. He backed this guy into a corner, towering over him, scaring him, telling him to apologize. It was… I don't know… sadistic. And I think he thought it was impressing me."

"Remember our softball team, when he yelled at that ump?"

"This is what I'm talking about. It wasn't very often, but he would get this rage. There was something…dead in his eyes. And as nice as he was being, I feel like he had those same eyes today."

"Maybe he just had a bad day. Or maybe, you're looking for a reason to stress over something."

"I don't know. Maybe. Do you like this?"

Robbie held a blouse in front of her.

"I like anything you wear."

"You are useless," Robbie said with a laugh. He would never be a help with fashion, but she still wouldn't trade him for anything.

* * * * *

Robbie wanted a sip of wine. It was a Chateau LaForge merlot, but she wasn't sure that meant anything. It could've been a two-dollar bottle from the grocery store and it wouldn't have made a difference. But no, she was stronger than that.

Eric was cleaning the dishes after dinner. Danny was in helping him, but she was sure they were talking about sports and not anything important. Robbie sat at the dining room table with Eli, Eric's younger sister, and Eli was on her fourth glass. Robbie was jealous of every sip.

"Come on, you can't tell me he doesn't seem a little mopey to you." Eli was probably drunk, legally speaking, but she wasn't slurring or talking loudly. She was drowning some sorrows, though Robbie wasn't quite clear what they were, other than Eli's husband and his less than gregarious persona.

"Danny has always been a bit aloof."

"Trust me. This is different."

"Didn't you say one of his students died?"

"Yes. A few weeks ago. But I think he's been acting strangely since before that."

"Have you tried talking to him? I know that sounds crazy, but sometimes it works."

"Oh, I've tried. Danny tells me things when he wants to tell me things."

Eli was a little more forthright than usual. She and Robbie were close, but not that close. They were family, so they never shared too much. At least, that's how Robbie saw it. Eli was a talker though, like a lot of women in their early 30s she could carry on a conversation completely on her own. Robbie just had to nod and say "uh huh" occasionally to keep her going.

Robbie could tell something was wrong, though she didn't want to admit it. Danny wasn't very talkative, not that he ever was, but she could see his mind was completely elsewhere. They sat at dinner-Robbie made lasagna with green beans-and Eli vented about her job and her boss. Robbie and Eric updated them on the kids, but Danny played with his food and drank his beer and didn't offer much besides a few grumbles.

Robbie had never met Bridget, the girl who had taken her own life, but she followed the news pretty closely. This was third, maybe even fourth, student she had heard that had taken their own life in the past year or so. Scott's school had a few cases as well. It broke her heart. She wanted to send a note to the girl's mother, offer some condolences, but she didn't know her and couldn't find any reason it would make sense. If one of Robbie's children died, God forbid, a note from a stranger wasn't likely to offer her any relief.

Robbie continued to listen to Eli droning on, but her mind went down another path. She thought of Scott, he knew the girl, it was his friend, Javi's, girlfriend. But he said they weren't close. He felt bad for Javi, that was obvious. And she tried to talk to Scott about it, but he was a teenager, and the last thing he was going to do was share his feelings with his mom.

Robbie watched Eli take another sip. It had been twenty-two years since her last drink, and for the most part she didn't miss it. Tonight, though, she really wanted a drink. The moment would pass. She knew that. It usually did.

* * * * *

The air was thick and cold. There was no snow on the ground, but the wind chill made it below freezing. Robbie hated this weather. A few days earlier it was in the sixties, and then, winter came roaring back. She pulled her scarf off as she entered the Target, the one on Saddle Creek Road that they referred to as Targhetto, because it wasn't as nice as the one in West Omaha (that was Targét-said with a French accent and silent "t").

Eric called as she was on her way home. They needed dish soap. This was her life. Dish soap, moody teenagers and bad weather. Robbie wasted time going up and down the aisles. There was always something else she could use. As she came around the corner in the grocery aisle she saw a teenager sneaking a pack of granola bars in his coat. It startled her, but she said nothing and when her cart made a noise, she looked down as if she wasn't paying attention.

The young man had a stocking cap on, but his hair was still hanging in his face. His facial hair was all scruff, and he moved with an awkward hunch. The granola bars probably weren't the only thing in his coat.

He went to move past her and that's when he really caught her eye.

"Oh my gosh, TJ?"

The boy looked at her. It was TJ, she was sure. It had been a few years, but he looked mostly the same.

"Mrs. Jetter. Hi."

"Please, it's Robbie. How are you? I actually ran into your dad a few days ago and we were talking about having you guys over for dinner."

"That's great, I guess. Sorry, I'm actually late to meet someone."

"Oh, sure. Good seeing you."

TJ moved past her and walked away. Robbie thought for a second and then took a look around the other aisle. TJ was making his way towards the front of the store. He didn't look back.

Robbie ditched her cart and walked towards the front from the other side. She ducked behind a magazine rack as she watched him shuffle towards the front doors. Robbie hurriedly headed towards the same exit.

The wind smacked her when she stepped outside. She didn't see TJ in the parking lot. She looked left and then right, just in time to catch him walking around to the back side of the store. Robbie pulled her scarf around her head as she continued to move faster. She hoped she could catch him before he got into his car, but she was more surprised when she saw him crouch on the other side of a large dumpster.

She slowed her pace long enough for him to light a cigarette. When she stepped in front of him, he was taking a long drag, while the smell of garbage mingled with his smoke.

"So, do you want to tell me what you were doing in there?"

TJ stood up. He was taller than Robbie, but only barely.

"What? Nothing."

He took another drag.

"Are you okay?"

"I'm fine. What do you want?"

"I saw you in there, TJ. And I'm sure we can go back and forth on what you want to tell me you thought I saw, but it's really cold out. So, why don't you grab your backpack that I can see hidden back there and you can come home with me. Eric is making pork chops for dinner and he always makes too many, and we have a couch, in case it gets too late."

"I don't..."

"Look, you don't have to tell me anything. I have two kids at home who never tell me anything. That's fine. But you and I both know I'm not going to leave you out here. So, you can get in my car, no questions asked, or I can take you back into the store and let the police shake the truth out of you, and whatever else you may have shoved in your jacket, and you can spend a night in a warm cell. Either way, you're not spending another moment out here."

TJ stared at her a moment. He was obviously freezing. His coat was not nearly warm enough for wind like this. He took another puff off his cigarette.

"Okay," he said.

"Good," she said, reaching out her hand. He took it and she shook it, while using her other hand to rub his shoulder. TJ grabbed his backpack, while awkwardly slinging it over his shoulder and trying not to let the contents of his coat spill out.

They walked towards Robbie's car.

"Now, I'm not your mother and can't tell you what to do, but can this smoking maybe be one of those things you sneak around and do without anyone knowing? I imagine you're pretty good at that."

"Yeah, sure."

Robbie rubbed his back. The dish soap would have to wait.

On the drive home, they sat in silence mostly. TJ stared out the window, while Robbie wondered what the hell she was going to tell her husband about their new house guest.

13. ABBY

"I just don't think she did it," Abby said. "None of it makes sense. She wasn't depressed or sad, even. She was…determined. She wanted to get out but not this way. I just… I know it."

Dr. Gant looked at her. He had his pen in his mouth like he often did when he was waiting for Abby to stop rambling. Was she rambling? She felt like she was talking a lot, but that was kind of the point of this whole thing, right?

"You seem agitated," Dr. Gant said in that soft manner that he said most things. Sometimes it was soothing, but other times, like now, it was really frustrating.

"Yes, I'm agitated. Everyone is acting like she was some sort of saint and this is all a big tragedy but no one is actually trying to figure out what happened."

"But why does it bother you so much? You weren't friends, as you've said. You have no vested interest in the outcome, whatever it may be. Why are you so emotionally connected to this situation?"

"When I… did what I did… I wasn't thinking this was going to end it all. This was it. I just wanted it to stop."

"Wanted what to stop?"

"Everything. The rumors. The talking behind my back. The feeling that I had no friends. The pressure of school, of being popular, of wearing the right clothes, liking the right things. Everything. It was just… I wanted it to stop. But it didn't stop. It just got worse. Everyone still talks, if they notice me at all. I still don't feel like I have any friends. I feel so alone. And then Bridget comes along, this girl who has everything I want. She's popular. And beautiful. She has friends. She has MY friends. And she's so mean. And terrible. And this happens and everyone acts like she's Miss Perfect and no one will say anything bad about her and I'm just over here realizing that it's not real. None of this is real. She's not a martyr. She's a victim. Someone did this to her. Because if they didn't, if she really did this, then what the hell am I doing here?"

"Do you think that if she did kill herself that it somehow invalidates your own suicide attempt?"

"No. I don't know. That's not what I'm saying."

"What are you saying?"

"There are signs to these things. Cries for help."

"Did you show any signs?"

"Big, neon ones. No one could see them."

"And you don't think Bridget showed any signs?"

"No."

"Because if she did, you think you would be able to recognize that, because of your own experience?"

"We weren't friends. She wouldn't open up to me."

"You said the night she died that you two had a somewhat pleasant talk."

"Yeah. Something like that."

"And that when you talked to her friend, Kira, that she said Bridget had a conversation with her about their friendship, almost as if she was saying goodbye."

"That's how she put it."

"And she gave your friend Breck an expensive necklace."

"Yes."

"These are some of the warning signs. Big gestures."

"I suppose. But it still doesn't make any sense."

"Sometimes it doesn't. But all of this goes back to my earlier point."

"Which is?"

"None of this has anything to do with you. Why are you getting so emotionally connected?"

"I don't know. I really don't."

Abby wasn't lying. Dr. Gant was right, she was getting deeper into the whole Bridget situation. Maybe it was reading her journal, something she wasn't quite sure she could share with Dr. Gant. Reading Bridget's journal, her private thoughts in her own words, made her feel some sort of connection to her. The Bridget character she read about was such a far cry from the Bridget that she had interacted with. She was confused and unsure of herself. She was frustrated with school and her friends and family. The Bridget she knew seemed so happy with everything. She was popular, a cheerleader even-the upper echelon in the high school hierarchy, and always acted like she was better than everyone, especially Abby. Abby didn't like the Bridget she talked to, but the one that she read about, that one she felt like she could've been friends with. If things had been different.

* * * * *

"This was really the only place we could meet?" Abby asked as she slurped on the pop she got in the food court. She hated the mall. It was just so typical teenagery and it only served to make her feel more out of place.

Kira was flipping through the dresses hoping she could find something acceptable for homecoming.

"Homecoming is so lame," Abby said.

"Well, it's kind of a big deal. Besides, I wanted to get out the house."

They agreed to meet at the Crossroads Mall after school that day. It was on the corner of the busiest intersection in town, and somehow served as a midway point between everything-Abby's house, Elysian Park, the schools, Mr. Sutton's house. The first time that Abby and Kira spoke was one of the more awkward conversations Abby had ever had. Kira had showed up at her house, no warning, and wanted to talk to her about Bridget. But not only Bridget, Kira asked about Abby's past. The whole incident. It was the first time someone her age really brought it up directly. Abby was honest, which was weird. It's not like she and Kira were even friends. They went to the same school last year but as Breck and Kira grew closer, Abby felt left behind, and had always resented Kira for that, even though she knew she didn't do anything directly. She even told her as such their last meeting. Kira apologized, and Abby accepted even though she didn't really feel like it was sincere.

Abby was relieved to have someone her age to talk to. They weren't friends, but they had the Bridget situation to talk about, and while Abby was quick to point out that it wasn't her loss to bear, she also ended up telling Kira about her belief that Bridget didn't jump off that roof herself.

Kira wasn't so sure. She told Abby about Bridget's weird conversation the night of the party, how it felt like a goodbye. She told her about this necklace that she left Breck. These things pointed to suicide. Abby told Kira that it didn't feel right to her, but she left out the part about the journal. She couldn't think of any reason she could tell her that she had it. And she had even less reason to read it.

The whole conversation that first time was uncomfortable, with Abby not being able to fully articulate everything. She did ask Kira if Bridget ever mentioned anything about Mr. Sutton. That seemed to weird her out even more and she ended up leaving. But not before they decided to meet again. If Abby knew it was to look at dresses she might've passed.

"So, I've been thinking about what you said," Kira offered, while continuing to rifle through the brightly colored lace and chiffon numbers. "And I don't know if I'm ready to believe it. I don't see her making anyone that mad that they would hurt her."

"I mean, it could've been an accident."

"If it was, someone would've called, right?"

"Well, someone did. On the news they said they were alerted to the scene by a 911 call. And it's not like anyone would've just been passing by a closed park after hours in the middle of the night."

"Look, I'm not saying I'm ready to get on board with this whole thing, but there are a couple things I thought might be worth talking about."

"Like what?"

"Well, okay, I saw her sneaking out of her house late at night. Like, a few days before…you know, before it happened."

"What time?"

"It was late. After one, I think. And I saw her putting on lipstick so I don't think she was just going for a ride or anything like that."

"Maybe she was sneaking out to see Javi."

"Maybe. I didn't want to ask him about it. Not yet at least. Besides, what if she wasn't?"

"Why else would she put on lipstick? But she never mentioned anyone else. And there's something else."

"What's that?"

"I've been helping her mom out. After school. Like cleaning and dishes and stuff. And I've known her mom practically my whole life. They live right across the street and our parents used to be friends, but she is not handling this well. She started talking to me like I was Bridget."

"That's messed up."

"I know."

"Was she drunk or high or something?"

"It was like four o'clock in the afternoon."

"You can do those things during the day."

"Maybe. I don't think she's gone back to work since Bridget died. But it wasn't just that she acted like I was Bridget, the way she talked was completely different. Like aggressive kind of."

"You don't think she could've done this, do you?"

"Oh no, nothing like that."

"Maybe she didn't have the best relationship with her mom."

"She never said anything to me. And they were always so close. They weren't as close recently but no, I can't see that."

Abby was stuck. She knew from the journal that Bridget did have issues with her mom. She mentioned getting slapped and some of the cruel things that Vanessa had said to her (Bridget only referred to her mom as "Vanessa" in the journal), but none of that seemed to fit with this idea of mother-daughter closeness that Kira recalled. But Abby knew from her relationship with her own mom that things were complicated. She was sure she could've written down that she hated her mom at one point, especially as she was going through everything the year before, but her mom was also super supportive afterwards. Abby and her mom didn't always talk like they used to; Olivia was busy being a single mom to two teenagers. She wondered how their relationship would look from the outside.

"Also, I did hear her talking to the cops."

"Who?"

"Bridget's mom. They told her they thought it was a suicide too."

"But the case is still open."

"Is it? Maybe they say that so they don't have to keep looking. And why did you ask about Mr. Sutton?"

"I don't know. Something always seemed off about him," Abby lied. She only thought he seemed off because Bridget mentioned a crush on a teacher. Abby did witness first hand Bridget and Mr. Sutton's dynamic in study hall, but was it really any different than how he seemed to treat any of the popular kids?

"Here, I don't look good in green, but I think you would actually be on fire in this thing." Kira handed Abby a dress. It was simple and elegant, sleek and not as puffy as some of the others.

"We are not here looking for me. No one has even asked me."

"So, no one has asked me either."

"Then why are you looking for a dress."

"I like to be prepared."

Kira forced the dress on Abby and she reluctantly took it and walked to the dressing rooms. She pulled the curtain across and started to pull off her clothes. She was still in her school uniform and there was something so perfect about letting her Catholic plaid skirt fall to the floor to put on a tight, low-cut dress that instantly made her look five years older. Abby squeezed into the dress. It was a little tight in the butt, and a little loose in the top, and it looked kind of weird with Abby's black bra underneath, but it wasn't the worst Abby thought she looked. The light in the dressing room was harsh and bright, so Abby stepped back outside.

"Oh my god, come here."

Kira was waiting outside and pulled Abby to the three angled mirrors towards the front of the store.

"Look at you, girl."

Abby did. She was surprised by how much more beautiful she felt with the dress on. She pulled her hair up, imagining it in some up-do arrangement that left her shoulders and neck exposed. Abby twirled around. She was actually enjoying this. So much, that it took her a moment to even notice the boy staring in the window from outside the store.

Abby gasped, which caused Kira to look. It was Percy, who offered a smile and a weak wave. Instinctively, Abby clenched up, covering up her chest with her arm.

"Do you know him?" Kira asked.

"It's Percy Van Allen," she answered. "Doesn't everybody."

Percy started to walk into the store.

"Be careful with that one."

"Why?"

"He's not right. He may seem all smiles and broad shoulders, but I know for a fact he's a drug dealing lowlife."

"How do you know that?"

"Everybody knows that. I know tons of kids that have his pager number. You want to look at someone shady, look at him."

Abby smiled as Percy walked up. Kira rolled her eyes.

"Ladies, how are you?"

"Fine," Kira said tersely.

"We're just looking at dresses," Abby said.

"Well, if you're on the fence, I definitely think this one is a keeper."

Percy was being sweet, but it still made Abby uncomfortable. More so, because Kira was there.

"Oh, she made me. I'm not really looking. I can't even imagine how much something like this…" she pulled the tag out from the shoulder "Holy God it's how much? Never mind, sorry. I should probably get this off before I pull a thread."

"Yeah, we should say our goodbyes now," Kira said, pointedly.

"Hey, I get it. I was only walking by when I saw you. But really, you look great."

"Bye now."

"Kira, come on," Abby said.

"No, it's okay," Percy returned. "I'm supposed to meet someone in the food court."

"Don't want to be late."

"I'll see you later," Abby said, as Percy turned around and walked out.

"Good riddance," Kira snarled under her breath.

"You really don't like that guy, do you?"

"I'm pretty sure Bridget got some stuff off of him one night. I didn't do it, but she had taken some pills that had her bouncing off the walls. The next day she was throwing up everywhere. She said it there was something wrong with it. She wouldn't tell me where she got it, but I know it was that guy."

"Well, you're not a hundred percent sure it was him, are you?"

"Are you into Percy or something?"

"What? No. Gross. I'm just wondering if he really is someone we should be looking into."

"Well, I can promise if you do, you'll find something. I don't know if it's about Bridget, but there will be something."

Abby watched Percy walk away. He didn't look back. She wasn't into him, was she? He was nice, but come on. That's silly. He's a senior. He's way better looking than she is, and then all this other stuff. No, of course she wasn't. But like Kira said, maybe he did warrant a deeper look.

* * * * *

Olivia looked up from her desk and was surprised that Abby was standing in the doorway to her office.

"Hi, Mom," Abby said with a smile. She had made her way past reception. They were used to her coming in every so often. Abby wanted as little fanfare as possible. She purposefully avoided the section where she knew Percy sat and walked out of her way to the other side where her mother's office was. She waited until she was off the phone before knocking.

"To what do I owe this honor?"

"I was in the neighborhood. I needed to look some stuff up at the library and the downtown one has so many more archives."

"School project?"

"Yeah, murder case."

"Well, that sounds kind of morose."

"It's ancient history, you know."

"Did you want to grab a coffee?"

"Maybe, actually I was wondering if I could talk to you about something."

"Of course."

"Our computer is so old and you have these new ones here. Do you think it would be possible for me to come in here after school and use one to type up my paper? It's a long one and I don't want to risk losing it."

"I'm sure I could find one, but if you're only doing a paper, I'm sure the computer at home can handle that."

"Yeah, I know. But if I'm here I can be more focused and maybe we could go for coffee more often. I miss you, you know."

"Who are you and what have you done with my daughter?" Olivia said with a laugh in her voice.

"Never mind."

"No, dear, of course, it's fine. Do you want to start now? I can probably find an empty cubicle for you if you want some quiet."

"Yeah, that would be great. I don't need to start now. I'll come by tomorrow."

"It would be nice to see your face around here more often."

"And it won't get you into trouble with anyone?"

"It'll be fine, sweetie."

Just then, there was a knock at the door.

"Olivia, do you have the folder on… oh, sorry. I didn't think anyone was in here."

Abby turned to see a familiar-looking, young, blond woman with a stack of folders.

"It's okay, Eli, come in," Olivia said. "This is my daughter, Abby."

Abby smiled and reached out her hand to shake Eli's.

"Abby, hi. Eli Sutton, I haven't seen you in forever."

"Hi, I don't remember ever meeting you."

"Oh, why would you. I'm no one."

"Actually, I think your husband is my teacher."

"You go to St. Dymphna's?"

"I'm not wearing this get up for its style," Abby said pointing out her plaid jumper.

"I'm sorry, I guess I thought you were at AC High."

"I was."

"She transferred this year."

"Oh, right," Eli said. A look of some recognition went across her face. And she quickly excused herself, telling Olivia she would call her later.

"Well, she obviously knows everything about me," Abby said.

"It's not like that. Eli was very helpful through that ordeal."

"Does everyone here know?"

"No. No one else. But you don't have to be like that. Eli would never tell anyone. She was simply there when I needed someone to talk to. In fact, she was the one that recommended Dr. Gant."

"What do you mean?"

"She gave me his number. Said he helped her a lot."

"She was a patient of his? Why?"

"I have no idea. That's none of my business. When I said I was looking for someone for you to talk to she passed his info along. That's it."

"This is too weird."

"It doesn't have to be."

"I know, I'm sorry. Just threw me for a second. So, do you want to grab that coffee?"

"Of course. Let me grab my purse."

Abby had a simple plan when she came into the office. She wanted to learn more about Percy. She can't believe that Danny's wife worked there. She was surprised this was something she knew and forgot about. And to learn that they shared a therapist. Abby's world got exponentially smaller in an instant, but instead of viewing it as a negative she tried to focus on the upside. This was nothing but opportunity. Not only could she learn more about Percy, but she could also learn more about Mr. Sutton.

Why would Eli be seeing a therapist? Marital issues? Of course. Maybe her husband was less than faithful. Maybe with a student. It was certainly possible. Abby didn't know this Eli woman at all, but she had a feeling she was about to.

* * * * *

Abby was exhausted. It had been a long day, but mostly fruitless. Percy had left the office before she got there, and when she tried to make small talk with Eli, she could tell she was busy. Even her mom was somewhat abrupt. Abby left the office early and did her actual homework at the library since she had already been downtown. It was dark by the time she got home but her mom still wasn't there. At least her car wasn't in the garage.

Abby dropped her bags in the living room where Jake was playing video games on the good TV.

"What are you doing?" Abby asked.

"Baking a cake. What does it look like?"

"Never mind then, ass."

"You got a delivery."

"What?"

"Some box. On the kitchen table."

"What is it?"

"Do I look like your secretary? It's a box. That's the extent of my knowledge of this."

Abby took a deep breath. She didn't have the energy to deal with Jake right now. Some days, he could be nice, but most days, like this, he was all attitude. Abby was grateful that his visits to her room seemed to stopped of late. It saved her the trouble of telling him "no." Even though she hadn't brought up the specifics in therapy, she was learning how to stand up for herself and had made the decision that this was no longer a relationship that she wanted to give any attention to. Of course, since she made that decision, Jake had stopped coming. She wanted to tell him off. She wanted him to know it was her decision, that he couldn't just tip-toe into her room whenever he wanted to feel close to someone, or he wanted to get off, whatever.

Abby wanted to talk about Jake in therapy, naturally. It was a complicated relationship. But she couldn't think of a way to talk about it that wouldn't result in the Doctor calling her mom, or worse, the police. Was it even a crime technically? Abby never actually said no to him before. And it wasn't like she hadn't wanted to. At least, at first.

Jake continued to tap buttons on his controller, oblivious to the turmoil swirling around Abby's head. He'll be gone next summer, she told herself. If nothing else, once he graduates, he'll be out of there.

Abby walked up to the kitchen and saw a large white box with a bright, red bow on the kitchen table. It didn't look like it went through the mail. Abby started to ask Jake how it was delivered, but she knew she wouldn't get a straight answer. There was a small card with her name and address on the outside of the box. She pulled at the bow and lifted the top off the box.

Inside was the green dress she had tried on a few days before. There was a note inside:

"Whether you wear it to the dance or somewhere else, I didn't want the mall to be the only place where you had the chance to wear this beauty. -P."

Abby smiled at the generosity, but at the same time felt a little creeped out by the gesture. They really hadn't spoken all that much and he's spending hundreds of dollars on a dress? That was weird, right? She wanted to hate it. She knew she probably should call and tell him off, but she had to admit, if only to herself, that there was something sweet about it. She couldn't think of the last time anyone went out of their way to do anything for her.

Abby quickly wrapped the box up and went up to her room and shoved it under her bed. She would decide how she felt about it tomorrow.

She laid back on her bed, and closed her eyes. But no matter how hard she tried, she couldn't stop the smile from stretching across her face.

14. JAVI

The scoreboard read "0-21," which was a pretty shitty showing for the homecoming game. Disappointed fans in the bleachers still cheered the AC High Cougars on. It was only second quarter, but there was little probability of coming back from this. The Cougars weren't a second-half kind of team. And they obviously weren't a first-half kind of team. Javi sat on the end of the bench. He hadn't seen much action in the game that evening, but he kept his helmet on. It let him feel hidden yet still in the center of everything. The quiet observer, a role he had perfected.

Javi clapped and offered a hearty "come on, guys," for the boys on offense, but he knew it wouldn't change anything. In between plays he prayed that the game would be over soon. He found the whole thing tedious.

More and more he was realizing just how little he cared about the entire situation. He had been on the varsity team since the year before but hardly felt close to anyone, except for Scott. Sure, some of the guys had offered condolences for Bridget, but there were more questions than anything around that. When your girlfriend kills herself there's always the underlying suspicion that you failed her somehow.

And he did, he could admit that. He didn't love her. He didn't really want to be with her. He liked hanging out with her and he liked how she fit into his world, checked all the appropriate boxes. But he didn't really know her. The Bridget he thought he knew would have never done something like this. The Bridget he thought he knew wouldn't put her mom through this, her friends, or even him. Javi couldn't imagine what could've happened to drive her to such a drastic act.

He asked God to forgive her. He knew that suicide was not accepted in the church. He had trouble believing someone who had been a good person her whole life would spend eternity in hell, but rules are rules, and the church was particularly unwavering in this regard. He talked to his priest about his concerns around Bridget, but it only made him more angry. What kind of institution couldn't offer the slightest help to someone who was asking for it? Javi's spirituality was so deeply ingrained in him that this entire incident, and, well, other things that were going on in his personal life, were really testing everything he thought he knew.

He tried to talk to Scott about all of this, but he wasn't helpful. Honestly, things had been kind of weird between Scott and Javi for weeks. They still hung out together, but were more quiet than usual. Neither one of them pushed conversations beyond small talk. Everything about their friendship just smacked of routine. Even tonight, Javi had showed up to Scott's after school to hitch a ride to the game. Although, he was a little surprised with how different Scott's home life had gotten.

Javi walked into the Jetter's basement-Scott's room was down there off the family room-and he expected to find Scott playing pool or video games, but instead he saw the strange kid from the Halloween party reading a book on the couch.

"Hey, is Scott around?" Javi asked.

"I think he's getting ready," the kid said without bothering to look up from his book. It took him a minute, but Javi remembered it was TJ Griffin. After the Halloween party, he had noticed TJ around school but he didn't really say "hi" or even a nod. He didn't know him at all. What the hell was he doing here?

Javi dropped his bag and awkwardly stood around the pool table for a bit in complete silence, until he decided to check on Scott. He went to knock on his bedroom door, but Scott walked out before he could.

"Oh hey, man," Scott said. "Ready to go?"

"Yeah."

Scott didn't say a word about the kid on the couch, didn't say goodbye to him, the two of them simply walked out to his car and went on their way. Javi asked about TJ, but Scott didn't offer much. Said their parents were friends and he was supposedly going to stay there for a little bit. Javi asked more questions, but Scott didn't have any more answers than that.

The rest of the ride was mostly in silence as Scott turned up his radio and sped towards the football field. Scott and Javi really weren't talking, not like they used to. Javi wasn't sure if it was about Bridget or something else. Maybe Scott was having issues with Breck. Javi convinced himself it had nothing to do with him.

He watched Scott come out of his shell in the locker room as they got ready for the game. Scott was laughing and joking with their teammates. It was all very superficial, and Javi didn't need to be a part of everything, but it did nag at him a little that something was off with them.

Javi sat on his own during the game. This wasn't unusual either. Javi always liked to spend more time in his head than actually in the game, even a game as important as the homecoming one. Javi was so lost in thought, he didn't even notice when a stray football came hurling towards him, a wildly out-of-bounds pass.

The ball bounced and whizzed right past his head which brought him back into the middle of the game. The crowd was cheering, it must've been an incomplete for the other team. Javi grabbed the ball and tossed it to the ref. As he stood up, he looked around.

The stands were a lot fuller than an average game. Maybe a lot of former students had come back. Javi saw Breck and smiled and waved, and he continued to scan until he stopped on another familiar face: Trevor.

Trevor had his coat zipped up to his chin, a scarf around his face, and a stocking hat pulled tight, but Javi still recognized his eyes. He didn't smile. He didn't like that Trevor was here. Trevor gave a slight wave, just a quick wiggle of his fingers really, but Javi kept looking on, pretending as if he didn't see.

* * * * *

Javi followed the rest of the team back to the locker room at half time. The coach offered some words that were meant to inspire, but Javi's mind was elsewhere. There was now an underlying frustration to everything. Every word the coach said annoyed him. It was all bullshit, he wanted to shout. It doesn't mean anything.

Of course, he said nothing.

When the coach finished, the team dispersed and started to file back out to the field. They were going to do the homecoming court procession and the team had to support their teammates who were also on court, which included Scott. Sometimes, it bothered Javi that Scott was popular and he wasn't. They shared a lot of the same friends but Javi was popular adjacent at best.

Javi waited until most of the guys had left and he caught up with Scott.

"Hey man, you cool?" He asked.

"What? Yeah. Why?"

"I don't know. Feels like you've been a little weird lately."

Scott was nonchalant, but Javi also noticed that he wasn't looking at Javi.

"Sorry, man, not sure what you're reacting to, but I'm cool. I guess things have been weird all around lately, you know."

"Yeah, I guess. But it just kind of seems like you're not talking to me."

Scott sighed.

"What would you like to talk about?"

"I wasn't trying to start something."

"No, really. Let's talk," Scott's tone got a little louder. And certainly was tinged with attitude. "What can we talk about? What is so important that we need to start a conversation? Right now? At half-time of the homecoming game. When I'm about to walk out in the middle of the field for Homecoming?"

"Dude, chill out. I didn't mean anything by it."

"I'm so chill. And really, you think I'm the one not talking? Whatever."

Javi was taken aback. What did he mean by that?

"What do you mean by that?" Did he know something? Was this about Bridget? Or was this about Trevor? Did Scott see Trevor there too? Did he know something? Or think something was weird there. Was that what he was implying?

Scott just shook his head. “Why are you being such a girl?”

“I’m not, I was just asking a question, dick.”

“Maybe I don’t appreciate this whole attitude you’ve got.”

“I’ve got an attitude?”

“What is your problem? God, I’m just trying to play some football here and you come at me with this. Leave me the fuck alone, weirdo.”

Javi was surprised that Scott seemed so agitated. Javi scoffed and walked out, saying a soft “screw you,” under his breath.

Javi pushed the door open, but then he took a deep breath. What the hell just happened? Maybe Scott was right and it was Javi that had an attitude. It was an innocent question, but it clearly wasn’t the time. Javi could admit that he was annoyed by everything, and he didn’t need to make things with Scott any weirder than they already were. And really, what did he mean Javi wasn’t talking? He definitely wanted to know more but he couldn’t figure it out if he needed to get another ride home.

He counted to ten and then went back. He could be the bigger person right now.

Javi turned the corner just in time to see Scott snorting something off of his finger. He stood there for a second trying to figure out what he actually saw. Scott inhaled harshly through his nose and then slammed his locker shut, which was when he saw Javi standing there.

“What are you…” Scott started.

“Hey, sorry man, I didn’t mean to…”

“Mean to what?”

“Be weird. I didn’t mean to come at you like that. It’s cool. I’m fine. Sorry if my questions made things awkward or something.”

"It's cool. I didn't mean to snap. Just hate to lose, you know."

"You okay?"

"Of course, bud. Couldn't be better, you know."

Scott slapped Javi on the back and gave a big smile. He was like a different person than the one he was arguing with not two minutes ago. The whole thing happened so fast, he couldn't even be sure what he saw.

* * * * *

The team managed to score one touchdown in the third quarter. It wasn't exactly the start of their comeback as the other team managed another one as well. At least it wouldn't be a shutout. Javi wondered if there was a mercy rule in football like they used to have in little league. They had lost by more points than this before so he figured he was doomed to stay the entire game.

He told his coach he had to run to the bathroom and jogged back down the hallway towards the locker room. He beelined for Scott's locker. Was he really about to do this?

Javi wanted to open it up, dig through his stuff and find something to make him a little more sure about what he had seen? Had he actually snorted something or was he wiping his nose? And what was he supposed to do with the information once he had it? He thought better of it. Things were already weird enough with Scott as it is, he didn't need to rummage through his stuff and risk alienating him even more. No, he wasn't going to do this. If something was up, he would figure it out in some other way.

As Javi walked out of the locker room, he was surprised to see Trevor standing across the hall.

"Hey," Trevor said.

Javi looked around the hallway and didn't see anyone else around.

"Hey."

"I saw you run off the field. Wanted to go into the boys' room, but I thought that might be creepy. For you. I've had plenty of dreams that were-"

"What are you doing here, Trevor?"

"You're playing my alma mater. I thought I would check out the game. And you in uniform."

"Stop it, okay? This isn't cool. Not here."

"Then where? You've been ignoring my calls."

"I don't always get my messages."

"Every day?"

"Why are you calling me every day?"

"Relax. I said I was Trevor from school and that we were working on a science project."

"Science project? I'm not even taking science."

"Chemistry? Physics? Whatever."

"This is too much. Okay."

"Look, I'm not trying to give you stalker vibes or anything. But I want to hang out. We have fun when we hang out."

Javi didn't want to agree with him, but it was true. In some ways, it was the closest he had ever felt to someone else. They hadn't done everything, but they had been close together, skin to skin, and if Javi could shut the rest of the world out, it would be so perfect. But the real world was still there. His parents. His brothers and sister. His friends. His school. Javi hadn't figured out what any of this was, and he didn't like feeling pushed into trying. No matter how nice it felt being with Trevor.

"I need you to leave me alone. I will call you when I'm not dealing with all this other stuff."

"What other stuff?"

"Just go, Trevor."

Javi returned to the field, but not before he punched a wall on his way out.

* * * * *

Fourth quarter wasn't going any better. There was still a pretty large delta in the scores. What a terrible game to lose, especially as this was three in a row. And Javi even thought they had a chance.

Javi avoided looking in the stands to see if Trevor was still there. He hoped he could take a hint. It wasn't even a hint; Javi was practically begging him to leave him alone. But what if he actually did? Did Javi want that? Everything was so screwed up.

Javi was still bothered by what Scott said. Did he know something? Did he suspect? What was there to suspect? Javi hadn't done anything other than mess around with some college guy that he worked with. He was drunk. It didn't mean anything. And they were friends. It wasn't weird that they were hanging out. Everyone hung out with friends from work. No. Scott couldn't know anything. There was nothing to know. There was one time. Twice, maybe. Trevor parked at Elysian at the far end of the parking lot. He had offered to give Javi a ride home. Perfectly normal. He had done that before, it didn't mean something was going to happen.

They talked in his car for a moment and it had started to rain. Javi made some stupid joke and then Trevor had put his hand on Javi's knee. Javi didn't push it away. He looked around the parking lot for other cars, but Trevor's was the only one around. Trevor's hand went further up Javi's thigh. He closed his eyes, when Trevor reached for his belt.

No one was around, Javi was sure of it. And even if there was, they couldn't see anything because of the rain, and the fogged-up windows. Right? It was the only time anything had happened in the park. No one could have seen. Scott didn't even work that day. Right? They closed the pool early when the rain clouds started forming. Scott couldn't have seen. But could someone else have?

Shit.

What if Bridget had seen? But that was months ago. She would've said something wouldn't she? Or asked him about it. Bridget had gotten distant though. Was this why? Javi's brain was spiraling through numerous scenarios, but everything came to the same result: he had cheated on his girlfriend, and she had killed herself. In that order. Did he have something to do with it? Was he refusing to think about it, because he wasn't sure he hadn't caused it?

Javi had gotten so lost in thought, he didn't see what happened to cause the rest of his teammates to jump off the bench and take the field.

Was it a fight.

Javi jumped up and followed them out.

"What happened?" Javi asked.

"He went to catch the ball but just collapsed. And he's like having a seizure or something," someone said.

"Who?"

"Jetter."

"Scott?"

The coach yelled for everyone to separate and he pushed through with the paramedics following him. When the group opened up, Javi saw Scott on the ground. He wasn't moving. The paramedics rushed to his side and knelt down.

Everything was happening so fast. Javi was in disbelief. He took a step back. The two teams formed a large circle around Scott as the paramedics started to give him chest compressions.

One.

Two.

Three.

Four.

Javi made the sign of the cross and clutched his hands together.

15. PERCY

Now, he was dreaming about Bridget. It started a few nights ago where he met up with Bridget at a park and they chatted while on a swing set. Percy asked her what happened to her but she was mad at him and didn't want to talk. She jumped off the swing and ran off. The next night they were at a concert. The band was some of his friends from school. He was dancing with Bridget and when he asked her where she went (from the previous dream), she jumped up on stage and started singing with the band. There was another one where he woke up next to her. He started talking to her, telling her everything he'd been going through after her fall, but when he turned back to her the bed was empty. Every dream there was a lost connection. Didn't take a psychologist to analyze those.

Percy knew from psychologists. He spoke to a few different ones when he was a kid. He was prone to outbursts, and after biting a kid in his fourth-grade class, his parents started him on a therapy regime. Percy learned early on that his family was different, and you just don't talk about things that happened inside of it, outside of it. He never really connected with anyone, but he stopped biting kids and that's all that his parents really wanted.

He actually wanted to talk to someone now. He wanted to talk about his dreams, his relationship with Bridget, what he could remember that night and what he couldn't. Maybe a professional could piece it together for him. But how was he supposed to do that without talking about how he made his money. And yeah, psychologists weren't supposed to turn you in unless there's a crime, but there were so many crimes happening around him, he couldn't be sure where he would actually be safe.

So, what was he left to do? He did what he always did, what he learned at a young age: suppress it, try to move on. Only, it wasn't so easy this time. This time, someone was dead.

He had successfully avoided all conversations with his mother over the past few days. And his father let him drive into work on his own now, so he didn't have to worry about any talking happening there. Harlan pawned him off on his subordinates for work assignments which let him avoid his dad altogether.

It's not like Harlan and Percy had a difficult relationship. They didn't really have any relationship. He remembered his physical back in seventh grade so he could play baseball. Harlan took Percy to the doctor's office on his lunch break, and he sat in the room in his suit, while Percy was in his underwear talking to the doctor. The doctor asked if they ever played catch together, and Percy and Harlan both jumped to say "yes" even though it had never happened. He just knew it was the right answer. Sure, Harlan bought Percy a glove. It was left on the kitchen counter before practice one day. And when Percy had a game, Harlan had a meeting. That's his childhood in a nutshell. He didn't even realize it was supposed to be different until he would see his friends with their parents-doting on them, taking an interest. In a way, Percy was grateful Harlan and Donna weren't like that. That always seemed a little too much to him. Percy got a car when he asked for one, that was good enough parenting for him.

Percy was always popular. Grade school, middle school, high school, he never had any trouble making friends and being one of the cool kids. He had status, because of his parent's money probably, and people were simply drawn to that. He never meant to become a drug dealer. He never really considered that's what he was. He just had enough money to procure some weed when his friends wanted some. And after a few transactions, he saw an opportunity to become that guy. It brought him more friends, more attention. It wasn't until this whole Bridget incident that he realized how little he meant to those he thought were friends. He had been around people for so much of his life he was only now dealing with being alone.

He wasn't a fan.

Percy didn't usually partake in the goods that he sold, but he did stash a few joints around before he got rid of the rest of his stuff. While pondering his loneliness, Percy grabbed one of his remnants and walked behind his house to the barely-used, wooden jungle gym that still sat in a lonely corner of their half-acre yard. Percy leaned against the ladder heading up to the slide and took a decent-sized hit.

He sat there, one with his existence for over an hour before he heard footsteps. He looked up to see Simon approaching.

Simon was eight, but he dressed like he was eighty. Khaki pants, suspenders, black sneakers that looked fancier than they were. He had the same blonde hair as Percy, but that was it for similarities. Percy was always skinny and slight. Simon wasn't fat, but was certainly rounder than Percy ever was. He had freckles and deep brown eyes. Percy's were hazel, leaning towards green. Percy liked sports growing up, and Simon was all about reading, something Percy still avoided like…well, if he read more he could think of a decent metaphor.

"Mom says we're about to eat."

"When did you guys get home?"

"I don't know. Now? What are you doing out here?"

"Thinking."

"Sounds awesome. Are you coming in?"

"Yeah, buddy. I'm right behind you. Hey, after dinner do you want to play a game or something? I've got time."

"I've got homework."

"Okay. Next time."

Simon trudged away. And Percy took a whiff of his clothes to make sure the smell wasn't too strong. This was his life. Dissed by an eight-year-old. Not even Simon wanted to get infected with whatever made Percy so toxic.

* * * * *

Leaning back in his chair, Percy wondered if he could get away with a legit nap at his desk. He was bored. He had looked for Abby but didn't see her around, and he finished his task list an hour ago. Before he could figure it out, though, a voice came from behind him.

"Hey, are you good with numbers?"

Percy turned around to see Eli Sutton standing there with a large stack of papers in her hands and a smile somewhere between sweet and annoyed. Eli was hot, Percy thought, even though her hair was a bit too short. She looked like that blonde chick from Melrose Place. In fact, he could imagine Eli taking a picture of that woman into her salon saying "give me that." She could pull it off though. Most women her age (she had to be at least 28) couldn't.

"Well?" Eli said.

"Sorry, what's that?"

"Are you good with numbers?"

"What does that even mean? I passed trig."

Eli rolled her eyes and dropped the stack of papers on Percy's desk.

"I need some data entry, but you have to compare the numbers on the paper with what we have in the system and then mark any difference."

"Wait, you can't just dump all this crap on me. I have other projects that-"

"-that you probably finished an hour ago and are now running out the clock. And I need this for your father, so if you want both of us can go ask him what he thinks the priority is."

Eli's smile grew. It certainly wasn't sweetness.

"Okay, I got it. Don't need to freak out."

"I'm not freaking out. Just under water."

"You don't seem the least bit wet."

Percy said it without even thinking. Maybe she wouldn't have even picked up on it.

"You know, junior, my husband is your teacher. So, maybe dial it back a bit."

"Sorry. It just slipped out."

"You Van Allen men certainly have a way of dealing with women, don't you?"

"I'm not anything like my father."

"Don't be so sure."

"And I don't know if you heard, but I'm not going to Dymps anymore."

"Yeah, actually I did. Sorry."

"No, it's fine. Not really missing it, you know?"

"Yeah, well, I know you've got a lot going on, but I could really use your help on this. Sorry if my approach was a bit abrupt."

"Don't worry, I got this."

"If you have any questions…"

"I know where you sit."

Eli smiled. This time it felt a bit more sincere. If he wasn't completely off the mark, he kind of felt like she was flirting with him.

* * * * *

Percy made it about halfway through the stack before he was interrupted again. This time by her voice. He was positioned near Olivia's office, so when Abby said hi to her mother, he knew she was around. He couldn't keep himself from smiling. He wanted to jump up and run over. But, no, he had to play it cool.

He sat for a moment, pretending to type. He didn't want the keys to overpower her conversation. He just wanted to sit back and enjoy her soft voice.

Percy counted to 100 in his head. It helped him focus. He made it to 47. Coffee. He could get coffee and maybe she would want some too. He stood up only to turn around and see Abby standing in the entry of his cube.

"Hey," she said.

"Hey."

"Working?"

"Yeah. You know. You?"

"Writing my Lit paper."

"Cool. Miss Salerno?"

"Yeah. Honors."

"Of course."

Abby sat on the edge of his desk. Percy leaned against the wall.

"I could use some coffee," she said. "Want to join me?"

"Yeah. For sure."

* * * * *

"So, are you just never going back there?" she asked.

They had been sitting for half an hour talking about nothing in particular when Abby started going in on school.

"Probably not. I can test out. And I might still be able to get into a decent school. One of the good things about Daddy's checkbook."

"Having money sounds like a real hassle."

"Sorry, I didn't mean anything."

"It's okay. But yeah, school is kind of weird. Ever since that whole Bridget thing, everyone is walking around all quiet or something. Hard to say. It's just different. Did you know her?"

"Yeah, I mean we had a couple classes, I guess. But I didn't know her that well."

"People are saying they don't think she jumped. Do you?"

What was this about?

"Why are you asking me about Bridget?"

"I didn't know her. You said you had a couple classes. Thought you might have some thoughts."

"I haven't really thought about it," he lied.

"It's just …people are saying she could've been killed. That someone could've pushed her."

"Why would I know anything about that?"

"I don't know. I was just asking. Maybe she said something in class. Maybe you had some random conversation with her. Like I did that night."

"You talked to her?"

"Barely. It was just idle chat over a smoke."

"That why you're so curious?"

"I guess. I just want to know, you know? Like, could someone in that school actually have done this? Do you even think it's possible?"

"Would you just stop asking about Bridget?" Percy snapped. His voiced had gotten loud enough that other people had turned to look at him.

"Sorry," he said.

"No, it's fine. People said you were kind of a jerk. I told them I didn't know that guy, so it's nice to finally meet the real you."

Abby stood up and put her coat on.

"Come on, don't be like that. Can't we just talk about something else?"

"Thanks for the dress," Abby said as she walked out of the coffee shop.

* * * * *

Percy dropped the stack of papers on Eli's desk.

"All done?" she asked.

"Yep. Everything's there."

"Thanks. This is a big help."

"Any time."

"You okay? You seem a little terse."

Percy was still agitated from his conversation with Abby. And clearly wasn't hiding it well. When he had gotten back to the office and went to look for her, her bag was already gone. She must've rushed out. He didn't mean anything by it, he was just getting flustered by all her questions. Did she know something? Is that why she was asking? No, that's silly. Percy knew he had to stop being paranoid. But he also knew he had to figure out what happened that night. Maybe it was about time he talked to someone about it.

"I'm fine. Sorry. Just something on my mind."

Percy wanted to stay and flirt with Eli some more. Not that it would go anywhere, but it was fun enough. But his mind was elsewhere. And he wanted the rest of him to be there as well.

* * * * *

Percy pulled up outside the house. It wasn't too far from his neighborhood, but it wasn't nearly as nice. These houses had character though. Old Victorians. Big, angled roofs, with three or more floors.

He had to apologize. He knew that. It wasn't just about shouting. But he made that crack about his dad's money. He was stepping in it all over the place. He could be better. He knew he could be better.

He parked in the street. There was another BMW in the driveway already (Percy's was newer, he thought, which only made him feel like shit again for being such a jerk).

It was starting to get colder so he pulled on a hat before he stepped outside. He rang the doorbell while going over his speech in his head. He worked on his smile, too. Abby had to know he was being sincere. He looked at his reflection in the glass of the screen door. Not too much teeth.

Don't look creepy. He settled on the perfect smile as the door opened.

It wasn't Abby, but her step-brother, Jake. He wasn't smiling at all.

"Percy?"

"Jake, hey, is Abby home?"

"What do you want?"

"I want to talk to Abby."

"I don't think that's a good idea."

"Excuse me?"

"Which part did you have trouble understanding?"

"No, I just…did she say something?"

"What would she have said?"

Jake was staring him down. They were in the same class, but they had never been friends. They had people in common, but Percy didn't think they had ever had a class together. Percy never really thought much about Jake at all, but it was clear that Jake had formed some opinion on him.

"Look, I didn't mean anything. If I could just talk to her."

"No, I don't think so. In fact, let me make it simple. Just stay away from her completely. Stay away from all of us. Leaving school was a good start, maybe just keep going."

"Are you serious?"

"Yeah. Stay away from Abby or I'll have to get involved."

Jake shut the door.

What did she tell him? Percy sauntered back to his car. Why was he even surprised? His family didn't want anything to do with him. His friends had ditched. Why would he expect Abby to be any different? Maybe Jake was right. Maybe he just needed to keep going.

16. BRECK

The news had an update on Bridget. There had been rumors and other talk for weeks, but no official word on anything. Now, the autopsy report was back and the five o'clock news featured the press conference. Breck watched on the small TV that her parents let her keep in her room. It only got local channels, no cable, but it was on every local news broadcast: the female reporter (it was always the female reporter) said there were no drugs found in her system and while they couldn't rule out foul play, they were inclined to believe it had been a suicide. They did note it was still an open investigation.

In other words: the update was- nothing new. Kira had already told Breck everything she had overheard at Bridget's mom's. Breck hated getting information like this-publicly and at the same time as everyone else. It was in the public interest, they would say, but the public didn't know Bridget. The public didn't care about Bridget. And Breck had enough to worry about than wondering what had happened that night. Now, she was more worried about her boyfriend. She couldn't lose him too.

Breck had been horrified when she saw Scott collapse on the field.

She didn't know what to think. She had gone to the hospital, and sat there in the waiting room with the rest of the Jetter family. She felt like an outsider, an intruder into their private moment, but she wasn't going any place. Not until she knew something. The first update was that Scott had sudden cardiac arrest (a heart attack! At eighteen!). He had lost consciousness, and his heart had stopped, but the paramedics were able to resuscitate him. He regained consciousness not long after, but was still pretty out of it. They were still doing tests when Breck went home.

Scott's mom was kind enough to give her updates. The whole weekend was a mess. He was up and down. Breck was able to visit him, even though it was technically family only, but he looked like such a different person with all the tubes and wires connected to him. Breck held his hand and told him to get better and that she was praying for him. She tried not to cry, but she couldn't help herself.

So many people had been calling. It wasn't like this happened in private. This happened in the middle of the Homecoming game. They canceled the game. The dance was the following night. There had been talk of postponing it but it was probably a tough call to shift everything for one student, even if he was on the Homecoming court (he didn't win, and Breck remembered thinking that it would be upsetting for him, but she forgot to even ask him about it). Breck didn't go to the dance, obviously. They did the crowning ceremony and Breck would be able to see the pictures in her yearbook class, and would have to remind everyone: Not Pictured-Scott Jetter.

Kira skipped the dance as well. She spent the night at Breck's, but they didn't talk much. They went to the video store and rented all the dumb comedies they could find. Breck forced her laughter. She mostly cried when they talked and Kira talked a lot about Bridget, but Breck wasn't really paying attention. She could only think about Scott and hoped that he would be home soon.

Breck's parents liked Scott, but they thought Breck spent too much time with him. They didn't like that he was a senior and she was a sophomore. They didn't understand why he wanted to date someone younger, but they didn't stop Breck from seeing him. They couldn't. She would just do it anyway.

Scott was the first everything for Breck. He was her first kiss, her first date, her first boyfriend, her first love. She knew she loved him. And she knew he was going to be other firsts as well. She was ready now, she decided. This whole incident drove home exactly how much she needed him. Every awkward time she pushed him away saying it was "too soon" would be over now.

The first day back at school was hard. She couldn't concentrate on her classes and everyone kept asking her the same questions. He's going to be fine, she'd say. He's not out yet, but maybe tomorrow. They're not sure what happened. It was exhausting. Breck had never had so much attention from so many people, and she was surprised at how many people, especially upperclassmen, knew who she was.

Breck sat there watching the news about Bridget, thinking about Scott, and ignoring her homework. Her mother called her down for dinner, but Breck wasn't hungry. Still, she had to be the good daughter and at least pick at her food or else they'd worry and stress her out even more.

Breck flipped off the TV and went to the dinner table.

* * * * *

Between the hospital and work, Scott's parents were being pulled in every direction. Breck offered to help them out where she could. As such, she got tasked with picking up Bernie from school. She was more than happy to do it. It made her feel closer to Scott, even though she had barely talked to him. Robbie said he was doing better, but he was getting oxygen or something and couldn't really talk much. She did say Breck could come for a visit tonight, though. Breck was excited, and nervous. She had never seen anyone like that.

She sat in Scott's kitchen while Bernie poured herself a post-school bowl of cereal. She felt so close to him and also like she was spying or something. Well, since she already had the guilt, she might as well go all the way with it. Breck busied Bernie with some TV and then slipped off towards the basement. The stairs were carpeted so she crept down quietly, even though it really wasn't a big deal.

The basement had a big family room that served multiple purposes. There was a couch and TV on one end of the room. A pool table and weight bench were on the other side. Part game room, part gym, all of it had a musty scent. Scott's room was off the other end of the big room.

Breck walked through the family room. There were piles of clothes strewn about. Breck knocked on Scott's door for some reason. Hoping this whole thing was a dream, maybe, and he would come rushing to the door with a big smile. No such luck.

His room was clean, unlike the mess she had to walk through to get to it. The bed was made. The books were perfectly categorized on his book shelf. He had a number of trophies behind his bed. It looked like the perfect teenager's bedroom, but there was also no personality to it. Breck could've just as easily walked into a stranger's room and saw the same thing. There was nothing particularly Scott about this place. It had only been a few days, but she felt so far away from him. And this place didn't make her feel any more connected to him.

Breck was startled when the door to the bathroom opened and TJ walked out with nothing but a towel wrapped around his waist.

"Oh, shit," TJ said as he hands grabbed the towel firmly.

"Sorry," Breck said. She first took in his half-naked self before turning away to fixate on the bookshelf. "I didn't know you were here."

"Just in the shower."

"I can see that. I actually kind of forget you were here at all. Sorry, that didn't come out right. I picked Bernie up from school. And I'm going to the hospital and wanted to see if there was anything he needed." It felt like a lie. Which it pretty much was.

"No, it's cool. There's a lot going on. But yeah, I've been sleeping on the couch out there. And it's easier to use Scott's bathroom than go upstairs, and since he's not here."

"It's okay. Don't let me keep you from getting dressed." Breck was uncomfortable. She had been with Scott without his shirt on, and it always gave her this rush of excitement. As innocent as this was, it made her feel like she was doing something wrong. Betraying Scott somehow.

TJ squeezed past her and walked out of the room. Breck sat down on Scott's bed. Scott had a mirror on his dresser just like she had in her room. But her mirror was lined with pictures of her and Scott, her and her friends, her parents. There was nothing around Scott's. It made Breck sad, almost upset, like he did something wrong, even though she knew he hadn't. They hadn't spent much time in his bedroom. As supportive as his parents were of their relationship, they still didn't want them hanging out in his bedroom, in the basement, all alone.

There was a knock at the door, and TJ was now standing in front of her in jeans and a t-shirt.

"Sorry about that," he said.

"It's okay. My fault entirely."

"How's he doing?"

"Better I think. I'm actually going to see him in a bit."

"It's weird. I was just getting used to living here with him and then he's not here and everyone else is gone. And… I don't know, it's just weird."

"Yeah."

"How are you?"

"I'm okay. It's been a lot."

"I can imagine."

"How is it? Living here, you know. Scott hasn't said much about it."

"I don't think he's a fan. He kind of hides in his room when I'm around."

"I'm sure it's nothing personal. He has a lot of homework."

"No, I know. This whole thing is…"

"Weird. Yeah, you said."

Scott didn't go into much detail about TJ's new living situation. All he said is that their parents were friends and he was going to stay with them for a bit. He didn't seem happy about it, that was true, but it didn't seem personal about TJ. Breck felt sorry for TJ. She wanted to ask what happened to create this situation, but she knew it was both none of her business and probably more than she could take on at this point. She was glad that TJ was going to be around and even made a mental note to include him in things if they were getting the group together. Maybe a movie or something once Scott was out. Get Kira, and Javi and Bridget.

It took her a second to realize how silly she was, that for an instant she forgot all about Bridget's death. There really was too much going on.

"I should probably go," Breck said, abruptly. She got to her feet and gave TJ a forced smile before darting up the stairs and out of the house, barely waving bye to Bernie as she did.

* * * * *

Breck parked at the hospital. She had stopped at the grocery store to get some balloons and flowers, and probably went a little overboard. She pulled the fluffy bouquet and four mylar balloons that had hearts and a giant "GET WELL SOON" message on them. The automatic doors caught one of the balloons when she tried to walk through, and it made a loud pop. It was the "SOON" so it wasn't a complete loss.

"Breck," a voice shouted from behind her. She saw Javi running up to her from the other side of the parking lot.

"Javi, hey."

"Do you have a sec?"

"Of course."

Javi pulled her back outside where they sat on the bench. The wind was starting to get crisper and Breck was glad she kept her gloves on.

"Did Mrs. Jetter call you too?"

"No, I don't think Scott wants to see me. I called your house and they said you were coming up here and wanted to catch you."

"Why? And why don't you think Scott wants to see you."

"We kind of had a little fight."

"He didn't say anything."

"No, he wouldn't. It was that night. Kind of right before it all went down."

"What are you saying? What were you fighting about? I don't understand."

It was all coming at her pretty fast. This whole conversation felt completely out of nowhere.

"Scott and I had an argument. It was no big deal. At least, I thought it was no big deal but then this whole thing and I don't know."

"What do you mean? I feel like you're dancing around something and I really can't read between those lines."

"Before he went down, in the locker room before hand, I could have sworn I saw him taking something."

"What do you mean 'taking something'?"

"Like snorting something."

"Drugs?"

"I honestly have no idea. I didn't get a chance to talk to him about it. And this. I just wanted you to know in case he said anything to you. Or if you could look out for anything."

"Anything like drugs? Of course, Scott isn't doing drugs. Don't be silly."

"No. I'm not saying that for sure. I just…I lost Bridget and I don't want to lose my best friend too, you know. I'm just worried."

Breck could see in Javi's eyes that he was being sincere. She didn't know what to make of what he was saying. Scott wasn't doing drugs. That's absurd. That wasn't him. She knew him better than that. There was certainly some explanation for what he saw.

"I don't want to miss visiting hours," Breck said. "Are you sure you don't want to come up?"

"No, thanks. Just let me know how he's doing."

"Okay."

Javi took off again and Breck braved the door with her three big balloons and one deflated "SOON" dragging behind her.

* * * * *

The hospital room was stale and a putrid green color. It smelled like decay and bleach. Scott had an IV in his wrist and other wires hooked up to his chest and nose. His face looked gaunt. Robbie had warned her, but it was still a jarring sight. Breck forced a smile.

Scott looked up at her with weary eyes.

"For me?" he asked weakly, barely pointing at the flowers and balloons.

"Of course, babe."

Breck set her gifts down and sat down in the chair next to the bed. She squeezed his hand.

"How are you?"

"Never better. About to run a marathon."

"You definitely look ready for it."

"Good to see you."

"I was so scared."

"I'm sorry. I'll be okay. Really."

"Do they know what caused it?"

"Some freak accident. My heart just kind of stopped."

"I thought you were dead."

"I think I might've been for a couple minutes."

Breck couldn't stop herself from getting teary. She could appreciate he was trying to make light of the whole thing, but if that's true this is a much bigger deal.

"Do they know why your heart stopped? I mean, you're eighteen years old, healthy, your heart shouldn't just stop."

"I don't know, they said a bunch of medicalese. I haven't been sleeping, been pushing too hard."

"And that can just stop your heart?"

"I can tell you're freaking out about this and I want you to know that I'm going to be fine. I'll probably be out of here in a day or two. They had to do some tests."

"And what did the tests show?"

"Mostly, that I'm fine. And that I'm lucky that we had paramedics on the sidelines."

Scott had a smile but his eyes kept darting away. Breck's entire conversation with Javi was playing over in her head. Something felt off about this.

"Is there something you're not telling me?"

"What is there to tell? I told you, I'm going to be fine."

"You've been in the hospital for nearly a week. That doesn't just happen when everything is hunky dory."

"They have to do more tests. What has got you so worked up?"

"Nothing, Javi was here and…"

"You talked to Javi? What did he say?"

Suddenly, Scott's entire tone changed. The lilt in his voice grew harsh.

"He didn't say anything. He's worried about you."

"Yeah, I bet."

"Did something happen between you two?"

Scott shook his head.

"Was this your plan? Come in here all sweet and then dump all this Javi bullshit on me?"

Breck was shocked. She knew Scott could have a temper, but it was mostly harmless. This felt like such a different boy in front of her.

"What Javi bullshit? He didn't tell me anything. Is there something he would have to tell me?"

Now Breck had the tone.

"I can't believe this."

"Can't believe what?"

"I can't believe that you give any credit whatsoever to what Javi said."

"Javi didn't say anything. He said to tell you he hoped you were feeling better. What an asshole. What else do you think he could've said?"

"Come off it, Breck. Javi was being all weird at the game like he thought he saw something."

"What did he think he saw? What is going on, Scott?"

"Nothing. I told you."

"Well, maybe you need your rest and I can ask your mom if she knows anything about it."

"DON'T," Scott snapped firmly. He dropped Breck's hand from his and leaned up in his bed. "You can't tell her anything, I swear to fucking god."

"Then tell me the truth."

"Okay, I took something."

"Something what?"

"It doesn't matter. I hadn't been sleeping and I took something to give me some energy. It was an important game and I needed the push."

"What did you take?"

"It was something I got from one of the others on the team, okay? I admit it. Nothing illegal, but I don't want anyone blowing it out of proportion. But you can't say anything, not to my mom or dad. Or Javi. Anyone. Okay?"

"Scott, if this is what landed you in here, you need to be honest with it. How are you supposed to get better?"

"I am getting better. It's out of my system."

"How do you know?"

"That's why I'm still here."

"But your mom didn't say anything about…"

"She doesn't know."

"How are the doctors not aware?"

"The doctors are aware, but I'm eighteen now so they legally can't say anything to my parents without violating some code. The only thing my parents know is what I've said is okay for them to say. But none of it matters because I'm getting better, I'm getting out of here soon, and I'm not going to do it again."

"Just like that?"

"Breck, I almost died. I know that. I'm not an idiot."

"No, clearly not."

Everything Scott was saying felt like it was coming out of someone else's mouth. The lies, the cover-ups, the manipulation. It all felt like a completely different person. Breck felt like a total stranger.

"I'm glad you're getting better," she said. And she meant it.

But she really had no idea what that meant for when he was better. Who was this guy she had been dating for months? And what else was he hiding?

17. KIRA

It was a nice enough night. Sometimes the end of November could get lost in a blanket of snow, but this evening was cool but mild. School was out for Thanksgiving break. Kira had gone over to Breck's to hang out but then the news report came on. It was the second news report about Bridget in as many nights, and Kira didn't really feel like hanging out after that. She decided to walk home. It wasn't too far.

The news report wasn't terribly important. They had found Bridget's car at some church in South Omaha. It had been parked there for weeks. There were signs of a break-in, and the license plates didn't match, but there wasn't any indication it was connected at all to Bridget's death. The police were still saying suicide. The only thing they knew for sure was that the car was not at the park when they found Bridget's body.

Kira wanted to tell Breck about Abby, that the two of them were… friendly? Trying to make sense of the Bridget situation. But she couldn't find the words and it felt silly to even bring it up. The police said the case was still, technically at least, open. They were investigating, right? Abby was convinced that Bridget was murdered, but Kira still wasn't sure.

Bridget had been acting so weird in the weeks before her death, and she had been shutting Kira out. It wasn't a stretch that she was going through something. If they knew what that was, maybe they could figure out if she did, in fact, take her own life.

It was only about a mile to Kira's house from Breck's, but even though it wasn't too cold, it was dark. Some of the streetlights were out, and Kira never realized how quiet the neighborhood could be, which gave it an extra eerie feeling. A gate would creek, someone taking the trash out to the curb, and Kira would jump. She had no reason to be afraid. It was only a little after ten at night. But she was black in a mostly white neighborhood.

There weren't many cars out, so when one crossed a stop sign up ahead it felt a little too slow. If Bridget was killed, that meant that a killer was still around. Maybe they targeted Bridget because she was black. Kira was pretty much the same as Bridget in every category. Young. Black. Female. They went to different schools, but other than that, they checked all of the same boxes.

There was a crunching of leaves behind her and Kira turned around to see a shadowy figure about a block away. It was a man, given the height and build. She couldn't make out much else, she just kept moving. At the corner, she crossed to the other side of the street even though it meant she would have to cross back in a few more blocks. She wanted to know if the person was actually following her.

Kira picked up the pace, occasionally glancing back to see the figure edging closer to her. As she approached a streetlight she wanted to see if would offer any illumination of the man following her, but when she took a look back she saw the man turn and walk up the steps to one of the houses she'd already passed.

Nothing to do with her. Now she was really starting to feel ridiculous. Kira still walked home as fast as she could.

* * * * *

Kira's dad has been on her case all day. It was Thanksgiving and they were hosting. The house had to be spotless. Kira spent most of the morning wiping down furniture and cabinets and shelves and shoving her clothes in whatever drawer or closet they would go in, clean or not. Her little brother, Timmy, was taking forever to clean up all his toys in the basement. Her cousin's family was due over in less than an hour and Randall and Georgina were busy in the kitchen basting the turkey and making too many side dishes.

Georgina had started to show, slightly. But she really leaned into it, wearing large, flowy blouses that didn't tuck in, and today she kept her apron loosely tied, making her belly look bigger than it was. Kira still hated the idea of a little half-sibling, but hadn't been dwelling on it much. She still had plenty of time to worry about that before Georgina was due.

Kira walked in the kitchen. At least the house smelled good. Georgina was mashing potatoes on the stove. Randall was loading the dishwasher.

"I finished the dining room," Kira said.

"Okay, thanks, baby," Randall responded. "Can you set the table?"

"I thought that Timmy was doing that."

"Well, maybe you could help him. There needs to be thirteen place settings at the big table. And six for the kids."

"And which table am I at?"

"Don't worry, you've graduated to the big table."

"Thirteen? Who's all coming?"

"Uncle Andre's family, Georgina's sister Claire and her boyfriend," Randall said.

"Fiancé," Georgina corrected. "Believe me, she will correct you."

"Oh, and I invited Bri… I invited Vanessa over," Randall said, catching himself.

"Oh."

"Is that okay?"

Kira was making a face. She couldn't help herself. She had nothing against Vanessa, but their last few encounters hadn't exactly been comfortable. But she did feel sorry for her. She shouldn't be alone on the first holiday without her daughter. And it's not like they hadn't been over for holidays before. Kira missed being able to sneak off to her room with Bridget where they could make fun of everyone else. Last Easter, they had confiscated a bottle of wine from the table that was still half full and finished it on Kira's floor while continuously giggling.

"Yeah, of course. Surprised you didn't mention it is all."

"Just kind of happened. Saw her in the driveway yesterday and got to talking."

"How's she doing?" Kira asked.

"Well as can be expected, I guess. I can't imagine what she's going through."

"Yeah, but I mean, did she seem, I don't know, off or anything?"

"Off how?"

"Never mind."

Kira wanted to suggest going easy on the wine with Vanessa, but she couldn't figure out a reason without bringing Vanessa's strange outbursts and that one time she thought Kira was Bridget. Thankfully, Georgina interrupted with a question about the gravy.

"I've got a pot on already with the gizzards from the turkey," Randall said.

"Splendid," Georgina responded. "This is my first big holiday meal I want everything to be perfect."

"You never made Thanksgiving dinner back home?" Kira asked.

"No, we're not so much with the Thanksgiving back in England."

"Oh, right," Kira said. "I should probably help Timmy."

Kira excused herself, before further embarrassing herself in front of her new soon-to-be stepmother.

* * * * *

The house had been noisy all afternoon, with the cacophony of children playing games in the basement and football blaring from the living room. Dinner was a hit. For the most part. Kira thought the turkey was dry and she much preferred her cranberry sauce from a can than whatever Georgina did to make hers.

Kira had a small plate, but didn't feel much like eating. Vanessa had taken the seat right next to hers, but was perfectly normal throughout dinner. When they held hands to say grace, Vanessa squeezed her hand a little too tightly, but there was nothing overtly wrong with that. Vanessa had asked her about school, and complimented her dress.

Kira had gotten the navy-blue dress on sale last year, but hadn't had any reason to wear it yet. She thought about it for Christmas, or one of the other big church holidays, but it was the only thing she didn't hate when she was trying on clothes.

"The color is so rich. I love it," Vanessa said, feeling the velvet sleeves. "It reminds me of Bridget's cheerleading uniform. It was such a great color on her."

The mention of Bridget was awkward for both of them. Vanessa had stopped fiddling with her dress and took another sip of her wine. Kira said thanks and excused herself. It felt wrong, talking to Vanessa without Bridget there. She didn't have the heart to correct Vanessa about the color of the uniform, since Kira had seen her in the white cheerleading getup plenty of times. There was navy lettering, but that was it. Kira was surprised she would make such a mistake, but she was often too busy to make it to the games.

While the majority of the adults retired to the living room to cheer on one team or another, Kira made her way into the kitchen to start on the dishes. The first part was getting all the food put away. Kira dropped potatoes and yams and cranberries into a variety of Tupperware containers, while her brain kept going back to that conversation on the uniforms. Was she wrong? Was it navy? Kira could swear it was white. Kira went to a game when they played at AC West at the beginning of the season. She remembered the stark contrast of the white against Bridget's dark skin and how it made her stand out even more as the only black cheerleader. Doesn't feel like a mistake that Vanessa would make.

"Here, let me help you with that, dear," Vanessa said, as if she was summoned by Kira's thoughts.

"Oh, thanks," Kira said as Vanessa took the glass casserole dish from Kira's hands and started to rinse it in the sink.

"Vanessa, we ran out of foil. Do you have some?"

"I'm sure I do. I can pop over and…"

"Oh, no, you stay there. I know where it is. I'll run over."

"Side door is unlocked."

"Thanks."

Kira wiped her hands on a dish towel and ran across the street without even putting on a coat. There was an easy way to settle her brain.

She ran in the side door of Vanessa's house and grabbed the foil from the third drawer down, next to the sink, before heading upstairs to Bridget's room. There were boxes in the room, and some of her stuff had been packed up, but her clothes were still in the closet.

Kira flipped through the closet until she found a hanger with a freshly laundered cheerleader uniform. She pulled it out to examine it closely. It was navy. Then what the hell was she remembering?

Kira sat down on Bridget's bed. There was no bedding. It had been stripped away and was probably in one of the boxes on the floor. Kira laid back and tried to tell herself she wasn't going crazy. She was sure it was white.

On the floor, with its twenty-five-foot chord that would let Bridget walk into any room upstairs, was Bridget's clear phone. Kira remembered the prank calls they would make back in eighth grade when the surest sign you liked a boy was trying to embarrass him on the phone. Kira picked up the phone and dialed.

She had used the number a lot over the past few weeks and was surprised she knew it by heart.

It rang three times before someone answered.

"Hello?"

"Abby? It's Kira. What color are the cheerleader uniforms at Dymps?"

"You know it's Thanksgiving right?"

"Did I interrupt something?"

"No."

"Then tell me."

"Blue for home games, white for away. Why?"

Of course. Kira let out a deep breath. She had seen an away game and Vanessa was used to home games. Easy answers. Kira was happy she wasn't crazy. And that she didn't correct Vanessa and make a whole thing of it.

"Hello?"

"Oh, sorry." For a second, Kira forgot she was on the phone. "It was just something Bridget's mom said."

At first, a moment of relief, but as she sat there, another uncomfortable feeling.

"Where is it?"

"Where's what?"

"Sorry, Abby. I just went through Bridget's closet and only her blue uniform was here. Where's the white one?"

"Maybe she left it in her car."

"But the police found her car and said there wasn't any of her stuff in there."

"Maybe the police have it."

"You said they cleared out her locker at school?"

"Oh yeah. I heard they had to get a crowbar because the lock number didn't match what they had in the office. I think it was just books and stuff. I talked to someone that watched the whole thing."

"What about her other locker?"

"What other locker?"

"She had one in the girl's locker room for cheerleading. I remember her talking about it because they put her away from the other girls because they were messing with her last year."

"They were?"

"Nothing serious. Teenage girl hazing I guess."

"So, wait, it's possible she still has stuff in there?"

"I guess."

"Kira, what are the chances you could get out of the house tonight?"

"Tonight?"

"I have a really bad idea."

* * * * *

Kira didn't like lying to her dad. For one, she wasn't very good at it. Her guilt always made her stammer. Now, deceiving him, well, that was a different story.

Randall had had enough turkey to keep him out. He was a heavy sleeper anyway. Georgina didn't spend the night. He only ever spent the night at her place, being proper he said, until they got married. Him and his pregnant girlfriend. Kira thought it was funny the lengths adults go to presenting something to their kids that is completely inconsequential. Although tonight she was grateful.

Kira had propped up pillows in her bed to make it look like she was sleeping. She left her car in the driveway. Her dad was planning on getting up early to get some good deal on something at the Black Friday sales. Even if she didn't make it back by the time he left, it was conceivable he wouldn't notice she was gone until well after lunch.

She left out the side door, the furthest away from her dad's bedroom and then walked up the street a block. She waited less than ten minutes before Abby flashed her lights and pulled up.

"Are you sure we should be doing this?" Kira asked as she hopped into the car.

"No. But I know that cheap ass school is not paying double overtime for someone to walk around on Thanksgiving."

They were at the school within a few minutes. They didn't see another car on the road the entire way. Abby turned her lights off as she went down the long driveway into the lower parking lot by the gymnasium.

There were no other cars around but they still sat and watched for any signs of life for nearly half an hour. Not another soul.

"Okay, so how do you suppose we get in?"

"Oh, that's easy. Come on."

Abby got out of the car, slung a backpack over her shoulder, and gently closed the door behind her. Kira followed.

"I still don't think this is a good idea."

"Shhh," Abby whispered. "And if you recall, I said up front that it wasn't."

They made it to the back door. Kira kept looking around for someone. There were priests that lived at the church, but it was up the street, far enough away and on the other side of a hill that there was no view to where they were. The window was made of nine smaller panes of glass. Abby pulled her glove tight and punched into the one on the lower left.

The glass shattered, loudly.

"Owwww," Abby howled. She rubbed her hand.

"What the hell?"

Abby picked out the rest of the glass from the window and reached her arm in and down. Kira's heart was pounding, but Abby pulled her hand out and then opened the door.

"Easy peasy."

"That was so loud. Are you sure no one is here? And that there are no alarms?"

"Pretty sure. And no alarms. They do have stuff up by the main office, but this school is too old and not wired properly. And I worked this out when I would skip gym class to have a cigarette. Even the emergency alarms don't work, which I'm sure is a pretty big violation."

"I really don't like this."

"Come on, this is the easy part."

The girls tiptoed into the hallway, careful not to step on any glass. Abby pulled a flashlight out of her backpack.

"You come prepared."

"Well, it's my first breaking and entering. I just wanted it to be special."

Kira hung close to Abby as she led her down the hallway.

"Look, if anything happens, make a run for it. Go across the field and hop the fence. Walk home and we will regroup tomorrow."

"What would happen?" Kira asked.

"You know, anything. Come on."

Abby pulled her down the hall and then down the stairs. Kira had been in the school before, and in the gymnasium specifically, but seeing it in the dark like this was a completely different experience. She felt like her heart was going to burst through her jacket.

"The locker rooms are down here, but you need a key to get inside. And they don't have anything I can break and reach in."

"Then how do we get in? Don't tell me, you can pick locks?"

"I wish, no. But I do need your help."

"With what?"

"A boost."

There was a point, in the corner of the hallway where Abby was able to step onto a railing and then onto a trophy cabinet and reach the ceiling. She pushed up one of the ceiling panels and pulled herself up and disappeared. Kira shook her head. She still felt like someone was going to come around the corner at any moment.

"What do you see?" Kira whisper-shouted. There was no response. Kira walked down the three steps to the door of the girl's locker room, where Abby had told her to wait. Every time she heard a noise, she would look up and down the hallway. It was still dark and ominous. It had been almost five minutes when Kira started to get worried. She heard rustling from the other side of the door.

"Abby?" She called. Still no answer. What if she fell? What if there was a janitor in there? Or security? What was she even doing here?

Then the door pulled open and Abby was dusting herself off.

"I can't believe that worked. One of the benefits of no one ever noticing you're around is that people will say anything and think they are being discreet. I heard a couple guys talking about sneaking in through the ceiling to watch the senior girls change and, well, here we are. From the mouths of pervs, eh?"

"Let's just get out of here."

"We've come this far. But, trying to figure out which one is hers may be a little more challenging. There are like hundreds."

Kira walked in as Abby handed her another flashlight. There were rows and rows of lockers, the cage kind where you could see everything inside them. Most were empty, but there were a few that still had locks on them. The doors were grated to where you could see inside. Abby and Kira walked up and down the rows shining the flashlight into the locked doors. There were other sports uniforms- basketball jerseys and volleyball shorts- but no cheerleader skirts.

"How are we supposed to know if it's hers?"

"Did she play any sports?"

"No."

They kept roaming up and down each row. After a few minutes, Kira found one locker that had a backpack with pink duct tape on one of the straps.

"Wait a second…I think this is her backpack."

"Are you sure?"

"Yeah, she tore the strap on our trip to Kansas City. I thought she got a new one, but maybe she used this one for something else."

The locker was protected by a small combination padlock.

"Any chance you know the numbers?"

"I have no idea."

Abby dropped her backpack and pulled out a pair of bolt cutters.

"Okay then, plan b."

She placed the bolt cutters around the lock and tried to squeeze the arms together but nothing happened.

"Let me try," Kira said, but she had no more success. Finally, they each took an arm and pushed them together. With a loud snap, the lock broke.

Abby pulled the lock off and opened the door. The backpack was hanging off a hook in the main compartment. Kira took the bag. There was another bag below that, which Abby pulled out. In the small cubby at the top there was some deodorant and a shower cap.

Kira unzipped the backpack. She pulled out the white uniform which was crumpled below some other gym clothes. In the front compartment there were some other toiletries. This must be what Bridget used to get ready for away games, Kira supposed.

"Kira, I think Bridget was planning on running away," Abby said.

Kira looked over and saw that Abby had been unpacking the other bag. There were clothes neatly sorted – t-shirts, underwear, jeans, sweaters. Abby pulled out an envelope of cash, hundreds. She handed it to Kira.

Kira counted. There was nearly two-thousand dollars.

"Where did she get all this? And what was she going to do with it?"

"Kira?"

Kira looked over when Abby called her name. She had pulled out a small box. It was too dark for Kira to tell what it was so she shined her flashlight over. On the back of the box in big, black letters Kira read PREGNANCY TEST.

"Holy shit."

18. JAVI

He was trying to eat his breakfast. His father had already left for work, but Javi's mom, Lucinda, was more than happy to lecture him as he ate his eggs. It wasn't entirely clear what she was on about, but there was an underlying theme of being careful (his "best friend" was in the hospital, his girlfriend had died). Javi still hadn't seen Scott or even talked to him since the whole thing went down. He asked Breck how her visit went, but she was cagey as well. Everything in his life seemed a bit sideways.

"Are you even listening to me?" Lucinda asked

"Sorry, Mama, I just remembered I have a homework assignment I need to finish."

"You better not drop the ball on your classes like you have everything else."

"I won't. I'm sorry."

"And you missed church on Sunday."

"Sorry, Mama. I'll be there this week. I promise."

"Don't promise. Be there."

Lucinda gave Javi a hug as he dropped his plate into the sink.

"Dishwasher."

"Yes, Mama."

It was true, he skipped out on church. He was having trouble with the whole thing, really. It was hard to worship and bask in joy when he was still so upset and confused about Bridget. One of the other kids in his class mentioned how when you kill yourself you don't get into heaven, which upset Javi. He couldn't imagine Bridget suffering in the afterlife. Nothing about that seemed right.

And then there was the Trevor of it all.

As Javi returned to his room and got dressed for school, his mind drifted to Trevor and their last meeting. He was somewhat annoyed that Trevor actually seemed to listen to him and kept his distance. No phone calls. No showing up. Nothing. Javi knew it was what he asked for, but it wasn't exactly what he wanted. All he wanted was for one thing in his life to be easy, but between school, work, church, friends and everything else, it all felt like a mess. A mess he had no idea how to clean up.

Javi sat on his bed. He had found a note from Bridget the other day. It was nothing special, just a little girlfriend message. It made Javi sad, and guilty all over again. He kept it tucked into the frame of the bed so he could read it every now and then. He wasn't sure why. It didn't make him feel better. But it did make him think of Bridget, which wasn't all bad. She ended the note with a simply drawn heart, and her signature "B," which kind of looked like an 8 with a line through it. He traced it with his finger.

Javi knew he had to figure out his life. He had to start with school. He would take advantage of his study halls to get caught up. He would make a note to get up for church with the family on Sunday. And if he was ever going to make sense of the whole thing with Scott, he was going to have to see him.

* * * * *

Javi paused for a second before he opened the basement door. Whatever happened with Scott, he didn't tell his parents. When Javi showed up at the house, Robbie was happy to see him and let him right in. Scott had only been home from the hospital for a day or so, and was anxious for visitors. Robbie said he could go right down.

Javi didn't know why it felt awkward. He had been going down to Scott's room for years, ever since the Jetters moved into this house. The sound of the TV was on, and Javi could hear that and the clack of buttons on Scott's Nintendo controllers when he started walking down. He was somewhat surprised to see that Scott was not alone. He was sitting on the couch, with his feet sprawled across the coffee table. A blanket covered his legs. His hair didn't look like it had been combed in months. TJ was next to him, playing some racing game. Neither heard Javi walk in the room.

He stood there for a moment, not wanting to interrupt. Finally, when there was a lull in the game, Javi knocked on the wall.

"Hey, your mom said I could come down."

They both turned. Scott sat expressionless.

"Hey."

"You look like crap. How are you feeling?"

"Better, I guess. This is TJ. He's…"

"Yeah, we met at Halloween. And Breck filled me in. Good to see you, man."

"Hey," TJ said, though Javi gave him little thought.

"Can we talk?" Javi asked.

"I can go upstairs or something," TJ suggested.

"Nah, keep playing. We can go in my room."

TJ returned to the game. Scott got up and moved slowly into his room. Javi followed, slowing his pace to stay behind Scott. In his room, Scott plopped on his bed. Javi closed the door behind them.

"Is that weird? Like an instant stepbrother or something?"

"I don't know. TJ is cool. You know, doesn't blow things out of proportion and spread lies about you."

So, it was going to be like that.

"Out of proportion? You almost died."

"And you got Breck in the middle of this?"

"I told her what I saw."

"What you thought you saw."

"Tell me then. What happened? What did I see?"

"I don't have to tell you shit. Whatever you think you saw, is my business. And it's really no longer any of yours."

When did Scott become such an asshole? Was he always like this and Javi just never noticed or is this something new?

"Just like that, lifetime friends are done? You can't be serious. That's just stupid, Scott."

Scott didn't say anything. Javi couldn't look Scott in the eye. He started to look around the room. It was a mess. Stacks of papers were all over his desk. His bookcase looked like it had been ransacked. Stacks of clothes were spilling out of the dresser drawers.

"Doing a little spring cleaning?" Javi asked.

"Seemed like the right time to get rid of some things, you know, that I have no use for any more."

"Why are you being such a dick?"

"Because I'm pissed off. How should I be?"

"What did I do to you? I was worried about you."

"Then where were you? When I was in the hospital like that? You're so worried about me you completely spaced me off. I almost died, like you said, and where the hell were you?"

"I didn't think you wanted to see me."

"Not to sound gay or anything, but you could've called. Something. I was scared. And you think I can talk about that with anyone? Yeah, I'm pissed. I was surprised by our fight, but I didn't think it was a big deal. And then you just blow me off. You're a bad friend."

"I'm a bad friend? You've been lying to me."

"Lying? Okay, fine, I took something. I had been studying for my Chem test and I didn't sleep for two days, and the game was a big deal. I wanted to stay awake. What's with all the judgement? We've smoked up before."

"It's not the same thing. And I'm not judging. I was worried."

"Well, no one asked you to. I didn't pass out because I took something. I have some weird heart thing I didn't know about. The two things aren't connected and now you got Breck all riled up. I don't know what's going on with you."

"There's nothing going on with me. I'm sorry, I didn't mean to make a big deal out of this."

"But you did." Scott got up and walked to the bathroom. "I gotta piss." He slammed the door behind him firmly.

Javi was confused by the entire interaction. Maybe he did misconstrue things. And maybe it was he who was pulling away from Scott. This whole thing with Trevor, he hasn't told anyone. He can't imagine ever telling anyone. They wouldn't understand. They'd make it into something it wasn't, although Javi didn't even know what it was. He wasn't sure if he should stay or go. He wasn't even sure what they were even fighting about any more.

Javi saw a stack of photos amidst the papers on the desk. There was one of Breck and Scott from Halloween in their matching costumes. Javi started flipping through them. There was one with Scott, Breck, Bridget and Javi from one of the rides at Elysian Park. Another showed Scott and Javi camping when they were, like, twelve. Javi was surprised he saved these. Scott never struck Javi as particularly sentimental.

There were notes strewn about the pictures. An "I love you, babe," note from Breck. Another missive that seemed about five pages long. Javi had turned in shorter papers in English class. He heard the toilet flush from the bathroom, and he tried to put everything back the way he found it but it doing so, an entire stack of crap fell off the desk. Javi leaned down to try and pick everything up when one of the notes scribbled on notebook paper caught his eye.

The handwriting was messy, and the paper was weathered. The note simply read "sorry to leave this on your windshield, but missed your call. If you can make it out, I'll be at our spot. Usual time." It seemed inconsequential, other than the signature.

It was B, scrawled quickly in what looked like an 8 with a line through it.

Javi quickly shoved the note in his pocket. And picked up everything else that had fallen. He was putting it back on the desk when Scott emerged from the bathroom.

"Sorry, I accidentally bumped into your desk and everything went flying."

"Leave it. I can get to it. Look, I'm sorry if I've been a dick. It's just been a lot. And my parents probably aren't gonna let me finish the season and I'm probably gonna have a ton to catch up on school, and I probably took some of that out on you. Sorry, dude. Can we just forget the last couple weeks ever happened? I could really use my best friend back."

Scott held out his hand. Javi had too much racing through his head to know how to respond. He shook Scott's hand and smiled.

"Sure, bud. We're cool."

* * * * *

Javi traced his finger over the words in the note. "Our spot" it said. What did that mean? Why did his "best" friend have a spot with his girlfriend? And with everything else Scott had been lying about, how bad was this.

Javi was trying to isolate his betrayal, and while it stung to know Bridget might've cheated, it wasn't like he was completely faithful to her. It was Scott, who he now figured had been lying to his face for months. All the while walking around like he's the greatest guy. Even though he was absent, there was a whole special mention about him at the Homecoming dance, even though he didn't win King. If voting hadn't finished before Scott's accident, maybe it would've been different. No doubt his hospital stay would provide the extra incentive for some students. Teenagers loved getting credit for doing something good. Javi grew angrier by the second.

He was in the computer lab, supposedly working on a paper, but he couldn't focus. He saw Kira approaching and he shoved the note back into his pocket. He wondered if anyone else knew about Scott and Bridget, and what there was to actually know.

"Hey," Kira said, taking the seat next to him. "Busy?"

"Not really."

"How are you?"

"Kira, I really wish I knew how to answer that. What's up?"

"I wanted to talk to you about Bridget."

Of course, he thought sarcastically.

"Of course," he said sincerely. "What about?"

"I know everyone is pretty set that she…did this to herself. And I don't know, maybe she did. But did she ever do or say anything that she might? I mean, it just doesn't feel right to me. But then I thought, maybe she was thinking of running away you know. Maybe she felt she had to get away and what happened was…something else."

At least Kira wasn't beating around the bush. Kira had been whispering, and Javi met her pitch. Anyone could be listening, even though they were in a secluded corner of the room.

"Something else? What do you mean?"

"You know there are rumors."

"What kind of rumors?"

"That she might not have done this herself. That someone did this to her."

"You think someone killed her?"

"Doesn't it make more sense? She didn't want to die. I really believe that."

"But who would…who could do this?"

"I don't know. But maybe we don't know because no one is asking the right questions. The police think she did this herself. Makes their job easier."

"But they still haven't closed the case. Not officially."

"But do you think it's possible?"

"That someone killed her? Yeah, I guess. Anything is possible. But I can't… wait, you don't think I had anything to do with this?"

"Oh, God, no. Of course not. I know you would never hurt her. I'm so sorry if I made you think that. But if this does turn into something and if the police do suddenly start questioning people, you know you will be the first person everyone thinks of and I just wanted you to be prepared in case something does happen."

"What could happen?"

"I don't know."

"And the police already talked to me. Did something else happen? Why are you suddenly so worried about this?"

"I was just thinking. If she was running away, and they thought that, they may look at everything a little differently. I mean, they found her car. Maybe something was there."

"I don't see it. She was happy here."

"Was she? Really?"

Honestly, Javi had no idea. They weren't really happy together. That was obvious. They were good at creating the appearance of being happy and normal. And Bridget never seemed to have anything nice to say about her mother. Even Kira seemed to annoy her sometimes, based on his phone conversations with her.

"She did seem to talk about leaving town. One day, you know, like college."

"And maybe something happened to accelerate her plan."

"What could have happened?"

"Look, Javi, people talk and I know it's just rumors and shit. But if the police start looking deeper then suddenly rumors become a bigger deal and I don't want it to come back on you."

"What rumors? What are you talking about?"

"Some people are saying, and I don't know if I believe this, but I heard some people talking and they said that Bridget was pregnant."

"What?" Javi's voice was suddenly loud. He looked up to see if anyone was listening, but the rest of the kids of the room were still pretty much ignoring Javi and Kira's conversation. "Who told you that?"

"I don't know, I just heard some people talking."

"It's not true." Or is it?

"I know it's not."

"I gotta go," Javi said, quickly gathering up his books. He wanted to scream out. His legs felt weightless and he just wanted to get away from Kira, from everything.

* * * * *

It was easy for Javi to lay low on the weekend. No one was calling him or asking him to hang out. He dropped off books for Scott and they talked for a minute, but Javi didn't stay long. He didn't know what to think about anything and didn't want to get in another fight with Scott when he wasn't completely sure. He spent Saturday doing homework of all things. On Sunday, he made it to church with his family, and resumed his role as the dutiful son.

That afternoon, while it was unseasonably warm out, Javi's oldest brother, Diego, asked him to help him with his car. There was a small garage attached to the house, but behind the yard there was another garage that faced an alley. Diego had gotten an old 1968 Mustang GT Fastback that he was continuously working on. Javi didn't know much about cars, but what he learned, he learned while hanging out with his brother in that garage.

Diego still lived in the house, but was hardly ever home. Javi generally only caught him coming or going, but when he asked Javi to hang out, Javi leapt at the chance. He loved his brother. He thought Diego was everything he wanted to be. He was always so cool. And funny. Nothing ever fazed him. Sure, he could have a temper, but that was always directed outward. Diego would never to do anything to hurt someone in his family. He was the best big brother.

They didn't talk much in the garage. Diego rolled under the car and asked Javi to hand him tools. Javi got most of them right on the first guess, even though it had been a while since they had worked on the car. It was forest green, although in desperate need of a paint job. Diego kept it covered on most days. The interior was in much better condition than the exterior, and the motor still wasn't doing what it was supposed to. But it was a sweet car.

Diego asked Javi about school, about football. Javi knew that even though he played, football was never going to be as important to him as it was to Diego.

Then, seemingly out of nowhere, Diego asked Javi about Bridget.

"How are you doing with that whole thing?" he asked.

"I'm fine. It sucks, but things are starting to get back to normal,

I guess."

"She was a nice girl, but I got to be honest, I didn't see it with you two."

Javi let out a chuckle. He wasn't wrong.

"Besides, this is your senior year. You shouldn't tie yourself down. This is when you need to go out and have fun with as many people as you can. Come on, everyone loves a football player, right? I know it seems wrong with all this hanging over you, but you will get through it."

"Thanks, man."

"And hey," Diego said as he wheeled himself out from under the car. "You ever need anything, you let me know. Anything. Beer. Weed. Condoms. I got you."

"Okay."

"You're my brother, Javi. I got your back. If anyone ever fucks with you or does you wrong, I will take care of them. No questions asked, just say the word. We are nothing without family, right? And I would kill or die for any of you."

Suddenly, Javi felt the conversation was a little more pointed than he was expecting.

"I know, Diego. I know."

"We look out for our own. No matter what. Now, can you hand me a flathead?"

Javi complied, and smiled at Diego. Diego smiled back and gave him a wink. It felt sweet, but also a little uncomfortable. Javi felt there was a subtext he was completely missing. His brother was aggressively loyal. And Javi couldn't help but feel like Diego was keeping something from him. Something he didn't want to say.

19. ABBY

She had to admit, only to herself of course, that his smile was absolutely intoxicating. Percy sat across from her at one of the tables outside the coffee shop. They were both wearing stocking hats because the wind was blowing, but even as they shivered sipping their warm drinks, Abby was perfectly content being with him. There were small scratches on his face, some on his neck. They seemed to grow smaller (is that an oxymoron?) every time she stared at him, which was becoming somewhat of a regular occurrence when they would run into each other at the office. "I completely forgot to thank you for the dress. That was entirely unnecessary," Abby said. It had been weeks since she had gotten that particular package, and at first it was awkward, but then not acknowledging it felt even more awkward.

"I bet you looked amazing in it at the dance," Percy said, gripping his coffee, his eyes darting away.

"I didn't go."

"Why not?"

"Well, no one asked me for starters. And going stag only works if you actually have friends. And want to hang out with a bunch of stupid high schoolers."

"I didn't go either."

"Yeah, I kind of figured when you assumed I went. And can you go? I thought you weren't a student anymore?"

"Well, my parents and I did talk to the administration. They are letting me go back next semester if I can test out of a couple things."

"Oh, that's great."

"I guess."

"You're not excited to go back?"

"I was kind of enjoying not being around a bunch of stupid high schoolers."

"Hah, yeah I can see that. Still, it'll be nice having one friendly face at Dymps."

"Oh, no. I can't be seen smiling at a sophomore. I have to go back to pretending I don't know who you are."

"Oh, really?"

"Totally. Nah, I'm just playing."

There was an ease to their back and forth. Abby knew he wasn't being serious. And she couldn't help but smile as she talked to him. His eyes were so blue. And he was funny. And smart. She couldn't believe he was having such a hard time of it. She thought about them next semester, walking hand in hand down the hallway. Her and a senior boy. It was almost too much for her to believe. And a part of her knew it was never actually going to happen. Things like that never happened for her. But right now, in this moment, it felt like it could. And that was enough.

Kira didn't like Percy. Certainly didn't trust him. She'd made that clear the last time they spoke. Abby and Kira put together a notebook on Bridget's death. They included all the notes they had compiled, and made pages for different suspects. When they discovered Bridget's bag at the school, it made it seem more obvious that something happened.

Kira wanted to go to the police with what they found, but they couldn't figure out a way to do so without incriminating themselves for breaking into the school. They decided to split up what they found. Kira kept the cash and the bag of clothes. Abby took the backpack and pregnancy test. They cleared out everything in her locker so that no one would realize anything was amiss. All they would find was a broken window, and maybe a loose ceiling tile in the girls' locker room. Surely, they would suspect some horny boy students were responsible.

When she went back to school after Thanksgiving there weren't even any whispers that something happened over break. The administration figured out how to keep it hush-hush. Probably because there wasn't any damage.

Kira had insisted on putting a page on Percy in their notebook. She made a point to list that he was a drug dealer. Abby still didn't see it. She had asked around, but while everyone had heard the rumors, no one she talked to admitted to ever buying anything from him. Maybe the whole thing was just a rumor, like most of the gossip in high school.

Abby wanted to ask him straight out. To ask him what he was doing that night, and to tell him about her investigation, if you could call it that. But even though she doubted his connection to the situation, she wanted to maintain some modicum of objectivity. That didn't mean she couldn't figure out ways to use him.

"We should probably get back," Percy said. It was true. They had been sitting outside for a long time. Abby wasn't on the clock, but Percy was and she didn't want him to get into any trouble. Not for this.

"Okay," Abby said, as she stood and grabbed her cup. "Before we get up there, though I was wondering if you might be able to help me out with something."

"Anything," Percy said. And Abby believed it. Though she was certainly about to test that theory.

* * * * *

"You haven't talked about Bridget much this session. Is she still on your mind?" Dr. Gant asked.

Abby fidgeted in her chair. She knew this was going to come up. She had decided a few sessions ago that she wasn't going to talk about Bridget anymore since she couldn't really share everything. Also, it was clear that he didn't understand her obsession or didn't want to even try to.

"I think I'm over it," she lied. "I think it was just bringing up a lot of last year."

Abby always spoke in euphemisms about her suicide attempt. She didn't like saying the words, not out loud. It felt wrong. Even with Bridget, most people talked around saying "suicide." It was a dirty word. Shameful. Maybe more so because she was in a Catholic school. Everything was shameful there.

She wasn't lying about Bridget's death bringing up a lot of stuff. Abby knew she was over trying to hurt herself. She didn't want that. But the things it took to break her down, to get her that low, they were still out there. She had talked through a lot of them, but she never felt like she fully purged herself from all of the demons. She wondered if she ever would.

"And how are things going with your mother?" he asked.

It always goes back to the mother with these guys, doesn't it? Abby actually was pretty happy with the state of her home life. True, her mom, her stepbrother and she herself were all so focused on their own things that they didn't overlap much at home. But turns out spending less time together was actually beneficial for her family. She saw her mom more at work these days and those fleeting moments were actually more positive. Maybe because Olivia was more focused on work and could only waste a few minutes with Abby, and thus was on her best behavior.

Abby gave Dr. Gant an abbreviated and somewhat exaggerated version of this. Her mom was great. They were seeing each other more at work. Fighting less. She was trying not to fixate on the clock, but it was getting close to time. Her heart started beating a little faster.

"Speaking of my mom, she asked me to make sure that the insurance was up to date. I have the card here, can you just check for me?"

"Sure, I can pull it up." Dr. Gant got out of his chair and walked to his desk. He turned on his computer and started to type stuff in. Abby looked at the clock again. She took a deep breath, hoping Dr. Gant wouldn't notice that her hands were shaking.

"I think you've been doing great these past few weeks, Abby. You really seem more sure of yourself. I like that."

Abby smiled.

Before she could say anything, there was a crash from outside and a car alarm started to blare. Dr. Gant moved to the window.

"What the hell?"

Abby jumped up and stood behind him.

"Oh my god, is that your car?" Abby pointed to a Chevy in the parking lot. There was a man in a ski mask standing by the car.

"Hey!" Dr. Gant yelled, even though the window was closed.

"Go, go," Abby said. "I'll call the police."

Dr. Gant ran out of the room. Abby waited until she saw him emerge from the front of the building and ran towards the car. She grabbed her purse and went to the doctor's desk. She dialed 911 on his phone.

"911, what's your emergency?" a voice asked.

"There's someone breaking into a car here."

"Can you tell me where you are?"

"Just off 90th and Pacific, um, I'm not sure of the address, it's like the third street down and then you take a right. There's a man at the car. He has dark hair, looks at least thirty years old."

As she talked, Abby had started to type on Dr. Gant's computer. She was opening files until she found one marked "Sutton, Elizabeth." She pulled a hard disk out of her purse and put it into the computer and started to copy the files.

"What kind of vehicle?"

"I don't know. It's a gray car. In the parking lot. It's my doctor. Just, please hurry," Abby said and hung up the phone. She went to the window and saw Dr. Gant at his car, the man in the ski mask was no longer there.

Abby jumped back to the computer.

"Come on, come on," she said to herself.

When the transfer was complete, she pulled up another file: Williams, Abigail. She went back to the window. Dr. Gant was walking back towards the building.

"Shit."

Abby stopped the transfer of her own file and popped the disk out. She closed out the files she had opened up. Put the disk in her purse, and threw the purse back next to the couch where she had it. She went back to the window just as Dr. Gant walked back in the room.

"Can you believe it? Out of all the cars in the lot, this joker smashed in my window."

"Did he take anything?"

"He ran when I got out there."

"I called the police. They're on their way. I couldn't remember your exact address, sorry."

"It's fine. I can call them back. Are you okay?"

"Yeah, why wouldn't I be? It was your car."

"I just can't believe it."

Abby watched as Dr. Gant went back to his computer. Every keystroke he typed in made her nervous. Could he tell that something was different? Would he blame her for the car if he figured it out? Would he still see her?

Abby walked to the couch.

"It looks okay to me," he said.

"What?" Abby asked.

"The insurance."

"Oh, yeah, sorry. I'm just so out spaced with everything going on. Can you write the account number down, please?"

Dr. Gant started to write. Abby sat back down and tucked her shaking hand behind her purse.

* * * * *

"So, how often can I expect you to ask me to do criminal things for you?" Percy asked. He was smiling at least. They had agreed to meet up at a McDonald's after the ordeal.

"It's not a common occurrence," Abby said. "But I appreciate your willingness to do so."

"You gonna tell me what this was all about?"

Oh, sure, Abby thought. She should tell him that she's trying to figure out who killed Bridget Kent, an investigation that had a fully dedicated notebook in her backpack which included a page on why Percy himself might be a suspect. Abby didn't believe it, couldn't believe that he would have anything to do with Bridget, but Kira insisted and so it was there. She was smart enough not to tip him off, on the remote chance something was up.

"I needed to get a copy of my own file from the doctor. I wanted to see what he was writing down about me."

"I think you can just ask for it. It is your file."

"Really? But this was so much more fun."

"For you, maybe. I wasn't sure if anyone was following me so I kept circling around before I ditched the ski mask."

Percy rubbed his hands through his blonde hair. Abby hoped that if he did get caught, her false description might get him clear. She didn't think about how bad it could've been if Percy had gotten caught, given everything else that was going on.

"Can we just limit it to like one crime a month?" Percy asked.

"No promises," Abby responded. There was something intoxicating about his willingness to be so boldly supportive of Abby's requests, without even questioning it. Abby wanted to believe everything good she ever thought about him. She didn't want to believe the rumors, that he was a drug dealer, that he might even be involved with Bridget's death. Those had to be lies, spread by jealous people.

"I should probably get going," Abby said. "But I appreciate all of your help."

"I'd say any time, but I really hope it's a little less frequent. The illegal stuff. Not hanging out. That's pretty fun."

Again, Percy smiled his million-dollar smile. Abby's heart was beating fast again, but this time for a different reason.

* * * * *

Abby didn't want to risk using the disk on her computer at home. Her mom, or Jake, could see and she would have a tough time explaining any reason she had Eli's files. She went to the library and printed out the pages, one by one. It would cost her a bit, but it would be easier to keep hidden. As she stood at the printer, listening to the ink cartridge squeal as it went line by line, she busied herself reading Bridget's journal, another document she didn't want to explore at home.

She had gotten away from reading it regularly. Mostly, she thought it was dull. There was nothing terribly exciting in it. There was a lot about her mother. Abby was going to have to bring that up with Kira. She did not paint a flattering picture of her mom, but Abby thought that if she had written anything down the year before, her own mother wouldn't fare too well. Parents are real easy to hate when the rest of the world sucks.

Bridget's journal referenced working at Elysian Park, and meeting Javi. It didn't seem like she thought much of him beyond thinking he was cute. Abby couldn't remember when they started dating, but this did seem to be a bit before that.

Abby flipped through a few more pages until she got to a rushed entry somewhere in the middle of this past summer. Bridget said she smoked pot for the first time. She always wanted to try it but was too afraid to risk getting caught. She had asked around and found out another boy at school was actually a hookup for the other kids.

Abby started to read more intently. Bridget referred to this boy as Richie Rich, because he had blonde hair and was one of the popular, rich kids.

“I always thought he was kind of jerk,” Bridget wrote. “Because he obviously came from money and privilege and didn’t seem to notice anyone else. But when I talked to him he was sweet. He had a nice smile. And he somehow made me feel important. Sure, I was buying drugs from him, but he didn’t even seem that interested in selling. Not as interested as he seemed to be in me.”

Abby felt a little sick.

Blonde. Nice smile.

Rich. Popular.

Sweet.

This was perfectly Percy. Coupled with the rumors of him being a drug dealer. Abby didn’t want to believe it. She flipped through the journal trying to find more mentions of Richie Rich. A few weeks later, there was another mention.

“I lost my virginity.” Bridget wrote. “Yep. Richie Rich was my first. I didn’t mean for it to happen, not exactly. We were at a party. We were stoned. He pulled me into a bedroom. We had kissed before, but this time he was more into it. He started to take my clothes off and I kind of felt like it was going to happen. It’s not like I would’ve said no if he asked me, but he didn’t. He just went for it. And I was cool going along with it. It was over in just a few minutes and he rolled over and passed out. I don't regret it. It felt weird it's just over like that. But I got dressed and left before he got up."

Abby flipped to the next entry. Another rant about Bridget's mom. The next page talked about going to the zoo with Kira and Breck. A few more pages and Bridget talked about her first date with Javi and how she just wanted a boyfriend.

Abby skipped through pages looking for any mentions of "Richie Rich," but she didn't find one until weeks later.

"Saw Richie Rich at a party. He acted like he didn't know me. I decided to find someone else to buy from."

The printer stopped and suddenly the entire library felt eerily quiet. Abby shut the journal. She would have to pick it up later. It wasn't true. It couldn't be. Percy wouldn't do that.

Would he?

* * * * *

Abby tried not to think about it all the way home. She blared the radio, sang along to an En Vogue song, even though she barely knew the words. She didn't want to believe it. She didn't believe it. It had to be someone else.

Besides, it had nothing to do with Bridget's death. There was still Mr. Sutton, right? Somewhere in Eli's file there was going to be something about him. Abby knew it.

She was surprised to see Kira's car in her driveway. Were they supposed to meet? Abby couldn't believe she would forget something like that, but with everything going on with Dr. Gant, Percy, the journal, she must have spaced it.

Abby walked into her house and down the hallway into the living room.

"Hey," she said when she saw Jake and Kira sitting on the couch. They were sitting next to each other. Like, right next to each other.

It looked like Jake had his arm around her but pulled it away when Abby walked in.

"Hi, Abby," Kira said. "How are you?"

"We were just watching a movie," Jake said. "Want to join?"

It didn't sound like he actually wanted her to join. Abby wasn't exactly sure what she was even seeing. But Kira was one of the only people that she could talk to, at least about the Bridget stuff. Was that all so she could get closer to Jake?

"I've had a long day," Abby said. "You kids have fun."

Abby walked up to her room and plopped down on her bed. She wanted to go to bed. Right now, even though it wasn't that late. She wanted to close her eyes and just be done with it. Be done with all of it.

20. BRECK

She hated being so behind on school work that it was eating into her Saturday, but Breck spent way too much time during the week obsessing about Scott. She had been taking him his assignments from his teachers, and things seemed mostly cool, but she still had a bad taste in her mouth from their conversation; the one when he first came home from the hospital. It was like he turned into a different person. She shouldn't have let Javi get into her head, but Javi has always been such a nice guy. Breck couldn't figure out what was happening with Scott. This whole incident, and the hospital, might've had a stronger effect on him than he was letting on.

Breck closed her English book. She had been at the library for a few hours, and had only progressed to the third paragraph on her paper that was due next week. It wasn't going to happen today, that was beginning to sink in. She saved her work, got her disk, and gathered up her things. She slung her bag over her shoulder and started to walk out.

The computer lab was on the top floor of the library. In the middle of the floor was an opening to the floor below, to all the floors really. You could see the eight floors down to the main floor, but you had a really good view of the tables on the seventh floor. At one of those tables, Abby had a notebook open and pictures, newspapers, and a stack of printed pages spread all over. Breck thought it was curious, Abby was never one for being so studious, much less on the weekend. After their last talk, she still wasn't sure where she stood with Abby. Maybe things were a little better now.

Breck wanted to go home. She was supposed to stop by Scott's later and she had a couple errands to run, but she couldn't help herself from pressing the 7th Floor button on the elevator. As the doors opened she walked over to Abby's table.

It was kind of strange, but when Abby looked up and saw Breck approaching, she got a strange look on her face. Breck smiled and waved. Abby waved back but started to hurriedly gather up her things.

"What's going on?" Breck said as she got closer.

"Oh, homework, you know. Finals coming up."

"Yeah. What's all this?"

"Just a research paper. It's exhausting. What are you doing here? I thought you hated the library." Abby stood up and dropped her backpack over some of the papers.

"The computers here are still better than that piece of shit my dad insists we use until the last possible second."

"I'm sure."

"You're not leaving because of me, are you?"

"Oh, no," Abby said. "I was getting tired."

Breck looked at one of the newspapers. It was a one from just a few weeks ago. "What's your paper on?"

"Crime. Some… it's hard to explain. If you're leaving, maybe we could grab a coffee?"

Abby started shoving everything into her bag. It was such a weird move, like she had been caught cheating or something.

"I should probably get home," Breck said. She noticed that when Abby picked up a file folder from the table a picture fell out of it and onto the floor. Breck reached down to pick it up. It was a picture of Bridget. Smiling. In her cheerleader uniform.

"What are you doing with this?" Breck asked. It wasn't an accusation. She was genuinely confused. Abby and Bridget weren't friends.

"It's an assignment for yearbook. I didn't want to say anything in case it was uncomfortable for you."

"Why would it be uncomfortable?"

"You were friends."

"We were friendly, I guess. But she was Kira's friend. I just knew her, you know? And even that I'm not too sure about."

"What do you mean?"

"I don't know. She didn't seem like the type. You know? To kill herself?"

"I think I know what you mean."

Breck realized her mistake as soon as she said it.

"Fuck, I'm sorry, Abby, I didn't mean anything by it."

"No, it's cool."

"No, it's not. I didn't mean to bring it up, or phrase it like that, I didn't mean anything by it, I just, you know what I mean, right?" Breck was stammering now. It happened when she got nervous. Of course, the implication was that Abby was the type but Breck didn't mean it that way.

"It's okay. Chill. I'm not mad."

"Why not? I wasn't a very good friend to you. Back then. Or since then, I guess. I didn't mean anything. I never mean anything. You know that, right? I'm really sorry that I couldn't be there for you."

"Breck, come on. I'm fine, okay. And what happened wasn't your fault."

"That's not what you said."

"What?"

"You don't remember? It was the last thing you said to me before… we didn't talk forever. You said everything sucked and it was all my fault."

"I didn't mean… I was pissed. You didn't think it was all because of you, did you? What I did?"

"I didn't know what to think."

"Well, you did open your big mouth and tell everyone about Jake."

"You keep saying that. I told one person."

"And she told everyone at my new school."

"What? I never told Bridget. I only told Scott."

"You told Scott?"

"You thought I told Bridget?"

"Well, she knew."

"I didn't even tell Kira."

"Why did you tell Scott?"

"I don't know. We told each other everything. And I was confused."

"You were confused."

"Abby, I'm so sorry. I swear I didn't tell Bridget. I had no idea. Maybe Scott told Javi and he told Bridget. I don't know. I was worried about you. And I was wrong. I was so wrong. I'm sorry."

Breck could feel the tears coming. She was prone to crying, did so almost on a daily basis, whether she was happy or sad or whatever, but this was definitely from being overwhelmed. She couldn't believe Abby held onto this for so long, and they were in the middle of the library finally talking about it. Thankfully, it wasn't too busy on a Saturday afternoon.

Abby had a look that Breck couldn't quite decipher, so she repeated herself.

"I'm sorry, really."

She reached out her arms to pull Abby in for a tight hug. Abby seemed willing, if a little reluctant.

"It's okay," Abby said. "I was getting tired of holding a grudge anyway."

"Maybe we should get that coffee."

* * * * *

Well, now Breck was late. She said she would be over to Scott's by 3pm, but after talking with Abby for over an hour, her entire day was behind. It was good, though. She needed to talk with Abby and she actually felt like she had made some meaningful progress. She still couldn't shake that Abby was hiding something, but after being so open and honest about her time last year, what else could she be hiding.

Breck felt she was being paranoid. She was already dealing with whatever was going on with Scott. She thought she was in her head too much about that. She loved Scott. She knew that. Yes, he was her first real boyfriend. Her parents always cautioned her not to get too into him too soon. But it was almost a year. Over a year really, depending on when you started counting.

They had their first real date in January. He asked her to the Winter Formal, and she was so excited as it wasn't something a freshman would normally get invited to. Breck had geometry right after Scott had trig with the same teacher, Mrs. McKenna, and they bumped into each other in the door one time. At Becky Whittaker's New Year's Eve party, Scott talked to her all night until he finally kissed her at midnight.

It was Breck's first real kiss. She had kissed a boy in sixth grade when she played seven minutes in heaven at some party, but that didn't count. It was barely a peck. With Scott, it was real, and warm, and something energetic. When he asked her to the dance she said "yes" without any hesitation. Her parents lectured her about dating an older boy, but they came around when they saw how nice he was.

Scott was a gentleman. He knew she was a virgin, and he respected that she wanted to wait. Not forever. She just wanted to feel ready. They've done some things, but as close as they were she didn't quite feel comfortable being naked with him. She didn't feel comfortable being naked with herself. Her thighs were too big. Her everything was too big. Scott had no trouble being naked. He would change clothes in front of her and think nothing of it. Breck was jealous he was so comfortable with himself. She wanted that. And she wanted to give him that. Scott wanted to have sex with her, he was very clear about that. He was not a virgin. And they had done stuff, but Breck wasn't ready for everything, not yet.

Scott had confessed that he slept with Marah Timmons, one of the football cheerleaders the year before. Marah was so skinny with the perfect body. Somehow, she had big boobs and a small waist. Her thighs probably didn't rub together when she walked. Breck knew that Scott liked her and she was being silly, but she couldn't help but compare herself to the popular girls. She didn't want to be a cheerleader or anything crazy like that, but no matter how much she worked out or how many sports she played, she couldn't seem to shake her thick thighs or get her belly flat. Bridget had gotten her belly button pierced and showed Breck and Kira one night, and Breck couldn't imagine doing anything that would draw more attention to her body.

Breck tried to shake all the negative thoughts out of her head. She knew they were no good, and weren't helping anything. She was having a good day. She didn't want anything to mess it up, and certainly not someone as dumb and inconsequential as Marah who would probably peak in high school and end up working as a waitress the rest of her life after having a kid right out of high school. At least, Breck hoped.

When she got to Scott's house, she knocked on the side door and then let herself in. She had been coming over often enough that it became her usual mode of entry. Scott's parents never minded. She also helped take care of Bernie, Scott's little sister, so they really treated her like part of the family. And she didn't want to make Scott climb the stairs. He was still recovering.

It was quiet when she walked in. There was usually some noise in the kitchen, but she figured Robbie and Eric must be out, maybe with Bernie too. Hopefully, Scott didn't take off because she was late. But then she heard a loud voice from the basement.

And then a thud.

Breck darted down the stairs to see Scott and TJ wrestling on the ground.

"Get the hell off of me!" TJ shouted.

Arms were flailing and Scott grabbed TJ's head trying to get him in a headlock, but TJ kicked him back. Breck ran over just as they separated and stupidly put herself in between them. They both had fire in their eyes and Breck held up her hands.

"Oh my god, stop. What is going on?"

"He was messing in my stuff," Scott snarled.

"I didn't touch anything. I just used the bathroom and then was looking at some of his books. Then he comes in and starts pushing me."

"He just got out of the hospital," Breck said to TJ as both boys got to their feet.

"Maybe he should go back."

"Maybe you should go to your own house, freak."

"Both of you, shut up. Please."

The boys huffed at each other. Breck moved closer to Scott.

"Let's just go to your room, okay?" Breck asked as she pushed Scott towards his bedroom.

"Fine."

"I need to get some smokes anyway," TJ said, as he grabbed his jacket off the couch and stomped upstairs.

Breck and Scott walked into his room and Breck shut the door behind them.

"What was that all about?"

"I don't like him messing with my stuff."

"He was looking at your books."

"So he says."

"What is the big deal?"

"This is my room, my stuff. Why is he even here? He's just always around. Right outside my room, whenever I leave."

"Your mom said his home life wasn't great."

"So, why does that make him our responsibility? We don't even know him."

"I thought you grew up with him."

"Our parents used to hang out. That doesn't make him our problem."

"Your mom seems to think otherwise. Just calm down."

Scott and Breck sat down on his bed. He held her hand.

"I'm glad you're here," he said.

"I'm glad I'm here too. I wish I came sooner. You could've gotten hurt."

"That punk couldn't hurt me."

"Scott, you just got out of the hospital like a minute ago. You shouldn't get so worked up."

"He just makes me so mad."

"That much is clear. Now, why don't we stop talking about TJ, and talk about you. How are you doing?"

"Well," Scott said while rubbing a finger on Breck's jeans, "I can think of something that could take my mind off of everything."

He smiled at her, and then went in for the kiss. Their lips met, and his tongue slid into her mouth. Scott pulled Breck down to where they were now laying on the bed, faces intertwined. His hand went from her shoulder, down to her side and caressed her along her hip. Breck used her elbow to bump Scott's hand back and pulled away.

"Scott, come on."

"What, he said he was going out. My parents are at a movie with

Bernie. When are we gonna have the house to ourselves again?"

"You just got out of the hospital."

"The doctor said I would be okay."

"You asked the doctor about this?"

"Well, not about this exactly, but he said physical activity was fine once I felt up to it. And believe me, I'm up for it."

"Not like this. Come on."

"Well, you can just blow me if you want."

Breck pushed back.

"Well, if you're gonna talk all romantic to me," she said while propping herself up.

"It's been forever."

"Is that all you care about?"

"I care about you."

Breck stood up.

"Nothing about this feels right."

"What's wrong with me wanting me to be with you?"

"You think I want to lose my virginity while you're still sweaty from fighting with TJ in the fifteen minutes before your family comes home? I thought you knew me better than that."

"Sorry, I was just trying to take advantage of the time."

"I know what you were taking advantage of."

"Is it a crime to want to have sex with my girlfriend? Oh, my god, lock me up."

"Now, you're just being a jerk."

"Is this about Javi?"

"What?"

"Ever since that whole thing you've been acting cold and distant. I told you it was nothing and I'm okay. I haven't done anything since that day. And you're, I don't know, punishing me or something."

"Oh, come on."

"No, really. I wonder. You think I'm some scary druggie and you don't want to go out anymore."

"You know that's not true."

"I don't know what I'm supposed to think."

"I'm not the one acting strange here. You're fighting with TJ, yelling at me."

"I'm not yelling," Scott said in a voice well above a whisper.

"You're something."

"Fine. I'm the asshole. I get it. Maybe you should hang out with someone else that doesn't freak you out so much."

"I didn't say that."

"You don't have to. Every time you pull away that's what you're saying."

Breck couldn't understand what was happening. She was stuck for how to respond. She wanted to fight back, stick up for herself, but everything Scott was saying just made her feel bad. Breck sat back down on the bed.

"I don't know what happened to get you so worked up, but I'm sorry."

Breck reached her hand out to run her fingers through Scott's hair, but he smacked her hand away.

"Ow," she said recoiling.

"Just go."

"What?"

"Get out!" Scott was definitely shouting now.

"Scott, come on." Breck could feel herself starting to cry. She didn't want to leave, not until they worked through whatever was going on, but Scott got up and walked to the bathroom and slammed the door behind him. The shower turned on.

Breck stood up.

"Scott, please."

There was a loud crash, and a shout from Scott.

"LEAVE."

Breck wiped the tears from her eyes and walked out of the bedroom.

* * * * *

He had punched the mirror. That's what he told her later that night when he called to apologize. Scott said he was still angry with TJ and was taking it out on her. Breck knew she shouldn't let it go so easily, but he was so sincere. And she saw how he was with TJ. It made sense. He was also frustrated being away from school. He wanted to go back, but his parents wanted him to wait a few more days. He still needed to nap to get through the day.

Breck was still getting his homework and taking it to him, even though TJ was at school. It made sense for her to do it. She knew the teachers better, and it would mean TJ having to be honest about his whole living situation, and no one seemed to want that.

Breck thought she should learn more about TJ, especially given his proximity to her boyfriend and his family. She didn't normally have lunch in the first section, but she skipped her study hall in order to approach him. She found him sitting alone in a corner of the lunchroom and went through the line and then sat across the table from him.

"Hey," she said, as he looked up from his Salisbury steak.

"Hey."

"Crazy weekend, huh?"

"I guess."

"Did you guys make up?"

"Make up? Like we were close or anything to begin with?"

"I don't know. Are things still tense?"

"Things are always tense. Your boyfriend is wound pretty tight."

"He's really not."

"He really is. I'm around him a lot. And he always seems to be seconds away from blowing up."

Breck didn't understand what TJ was saying. Scott wasn't like that. He was probably still sore from their argument. And she could understand getting tired of the new guy staying in the other room. Robbie brought TJ home without so much as a warning. Things must've been pretty bad for that to happen.

"Can I ask… why are you staying there? I know it's none of my business, but if you did want to talk about it, I can listen."

"It's okay," TJ said as he returned to his meal. "It really is none of your business."

Breck didn't mean anything by it. She didn't know TJ at all, but aside from being a little awkward and remote, he didn't seem like a bad guy. Maybe he needed more friends. She didn't want to push, but from what Scott said, he didn't really ever leave the house other than to go to school. He could use some social activity.

Then Breck had a brilliant idea. With things moving in the right direction with Abby, maybe the four of them could hang out. Having friends around might keep Scott from being so focused on sleeping with her. TJ and Abby would of course hit it off and they could both use the company. It would get TJ out of the house more, and maybe Abby could get him out of his shell. And it let her hang out with Abby without having to be weird because of everything last year. Everybody wins.

Even though TJ had started to ignore her, Breck couldn't help but smile. Maybe this lunch wasn't the right time, but she was definitely going to set this up. It was perfect. And even if it wasn't, how bad could it be?

21. PERCY

Abby opened the door to his car and sat down in the passenger seat. She smiled that sweet smile that Percy adored. She had a large backpack that dropped on the floor. Her hair was tucked into a stocking hat and her coat puffed up when she sat down, but she still had this air about her that was simply amazing.

"Hi," was all she said.

"Why did we have to meet here?" Percy asked. He kept the car running because it was still cold outside. He thought he was looking at her too long so he turned back to Elysian Park. They were the only two cars in the parking lot. It was night, so Percy turned his lights off. He was facing the tower and preferred it to fade away in the darkness. He hadn't been here since that night.

"I have to tell you something, and I didn't want to do it around other people."

"Does this have something to do with the crime that you asked me to do the last time I saw you?" Percy was saying it lightly, but he was relieved that nothing had come of him breaking into Doctor Gant's car.

"Well, yeah. Although, thoroughly impressed how quickly you agreed without knowing anything."

"Hey, you asked."

"Here's the thing, Percy…" she paused after using his name. He liked hearing it in her voice, but he wasn't sure what was going to follow. He was smitten with this girl. She wasn't like the other girls at school. She was smart, driven, focused, and had this sense of humor that eased into everything. He would do anything she asked, though he knew better than to tell her that right now. And she was beautiful. In her own way.

"It's fine. Whatever it is."

"I think it's gonna freak you out."

"Why would it freak me out?"

"Because… I don't know. Because everything is kind of a mess. And I know you're kind of involved, I mean, not involved, but you have a lot going on and some of it is connected and I just don't know how to tell you, but I feel like it's weird if I don't say anything."

"Abby, you're rambling. It's fine. You can tell me anything."

He meant it. He couldn't think of anything she could say that would make think any differently of her. He wanted to tell her, but he was still so wrapped up with everything else he didn't want to burden her. He wanted to just sit here and look at her face.

"Okay, here goes. I don't think Bridget killed herself. I think someone else was there that night. I think they killed her. And the police aren't doing anything so I've been trying to figure it out. There's just so much that the cops don't know. And I think I'm getting closer to actually figuring it out."

Percy could feel himself getting flush.

"What do you mean? What does that have to do with your shrink?"

What did she know? Was Abby trying to hint that she knew he was there. Is that why she asked to meet here? Does she think he did something to Bridget? What does she know that he doesn't?

"Well, my doctor happens to be the same as Mr. Sutton's wife's doctor. Who just happens to work with my mom and your dad. Small world, I know. But there's something about Mr. Sutton. He was close with Bridget. Closer than he was to other students. And she said she had a crush on him one time. And, get this, Eli, that's Mr. Sutton's wife, she admitted to our doctor that she thought her husband was having an affair."

"That's why I broke into his car? So you could steal her confidential medical files?. What if someone finds out, Abby? What if we get caught? I thought it was some prank. This is serious shit."

"Well, if I told you I was going to steal confidential medical files, would you have been so quick to say yes?"

"I don't know. What is wrong with you?"

"I'm trying to figure this out."

"Why? What are you, like, some Nancy Drew? If you think Mr. Sutton is involved, why don't you go to the cops?"

"Maybe I will. But I can't exactly say that I stole medical files, can I? I need to get something else. Something to help me get them to look in his direction."

"How do you know they haven't looked into him? They've questioned a lot of people. They questioned me."

"Why would they question you?"

Percy couldn't tell if she knew anything and was looking for him to confirm or if she truly wasn't aware of his involvement. He wasn't involved. Not really. He was just there. And he was attacked too. Maybe Bridget accidentally stabbed him and he pushed her. Does that make any sense? No, he couldn't have. It's all so foggy. Why can't he remember that night?

"Percy? Why did they talk to you?" she asked again.

"I knew her. Somewhat. Not really. I guess they were asking people she knew."

"And you didn't know anything?"

"Of course not."

Abby looked into his eyes. Percy tried to force sincerity into them, even though he knew he was lying. But he didn't want Abby to look at him differently. Not like everyone else looked at him. Like some rich fuckup loser, or worse a liar. Or worse, a killer.

"I think there's something there with Mr. Sutton."

"And how do you expect to find out?"

"Well, I think I need to look closer at Danny and Eli."

"Do you want me to buddy up with Eli at the office? I do know who she is, you know. And you can, I don't know, follow Mr. Sutton when he's out. Or I can. I guess. I don't know. I don't even know how any of this makes sense. But he was my coach freshman year. He definitely knows me. It would be hard to explain."

He was rambling. He stopped to collect himself. One word and he just jumped into doing whatever Abby asked. Was she playing him? Was this all a game? Was she that conniving?

"Look, you can't tell anyone I told you about this."

"Who would I tell? My friends have all ditched me."

"I'm serious. I shouldn't even be telling you."

"Why not? Do you think I had something to do with it?"

"Of course not. I know you couldn't do something like that."

"Why do you have such faith in me?"

"Because you were the only one that was nice to me."

"What? When?"

"At school. When I fell? You picked up my book."

"Oh, right. God, that seems like forever ago."

Percy forgot about that first meeting with Abby. When she spilled on the ice and her stuff went everywhere. He heard the other students laughing but didn't think anything of it. When someone falls, you make sure they're okay. That's normal. Right?

"You shouldn't trust me, Abby. You shouldn't trust anyone."

"I don't trust anyone. Don't worry."

"But really? Mr. Sutton? Why would he do something like this?"

"I don't know. Maybe Bridget was threatening to tell. Maybe they were a thing and he got her pregnant. That's something that would ruin his life."

"You think someone could go that far to protect their life?"

"I don't know. I don't even know why he's trying to save his marriage. Eli pretty much admitted she was having an affair too."

"What?"

"It was hard to tell with the therapy notes, but it seemed like her suspicions of her husband drove her into some other dude's arms. Or bed, really."

"I can't see that."

"Well, people always have two sides. Who they really are, and who they show to other people."

"So, you think everyone is hiding something?"

"Mostly"

"Then by definition, you're hiding something too."

"I suppose that's true."

"Well, then. Why don't you tell me what you've learned so far?"

"Seriously?"

"Yeah, I want to know everything."

* * * * *

Percy couldn't stop thinking about Abby. They sat in his car for hours as she talked through all of her research. Bridget's crush on Mr. Sutton, that she might be pregnant. She talked through weeks of poring over every newspaper article, and all of Eli Sutton's therapy notes. Abby said that she found a backpack that Bridget had stashed filled with clothes and money. The only thing she didn't mention was anything on him.

Was he really not on her radar or was this entire thing some ruse to get close to him and learn what he knew? Did she know about his dealing? She didn't say anything negative about him. Didn't ask him any questions about himself. How was that possible?

Percy had trouble concentrating on work, his mind kept playing the conversation with Abby over and over. Her intensity. Her concern. The way her hair kept falling into her face when she took her hat off.

NO.

He couldn't think of her like that. He had to put his little crush aside until he knew exactly what her intentions were. Percy wanted to believe her, to think she was just innocently looking into the Bridget situation without a second thought to his involvement, but if she could uncover so much info in such a short time, it seems like she would know something about him. Maybe she wanted to trip him up. Or maybe she thinks he can actually remember that night. Maybe he should tell her everything. Tell her that he woke up next to Bridget. That he'd been stabbed in the side and covered it up. That he actually has a mental block about anything that happened after he showed up at Elysian Park. He could tell her that Bridget paged him that night.

No. He really had to be careful to trust her with anything. The police still hadn't found his pager account or if they found it didn't connect it to him, and that was the closest thing that tied Bridget to him that night. Well, that and actually all the blood he left at the scene.

Percy pored over the budget numbers in the file that he was given from one of the accountants. He would focus on work now. All he had to do was match the checks against the invoices and balance them against the bank ledger. He did it all the time, but usually they matched exactly. Now, he was off by a large amount. It didn't make sense. He was either missing an invoice, a check, or the bank was off, none of which had happened before. He kept looking as he tried to keep his mind from wandering, pounding the keys of the adding machine hoping they would give him different numbers each time, but they never did.

He didn't want to ask the accounts payable team about it either. Marsha didn't like him and thought he was just some idiot whose dad ran the company, and he didn't want to add any fuel to that particular fire. No, this one he would figure out on his own. He went through the check numbers of what cleared the bank and this is where he noticed a missing check. Check 100479 had cleared, and check 100481 through 100495, but check 100480 wasn't anywhere. Maybe it was a mistake, or was still out there, but there was also no invoice that was connected to it. This was from Harlan's direct account, and not the one accounts payable used. Maybe the duplicate was still in the checkbook, Percy would have to check in his dad's office.

Percy didn't want to talk to his father. They had reached a nice equilibrium where they kept to themselves, and Percy stayed out of trouble and they didn't have to acknowledge each other's existences beyond a nod at the dinner table that his mom kept insisting they share. The office door was open, which usually meant that Harlan was inside and off the phone. Percy walked up as quietly as he could and put on his best smile for Darlene, Harlan's assistant.

"Is he in?" Percy asked as softly as he could.

"Oh, hi dear. No, he's out at a meeting for a little bit. But he should be back by three."

"Dang. Okay, well I can just leave him a note."

Darlene waved him in and Percy went inside. It felt ominous, as if Harlan had booby trapped the office. Percy walked behind the big, antique desk and sat in his father's chair. Nothing about it felt right.

Percy pulled the desk drawer open and saw the black leather binder of the checkbook. There were pages of duplicates going back years, and pages of new checks. Percy thought he could take one page, four checks, make them out to himself and leave town before anyone could put it together. Start a new life. It would certainly make it look like he did do something wrong, but who cares. He could get a new name, something without the legacy of generations attached to it. Something common, like Joe or Zack. Zack was cool.

It was a nice thought, but Percy knew he didn't have the balls to do it. He could leave his parents, no problem. But what about Simon?

He couldn't leave his little brother to fend for himself with Harlan and Donna. And Abby? He didn't want to leave her behind either.

Percy flipped back through the pages to find the missing check number. When he got to the right page, he saw that the duplicate was actually torn out as well. Going back years, there was no other duplicate that had been torn out. This didn't make any sense. In the margins, by the perforation, there was a small note in his father's handwriting "10/30-10k/BK, Eli dep."

What the hell did that mean?

Percy closed the book and shoved it back into the drawer. He didn't want to be caught looking at it until he could understand it. Why was the check torn out? And 10/30 was the day before Halloween, the day before Bridget died, and to see her initials was really curious. Sure, it could be Burger King or Billy Knight, a DJ his dad had hired before, but then why wasn't the actual documentation there. And what did the note about Eli mean?

Percy shut the drawer and walked out of his father's office. His mind was racing. His first thought was to call Abby. Maybe she could make sense of this. Maybe it wasn't him that she was looking into but his dad. But that didn't make any sense, what did his dad have to do with Bridget? He didn't even know who she was until the news.

Percy walked by Eli's desk, but she wasn't in. He didn't know what he would even ask her anyway. He needed some air. He wasn't feeling right. Percy grabbed his coat and went to the elevators. He kept pushing the buttons, but the doors wouldn't open, so he went to the stairwell. He could walk down ten flights of stairs. Beats waiting for the creaky, old elevator. He ran down a few levels, and then felt his heart start to beat faster. He slowed down. On the third floor he stopped completely and sat on the steps. Where was he going? What was he doing? This whole thing was silly. There was surely an easy explanation for this.

Percy heard voices. A few floors below. He didn't know anyone that worked on the lower floors so he wasn't worried about getting caught being away from his desk. Besides, he pretty much came and went as he pleased. The perks of being the boss' son. He didn't want to talk to anyone though. He could just wait them out and then go outside. As he sat there quietly, the voices began to echo. He couldn't make out what they were saying, but there was a familiarity to them. He stood up and peered over the railing. He could see two figures in the stairwell below.

It was his father. He had his back to Percy, but he could tell from the laugh, and the leather coat and scarf that was tucked around his neck. A woman's fingers ran through Harlan's hair, straightening it. Fixing the way it stood up in the back. Percy watched as his dad grabbed the hand and used it to pull the woman closer for a quick kiss. When she pulled away, Percy saw Eli smile as she set her hand on Harlan's chest.

Percy jumped back against the wall so they couldn't see him. He grabbed the door onto the third floor and walked into the middle of dull hallway with signs pointing out a doctor's office. He walked faster down the hallway, they followed the same pattern as the floor of his father's company, and made his way to the elevator bank. He didn't press the buttons. There was a chair next to the elevators and Percy plopped down and felt himself breathing harder and heavier.

What the hell was that?

His dad and Eli?

Shit.

22. ABBY

Percy was out of breath when he called her. She wasn't sure at first what he was talking about, he was yammering so much, but eventually he spit it out: Eli was having an affair. And he was pretty sure it was with his father. He begged her not to say a word of it, not to anyone, not until he knew for sure. Then what? What happens at that point? He didn't answer.

Abby didn't know how to take the news. She was surprised, but she wasn't shocked. Harlan had always been kind of a ladies' man. Abby heard stories from her mother, not specifically about cheating, but more talking around it. She wondered if her mother even knew. Was this an open secret? How long had it been going on?

It confirmed a couple things for Abby. One, that she was right to keep Mr. Sutton in her sights. Spouses who cheat oftentimes have spouses who cheat. Eli's affair gave credence to the hypothesis that Danny and Bridget were having an affair. An affair? Could you even call it that when one of them was a student of the other? The age of consent in Nebraska was sixteen so there wasn't anything statutory about it, but it was still wrong on a moral level. Wasn't it? In her journal Bridget wrote, somewhat recently, about having sex with someone that she shouldn't have. She didn't say anything beyond that. Didn't even give this guy a pseudonym. Sounds particularly scandalous, like with a student and teacher perhaps?

Abby tried to press Percy for more information, but all he said was that he saw them together in private and they looked like they were hiding something. She could wait for him to tell her more later. It made it easier to forget everything she had read about Richie Rich.

Abby finished Bridget's journal. She wanted more, but it was obviously a book without an ending. The most recent entry was about a week before her death. There were lamentations about being away from Omaha, but nothing concrete about her running away or having a specific plan. There was also nothing indicating she was thinking of jumping off a building to her death. There was only one more comment on Richie Rich in the journal. Something about being at a party and him completely ignoring her. It didn't feel like something Percy would do, but Abby knew that boys, even nice ones, could be duplicitous. Mr. Sutton never quite acted like he could be sleeping with a student, but it was possible. Her own step-brother, Jake, could smile at church on Sunday and sneak into her room in the middle of the night.

Thankfully, Jake had been keeping his distance from Abby. Maybe it had something to do with walking in on him with Kira the other night. She could admit that made her uncomfortable. Kira was supposed to be her friend. But was she jealous of Jake, or jealous of Kira? Her relationship with Jake was complicated. Obviously. And she was sure that Kira knew about Jake and Abby. If Bridget knew, wouldn't it have come through Kira? Breck said she didn't tell Kira, but should she even believe it. Sure, Scott could've told Javi and Javi told Bridget. In any case, Abby thought it was a bit unfair that sleeping with her stepbrother seemed to only have negative consequences for her. Jake never acknowledged it in daylight, so it never became a thing for him. She had to wear the scarlet letter. He could just shrug his shoulders and act like nothing happened. Not even after what Abby did.

Abby couldn't concentrate.

She had to talk to Kira. She had to share what she had learned. Not everything. Abby still wasn't sure how much she could trust Kira. And she didn't want to share everything she knew about Percy. Kira already hated him. If she knew about the Richie Rich stuff, she would for sure target him. No, she couldn't be objective about Percy. Not like Abby could.

Abby laughed to herself. She could try to convince herself that she was still being objective, but she knew that wasn't completely true. She was smitten with Percy. She wasn't quite drawing his name all over her notebooks with little hearts, but she thought about him. A lot.

But then there was the other thing. The thing Abby read in one of the last entries of Bridget's journal. It was clear and succinct: I HATE MY MOM. THAT FUCKING BITCH JUST ATTACKED ME.

That was it. There wasn't any more in that entry. In the next one, Bridget wrote about her eye healing everyone believing it was a cheerleading injury. Abby felt sorry for her, for the first time really. She never saw Bridget as a victim. Not before the alleged murder. But getting beat up by your mom, any parent, by the person that's supposed to protect you and keep you safe, it's wrong. Completely and utterly wrong.

Abby had never met Bridget's mom. Kira always said that Vanessa was a little strange, mixed up, maybe even an alcoholic, but she never said she was violent. But it does lend credence to the theory that Bridget was running away. This was something she would want to leave. She didn't talk a whole lot about her mom in the journal, maybe she was afraid she would find it, but there was never anything positive about her. It never struck Abby as strange because as great as her own mom was, she only ever felt like complaining about her. She took for granted all the positive moments. It's just something teenagers do, she thought.

She added a page for Vanessa in her own notebook, the one she kept of suspects. She had a hard time believing it, mainly because she couldn't imagine her mom climbing up to get on the roof of the bath-house. But then she couldn't imagine her mom beating her up either. And most violent crimes are committed by a family member. Abby read that somewhere.

She didn't know how to tell Kira this. For one, how could she explain that she had Bridget's journal without sharing it? And then Kira would read about Richie Rich and she would certainly put two and two together there. There were other things in the journal that would hurt people too. Bridget complained about Kira directly, for one. Stuff about not being able to rely on her, but also that she felt so much younger and didn't understand the real world. Bridget also talked about having sex with the wrong guy again, and the dates are firmly after she started dating Javi, someone who hardly showed up in her journal. Does that open up Javi as a suspect? Did he find out she was sleeping with Danny? He certainly hasn't acted like he's guilty, but then again, no one really has.

Abby knew the journal was too much. If anyone knew she had it, even Percy, it could actually be dangerous. Bridget obviously had secrets and though there's nothing too terrible in the journal, that doesn't mean that someone might not think there's something worse in there. If someone was willing to kill her, they would likely be willing to do something just as bad to keep from being caught.

Abby had to hide the journal. She made a plan to photocopy the important pages at the office tomorrow, and then she would figure out a secret spot where she could keep it safe. Even as her book of suspects grew larger, she still had only one that she was more and more sure of: Danny Sutton. She wondered if he had even been questioned by the police. She knew Percy had, he said so himself. And surely Vanessa had, as the victim's mother. Javi had been as well, but didn't say anything to suggest they thought he was a suspect. If the police knew everything Abby knew, maybe they would look more into Mr. Sutton. But was it enough?

Abby knew that before she did anything she was going to have to talk to Mr. Sutton herself.

* * * * *

Mr. Sutton had office hours fifth period. Abby skipped Biology and waited in the hallway until it was clear. His "office" was more like a closet, sandwiched between two classrooms. There were three desks along one wall-he shared with Mr. Guinan and Miss Booker-and there were bookshelves overhead, and barely enough room for a folding chair between the desk and the other wall. The door was open when Abby knocked.

Mr. Sutton had his head down at the far desk, and when he looked up to see Abby, she could tell he wasn't quite sure who she was.

"Hi," she said. "I'm Abby Williams. I was in your study hall."

"Of course, Abby. Hi. Were you looking for me or did you need one of the others?"

"I was hoping I could talk to you."

Mr. Sutton had a smile that seemed designed to put you at ease. Abby didn't trust that smile. She was suddenly all too aware that she was in a small room with a potential murderer. He motioned for her to come into the room, but she only got to the second desk which she leaned against. Without noticing both her hands were squeezing the straps of her backpack.

"What can I help you with?"

"I wanted to ask you about another student."

"I'm not sure what I can talk to you about, but I can help however I can."

This was harder than she thought. His eyes were soft an easy. Even looking down on him, he was seated as she was leaning down but still above him, she felt his authority and control. It had been so easy for her to ask other students about Bridget. She could confront Percy or Kira or Breck with questions and allegations, but this was different.

"It's, um, Bridget. Bridget Kent?"

"Why would you be asking me about her?"

"You were her teacher?"

"She was in my class last year, yes. Is that what you needed? What's this about?"

"Um, I am on the yearbook and we are thinking of doing a feature and I was just wondering if you wanted to say something about her. Being her teacher."

"Former teacher."

"Yeah, whatever. She was also in your study hall this year. I had the same study hall first quarter."

"Yeah, I left that study hall when I took another class."

"Right."

"A yearbook class. I became an advisor for the photography team."

"Oh."

"And funnily enough, I don't recall you being in that class."

"Well, I'm not, it's more…"

"Actually, underclassmen aren't even allowed in yearbook class so I find it curious that you would not only presume to know what we would be doing stories on for yearbook but that you, a sophomore, would be asked to do a story on a senior, especially one who took her own life. Did you forget this was a Catholic High School? We will not be doing a story on Bridget Kent. So, do you want to tell me what you are actually doing in my office?"

"I'm sorry. I didn't mean to."

"Mean to what? Lie?"

"It's not like that."

"Miss Williams, I think you should leave and we can both forget this conversation ever happened, since I have no idea why you would think I would be able to answer questions about any student, much less one that I had last year and barely knew. And I'm pretty sure you don't want me thinking too hard about it."

His eyes were no longer kind and forgiving. He also didn't seem the young, cool teacher he always felt like. He was old and intense. And Abby was more than a little freaked out by the entire exchange. She should've planned better. She should've researched her story and built a trust, before she went in on him about Bridget. She needed to catch him in a lie, instead she merely tipped her hand that she was somehow enmeshed in Bridget's life, something everyone else seemed to overlook.

Abby apologized quietly, and without looking back turned to leave the room. She stumbled over the feet of one of the chairs because the aisle was so small and she pulled the door shut behind her so he wouldn't follow. Abby darted into the girls' bathroom without looking to see if Mr. Sutton was following her.

Her legs were shaking when she sat down. She tried hard to breathe normal so that she wouldn't start crying.

She went about this all wrong. She had no business confronting Danny directly. This was not her job. Abby was going to have to figure out another way to get Mr. Sutton.

* * * * *

The headquarters of the Omaha Police Department was downtown, just blocks away from the library, blocks away from Harlan's office. Everything in downtown was just blocks away. Abby found a meter and parked on the street and watched people go in and out of the building surrounded by a white, stone grid, some design choice that made it feel more like a prison. After working up the courage to go in, Abby trudged across the stone courtyard and entered the building.

There was a group of chairs immediately as she walked in and a bullpen surrounded by plexiglass in front of her, a less welcoming DMV of sorts. A woman in a police uniform motioned for her to come to her window. Unlike the DMV there did not appear to be a long wait.

"Can I help you?" the woman asked.

"I, uh, need to talk to someone about a case."

"Can you be more specific? Are you the victim? Or a witness?"

"No, nothing like that, I had information, or wanted to see if you had some information I guess. About Bridget Kent, she was a young girl who-"

"Yeah, I know who she is. Have a seat and I can get one of the detectives. Can I get your name?"

"Um, Becky. Becky Watson."

"One minute, Becky."

Abby took a seat by herself, and tried not to make eye contact with the homeless-looking man on the other side of the room. Was this a mistake? She wasn't sure what she hoped to accomplish here. She didn't want to risk anything getting back to Mr. Sutton, thus the fake name, and she purposely left her ID in the car.

Abby second guessed herself for about five minutes until the door buzzed open and a young man in his 30s, with a striped shirt and tie, and a five o'clock shadow stepped out.

"Becky?"

Abby lifted her hand and followed the man as he motioned at her. He was handsome, although barely taller than she was. There was a thick belt across his waist with a gun on one side and a radio on the other. The gun made Abby nervous, even though it was strapped in. Something about it just left her uneasy.

The noise level increased when she crossed the threshold with dozens of people walking around, talking on the phone, taking statements, all amidst a bank of desks that were spaced throughout the large room.

"I'm Detective Anthony. We can talk in here," he said, motioning to a room off the big, main room. “It’s not as scary as it looks.”

The room looked pretty bleak. Cement walls, with a table in the center, pretty much like every movie used for angry policemen questioning nervous witnesses, exactly how Abby was feeling.

“Can I get you some water? Coffee? I’ve got to grab the file anyway,” he said.

“I’m fine.”

“Coffee stunts your growth anyway. You’re what, fourteen, fifteen?”

“Seventeen,” she lied. “I guess I just look young.”

Detective Anthony motioned for her to grab a seat and walked away without closing the door. Abby looked around the room. There wasn’t a mirror anywhere. She expected to be watched by some greasy, old, grizzled cop who was mistrusting. They sent the young, handsome cop out to disarm her, but he was watching, ready to pounce. He was probably only offering her something to drink in order to get her fingerprints so they figure out she wasn’t Becky Wilson at all. Or did she say Watson? Shit.

The detective returned and sat on the other side of Abby with a large, stuffed file folder, with papers practically spilling out, a notebook, and two bottles of water. He set one in front of her.

“Just in case,” he smiled. “Now, you said you wanted to talk about the Bridget Kent case?”

“Yes.”

“What exactly did you want to talk about?”

“I was wondering if you had talked to someone, you know, like already figured out if he had an alibi?”

“Well, I can’t comment on the case, because it’s technically still open.”

"But the news said you believed it was a suicide."

"I can't comment on the case. But why don't you tell me who you're thinking of and I can talk to the other guys and see if it's something we've looked into."

"If I'm wrong, I don't want to get someone in trouble."

"Look, miss, we're not going to do anything to anyone unless we have proof of something. Do you have proof of something or is this simply speculation?"

"I don't know. Speculation, I guess."

"Why don't you tell me what you have and we can do our job and see if there is anything there. Okay?"

He smiled again. He was good. Abby wanted to tell him everything. She almost wanted to confess to breaking into the school and killing Bridget herself. But, no. She had to stay focused.

"I think she was having, you know, like, an affair with one of her teachers."

"You think?"

"She was a friend of mine. And she told me. She said she slept with her teacher."

"Did she say which teacher?"

"His name is Mister Sutton. Danny. Daniel Sutton."

Detective Anthony opened the file folder and flipped through some pages. He set the folder back down and closed it again, scribbling some notes on his notepad.

"And she told you this directly?"

"Yes."

"I need to grab something else. Can you wait here a moment?"

"Yeah, sure."

Abby watched the detective walk out and walk across the room and talk to another man, obviously another cop. From her peripheral vision she could see Detective Anthony turn his head back in her direction. The door was still open, but the angle meant Abby was only partially visible, and the other side of the table was blocked. Abby watched as Detective Anthony went into an office with the other detective and closed the door. Hurriedly, Abby grabbed the file folder and turned it to face her.

A picture of Bridget was the top picture, her school picture in her cheerleader uniform, the one they always showed on the news. On the left side was the first police report. Abby scanned quickly. She saw "TIME OF DEATH: est~ 2:30am." She flipped up the page but when she saw a picture with a pool of blood, she quickly slammed her hand down. She was not ready for that. The right side of the file folder had a bunch of disparate notes. Abby flipped through looking for anything interesting. Her eyes stopped when she saw "PERSON OF INTEREST – PERCY VAN ALLEN." There were notes scribbled below it: says he was home, ambulance to Underwood house 3:47am, son of Harlan Van Allen. Lawyer: L. McKenzie.

She heard Percy had an accident, but didn't realize it was so close in time to Bridget's death. He said it was Sunday, which was technically true, but the difference seemed like a day, and not a couple hours. Maybe they had nothing to do with each other, the police obviously questioned him, they had his lawyer info already, something Harlan probably forced. Abby heard a door shut, and quickly flipped the file closed and turned it around. In her haste, a cassette tape had fallen out of the file, bouncing off the wall and landing near her feet. The case fell open.

Abby looked over but the door was still closed where Detective Anthony went. Quickly, she picked up the tape. In black marker, scrawled across the front: "911 log 10/31 pm". Abby slid the tape into her coat pocket, but put the case back in the file. She straightened everything back to normal and looked back at the still closed door.

She said what she had to say. They would look into Mr. Sutton. They didn't need her anymore, and she didn't have to risk being identified and Mr. Sutton seeking revenge. It would all work out. She would be safe. She just had to leave.

Abby stood up and inched closer to the door. There were dozens of people in the big room, and none of them were looking towards Abby. She walked back to the hallway towards the front room. She saw a large button that said PRESS TO OPEN DOOR and she did. When the door opened she practically sprinted through, and bolted right through the front door.

Even the fresh air didn't make her feel calm. Instead of walking directly back to her car, she turned the corner and walked around the block, took her coat off and shoved it into her purse. She grabbed her hat and pulled it on, tucking her hair into it. She continued walking, continuing to look behind her to make sure she wasn't followed.

About fifteen minutes later, she returned to street of the police station, this time from the other side. She expected Detective Anthony to come running out and chase her down, but the door didn't open. She walked quickly towards her car and drove away quickly.

She did it, she thought. She told them. Now, she just had to wait.

23. KIRA

"I never saw anything like that," Kira told Abby.

She still couldn't believe what she was hearing. Sure, Bridget had complained about her mom. What teenager didn't hate their parents every once in a while? But Bridget never even suggested her mother was anything other than a normal mom that was a little overbearing sometimes.

It also didn't gibe with what Kira knew herself. Vanessa was weird, okay, that much was clear. She may have a drinking problem, but Kira only noticed that after Bridget had died. Any parent could be excused for acting out of character if their kid was brutally killed. Or killed themselves. Kira was still waffling on what she believed was the real story.

It was easier for her to believe that Bridget was killed than she took her own life, but if she was killed, that meant there was a killer. And if there was a killer, and if Vanessa had been violent toward Bridget, that meant it was possible she was the killer. And Kira just couldn't get there.

"How exactly did you hear about this?" Kira asked.

Abby was shivering even though they were inside a well-heated mall.

They were on Christmas break and having hot chocolates in the food court, ostensibly trying to kill two birds with one stone: solve a murder and finish Christmas shopping. Abby took a sip of her hot chocolate, but kept avoiding looking at Kira.

"It's from a reliable source," Abby said.

"No, that's not good enough, not for something like this. You have to tell me."

"Do you think it could be true?"

"Depends on where you heard it."

People kept walking by in their puffy coats with bags of presents. Kids were screaming in line for Santa on the level below, but Kira stayed focused on Abby. There was something she wasn't telling her. Kira could tell. Abby finally looked over at her and Kira raised her eyebrows, urging Abby to continue talking.

"I went to Mr. Sutton. I went to the police. I need to know if I could've been wrong."

"I can't believe it. Bridget never said anything like that. Maybe whoever it was misunderstood. I'm sure it was nothing. Maybe they exaggerated. Bridget would never say her mom hit her."

"Bridget did say it."

"How do you know?"

"Because she did."

"To you?"

"Not exactly."

"Where did you get this?"

"Look, you're not gonna like this."

"Just tell me."

"Bridget kept a journal."

"I know, but it wasn't in her room when I looked through it. And it wasn't in her school stuff."

"That's because I took it."

"What?"

"Before she died. I stole it out of her backpack. I forgot I even had it until this whole thing."

"And you didn't tell me?"

"She doesn't say anything about you."

"I don't care about that. But she says her mom hit her?"

"Yeah."

"What else does it say?"

"Lots of stuff. And nothing. Nothing about wanting to kill herself. Nothing to indicate she was thinking of running away. But maybe I took it before that whole plan."

"I want to see it."

"I don't know."

"What? It's not yours."

"It's not yours either. And you were close with her. I know that what I did was wrong and an invasion, but if anyone finds out we have it and didn't give it to the police, especially with everything else going on… well, I don't know what it could mean."

"Does it say anything else? About anyone else?"

"It says she was sleeping with a new guy. One that was a big secret."

"And you think that was Mr. Sutton? Is that what she was doing when she was sneaking out of her house?"

"I don't know."

"Abby, come on. Maybe I can pick up on something that you can't because I did know her."

"I don't know, okay. I don't even have it here."

"Where is it?"

"Somewhere safe. I didn't want to risk it. I don't know. If the police figure out it was me that pointed them to Mr. Sutton, maybe they come search my house."

"I don't think that's how it works."

"I don't know, okay. This whole thing is getting out of hand."

"You think?"

* * * * *

Abby's words kept running around Kira's head. She didn't know whether to be mad or concerned. Both? If Vanessa did have something to do with Bridget's death, then her complete and continual emotional breakdown might make sense. The guilt could destroy a normal person.

Kira had no reason to go to Vanessa's house. She had stopped going regularly. Not for any particular reason. For one thing, Vanessa seemed to be getting back to normal. The dishes were getting done. She was making it into work. For another, Kira had gotten sidetracked. School, the investigation, whatever was going on with Jake, all of it was taking her time.

Georgina had been making Christmas cookies all afternoon, so Kira took it as an opportunity. She grabbed a tin and put a bunch of her soon-to-be Stepmom's baked goods in there and walked over to Vanessa's house.

She still had a key, but didn't feel right just walking in. She rang the doorbell. It took a moment, but Vanessa came to the door and smiled when she saw Kira.

"Oh my gosh, girl, it's so good to see you. Where you been?"

Vanessa's effusive nature threw Kira. The last time she saw her, she had been half asleep on the couch, in a robe that she had been sleeping in for days. Now, Vanessa had her hair done and was wearing what looked like a new dress.

"Hi, Mrs. Kent. I just wanted to bring over some of Georgina's cookies. I thought you could use some Christmas cheer."

"You know better. Call me Vanessa. Come in, come in. That's so sweet."

Kira handed her the tin and followed Vanessa into the living room. It was clean. Probably the first time Kira had seen it so pristine, even since before Bridget's death. The pillows on the couch were straight. The mirrored coffee table didn't have a single fingerprint.

"I don't know that I need any more Christmas cheer in the form of calories, but I'm sure I will eat every last one of these," Vanessa said as she set the tin down in the kitchen. "Can I get you anything?"

"Oh, no thanks, I'm fine. I was only checking on you."

"Thanks, dear. One day at a time, you know."

"Yeah."

Kira could see the hurt in Vanessa's eyes. She still couldn't believe this woman in front of her, this sweet, sad, struggling mom, would ever raise a hand to her daughter. Kira was beginning to doubt Abby even had a journal in the first place. Maybe she was making the whole thing up? Maybe that's why she wouldn't let her read it.

"So, tell me, sweetie, how is school?"

"We're on break now, but it was good. Think I did well on my midterms."

"Good, good. That's important."

So, now it was like this. Small talk. Kira appreciated the simplicity of it. She didn't have the energy to face the sad, lonely and confused woman she had been seeing in the days after Bridget had died. For the first time, Kira thought that Vanessa might actually see her way through this ordeal. And if she could, Kira knew that she could herself.

The two spent a few minutes catching up, until they were interrupted by the phone ringing. Vanessa went into the kitchen to answer it and while Kira could hear her voice, she wasn't paying attention to the words. Her voice was cheery. This wasn't like when the cops visited.

Kira focused on the photos on the bookshelves. One of them was pretty much a shrine to Bridget. It always had been. Bridget as a little girl in that awful plaid jumper. Bridget's class picture from last year. A picture of her cheering. A baby Bridget crying on the Easter bunny's lap. Thirteen-year-old Bridget with Vanessa, both of them smiling with their arms around each other, waves crashing from some ocean in the background. Kira never paid much attention to these pictures before. They'd always been there. They'd been background noise. But now they're all that's left. Bridget will never take another picture. Never smile in front of another ocean. Never put her own daughter on some scary rabbit's lap.

Vanessa returned, pulling Kira out of her thought. She was pulling on a coat.

"I'm so sorry, dear, I completely forgot I was supposed to meet someone. Can you do me a huge favor?"

"Sure."

"I have a load in the dryer that needs to come out as soon as it dings and get hung up or they will absolutely be ruined. Should be done in like twenty minutes. Could you please, please, stay and help me out?"

"Oh, of course."

"Stay as long as you want. Eat whatever you want. Just lock up when you leave."

"No problem."

And with that, Vanessa was off. Kira waited for the garage door to go down and watched Vanessa's car pull away.

The house was quiet again. Quiet enough that Kira could hear the hum of the dryer from the basement. She turned on the TV, and went to the fridge. Maybe she had some good food. Kira wasn't above a little snack. While the house may be clean, it didn't look like Vanessa had done much grocery shopping. Eggs. Milk. The staples. Kind of boring.

Kira turned on the TV and waited for the dryer to ding. She helped herself to some crackers she found. As Wheel of Fortune droned on, Kira shouted out the answers. They were too easy: All That Glitters Isn't Gold. Kiss and Make Up. Read Between the Lines.

Kira gave up before the final round and went into the laundry room, hoping her presence would make the dryer move faster. The room was a small alcove between the kitchen and the garage. The dryer was grumbling and shaking. Kira finished the sleeve of crackers she was munching on and went about hiding the evidence in the trash can. There was a magazine on top of the bin, so she pulled it out and crumpled up the paper, and went to hide it underneath. It was then she saw the pill bottle.

She grabbed it out of the trash and held it up to the light. It was a small, brown prescription bottle. Empty. It read: Thorazine generic for Chlorpromazine. It had Vanessa's name. Was she sick? Kira hadn't heard of the drug before, but it's not like she was familiar with any prescription drugs really. Still, it was curious.

The buzz of the dryer startled her and she jumped back, shoving the pill bottle in her pocket. Quickly realizing she was still alone, Kira chuckled, but kept the bottle. She put the magazine back the way it was in the bin and then went about emptying the dryer.

* * * * *

"My dad is right upstairs," Kira said as Jake moved in closer.

They had ostensibly been watching a movie, but halfway through E.T. (it was the only non-Disney movie Kira had), when Elliott seemed to be dying, Jake scooted closer and put his arm around her. Kira liked it, but she felt scrunched and didn't know what to do with her arms. She held them in her lap, but it seemed unnatural to her.

Then Jake tried to kiss her. Kira kissed him back, quickly before pushing him back.

"We'll hear the door open won't we?"

"Maybe, but that doesn't mean he won't try and murder you when he gets down here."

"Your dad doesn't seem that bad."

"That's because you haven't pissed him off yet."

Jake pulled back.

"Is everything okay?"

"I don't know. Everything is just weird right now."

"Want to talk about it? I give good listen."

Jake was flashing that charming smile that Kira found adorable. She was still having trouble believing that a senior boy was sitting next to her. It started normal enough. She went to Abby's and he was there. While she waited, they talked about school. She complained about doing bad in math, and even though he went to a different school, he still offered to help. After a couple weeks he asked if she wanted to hang out sometime. She said "yes," of course, and this was now the third instance of them officially hanging out. She wasn't sure what it meant. What it was supposed to mean, even.

But the kiss was something new.

"I don't know. There's just a lot going on," Kira said. "Abby was saying something that kind of made me feel, I don't know, weird I guess."

"So, I try to kiss you and you bring up my stepsister? That's a new one."

"I'm sorry."

"No, it's fine. She tends to ruin things when she's around, why should it be any different when she's not?"

Jake held his hands back, giving up. The mood has officially been killed. Kira didn't intend that, but she couldn't legislate how her brain worked.

"What did she say?"

"It's nothing."

"If it's got you stressing about it, I wouldn't say it's nothing."

"I know. Look, can we just go back to movie."

"Fuck E.T. He goes home. Seen it a million times. Talk to me."

"Abby hasn't said anything to you about what she's doing?"

"What she's doing? What do you mean?"

"She's got it in her head that someone killed Bridget. And she thinks she can figure it out."

"What?"

"Yeah, she was all sure that it was Mr. Sutton, this teacher Bridget knew, but then she told me she found Bridget's journal and that Bridget said her mom hit her. And I didn't believe her, but then I found this pill bottle and, I don't know, maybe her mom was sick."

"Woah, woah, woah. Settle down. That's a lot to take in."

"Please don't tell her I told you."

"It's okay. Abby and I don't really talk much. But, can I give you some advice?"

"Of course."

"Abby lies. You can't believe anything you hear from her. I don't know if it's attention or what, but she's always in the middle of some drama."

"And you think that's what this is?"

"I don't know. Look, I didn't know Bridget, and I'm pretty sure Abby didn't know her. Why is this something she's spending any time on?"

"I don't know."

"Is this why you've been hanging out with her?"

"Kind of."

"I knew you couldn't be friends. Not real friends. You're way too cool for her."

"Abby's… nice?"

"Abby's a lot of things, but I don't think anyone would say 'nice.' Look, just be careful, okay. Don't let her pull you into her chaos bubble. I've been there. It's not pretty."

"Okay."

"And what's this about her mom's pills?"

Bridget's backpack was sitting on a chair across the room, so she got up and walked over and pulled the bottle out. She handed it to Jake.

"Wow. Heavy stuff."

"You know what this is?"

"Thorazine? Yeah. My mom was on this."

"What's it for?"

"Well, I don't know if it works for other stuff, but my aunt took it for her… episodes."

"Episodes?"

"She was schizo. I guess they say bipolar now or some shit like that."

"What kind of episodes."

"Believe me, you don't want to know."

"I really do. Could it be something violent? Could that be what happened with Bridget and her mom?"

"I don't know. Look, you're getting spun out again."

"I know. I'm sorry."

The door creaked open from upstairs.

"Kira," a stern voice shouted down.

"Yeah, Dad?"

"It's getting late."

"Okay." Kira turned to Jake, shrugging her shoulders.

"I guess that's my cue," Jake said. "Need to stay on his good side."

"I guess so. But hey, thanks for the info."

"It's okay, but like I said, be careful with Abby."

"I will. And please don't tell her I said anything."

"I won't. That would for sure get you on her bad side. And you don't want that."

* * * * *

Kira was hiding out in her room. After Jake left the night before, Randall proceeded to give her a lecture about dating someone older and what being respectful means and that Kira had to be extra careful. Basically, boys were evil and Randall wanted to keep his daughter hidden away until she graduated college. Kira was still annoyed and didn't feel like hanging out. She had her headphones on, and was trying to zone out to the music when her door swung open.

"Dad, come on, don't you knock?" Kira snapped as she pulled her headphones down.

"I did knock. Maybe those things on your ears were a factor."

"Whatever."

"You have a phone call."

Kira darted to the phone and picked it up, answering happily, hoping she would hear Jake's voice. She was surprised, and somewhat disappointed, to hear it was Abby.

"Hey, Kira. It's me."

"Hi, Abby."

"Are we getting together later?"

"I don't know. My dad is kind of mad at me."

"Okay. Maybe tomorrow?"

"Yeah, okay."

"Anything new?"

"What do you mean?"

"You said you were going over to Vanessa's. Was she being weird again? Did you find out anything?"

"Oh. No. I don't think there's anything there," Kira said.

She wasn't sure why she lied. Maybe Jake was right and this whole thing was Abby rustling up drama. Maybe something did happen with Vanessa. Maybe she was sick, only not in the way Kira originally thought. But she wasn't sure letting Abby in on the truth, at least yet, was the right thing to do.

"I'll call you tomorrow," she said, knowing she wouldn't.

24. JAVI

He couldn't concentrate on the movie. The theater wasn't that full but he kept worrying someone was going to see him. Trevor had talked him into seeing a movie, but Javi would only agree if they went to the Q-Cinema 9 out west, where he was unlikely to run into anyone. Still, Javi kept looking around the theater to be sure.

He wanted to see A Few Good Men, a military movie. It wouldn't be weird at all. But there weren't any tickets left. The Bodyguard was at the right time, but it felt wrong to Javi. Trevor begged and he acquiesced. But still. What if someone saw them? A couple guys at an army movie was fine, but two dudes at The Bodyguard? That was suspect. And they were sitting right next to each other. Sometimes, when he went to the movies with his guy friends they kept a seat open between them. Why never made sense. It just made Javi talk louder when he wanted to ask a question.

At one point, Trevor reached over and set his hand on top of Javi's. It immediately made Javi's heart beat faster. He wanted to pull it away. What was Trevor doing? They were in public. Sure, no one else was in their row, but someone could see. He didn't move his hand, though. He took a deep breath, kept looking forward at the screen and sat perfectly still.

Trevor's hand was warm. Javi felt like his was clammy, but in the palm, and Trevor's hand rested on the top of his hand. Everything about this made Javi sweaty. His heart kept thumping, and when Trevor grazed his fingers up Javi's arm, he immediately jerked it away and scratched his neck.

"Sorry, I had an itch," Javi whispered.

"It's okay."

Trevor's hands rested in his lap, but he smiled at Javi and then turned back to the screen.

During one of the musical numbers, Trevor leaned over to Javi and whispered something, but Javi didn't hear.

"What's that?" Javi asked as he leaned closer.

"I said 'no one is watching'." Trevor responded and then kissed Javi. Javi's heart raced. It felt right, and very wrong. But he kissed him back. Trevor's face was scratchy. It was so different from all the girls Javi had kissed (well, all six of them). It wasn't the first time they had kissed, but it was the first time that wasn't in the back of Trevor's car or some other secluded place. And maybe the first when no alcohol was involved. When Trevor put his hand on Javi's thigh, he pulled back and pushed Trevor away.

"I want to see what happens."

"Okay."

Trevor set his arm on the armrest. Javi set his hand on top of Trevor's. He didn't look over at him, he stayed focused on the movie, but he could feel Trevor looking at him. And smiling.

As soon as the credits started to roll, Javi stood up and motioned for Trevor to join him. He wanted to escape the theater while it was still dark.

"That was awesome," Trevor said as they pushed the door open into the large hallway. "I have to pee."

Trevor took a sharp turn into the bathroom and Javi walked a few more yards before leaning against a wall. More people filed out of the theater. Javi pulled up his head so he could watch everyone leaving without risking eye contact.

"Javi?"

Javi recognized the voice but didn't turn immediately, but then she was standing right in front of him: Abby Williams. She used to be a friend of Breck's, and went to his school last year, but she transferred out and he hadn't seen much of her since. Her hair was longer than he remembered, and it was pulled back into a pony tail. Her sweatshirt and sneakers completed a look that suggested she wasn't here on a date.

"Hey, Abby."

"Trying to catch up on movies before Christmas too, eh?"

"Yeah. I guess."

"Are you coming or going?"

"Going. I just, uh, saw A Few Good Men."

"Oh, that's awesome. 'you can't handle the truth!'"

"What?"

"It's a line from the movie."

"Must've been when I went to the bathroom."

"How is everything?"

"Oh, fine. You know."

“Yeah.”

Javi was trying not to engage, but Abby didn’t seem to be moving, and of course, Trevor walked up before he could get rid of her. Javi’s immediately got nervous.

“Ready?” Trevor asked.

“Hi,” Abby said, acknowledging Trevor. “I’m Abby. I used to go to school with Javi.”

“Trevor Rhodes, I’m—”

“He’s my cousin,” Javi interjected. “Here for the holidays. And we should probably get back before my mom starts to freak.”

“Oh, sure. Merry Christmas. So good to see you,” Abby said.

“You too,” Javi said as he turned to walk off.

“Nice to meet you!” Trevor shouted back as Javi pulled him away.

Javi beelined for the exit doors and kept his fingers crossed that no one else was going to make an appearance. Did he really have to worry about Abby? Why wouldn’t she buy the cousin thing? And what would it matter if she didn’t? Did she even talk to anyone anymore?

And if she did, what would she say?

* * * * *

“Javi, you have a visitor,” Lucinda shouted from upstairs.

Javi was still in his bedroom. He had been up too late the night before. Mostly staring above and trying to slow his brain down, but nothing worked. He probably didn’t doze off until after 4am, since he distinctly remembered looking at the clock around then when his brother was snoring. So, it wasn’t crazy that he was still in bed at 11am.

“Be right up.”

He pulled on some clothes that were on the floor, whatever was closest to the bed and walked upstairs. He wasn't expecting anyone. Was it Scott? Coming to admit something about messing around with Bridget? Or Abby, further questioning what she saw the other night? Did she even know where he lived?

When he made it upstairs, he was somewhat surprised to see Breck there. She had a stocking hat and thick coat on. It must be cold outside.

"Hi," she said. "We need to talk."

"Okay."

"Good to see you again, dear," Lucinda said as she returned to the kitchen where the younger kids were making noise. "Not in your room, Javier."

"I know, Mom."

Breck and Javi went into the living room and sat on the couch. As if she had to be worried about something happening between him and Breck. For a number of reasons.

"What's this about?" Javi asked, wondering if Abby had started talking and Breck was going to have questions about his "cousin."

"Scott," she responded, to his relief.

"What's going on?"

"I don't know. He's getting worse."

"Worse how?"

"Javi, look, I'm not sure what all he's told you, but we haven't exactly been getting along lately."

"Yeah, I haven't talked to him much either."

"You know he took something, don't you?"

"Took something?"

"Come on, Javi. You told me you saw him snorting something. And then he wound up in the hospital. And ever since then he's been more, I don't know, not himself. He's down one second and then angry the next. We got in an argument the other day and pushed me."

"Are you okay?"

"I'm fine. It's him I'm worried about. He punched the mirror in his bathroom and cut his hand all up, and he told his parents it was an accident. It just feels like he's lying all the time about everything."

She got that right.

"Yeah, I saw his hand. What do you want me to do?"

"I don't know. Really. I just wanted to talk to someone. I don't know anyone else that actually cares about him. I don't want to tell Kira or Abby. They don't know him like we do."

"You still talk to Abby?"

"Yeah, we kind of made up a few weeks back. But she's got a lot going on."

"Like what?"

"She hasn't talked to you?"

"Why would she talk to me?"

"Oh, I figured she would reach out."

"Why? Why would she want to reach out to me? What did she say?"

"I probably shouldn't say."

"No, come on, Breck."

"It's about Bridget."

Javi exhaled.

"What about Bridget?"

"She thinks someone killed her. That it wasn't a suicide."

"What? Why?"

"She thinks she was seeing someone else. I'm sorry. I really shouldn't be telling you this. It's only been a couple months and you're probably still dealing with it. I really just wanted to talk about Scott."

Maybe they really were talking about Scott. Javi couldn't believe that Scott was capable of anything like murder, but Breck said he was strung out, and violent. And Kira said Bridget might've been pregnant. Maybe Javi should tell Breck about all the secrets Scott was keeping.

"Javi," Breck said, probably realizing his mind had been drifting. "What are we gonna do?"

"I really wish I knew."

* * * * *

Javi couldn't sleep again that night. He was worried about everything. About Scott. And what Breck said about Abby. He wondered why Abby hadn't talked to him. Did she think he did it? Did she really know anything? He wanted to talk to her. To find out what she knew, but he was worried that she would bring up Trevor. She was obviously into snooping.

Javi couldn't get his brain to shut off. He had a hard enough time believing that Scott and Bridget were getting together behind his back, but to think that Scott may have somehow had done something to cause her death was a bridge too far. Maybe it was an accident. Even if something happened, that was the only logical explanation. Scott was so focused on grades and sports that he could easily keep up the lie to ensure his status was intact. Maybe that's why he was using to begin with. Something like this could eat someone alive from the inside out.

The door creaked open and Javi listened as familiar footsteps came stomping down the stairs. It was Diego. His steps were heavier than

Antonio. Besides, Antonio hadn't been around the last few days. It was hard to keep track of the brothers. There was no expectation that they had to be home every night. His parents were focused on the younger kids. The older ones were free to fend for themselves.

"Hey," Javi said as Diego plopped down on the couch.

"Sorry, bro, did I wake you up?"

"Nah, I was up. You all right?"

"I'm good, man, just had too many. Buddy of mine dropped me. Got tomorrow off so I can sleep in. Let this be a lesson to you, don't drink and drive. It's bad."

"Got it."

"You can call me if you need to, you know that."

"Yeah, man."

"No, seriously, bro, for like anything. I got you. You can't trust anyone else in this world, but you can trust me."

"I know, it's cool. Thanks."

"I got you. I swear."

Javi couldn't tell exactly how drunk Diego was. He was usually good about holding his liquor, so this must've been a pretty decent bender. At least he didn't drive. Even drunk, Diego had a way of keeping his head about him. He knew he could trust Diego. He wanted to tell him about Scott, about the whole thing, but wasn't sure what good it would do. Diego was overprotective even sober, and if he thought Scott had done even half the things Javi was thinking about, Diego was bound to get right back up and give Scott a visit. Javi didn't want to risk it. Not until he had some real answers.

"You have to get out of here," Diego muttered, almost to himself.

"You're so much smarter than the rest of us. So much better. You need to escape this place before it swallows you up like the rest of us. You need to get out and go make something of yourself. Because you can."

Javi wasn't even sure what he was talking about. Diego always seemed to talk Javi up like this, and Javi wanted nothing more than to be elsewhere sometimes. But he had no idea how to get anywhere. Especially not with everything that was going on.

Only a few minutes after arriving, Diego had drifted off, still in his clothes, and laying on the couch. He was snoring before Javi could even think about saying anything more.

* * * * *

"So, are we gonna talk about what's going on here?"

"What do you mean?" Javi asked.

Trevor was buttoning up his shirt. The two of them were in his dorm room. Javi wanted to talk to someone, but when he got there Trevor offered him a drink and it actually felt good not to think about everything for a bit. Javi had a few drinks and then the two of them were making out on Trevor's twin bed. Javi knew it was wrong, but then why didn't it feel wrong?

"I mean this," Trevor said. "The two of us. I like you, Javi, but I feel like you're not ready to admit that you like me."

"I like you. You've been a really good friend."

"Oh, come on. This isn't being friends. You suck off any of your other friends?"

"Keep it down, Trevor."

"Or what? Someone might think I'm gay? Oh, no. I'm out, Javi. And you tell your friends I'm your cousin?"

"It's not that simple, Trev. I'm not gay, I'm just, I don't know, having a little fun. It's not a big deal."

"Javi, I think it's a bigger deal than you're ready to admit."

"Look, I've got a lot going on, okay? My girlfriend just died."

"Is that why you're having such a hard time with this? Do you feel like you're betraying her memory or something?"

"It's not like that."

"Because, believe me, Javi. She's not worth it. She may have been nice, and no one deserves to die like that, but that doesn't mean she was a good person. And she certainly wasn't good to you."

"Why do you say that?"

"Never mind."

"No, what?"

"I don't know. I saw her fighting with Scott. Something was obviously going on with them. I don't know what it was about, and I didn't want to tell you like this, but you keep beating yourself up over this girl, when it's pretty obvious neither of you wanted to be with the other person. Not really."

"Wait, you saw them fighting?"

"Yeah. That night. The night she died."

"What was their fight about?"

"I don't know. I couldn't hear them, but the way they were acting. I was on the terrace and they were over in the corner by the bathhouse."

"What time was this?"

"I don't remember. Why?"

"I don't know. It doesn't matter. Are you sure?"

"I know I saw them. And I know they were trying not to be seen."

* * * * *

Javi left Trevor's before they could make any real headway on their discussion. Trevor was right about one thing: Javi wasn't ready to deal with whatever was going on with Trevor. He liked him. Liked him liked him. But what did that mean? And what would his family say? What would his friends say? Everything he was taught said that God would punish him. And is that what happened with Bridget? Was she the sacrifice for Javi straying from his faith? That was a stretch, Javi knew, but all of this was rolling around his head, along with everything else going on with Scott.

Trevor saw them. That night. He wouldn't make something like that up. And he didn't even know everything Javi knew about the situation. It was becoming more and more clear that he was going to have to do something about the whole thing.

Javi tiptoed down the stairs into his bedroom in case his brothers were asleep, but the light was still on, and he was the only one there. Good. He didn't have the energy for another conversation with Diego, drunk or sober.

There were some envelopes on Javi's bed. His mom was always throwing the mail there to make sure he got it. He wasn't in the mood to dig through it, but the big envelope on top was curious. It was from the University of Colorado-Boulder. Javi had applied for early admission there back in October but he wasn't expecting to hear anything before the new year. He tore open the envelope and read the first few words: "We are pleased to invite you to attend…"

He got in.

Javi had never really thought about actually going away to school.

He didn't think he would actually have the option. Getting in was one thing, affording it was another, but for a moment Javi let himself bask in the joy of the opportunity. He got in.

He actually could go away to school. Start over. Become who he was supposed to be. Figure out who the real Javi is. He couldn't keep himself from smiling. Suddenly, all of the other bullshit with Scott and Breck and Abby seemed irrelevant.

He got in.

He wished there actually was someone there to share the news with. His parents were obviously asleep. It would probably have to wait until morning.

Javi grabbed the rest of the mail and flipped through it. There was another envelope that just had "JAVI" written in thick black marker on front. Javi opened it.

It was a xeroxed copy of a notebook page. And he recognized the handwriting immediately. It was Bridget's. She had written him enough notes and always had a way of doing her "i's" lower case with an open circle instead of a dot. But this wasn't a note to him. It was a note about him.

"I don't think things are working out with Javi. He's nice and all but he's not the one. i know that. But the one is with someone else. And even though i have told him that, i have said i love him, he says we can't be together. Not ever. But maybe love will find a way."

What was this? Her journal? She talked about writing one, but obviously he had never seen it. And why send this to him? There was nothing on the other side. Nothing on the envelope. Someone must've put it in the mailbox or left it in the door. Was someone fucking with him? Someone else knew that Bridget and Scott had a thing. But what did that mean?

The high of the college acceptance had worn off. Now, he was left with an entirely new thing to keep him awake.

25. PERCY

It was the day before Christmas. Snow was falling, but while it made for a nice sheet of dusty white over the lawns, the corners of every street had large, packed piles of dirty black sludge. Every step Percy took on the sidewalks splooshed against his boots. He hated the snow. It was fun when he could go sledding or have a snowball fight with his friends, but now it was just an annoying, inconvenient mess that messed up the whole town.

Percy went to the mall to get his Christmas presents. Like most things, he was doing it at the last minute. It was all so stupid. He was buying presents for his family as if everything was normal. Nothing was normal. He spent the last couple months out of school because of rumors about a murder, a murder he was pretty sure he didn't do, but since he was drunk and had a mild blackout, he couldn't be a hundred percent certain. His mother was intent on presenting everything as it was before, even though the whispers on his involvement was affecting her social standing. His father was banging Eli, a woman that worked for him and just happened to be married to one of Percy's teachers. A teacher, incidentally, who may have been sleeping with the murder victim. Allegedly.

In the middle of all of this was Abby Williams, this fierce, amazing fireball of a young woman who he couldn't stop thinking about, but who seemed both interested in him and uncomfortable around him.

It was a lot.

Percy wanted to get through the next few days as quickly as possible. Just forget this entire year, and start over in 1993. But then he remembered that along with the new year was the fact that he would be returning to St. Dymphna's, and was likely to face a whole slew of new rumors and dickhead students talking shit about him. Maybe it wasn't too late to get out of it. But then again, Abby went to school there as well. So, at least he had that to look forward to.

When he walked into his house, he dropped his bags by the twelve-foot-tall Christmas tree that faced out of their front window. He paid extra to have everything gift wrapped. He wasn't about to extend the effort to actually wrap them himself. He just wanted to get high and go to bed, even though it was only about three in the afternoon. And neither smoking nor sleeping was in the near term.

He heard some rummaging in the kitchen, and steeled himself up for a conversation with his mom but was surprised by the dark-haired girl in front of him, eating cereal out of a coffee cup.

"Bailey?" Percy asked, knowing full well it was his sister. "I didn't think you were coming home."

"Yeah, well, couldn't really get a better offer."

"Staying at school isn't a better offer?"

"Oh, it for sure is, but they actually shut down the dorms for a week. Such bullshit."

"Are we supposed to hug or something?"

"No, wait until Mom and Dad are home so they can pretend we all love each other."

Percy smiled. It was the first time he'd felt a connection to his family in forever. He wasn't particularly close with Bailey. They always fought growing up, her being their father's obvious favorite, and Bailey feeding into that sentiment. That changed when she was in high school and was no longer the angel she was raised to be. Now that she was away, he realized she was the only other person in the world who could understand him.

"So, what's the deal, you kill that girl? Bridget? I don't remember her."

"No, I did not."

"Guess I'll have to return that shiv I got you for Christmas."

"Don't worry about it. I didn't think you were coming, so I didn't get you anything."

"Fair enough."

"Is Simon home?"

"No, he's with Mom somewhere."

"Wanna get high?"

"I really do."

* * * * *

Percy and Bailey shared a joint in his bedroom, sitting near the window, with the cold air blowing in. A candle was burning in an attempt to mask the weed smell with apple cinnamon. It was a lot of effort even though neither Harlan or Donna had come down to Percy's room in weeks.

"Hey, I think I should tell you something," Percy said, leaning back in his chair with his feet up on his desk. Bailey was splayed out on his bed with in an oversized sweater.

"What's that?"

"I think… I mean, I'm pretty sure, Dad's having an affair."

"Oh, yeah? Who is it this time?"

"Wait… what?"

"Oh, sorry. Did you think this was the first one?" Bailey was laughing. Not only was this not news to her, it wasn't even off putting.

"Are you serious?"

"Please. He's bedded more women here than that hotel downtown. What's that called?"

"The Red Lion?"

"Yeah, yeah. For sure. And I know every business trip is just an excuse for him to dick down some out-of-staters. He probably has other families somewhere."

"Wonder if he likes those kids."

"I don't know, is he even capable of that?"

"Do you think Mom knows?"

"They probably have some sort of arrangement."

"You think?"

"Yeah, you don't think she wants to fuck him anymore, do you? She doesn't want to risk losing the Van Allen name. Or she'll have to go back to being the girl from South Omaha, and working at the bowling alley. They were probably just staying together until we went off to school and they could fight over who gets the house."

"Simon really fucked that up, didn't he?"

Bailey rolled over and sat up on the bed. She no longer seemed interested in joking about their parents' possible divorce.

"So, who is it? You didn't say."

"Eli Sutton. She's…"

"Eli? I know who she is. From the office?"

"Yeah."

"Shit."

"What?"

"Nothing. I don't know. I shouldn't be surprised. It's not the first time he had a fling at work."

"For real? Who else?"

"How much time you got?"

"This whole thing is blowing my mind."

"Yeah, well. Merry Christmas from the Van Allens."

"We really are fucked up, aren't we?"

"You have no idea."

But he was starting to. It wasn't like he held his parents up as some paragons of virtue. He went to Catholic school because that's where his father went. They went to church because they had to be seen going to church. It wasn't like his parents ever talked about religion beyond that. His father's affair wasn't a betrayal of Harlan's persona, it was further example of it. Percy wasn't sure if he was upset, much less why. Was it because it had happened before. More than once according to his big sister.

Talking with Bailey didn't make him feel any better. He was happy to finally have someone to share the news with who might possibly understand, but Bailey seemed to have reached these conclusions about the family long before Percy got there. While he was excited to see that she was home, talking with her only seemed to further isolate Percy from his family. Well, from his parents at least.

* * * * *

There was no one in the office on Christmas Eve. Percy turned the alarm off himself and told Abby to meet him there. There was some reluctance on her part, but he finally convinced her. He said it would be quick, but he had to show her something. About the case. As long as he made it about the case, she was on board.

It was the missing check.

He first discovered it right before he discovered Eli and Harlan's affair. That occupied his brain space in the immediate aftermath and by the time he thought back on the check, he still wasn't sure what it meant, but it was complicated further with Harlan and Eli's relationship. He tried to explain to Abby what he found, but he muddled the details and thought it would be easier to show her.

The office was closed, and once he and Abby were in, he went into the security room to turn off the cameras. There were a few scattered around the office, and Percy wasn't sure what they were supposed to capture, but he didn't want to answer questions as to why they were at the office after hours, on a holiday no less.

They had made their way into Harlan's office, Percy knew where the key was, and he showed her the ledger with the note: 10/30-10k/BK, Eli dep.

"Did you ask anyone about this?" Abby asked.

"No. I went to ask Eli, but she wasn't in, because she was with my father in the stairwell. That's when I found them. What do you think it means?"

Percy watched Abby scrawl down the note in her notepad.

"I don't know. But it is a little curious."

"That's what I thought."

"I mean, it's just initials, right? It doesn't necessarily mean it was Bridget. I mean, it could be Burger King or Ben Kingsley."

"I'm sure my dad was writing a ten-thousand dollar check to Oscar winner Ben Kingsley."

"You should ask her."

"Eli?"

"Yeah, ask her about the check. Even if she doesn't know anything about it, her reaction to it, or to you asking might trigger something for her."

"You think she might tell me she's banging my dad?"

"No. Nothing like that. I don't know. But you have to ask her."

"Okay. But I won't be able to until we're back in the office on Monday. I can't just call her."

"I know."

Percy put the ledger back in the desk and straightened everything to how it was before. He moved towards Abby, but she kind of flinched when he approached.

"Is everything okay?"

"I'm just a little on edge."

"Yeah, this whole thing has got me kind of skeeved out."

"It's not just that."

"What?"

"My locker was broken into at school."

"What? Why? Did they take anything?"

"Yeah. It was…a book. Kind of."

"A book?"

"About Bridget. Well, from Bridget."

"You're not making any sense."

"I had a journal of Bridget's. And I was keeping it at school. And someone broke into my locker and took it."

"Wait, for real?"

"Yeah, except it wasn't exactly broken into. Someone must've known the combination."

"Did you tell anyone?"

"No."

"Then how do you know it was taken."

"Because it was there. And now it's not."

"Are you sure you didn't have it somewhere else?"

"Very sure. And it wasn't the only thing that was taken."

"What else?"

"Well, I had a notebook where we, me and Kira were keeping notes about this whole thing and, you know, suspects… and that's gone too."

"Are you sure Kira doesn't have it."

"No, I always kept it."

"Did anyone else know about it?"

"No, but…"

"But what?"

"It was after I talked to Mr. Sutton. And after I went to the police. It wouldn't be out of the realm of possibility that a teacher could get access to a locker without breaking into it. Or the police. They could've figured out who I was and gone in there. And no one knew about the journal and

I could get into real trouble if it gets out that I had it."

"It'll be okay, come on. How bad could it be?"

"If Mr. Sutton killed Bridget, and if he was willing to break into my locker. What else would he do?"

"Are you worried he might come after you?"

"I don't know. But…hey," Abby said as something seemed to click in her mind. "I have another question: how far back do those security tapes go?"

* * * * *

There was one VHS tape for every day of the month. It captured a screen that had a feed of six cameras: the main entrance, the back exit, Harlan's office, the HR office, and a wide view of the finance department.

"It only goes back a month," Percy said. "They record over the tapes."

"Yeah, but November only hath thirty days."

"Yeah, so."

"So, the tape from October 31st is still there, right?"

Percy grabbed the tape marked "31" and put it into the VCR. The timestamp in the corner showed "10/30 10pm."

"I guess they start the tape the night before when security goes home," Percy said as he looked at the feed on the big screen. Abby sat on the chair next to him and they began to watch together. The individual screens were kind of small on the screen so Percy flipped the setting to have a running scroll flipping through each camera view so each one appeared full frame. He used the knob to fast forward through the video and it started to move through about a minute at a time.

"You really know your way around a security machine," Abby said smiling at him.

"Yeah, a couple years ago one of the security guards was being nice to me and showed me how everything worked."

"You should thank him."

"Pretty sure my dad fired him for something."

"Such a swell guy. I'm glad the apple seems to have rolled down the hill a bit from that tree."

"What?"

"You don't seem like …never mind."

Percy and Abby were now locking eyes. She was smiling again. It was always hot and cold with her. When she was talking about the missing journal, Percy almost felt like she was going to accuse him of taking it, but now he felt a different vibe. It was in her eyes. She was looking at him, really looking at him, and actually seemed to see him. Percy didn't want to wait anymore.

Impulsively, he moved forward and kissed her. At first, just a peck. Then he rested his lips on hers. He pulled away slightly, enough to see that her eyes had closed. And he kissed her again. This time with intensity.

Her felt her hands on the back of his head, running through his hair as he slipped his tongue inside her mouth.

His right arm started to caress her shoulder and his left moved gently down her hip. She pulled back for a moment and they locked eyes again. They were both breathing heavy. She pushed him and straddled him on his chair. When he started to rub her legs, his penis immediately stiffened in his pants and he tried to shift so it wouldn't be too noticeable. Abby began to unbutton his shirt and kiss on his neck. Percy's eyes closed and he continued to kiss her more. She let out a little moan when he kissed her neck but then suddenly everything changed.

"No!" Abby shouted.

Abby jumped off him and Percy instantly held his hands out.

"Sorry, are you okay? I didn't mean…"

"I can't do this," Abby said, straightening her clothes and darting out of the room.

Percy leaned back. His shirt was askew and his hair mussed. He felt happy and strange and sad and confused. Did he do something wrong? He wanted to follow her, but he heard the front door close. Maybe he should let her be.

Percy turned back to the security system. The screen was still flipping through the evening of October 30th. It was now showing 11:17pm and Percy was surprised when he saw his father entering the office. He slowed the tape down to normal speed.

Percy hit the button to make the screen go back to showing all six camera views. He tracked his father walking in the front, past the HR office, and into his own. Harlan unlocked his desk drawer and pulled out the check ledger, scribbling a check and tearing it out of the book. He paused for a moment and then made a phone call. Percy wished there was audio on the security cameras, but it was only video. He watched his father hang up the phone and then turn and face out the window.

Percy fast-forwarded the tape, watching his father move about the office. Was he waiting for someone? About half an hour later, Harlan put the ledger back in the desk and locked it. He left his office and went to the lobby. Percy slowed the tape back to normal speed and switched the view to the front lobby only. He watched as his father opened the door.

And in walked Bridget Kent.

"What. The. Fuck?"

Harlan smacked the check down on the secretary's desk that sat at the entrance. Bridget grabbed it and seemed to examine it. They had words for each other, but Percy couldn't figure anything out. Bridget was upset, and Harlan appeared to be yelling, gesturing emphatically. And then, Bridget left.

With the check.

The day she died.

Well, there goes the Ben Kingsley theory. It was Bridget. But…why?

Why did Harlan write Bridget a check for ten thousand dollars in the first place? And why didn't Bridget seem that happy to get it? Percy wasn't sure what was going on, but he suddenly felt the urge to get the hell out of there as soon as possible.

He buttoned up his shirt. He took a deep breath before ejecting the security tape. He set it on the counter. He took the tape labeled 24, the tape from today, and rewound it to before he showed up. He recorded over everything from his entrance to walking into the security room and turning off the camera. Then, he pulled the actual tape out with a yank, severing it in two. He shoved the tape back into the VCR.

Security probably wouldn't be back until Monday morning. Maybe they would figure the tape was eaten, as VCRs were wont to do sometimes.

Percy grabbed the tape marked "31" and shoved into his coat, before erasing any evidence that he was ever in the building.

* * * * *

Percy arrived back at home, but sat in his car for a moment. He felt the tape in his jacket. He wanted to leave it in the car, not even take it in the house, but he was worried the cold could damage it. It would be fine, he thought. They weren't going to strip search him.

Percy opened the door and heard his family in the kitchen laughing, which had a weird echo in the hallway. He walked into see his mom and dad sitting on one side of the island while Bailey and Simon sat opposite. They were playing a board game. Monopoly? Really? At least it wasn't Clue.

"Hey, son, where've you been?" Harlan asked with a smile. It felt sincere, and yet still made Percy uncomfortable.

"Just had some running around."

"Someone left a card for you," Bailey said. "I threw it on your bed."

"Thanks."

"Come on, join us," Donna said, as if this was a perfectly normal occurrence. He can't remember the last time his family played a game together. Harlan waved him in as well, but all Percy could see was Harlan arguing with Bridget.

"Yeah, sure. I'll be right back."

* * * * *

Percy ran into his room and shut the door behind him. He saw a card with a red bow sitting on his bed. He looked around his room trying to think of a good hiding place, but was coming up empty. So, he thought maybe he should hide it in plain sight. He went to his shelf of movies grabbed Return of the Jedi. He pulled out the actual tape and threw it in the trash, burying it beneath papers and tissues. He could always buy it again if he really needed to see some Ewoks. He took the tape marked "31" and put it in the Jedi case.

Okay, that was it.

He wanted to call Abby. To tell her about this. But he didn't know what she would say. He wasn't even sure what he thought. He didn't know his father was having an affair. What if he was keeping something else secret? Could he actually have something to do with Bridget's death? And why was he giving her money in the first place?

Percy leaned back on his bed, forgetting the card that was there. He pulled it out from under him and tore the envelope open. It had his name written on the front, but no address or anything. Someone must've left it for him. It was a normal Christmas card, not signed, but inside was something else. It was a folded-up piece of paper. Percy unfolded it to see his name on top: Percy Van Allen – Suspect.

Below it was a list of notes: drug dealer? Lied about Bridget. Mysterious injury that weekend. Police questioned him. Richie Rich.

Percy didn't know what the last one meant, but the rest of the list made sense. It was from Abby's book. The one she mentioned getting taken from her locker. And something she failed to mention: he was on her list of suspects.

It was a photocopy. Whoever stole it wanted him to know there was still a copy out there. In all their talks, Percy never talked about dealing drugs, and he only alluded to his injury. Abby must've been keeping tabs on him the whole time.

Is this why she freaked out? Because she actually thought he killed Bridget and she was trying to, what, get him to confess or something?

"Percy, come on, you can be the thimble," Bailey shouted from upstairs.

Clearly she needed backup for dealing with their parents. Percy wasn't sure he could, but he forced himself to anyway.

"On my way," he shouted, as he took a deep breath.

He put the note in his drawer and pushed a fake smile onto his face. Everything was fine, he said to himself.

Everything was going to be fine.

26. ELI

"Thank you for seeing me on such short notice," Eli said, pulling the door closed behind her. She bolted into Dr. Gant's office, but didn't take a seat even when he offered it to her.

"You sounded distraught on the phone."

"I need to pace," she said. "I can't focus. I can't think. There's so many things going on. So many things. So many things. I don't even know where I would attempt to begin."

Dr. Gant sat behind his desk. Eli paced between the chair he usually sat in and the couch that was her territory. The block heels of her pumps dug into the thick, woven rug with every step. She hated that stupid rug. It was a blue and white weave, clearly set up to match the blue and white pillows on the couch, but the blues were off and the whole thing clashed. Clearly not anything designed by a woman.

"It's okay. Take a deep breath. Why don't you tell me what set you off? You were having a normal day and then?"

"A normal day? I can't even remember the last normal day I had."

"Okay, why don't you tell me about today?"

"I'm sorry. I'm fine. I'll be fine. This, this is what set me off. This is what is freaking me out."

Eli pulled out a small, white, plastic stick. There was a bright blue + sign on it.

"I'm pregnant."

"And this is not news you wanted?"

"Did I want this? Oh, god. Not like this. How do I answer that? Did I want this? A baby? A family? Of course. But this? Not really. I mean, I always thought I would have a family one day. Like, down the line. I know I'm almost thirty and most of my friends already have kids, that's just what you do, but it never felt like something I had to do right away. I got married right away. You know, I was twenty-four-years old. I'd been out of college, dating this guy and it's what you do. Danny was nice and sweet. And we had a great time together. Neither one of us particularly liked it here. But I started working for Harlan Van Allen, decent money. I was making way more than my friends. They were waitresses or working retail. No one had dreams to be anything other than here. This place, this city, it has a way of sucking you in and keeping you here. I should've gone away to school. I couldn't afford it. My parents died when I was young, and it was just me and Eric, my brother, and we made do with what we had. I don't resent that. I don't regret not going away. I wish I did, but it was fine. One day. I was going to leave one day. And then I met Danny. We talked about it. Leaving. Then I got a job. He got a job. He liked teaching. I never quite understood that. I couldn't wait to be done with high school, to put all of that behind me. And here's this guy, and he's back in that world, with its jocks and cheerleaders and popular and unpopular and everything, and he loves it. And he doesn't want to go. So, we get married. Not because we wanted to. I mean, of course I wanted to. But it was the thing you do, you know? You date a guy for a few years, you get married. You have kids. You buy a fucking house in the suburbs and talk about the weather and spend the next seventy years slowly dying every day."

Eli took another breath. She knew she was rambling, but it felt good to say these things. She'd been going to Dr. Gant for a couple years, ever since she and Danny first started having problems, but she wasn't ever really honest with him. Not like this.

"This is just one more reason to stay, right? This baby? That's all it is. I thought with everything going on, one of his students died and that really seemed to upset him, I thought that would make now a good time to push leaving again. Now, he might want to switch schools. Move to a city on the coast. By the water. Or in the Pacific Northwest with mountains. Just something, something different."

"And you don't think he would move?"

"I don't know. Part of me thinks he would do anything I asked. But another part of me thinks he wants out of this marriage every bit as much as I do. That's the problem. That's what I haven't been saying. Not to you. Certainly not to him. And not even really to myself. We shouldn't have gotten married. I know that now. I love Danny. I really do. I love his terrible jokes. And the weird hair on the back of his neck that I have to cut for him because he can't see it. I love him. But we weren't meant to be married. Good friends? Sure. But this is not the life I want. I do not want to be here."

"Do you think this pregnancy news means you are getting more stuck here?"

"I don't know. Not really. Yes and no. The thing is, it changes everything. In some way."

"That's what pregnancy does."

"Yeah, but not in the way you think," Eli said with a chuckle, even though her eyes were failing at holding back her tears.

"It's not his. Danny's. This is not his baby. I know it's not. I don't know if he will realize it. We really haven't been sleeping together at all, but we did a couple months ago and if I don't talk too much about the timing, he probably won't put it together. Can I do that? Can I lie to him? I honestly have no idea. That was my first thought, of course. That this baby would just be his baby, you know? It's an easy lie to sell. He's my husband. The real father doesn't want any more kids. I don't think he even wants a life with me. I can't even imagine a life with him. All of these things are just hitting me all at once. My period was late, I thought, I can't be pregnant. Not like this. I know I'm not on any birth control. I probably should be. I obviously should be, but what? I just go back on the pill now? And condoms? You think I'm going to convince a fifty-year-old man to start using condoms?

"So, yeah. This kid, is this the thing that might save my marriage? When has a kid ever really done that? And what kind of pressure is that to put on a kid? So, what, we divorce now? When I'm pregnant. I can't do this on my own. This I know. I am not built for that. I'm not one of those women that always dreamt of being a mom. I never had a good role model, you know. My mom wasn't bad. She tried. But she wasn't warm. She wasn't the bake cookies and talk about your problems kind of mom. When my dad died, that was tough. On all of us. He was a cop and died in the line of duty, as they say. He was shot. Some teenager. It was so stupid really. But I still remember the doorbell. It just sounded different. I was in the kitchen watching cartoons on this little TV. It was Saturday morning. He worked overnights sometimes. It wasn't strange that he didn't come home the night before but when I heard the doorbell, it sounded off somehow. I peeked out of the kitchen towards the front door and saw my mom let out this little shriek. There were two officers standing in the doorway and they just said, "I'm sorry." She knew right away. I think she always knew that it was going to happen. It's sort of the deal you make with yourself when you marry a cop. You know it's a possibility.

"After my dad died, that was kind of it for my mom. She was pretty much dying from that day forward. She got us to school on time, made sure we were fed, but she was never quite the same. Cancer got her. I was, like, nineteen, but she had been really sick all throughout high school. I think it did keep me from getting close to some people. I didn't ever want to have anyone over. My mom was always looking sick, coughing. I had gotten used to it, but I didn't want to have to explain it to someone. How shitty is that? I thought my mom being sick said something about me. So, obviously that had an effect. I knew I was never going to marry a cop. That's for sure. I never wanted to hear that doorbell again. I also know that I can't watch someone die. Not like that. Not every day for years. And yet, I still got involved with a man almost twice my age. While we are both married. He's not my first bad decision. But maybe the first one I'm stuck with.

"I know, I have options. I'm sure that's what my friends would say if they knew the whole story. I have options. But I really don't know. I have nothing against abortion. Freedom of choice and all that, but it's not for me. Not now. Maybe when I was younger. When I knew I couldn't deal with it. Or knew it would completely derail my life. Not now, when it's an inconvenience, sure. But not something I can't figure out. I figured out how to make a marketing degree work for a finance job. This is nothing compared to that. It's all just happening so fast."

Eli's thoughts were racing, but she had slowed down in her talking. She no longer felt manic like she did when she first walked in. She sat down finally. She smiled at Dr. Gant, looking him in the eye for the first time in the session.

"I'm sleeping with my boss. Harlan. He's the father of my baby. I wasn't going to say anything when I came here. Couldn't risk it getting out, you know, but I know you can't say anything. I was also worried about what you would think of me. How screwed up is that? I felt like such an adult coming here, talking about my problems in my marriage, my lack of trust, my inability to trust, and I'm really just in some pedestrian soap opera. I haven't told anyone. Not a soul. About me and Harlan. I know that's part of why it felt so good to be with him. Because it was something that was just mine. I know I told you months ago that I was thinking of other men, of being with other men, but it had already started before that. We were out of town at some conference. Of course. Everything about it is so trite and typical. I'm sleeping with my boss. My married boss. I'm pregnant with my married boss' baby. What a god damned cliché.

"I can't even begin to think of what I would tell Harlan. I feel like he would be mad at me. Like it's entirely my fault. But I mean, you should see the kids he has now. If I had those kids I wouldn't want any more either. Certainly not with some woman that wasn't my wife. I think he would want me to go away. He hates his family, never really has anything nice to say about them, certainly not his wife. She's such a shrew. And yet, I know he's never gonna leave her. She represents something. Something I will never be. With all of her projects and boards and shopping for the latest fall styles and always wearing the best suits and having the best hair. I don't want to be Harlan's wife. Ever. I want to be Harlan. I want to be the one in charge. The one calling the shots. The one that walks into a room and everyone shuts up. I don't want to be close to power. I want to have the power. And I'm not in a bad position. Not that I think Harlan would ever want to put a woman in charge, but I am the youngest department head. I could advance at this company and become one of the youngest vice presidents at least, before moving on to some other organization. Take over as CEO. It won't happen now, of course. Women that sleep with the boss seldom win in the long run. I know that. I knew that going into it, and yet I still let it happen. Let it happen, I pretty much seduced him. Sure, he probably would've made a move at some point. I know I'm not even the first woman at the office that has been in this position. But that night, at that hotel bar in Chicago, it was me. I made the first move. I had a fight with Danny on the phone and I just decided I wanted some other man's arms around me. And I chose Harlan.

"We swore it wouldn't continue. Couldn't continue. Someone would find out. We've been careful. For the most part. I don't think sneaking off for a hotel tryst in the afternoon is really something people won't pick up on at some point. There is evidence now. I paid cash for a hotel room at two o'clock on a Tuesday. He couldn't do it. Someone might recognize him. But all that running around, sneaking around, cheating on Danny, betraying him with someone he doesn't even like. I'm not sure I even like Harlan. But I like being with him. He makes me feel sexy. And wanted. All things I'm sure a baby will really help.

"No. I'm not going to tell him. As far I'm concerned, as far as the world is concerned, this is Danny's baby. I can break it off with Harlan. Shit, we talk about breaking it off every time we're together. 'We can't do this anymore' one of us inevitably says, still naked and sweaty. So, yeah, I can break it off with Harlan. We can both go back to our lives. He can find some other young woman in the office to be his side piece and I can go back to Danny, pregnant with his child. Which brings me back to the beginning. What does that mean for us? For me and Danny?

"Do I tell him I'm pregnant, assuming he doesn't pay attention to a calendar, and see if this is even news that excites him? Do I use this as an excuse to leave? Start over. Maybe Danny would even go with me. Not that I'm sure I want that. Not now. Not the way things are but a new place, new city, new child, maybe that would help us. Maybe that would be a spark that could reignite the flame of our marriage. I know it's silly, but what do I honestly think is possible? We're not going to get divorced when I'm pregnant. Maybe a year or two down the line when he realizes we probably aren't meant to be together. Maybe he even realizes it now, but he's too good. He wouldn't leave me when I'm pregnant. That's too much.

"And it's not like he's perfect. He very well could be cheating on me too. I know that. I've told you that before. If nothing else, his mind has been somewhere else for a while. Oh, I didn't even tell you this part. You know his student, the one that died? There's something about her and him. Something I don't know the whole story about. It had been a thing with him even before she died. He seemed particularly fixated on this girl. Not in a sexual way. I don't think. I think if that were the case he wouldn't have told me about her in the first place. He said she was having problems at home and he was trying to help but there's only so much a teacher can do, you know? But it weighed on him. It would come up at weird times. When we were in bed. His student. We would fight about it, but he swore it was just concern. And then she died. What am I supposed to do with that? I can't say anything bad about her now. Especially because she killed herself. He's worried about this girl and she kills herself and he can't think of anything else. And for a while that was fine. It's tragic. I'm not saying it's not. But she's gone. And I'm here. And he doesn't care. And even if he did, I don't know that it would make a difference now. And he says it's nothing. It never was anything, but then I found it."

"Found what?"

"Yesterday, I was looking for a pen. And…okay, that's a lie. I'm trying to be honest here, so I'm just going to be honest. I went through his stuff. How great is that? I'm the one cheating. I'm the one that betrayed him and it has just made me all the more mistrustful. I cheated so I don't trust him. And I went into his briefcase. He has this old leather briefcase he takes into school every day. I don't know why, I think he likes the way it makes him look, but it really doesn't feel right for a high school teacher. Maybe an English professor. But anyway, he lugs this thing back and forth, and it has files and books and everything, but he doesn't ever use it, you know? He walks in the door and throws in on the chair in the dining room, and then picks it up the next day and slings it over his shoulder. It just feels like it's all for show. So, I pretend I have to look for a pen. I just want an excuse to dig through it. Sue me. And I'm seeing files with grades and stuff, stupid shit that he does not need to be transporting back and forth. And there's a book, but not the one that he's reading, the one that he keeps by his bed every night and flips through when I'm trying to sleep. No, this is a handwritten diary type thing. Only it's a mess. Frayed edges. Pages have been torn out. And so, I start reading it. I know I shouldn't. It's none of my business, but I think it's harmless, right? Some lovesick teenage girl… with a crush on her teacher. It was a journal. That Bridget, the dead girl, it was hers. Why did he have it?"

"Did you ask him?"

"Of course, I asked him. And no, probably not in the most constructive way, but I was curious. And angry. Why did he have this? Sure, he first started yelling and ranting about me going through his things. We had to fight about that. But once we got through that, I asked him again. Why do you have this? How did you even get this? He said someone left it for him. On his desk. No note. Nothing. He didn't want to leave it at school, not until he knew for sure who sent it to him."

"Do you believe him?"

"I don't know. That's the thing. I always trusted him implicitly. He would never lie to me. Then I started lying to him. And now I don't trust him. I know we've had our problems, and it's been a rollercoaster this year, but with Christmas and New Year's and everything, we were actually getting along. We felt more simpatico, you know? It may have been a show, presenting a good marriage for my brother and his family, who, let me tell you, are going through their own thing right now. But Danny and I were at least getting along. It didn't take much to get us to fight this year. Seemed like every little thing would lead to some spat. He didn't like my perfume. I didn't like him leaving his socks on the floor. Stupid stuff like that. But here come the holidays and we're opening presents and kissing at midnight, and even though I know it's all an act, that we've got something going on we have to figure out. It still felt a little better. But then I find this journal and it all comes back, you know? And I'm yelling and he's yelling and it's all back to that. He didn't come home last night. I know burying the lede with that one. I'm rambling on about pregnancy and my affair and I'm not a hundred percent sure that my husband hasn't already left me.

"I know that's probably why I was so freaked out to begin with. I expected him to leave, blow off some steam and come back and we'd be back in our status quo. All this time I've been thinking about me leaving him. My choice. My action. And then he runs out the door and I go to bed alone. He probably spent the night at his buddy's house. But I'm not gonna call him. He can call me. So, when I woke up this morning, he's still not there. And I'm still late. I'm like never late. It's a thing. I'm like right there on track. The first month, I was like, it's stress. All the running around. The lying. The fighting. Everything with this student. Okay. I missed a month. I made sure to sleep with him then. Just in case. I mean, I had an idea, but denial is really easy sometimes. So, I waited. Put it out of my mind. And kept pretending everything was normal. And then I took another test. Last week. One of those at home things. This one I showed you. Then I called my doctor.

"My appointment was this morning and she confirmed everything. Even the number of weeks. And math has always been my strong suit. It didn't take much to count back and realize that Harlan was the only one I had been with around the time of conception. I went home, not sure what to do. Didn't matter. Danny still hadn't come home. My mind started jumping around. And that's when I called you. That's when I came here."

"That's a lot to get off your chest. Does it help?"

"I don't know. I guess. Talking it out, saying these things, finally, admitting all of these things. It helps. I know, what a shock."

"So, talking helps. Keep going. What are you going to do about this?"

The question hung in the air there for a moment. Eli wasn't sure how to answer. It was enough to admit everything in the first place. To actually figure out what to do was a whole other thing. She continued to talk. Once the floodgates opened, she found it easy to keep going. To admit her feelings about everything, her husband, Harlan, this baby. It felt good to say all of these things. To declare them out loud, especially to someone who was legally bound not to share the information. But it didn't make it any easier to think about what would happen next, or even admit what she wanted to happen next.

* * * * *

Eli had gone to the store, a little gift market near the donut shop. She'd suddenly had a craving. She bought a little gift box, one that was probably meant for a pen, ironic, she thought, since the imaginary pen was what started their fight in the first place. She picked out a ribbon. She went with gold. She wanted blue, but that felt a little too on the nose. And blue and pink had specific connotations in these situations.

She got home and put the pregnancy test in the box, surrounded by tissue paper so it wouldn't float around. She wrapped the box in silver wrapping paper she had bought for some anniversary gift for Robbie and Eric last year. Maybe it was the whole New Year's glow. It was 1993 now. New beginnings. She was careful to make sure the edges were perfect and didn't use too much tape. She tied the gold ribbon around the box and frayed the edges. The package looked perfect, like it had been wrapped by one of the old ladies in the mall they also brought on at Christmastime. She put the box in her purse.

In her head, Eli thought about giving the box to Harlan. It was his child after all. But she played out that scenario to its inevitable conclusion and it ended with her hurt and alone and out of a job. No, this was the right thing to do. This was the right step. She and Danny had their issues, she wasn't lying to herself about that anymore. But she was starting to enjoy the idea of a child, and this was going to be Danny's child. It may not have his eyes or his chin, but it was going to have his love.

This was the step that their marriage needed. She was going to end things with Harlan. She was going to forget everything about that stupid journal. She was going to tell Danny they were going to have a baby and then she was going to talk to him about moving. Maybe to Denver or Indianapolis. It didn't matter where. Just somewhere different where they could start over, the three of them. She'd want to be close to Eric. He was the only family she had. But so long as they could drive the distance in a few hours it would be fine.

She put on a nice dress. It was still winter, but she wasn't actually going out, so she opted for a dark blue polka-dotted number that she usually wore in summer, but she finished with a cardigan sweater so it looked more in season. She put on make-up and did her hair. Maybe this was the problem, she had stopped putting in the effort. She looked in the mirror, happy with how she looked.

She wanted to make dinner, but there was only so much she could do. It was already past seven o'clock, and maybe he would eat before he came home. That didn't need to be part of the whole plan. One thing at a time. In the back of her mind, it was starting to creep up on her that maybe he wasn't going to come home again. But he just wouldn't do that to her. One night, sure. That's allowed. But he was going to have to come back sooner than later.

The doorbell rang.

It was him. The thought made Eli smile, even though she knew it was strange that he would ring the doorbell. This was his house too. They could talk through that. They were going to get a new house with their new life and their new family in the new city.

Eli opened the door and was surprised to see two policemen standing in front of her. Their car was in the driveway, the red and blue lights still waving.

"Elizabeth Sutton?"

"It's Eli, yes."

"I'm afraid we have some bad news. There's been an accident, a car accident. Involving your husband, Daniel," the first policeman said.

Eli didn't quite register everything at first. He got in an accident. Okay. He probably had too much to drink and got in a fender bender and slept it off in jail. Of course.

"What kind of accident? What happened? Is he okay?"

"He was driving and it appears that he hit an ice patch and his car swerved off the road, and into a tree."

Both policemen looked stern. Afraid to make an expression. The old one that was talking had a mustache that appeared to be three different colors. But the young one, the one that looked barely older than Danny's students, finally spoke.

“I’m sorry, ma’am, but I’m afraid he’s gone. He died.”

“I’m sorry, what?” Eli was sure she misheard that.

27. ABBY

She didn't want to go back to school. It felt wrong. Everything had gone to shit over the break. Abby was still upset for freaking out on Percy. He finally stopped calling, but she wouldn't know how to explain even if he did get through. She liked him. She could admit that. But she also knew he lied to her. A lot. And then Kira was being weird. She didn't believe Abby when she said Bridget's journal and the suspect book was stolen. Kira ended all involvement with their "investigation," such as it was. It didn't matter anyway; Mr. Sutton was gone.

Abby still had trouble believing that. Mr. Sutton died. They say it was a car wreck, but there were already rumors that he drove into that tree on purpose. Abby heard it from Breck, who heard it from Sandi, whose dad was an EMT. Breck didn't believe it, because she had seen Mr. Sutton over break and he was happy and normal. He was married to Scott's aunt, Eli, and they saw each other around Christmas. But Breck didn't know what Abby knew.

Abby knew that there was something between Mr. Sutton and Bridget. Abby hinted at that to Mr. Sutton herself. Abby knew that she gave the cops a heads-up as well. Abby knew that Mr. Sutton's wife was cheating on him and that she thought he was cheating on her. Did the cops confront him? Did Eli break it off? Was he guilty because of what Abby said? Any number of things could have happened to send Danny off the edge, literally speaking. And all of it was Abby's fault.

Everything she touched turned to crap. She was like the worst version of Midas. Abby knew one thing. She was done with all of it. She was done with Mr. Sutton. And Bridget. She was done with Percy; he wouldn't want her anyway if he knew what she knew. She was done with her family. Done with Breck and Kira. She wanted to be done with St. Dymphna's, but there was no way she could convince her mom to go to another school in the middle of the year. She would have to stick it out this last semester and then maybe a transfer out west.

Abby was done being Abby. She didn't want to look like Abby any more. She quit wearing her contacts and pulled out the dark-rimmed glasses she hadn't worn in a couple years. She dyed her hair black and straightened her out-of-control curls. Cut off a few inches. Her hair was now a straight bob that was above her shoulders. She still had to wear the uniform, but she opted for thick fishnet stockings and dark boots that went up to her knees. It took her forever to tie the laces, but the thick heel made her a couple inches taller.

As she walked into Dymps, she could feel the looks. Maybe they thought she was a new girl. No one really knew her before anyway. She ignored everyone and just went to her locker, and shoved the thick, black canvas jacket she stole out of the bottom of Jake's closet in there. He quit wearing it last year so she didn't think he'd care. Or notice. And she knew all of his hiding places. The jacket tied her new look together, and if Jake got mad later, so be it.

Abby made it through two periods without talking to anyone, other than alerting teachers that she was, in theory, present. Her mind was always elsewhere. During her free period, she went down the hall to Mr. Sutton's office. The desk had been cleared of all books and other things, but there were flowers and cards that other students must have placed there. It only made Abby feel worse. Even if he did have something to do with Bridget's death, she didn't want this. Not without knowing the truth. She wanted him to admit what he did and then to go to jail. It wasn't fair that he could just end it all like this and still leave behind an adoring fan club of students and teachers that had no idea what a scumbag he was.

Or might've been.

That's what bothered Abby the most. That she still wasn't sure. She was pretty sure. The evidence was there. Well, at least it was until someone stole the journal. Now, it was just her saying what she read without any proof. Kira already didn't believe her about what Bridget wrote about Vanessa. What if she was wrong? What if everything she stirred up pushed him over the edge and he had nothing to do with anything? All she really knew was that Bridget had a crush on a teacher. And because Abby stuck her nose where it didn't belong, Mr. Sutton was gone.

Abby stared at Mr. Sutton's desk. She remembered their confrontation and how differently it went from how she wanted it to go. Now, what was she supposed to do? Just forget everything and go back to normal? What was normal anyway?

"Hey," a voice called out and Abby turned to see Percy standing there. He had his school sweater tight over his shirt, almost like he grew over break. His lips kind of crinkled into a smile, but it was like he forced it to stop. "I like your hair."

"Hi," Abby said.

"Pretty weird, huh?" He said nodding to Mr. Sutton's desk.

"I can't do this," Abby said. "Not right now."

"Abby, wait," Percy called after her but she jumped into the girl's bathroom, where he wouldn't follow her. Abby walked to the end and slammed the stall door shut. The bell was going to ring soon, and Abby didn't want to see if Percy was waiting for her outside, so she decided to stay who knows how long. She could skip English.

Unfortunately, the last thing Abby wanted was to be alone with her thoughts. She had to believe that Mr. Sutton was guilty because otherwise she got an innocent man killed. And while she believed that he did something to Bridget, she couldn't deny that there were other possibilities: Vanessa, in some violent outburst. And yes, even Percy. She didn't believe that, but she couldn't ignore that it was a possibility. She couldn't think of a motive. Didn't want to. But she couldn't deny it was possible.

Abby stared at her watch and wished that it would move faster. She really wanted this day to be over.

* * * * *

Abby walked through the mall with a little more effort than it took to walk to her classes. The new Walkman she got for Christmas was coming in handy as she had her headphones on and the sad melodies of Toad the Wet Sprocket were blaring in her ears. She could see other girls in small groups giggling and gossiping as they hopped from store to store. Abby both envied them and was grateful she wasn't with them.

She wanted friends, wanted to feel a part of something, but really didn't like or understand girls her own age. They seemed so fixated on unimportant things: boys mostly. But they probably weren't dealing with the idea that they could've gotten someone killed.

Abby wandered around the mall without ever going into any stores. She watched from the windows and sipped on her pop while listening to the music. It was helping her zone out. Outside of the Younkers, the cornerstone of the east side of the mall, Abby fixated on a mannequin with a bright pink, sleeveless pantsuit. The mannequin had her arms angled on hips and looked skyward. Abby thought she looked regal. Powerful. It was the complete opposite of her current look, and the slouched shoulders that she couldn't seem to shake. She tried to imagine herself wearing something like this. And holding such a powerful pose but her brain couldn't make it work.

She was so focused that she didn't notice, at first, the hand waving in front of her face. Abby focused to see Breck gesticulating. She pulled her headphones down.

"Earth to Abby," Breck said. "Oh my god, you were so someplace else. I like wasn't even sure it was you at first but it totally is. Wow. I'm digging the new look. It's very, I don't know, Shakespears Sister."

"Hi, Breck."

"Are you okay?"

"Yeah."

"No, I mean really. Never mind the new look, but you seem kind of out of it."

"Just a lot going on. You know, Mr. Sutton. How's Scott and everyone?"

"I think they're still in shock. Scott isn't really saying much but I don't get the feeling they were that close. But still, gnarly accident."

"Yeah."

"Is that what's got you all broody and dark?"

"I'm not broody and dark."

"You might want to tell that to your hair. But you've been like this for weeks. Every time I call you seem distracted. I mean, are you like still mad at me? I thought we talked through that."

"No, I'm not mad at you. It's not about you."

"Then what's it about? Come on, Abby, you can talk to me."

Abby pulled Breck onto a nearby bench, where no one walking by was likely to overhear them.

"Okay, fine. Look, I'm tired of this anyway. Remember you found me with all that stuff on Bridget at the library?"

"For your yearbook story?"

"Yeah. Only I'm not doing a yearbook story."

"Then what are you doing?"

"I don't think Bridget killed herself."

"What?"

"And the police weren't looking into it, and there were just so many things pointing to something else happening."

"Signs? What kind of signs?"

"Look, I can't get into this right now. But Kira and I were trying to see if—"

"You and Kira? Since when are you guys friends?"

"We're not. Not really. But she was helping and—"

"And you didn't want to talk to me about it?"

Abby couldn't tell if Breck was hurt or angry. And it didn't really matter. It did feel good to finally talk about it.

"I'm sorry. I wanted to, but the more people that knew we were looking into it, the more trouble we could get into."

"So, who do you think did it?"

"I don't know, that's not an easy question to answer."

"Well, I mean, you have to have some theories right?"

"There's a lot of things you don't know. It's not that simple."

"What kind of things? This is too weird."

"I know. And I'm sorry I'm just dumping this on you. But this whole thing has just been freaking me out."

"Yeah, I'm sure. But you really think Bridget didn't kill herself?"

"No. Or yes. Someone did this to her."

"Oh, wait, you don't think Javi had something to do with this, do you?"

"No. Not really. I mean, I haven't really talked to him."

"Then who?"

"It's complicated, but before he died there were some thoughts…"

"You think Scott's uncle had something to do with this? No way. No. That's not possible."

"I don't know anything for sure."

"Well, he didn't."

"How do you know?"

"I don't know. I just can't see it."

Abby understood that feeling. It's how she felt about Percy. She wanted to tell Breck everything. Tell her about Vanessa. And all the affairs. But just thinking about it she didn't know where to begin. Bridget had a crush on a teacher, but never mentioned it again. She was dating a boy she wasn't sleeping with, and slept with a rich kid that she wasn't dating, but she broke it off with that one to begin another secret relationship which may or may not have been the aforementioned teacher. It was a lot. And Breck would certainly put it together that Percy was the rich kid. She didn't want to think about what Breck would do with that info.

"Look, please don't tell Scott about this."

"I wouldn't. I don't think he would take this very well."

"I didn't mean to lay all this on you. And I swear, I will tell you everything but I can't right now. There's just something else I have to take care of."

"Right now?"

"Yeah, I really have to go."

Abby hugged Breck quickly before returning to her car and working up the urge to do what she should've done weeks ago.

* * * * *

The house was massive. The front entryway felt bigger than Abby's driveway. The tile was pristine white and echoed with even the softest step. Donna had given Abby a look that Abby interpreted as mistrust or disgust when she opened the door. Nothing good. Abby still smiled.

"Is Percy home?"

She waited in the entryway, alone, while Mrs. Van Allen disappeared down a hallway. Abby had a perfect view of the living room to the right, the dining room to the left, and a staircase leading to what was easily another wing of the mansion. She could already feel herself chickening out. When she went to confront Mr. Sutton, she couldn't get the words out. But this was different. This was Percy. And if she didn't ask him, she would never let herself kiss him.

And she really wanted to kiss him again.

"Hey," he said, when he came from another corner she didn't even realize existed.

"Hey," she smiled, even though it went against everything she was telling herself. "We need to talk."

"Come on downstairs."

She followed him down. He was wearing a plain t-shirt and sweatpants. He looked like any other kid her age, even though he wasn't anything like them.

"Did you kill Bridget?" she thought to herself, trying to will the words to come from her mouth. They didn't. He showed her into a small living room area and sat on the brown leather chair and motioned for her to sit on the couch.

"It's kind of a mess," he said. "I broke the coffee table a while back and my parents still haven't got a new one. Guess they got busy with other things."

"I can imagine."

They sat there nodding at each other. Abby thought it was weird to be alone with him. What if he was a murderer? Was she in danger? His mom was upstairs. Surely he wouldn't risk anything. If something did happen with Bridget, and Abby still couldn't get there fully, but if it did, it surely had to have been an accident. Right?

"Did you need something?" Percy finally asked.

"Sorry," Abby said. "Actually, that's part of why I came here. I wanted to apologize for, you know, the last time I saw you. Running out like that. I didn't mean to."

"It's okay."

"No, it's not. It's just, I don't know, it was happening so fast."

"It's okay. I don't ever want you to feel uncomfortable around me. If I did anything to make you feel that way, I'm sorry."

"Stop it, okay? Just stop being so nice to me."

"Why wouldn't I be nice to you?"

"Because I don't deserve it."

"I don't know who put that into your head, but you deserve anything that will make you happy. I know there's a lot going on and maybe it was the wrong moment, but I'm not sorry I kissed you. I wanted to kiss you. I'm sorry if I scared you or pushed too hard, or if I misunderstood the signals. I just felt like we were…connecting. You know?"

"I can't do this."

Abby stood up. She couldn't look Percy in the eye.

"No, please. Don't run out again. Just talk to me. Okay? I promise I won't do anything."

Abby felt like crying. She felt this tangle in her stomach that was a mishmash of want and affection, and then this alarm in her head that kept shouting that he might be a killer. But then, in a way, so was she.

"Did you find anything on the tapes? After I left?" Abby said, relenting. She sat back down.

Percy didn't answer right away. He kind of let out a weird sigh.

"Sorry, is it okay to ask about this? Your parents can't hear us, can they?"

"No, don't worry. They're practically in another zip code upstairs. Besides, we'd hear the door open and the steps creak if they even thought about coming down."

"So, was there anything on the tapes?"

"Nothing really. What about you? Now that Mr. Sutton's, you know, dead, is this whole thing over?"

"I want it to be. I wish it was. But I'm not a hundred percent sure."

"So, you're not giving up?"

"Not until I know for certain. No matter what I find."

"Yeah. I get that. Um, hang on a sec."

Percy got up and walked out of the room. He went down a hallway. Abby heard a door open, and after a few seconds he came right back in. He was holding a wrapped package. It was red and green, with a gold bow.

"I got this for you. I mean, I wanted to give it to you before Christmas, but then… you know."

"Percy, you really didn't… I mean, this is… I can't."

"Open it, please. If you don't want it, that's fine, but just open it."

He handed the package to Abby. It was a box, about the size of a really thick book, but heavier. She undid the bow and tore open the paper. The brown box beneath was nondescript so she ripped open the side and lifted the lid. It looked like an electric razor. About eight inches long, metallic black, with prongs at one end and a grip with a red button.

"I don't…"

"It's a stun gun," he said. "I figured if you kept digging around this you might get into something dangerous, and with your penchant for lying to cops, and stealing files from doctor's offices, who knows what other shit you could get into. I just wanted you to be safe. And it's not exactly legal, but it's safer and better than having a real gun, I guess."

"I don't know what to say. This is so strange, and so sweet. I don't think anyone has ever cared so much about what happened to me before."

"Look, no pressure or anything. Like I said, I just want you to be safe. I know what's out there."

"Because you're a drug dealer?"

Abby's words hung there for a moment. The sincerity in Percy's eyes kind of softened. He didn't seem angry, more sad.

"I guess I couldn't expect that to stay quiet forever."

"Guess not."

"I should've told you. I know. I just didn't want you to think less of me. I know that's stupid, but I care what you think."

"It's not stupid. But with all that's going on, the more I know the better."

"I wanted to tell you. The truth is I got rid of everything when the whole thing went down with Bridget. I haven't done anything since. I swear. Well, okay I did some stuff for Scott, but he got some other shit somewhere that put him in the hospital. I had nothing to do with that."

"Wait. What?"

"Oh shit. I thought with you and Breck being friends that you knew all this."

"I had no idea. What did Scott buy off of you?"

"Over the years, a ton of stuff. He was mostly into speed."

"Over the years? How long has this been a thing?"

"Well, since we were sophomores at least."

"I didn't even know that you knew him."

"Yeah, well, discretion is part of the job."

"Oh my god, this blows my mind."

"Yeah, that dude is fucked up. I thought I was wound tight."

"Does Breck know?"

"I have no idea. I told Javi I wasn't gonna say anything to anyone."

"Javi knows?"

"I think he was worried about him. He came at me all agro but I told him I was out and that Scott must've found another resource."

Abby shook her head. This was a lot of information coming at her. What did this mean? And what did Breck know?

"I can't believe you didn't say anything about this until now."

"Well, you didn't really ask. And I wasn't exactly trying to shine a light on my prior criminal history. Besides, this doesn't have anything to do with Bridget. Does it?"

"I have no idea. But I think I know someone that might."

* * * * *

Everybody lies. Everybody had secrets. That's what Abby was taking away from all of this. Percy had lied to her. She had lied to him too. Scott was a liar. A big one. Abby thought she had things figured out, but she really only had a few pieces of the puzzle. There was something about Scott's deception that felt off to her. She wanted to rush over to Breck, but could she trust what answers she would give?

Abby had a different target in mind: Javi.

He knew things he wasn't sharing. About Scott. What else was he hiding? Given that Bridget was dating him, however hollow that relationship was, it put him right in the middle of this. There had to be more.

Abby kept the stun gun. It was thoughtful, sure, but it also made Abby feel safe. Maybe she wasn't any safer than she was without it, but if she had it when she confronted Mr. Sutton, maybe she would've been more direct. And gotten more answers. Abby felt the stun gun in the pocket of her coat. She rubbed her finger along the grip. It was cold.

Percy had showed her how to use it, and she kept it with her at all times. She wanted to confront Javi that night, but decided against it. It was late. She parked outside his house, maybe a block away and sat there for hours while she watched him and his family come and go.

There was something exhilarating about watching someone that didn't know they were being watched. They carried themselves differently. People seldom looked around to actually see what was right around them, or in this case, a house down and across the street. She sat in her front seat and scrunched down whenever someone came or went. But they never looked her way.

She went back the next night.

Tonight was her third night. She still hadn't seen anything that gave her any particular insight into Javi and his family, other than there was an enormous amount of them. She kept notes as to when Javi and his brothers would come and go in case there was any pattern worth exploring. It was after ten when she saw Javi emerge from the front door. He put a hood up and walked up the hill, away from where Abby was parked. Her car was running, it was cold out, so she waited until he was far enough away and she turned her lights on and pulled out.

He turned a corner and then walked towards the 7-11 parking lot. Abby turned her lights off and parked across the street, where she could continue to watch him. He walked into the shop, lingered at the soda fountain for a moment before grabbing a bottle from the refrigerator case, and took it up to the register. Another car pulled into the parking lot. Abby crouched lower in her car. She recognized the boy in the new car. It was Trevor. Javi's cousin.

Javi came out of the store and got into Trevor's car. Abby could see the way Javi smiled when he looked at Trevor. And then it all made sense.

* * * * *

"He's not your cousin, is he?" Abby said, startling Javi.

She followed the two boys to the university library downtown. Her car was illegally parked, but she could deal with a ticket later. She had followed them inside and sat at a nearby table, ducking behind a book so she could watch them. They appeared to be studying, but there was a playfulness between them. Abby was almost jealous.

Abby waited until Trevor excused himself and went into the bathroom before walking over and talking to Javi.

"Abby? Jesus, I didn't even recognize you. That's quite a new look."

"Yeah, we can talk about that, or we can talk about what's going on with you two."

"What? There's nothing going on. We're studying. I told you, he's my cousin."

"Yeah, you can keep saying that, but he's going to come back soon and if you don't want me to make an enormous scene, you'll leave a note saying you'll be right back and you'll come over here and talk to me."

Abby pulled Javi into a long row of books that stood twice as tall as she was.

"What is going on? What are you even doing here?" he asked.

"Never mind that. I need information from you."

"On what?"

"On Scott."

"What about him?"

"Tell me about his little drug habit."

"What? I'm not telling you shit."

"You could play it that way. And then I guess I could just ask him about you and your cousin over there. I'm assuming your best friend knows about your study buddy, right?"

"What?"

"Look, I don't want to blow up your spot here. This is your business and none of mine. I know that. And I want you to trust me. But I have nothing else I can use to get you to trust me. So, please. Just tell me what I want to know and I swear I will go back to pretending I don't know about you and him. Because, Javi, it's really okay, you know?"

"What do you want to know?"

"I want to know about Scott."

"What about him?"

"How long has he been using?"

"Using what?"

"You know what I'm talking about."

"I know, but I don't know the details. I know that he was on coke or something like that when he had his episode at the football game. I know that he's still on whatever he's on because he's not at all himself. But that's all I know. I told Breck everything I know."

"So, Breck does know?"

"Yeah. I figured she told you."

"No. She didn't."

"Then what are you.."

"It doesn't matter. Look, I'm sorry. I know that you and Bridget had your issues."

"Abby, real talk, you don't know shit about me and Bridget."

"I think I know a little more than most people." Abby motioned her head back in the direction of the table Javi was sitting at. "Also, I found Bridget's journal."

"Wait, you had her journal. Did you send me that page? That's fucked up."

"What page? What are you talking about?"

"I came home the other night and there was a copy of a page from Bridget's journal. How she didn't love me."

"I know the one. But, no, I didn't send it. Someone stole the journal from me. When did you get it?"

"I don't know, last week sometime."

"Was it before or after Mr. Sutton died?"

"Before I think. Why?"

"I don't know. Look, is it possible that Scott knew something about his uncle? That maybe he was helping him cover it up. Were they close at all?"

"Cover up what? What are you talking about?"

"I don't know. The suicide. Or supposed suicide. Look, Javi, I don't think Bridget killed herself."

"Yeah, Breck told me that too."

"Well, Breck doesn't know everything I do. Okay? I know that Bridget was sleeping with someone new. Someone she didn't want anyone finding out about. I know you don't want to hear this, but it wasn't the first time she cheated on you."

"There was more than one guy?"

"Yeah. And we found a pregnancy test in her stuff. And I know you and her never, you know. I know you couldn't be the father."

“What does this have to do with Scott?”

“Maybe nothing. But his uncle did know something. And maybe Scott knows what that is.”

“What is going on here?”

Abby and Javi both turned to see Trevor standing there.

“Oh, nothing, we were just talking,” Javi responded.

“Yeah, I’m surprised you didn’t get shushed. Jesus H. Tapdancing Christ, the whole floor could hear you just talking. Woah, like what the holy hell? You’re the girl from the theater. Are you stalking us?”

“No, I… it doesn’t matter anymore. Javi, I’ll talk to you later.”

Something about what Trevor said triggered something in Abby. He didn’t say it meanly, or even aggressively, but there was something about how he said it. Abby could hear Javi calling back to her but she ignored it as she left the library.

She had to get home.

* * * * *

Abby went digging in her closet. She hadn’t used her Walkman since she got her new one, but she needed the cassette player. She locked her door. She didn’t know why, no one else was even home, but she wanted to feel safe. She plugged her headphones in. She still had her coat on, and the stun gun still in her pocket.

She pulled the cassette out of the case she had hid it in and put in the Walkman. She knew the time by heart, she had listened to it over and over again. That’s why it sounded so familiar, what Trevor had said. She fast-forwarded it until she could find the right spot.

It was the night Bridget died. The 911 call log. Before each call there was a note on the time. She went to one thirty-seven in the morning.

The clocks turned back that night, so the log actually had two different one-o-clock hours. Before and after the clocks changed at 2am to go back to 1.

Abby found the clip she was looking for and hit play.

"There's a body," the voice said nervously, rushed and spastic. "At the party. Elysian Park. One of the kids, from the party, they fell. Or jumped. I don't fucking know. I think they're dead. Oh god, they're dead. What the hell, man, you know?"

"Just take a deep breath. And can I get your name?

"What do you need my name for? I don't know them. I don't know anything. I just… I saw it. I saw the body."

"We just need your name for documentation."

"Jesus H. Tapdancing Christ, I'm telling you, I have nothing to do with this. Just get someone out there. They're dead. I know they're dead."

She didn't recognize the voice before but now it was unmistakable. She had just heard him say the same exclamation, with the exact same inflection.

Trevor was the one who made the 911 call.

She listened to it again. And again. It was him. No doubt about it. He sounded surprised on the call, so he could've just run into the body. All that it meant for certain was that Trevor was there that night. After the party was over. After Bridget was a body on the ground.

Abby leaned back in her chair, as her thoughts raced around and around. Could Trevor be involved? Maybe her angle was all wrong, was this a jealous lover thing? Maybe Trevor thought it would be easier with Javi if Bridget was out of the picture.

Is that really a thing people did?

Abby started writing notes down. She had to recreate everything since she lost her book of suspects. She had to recreate the timeline. She was writing everything down from memory, while random 911 calls continued to play in her ears. People complaining about neighbors' loud parties. Vandalism calls. It was Halloween, so there was plenty of mischief to go around.

Abby wrote her list of suspects again. She wrote Mr. Sutton down, and followed with what she could remember. She wrote Vanessa down. Couldn't rule her out. She wrote down Trevor, and put everything she knew about him. He was clearly a student at the University, so she was going to have to do some more digging on him. She could ask him, but then she remembered what she was thinking earlier, about how everyone lies. Maybe it was better not to tip him off that she knew anything, not until she found out everything she could. Everyone lies, so she couldn't believe anything he told her anyway.

She continued to write as the 911 calls continued to play. She had never listened to the rest of them before. It was kind of funny, some of the callers were clearly drunk or stoned, some were just stupid. And then she heard his voice.

Percy.

"I…need an ambulance. I fell. Cut myself. Losing blood. 6616 Underwood. I'm… in the basement."

It was time stamped at 2:54am. After the time change. She knew he had an accident that weekend and landed in the hospital. She had seen his scars. He said he was drunk and fell when he came from a party, but she thought he said it was Friday. He said he wasn't at the Elysian Park party and didn't even know about it. But this call was only a couple hours after Bridget's death.

Abby continued to write on her list of suspects. She was hesitant at first, but she had to be honest. She didn't know for sure.

Abby wrote Percy and underlined it. She was going to get the truth. One way or another.

28. ROBBIE

"I want to talk to my son," Adam snarled.

The air felt like ice, but Robbie stood outside the door, not wanting to give way to Adam. She clutched her sweater tight. Adam stood down the steps. He had pounded on the door, but Robbie wouldn't open it until he took a step back.

"I told you. He's not here."

"Bullshit. I know he's staying here."

"He is staying here, but at present he is elsewhere."

"Don't talk to me like I'm an idiot."

"Then stop yelling like one."

It was a long time coming. TJ had been staying in her basement for weeks. Robbie made sure that he called his dad to tell him he was okay, but Adam had hung up on TJ before he ever got specific. It was too small of a town for it to be a secret for any length of time anyway.

"You can't keep him from me."

"I'm not trying to keep him from you. I'm trying to keep him out of juvie. If child protective services got involved they would snatch him from you in a heartbeat."

"You saying I'm a shitty father?"

"I'm saying you have to figure your shit out. When you can come over without screaming and smelling like an ashtray with day-old beer at the bottom of it, then we can talk. Like adults. If you have a problem with that, then call the police. I like my chances with them."

Robbie turned around and walked back into her house. She shut the door behind her and shuddered when she heard a smash against the door outside. Probably the bottle Adam was trying to keep hidden in his back pocket.

"Everything okay?" Scott asked as he walked into the room.

"Yes, just stay inside right now."

Scott looked out the window.

"TJ's dad?"

"Yeah. Is he still there?"

"Looks like he's driving away. I can probably catch him. Go fuck him up."

"Scott, language."

"Mess him up. Whatever."

"No, I don't want my eighteen-year-old son to try and fight a grown man with anger issues who is half in the bag already. Don't you have homework?"

"Should I call Dad?"

"He's gone. It's fine."

"What did he want?"

"He wanted his son."

"Well, it begs the question, how long is Little Orphan Asshole gonna be here?"

"Scott, not now."

"Hey, I'm the one that has to put up with him more than anyone else. He's outside my room. Sharing my bathroom. I take him to school and everything."

"And we appreciate your sacrifice. Where is he now anyway?"

"He was working on some project after school with Breck."

"Why didn't they come here?"

"I don't know."

"Everything okay with Breck?"

"Yeah, sure."

Scott responded as he walked into the kitchen. Robbie followed him but stood in the doorway while he pilfered through the cupboards.

"You know, Scott, if you wanted to talk to me, you can."

"Aren't we talking now?"

"I think you know what I mean. I'm here. If you ever decided you wanted to share what's going on in that vast abyss of a mind you have."

"I'm fine, Mom. Just hungry."

"I can make something."

"I'm good. I'll just have some chips."

Scott grabbed a bag of Ruffles and returned to the depths of the basement from whence he came. Robbie knew she shouldn't have pushed. She had him. It was just a moment, but he was engaging her without effort. She should've let it keep going but she had to push and then he was off again.

Robbie missed her son. They used to be so close, and would joke around or talk about random things, but lately he seemed to view her as a nuisance. Every time she tried to reach out, he's busy. She knew it was an expected part of adolescence, but it's just such a shitty part.

What happened to the sweet boy he used to be?

* * * * *

The ballroom was elegantly decorated with everything white, tinged with gold. The napkins had gold trim. The tablecloths had gold centerpieces. Big, gold-framed mirrors in every direction. None of it could hide the gaudy hotel carpet they were walking on.

Robbie thought the entire thing was a tacky waste of money, but then, she wasn't even supposed to be here. She promised Eli she could sub for her in this Working Women of Omaha seminar that seemed as silly as it was useless. Was it a networking event, or just a way for women to get together and gossip without their bosses? Because the bosses were all still men, and not here.

Robbie wanted a drink.

Her dress was a rich, forest green, sleeveless thing. Her hair was up, her jewelry was plentiful, and her makeup was impeccable, but she still wondered why anyone would go to all this trouble. She walked over to the bar, where she gave a nod to the young bartender, the only man in the room.

"Can I get a sparkling water, please?"

The bartender nodded and quickly set a glass in front of her.

"Lime?"

"Why not."

Robbie took a swig and mustered up the strength to continue mingling.

"Robbie Chancellor?" a voice called from behind her.

She turned to see Donna Van Allen, her former sorority sister. Donna, naturally, looked flawless and even more made up and put together than Robbie. She would've been jealous if she cared about any of this.

"I think you know it's Jetter now," Robbie said. "You were at the wedding."

"Right, right, how is my ex-boyfriend?"

There was the obligatory kiss hello, even though nothing about their interaction felt cordial.

"Settle down, you had two dates. And Eric is wonderful. We really couldn't be any happier. Scott is lettering in three sports, looking at colleges. Bernie is really just a musical savant. How is your family? I don't think I've heard anything lately."

It was beneath Robbie to be so catty, but Donna just brought it out of her.

"Oh, everyone is fine. We were planning to winter in Palm Springs, but Harlan had to stick close to home because he has so much going on at work."

"Is that why? Well, that's a shame."

"We made do."

"Well, it was lovely to—" Robbie tried to remove herself from the conversation but Donna steamrolled right over her comment and kept going.

"You know, speaking of exes, I swear to god I saw your ex the other night. He was on Pacific Street, and the cops had pulled him over. And he was trying to walk back and forth but kept slipping. Must've been icy."

"He's been going through a rough time since his wife passed."

"Oh, do you still keep in touch?"

"I wouldn't say that."

"Well, I just feel for his family. That has to be difficult to deal with."

"I'm sure. But I wouldn't worry too much. The older kids are away, and his youngest is actually staying with us."

"You don't say."

"But you knew that too, didn't you? That's what this whole thing is about, isn't it?"

"I don't know what you're talking about."

"You made a beeline over here to, what, try and make me feel bad?"

"I swear to you, I meant no offense. But yes, I had heard about Adam's son. I just can't imagine that it wouldn't be awkward for everyone."

"It's not, I can assure you. But I appreciate your concern. And it was lovely to—"

"Robbie, I'm sorry if I made the wrong impression. My foot loves hanging out in my mouth, you know. I saw Adam getting pulled over and I didn't know how involved you were with everything. With his son being at your place, and given how nice you are, I wouldn't be surprised if you were his lawyer or something crazy like that."

"I'm not even practicing, Donna. But I am working, which begs the question, what are you doing here? You're not an actual working woman of Omaha, are you?"

"Nice try, dear, but I'm on the committee that put on this affair. And isn't the décor just lovely?"

"Yes, it's wonderful. Well done."

"Thank you. And good luck with… everything you have going on."

"Thank you, Donna. Wonderful to see you."

"We should definitely get lunch sometime and catch up."

"Well, you know where to find me."

Robbie's fake smile was about to break her face, but thankfully Donna finally got the hint and excused herself. Robbie downed her water and decided she needed another moment to herself.

She wasn't surprised about Adam, assuming Donna was even telling the truth. He had been teetering closer to the edge every day. It was an unfortunate situation that was untenable in the long run. TJ couldn't live with them forever. Adam either needed to get help or get lost. And what about the other kids? How much was Robbie prepared to take on in this whole ordeal, that had, she knew, really nothing to do with her.

She ordered another sparkling water with lime and wished she didn't secretly want it to be mixed with large amounts of vodka.

* * * * *

"You'll never guess who I ran into tonight."

Robbie was in the bathroom, washing the makeup off her face. Eric was in bed, with his nose in a book.

"I can't imagine," Eric said.

"Your ex-girlfriend."

Robbie saw Eric set his book down.

"You can just say Donna."

"What did you ever see in her?"

"We went out twice. It was college. I wasn't looking too deeply."

"Um, excuse me, we met in college."

"Yeah, and I only went out with you because you were hot. I married you because you were amazing. But I didn't know that at the time."

"Nice save."

"I think it was pretty good."

Robbie finished drying her face and returned to the bedroom.

"She said she saw Adam getting a DUI."

"Well, I can't say that doesn't make perfect sense."

"She thinks this whole situation is pretty weird."

"Well, she's right there, but are we really going to concern ourselves with what that stuck-up…socialite thinks?"

"Of course not. But are we okay?"

"Yeah. What's this about?"

"You know this has nothing to do with Adam, right? I saw someone in need and I helped them and I would've done that for anyone."

"Come on, what are you doing?"

"Do you think this does have something to do with Adam?"

"Look, I'm not jealous or anything, but come on, I don't think you would've done this for just anyone."

"Do you think he ever hit TJ?"

"There it is."

"What?"

"You saw him yell at a couple people twenty years ago, so now you think he's abusing his kids."

"I tried to talk to him, but he's about as open as our own kids."

"Robbie, you can't do that."

"Can't do what?"

"Create this storyline in your head so you have a reason to keep yourself involved."

"That is not what I'm doing."

"Well, it sure feels like it sometimes."

"Trust me, there are no feelings there."

"I know there's not any real feelings there. I'm not threatened by Adam, but you could've let this go a while ago. Called child services and be done with it."

"I couldn't do that."

"I know. Because it's Adam."

"Adam is not the reason. Not exactly."

"Then what exactly is it? Because I can only suggest what it seems like."

Robbie sat down on the bed. She had always been honest with Eric, but that didn't mean she always told him everything. Some things were easier to let go.

"We were at a party once. You were there, we had been dating awhile, and Adam had just met Maureen. I think it was Devin's engagement or something, it doesn't matter. You were telling some story about Adam from high school, something about the wrestling team and how he was trying to make weight."

"Yeah, and he ended up drinking that syrup that makes you puke and he didn't think it worked, but then he was making out with some cheerleader and ended up puking all over her."

"That's the one. Lovely story, by the way. And he was laughing along with everyone. And I made some comment to Maureen to be careful. Something like that. He had cornered me in the bathroom later and grabbed my arm and squeezed as hard as he could saying 'you will not disrespect me' and he was shouting it. I told him he was scaring me, and hurting me and he shoved me down and walked away."

"What? You never said anything. I would've fucking killed him."

"And that's why I never said anything. He had two sides. He could be sweet. And he could be dark. And I've seen that."

"He's not your father, Robbie."

That stung a little. Robbie's relationship with her father was complicated at best. He was an old-school alcoholic good ole boy from the South. Everyone loved him. Except for his family, they lived in fear of him. At least when he was drinking, which was most days. Robbie had escaped his circle of influence when she moved to Omaha for college and never looked back. They hadn't spoken in years when she heard about his heart attack. Robbie didn't want to continue down this line of discussion so she tried to calmly move out of this conversational landmine.

"I'm not saying that."

"You didn't have to."

"Anyway, I can admit there's something about trying to fix him. Because I know he can be better."

"Do you really think that?"

"I don't know. But earlier this week he came to the house, shouting and yelling for me to give his son back, and I saw his eyes and there was just nothing there."

"Robbie, you have to tell me these things."

"I am telling you."

"How many days later? Do I need to worry about not being here? Do we need a restraining order or something?"

"No."

"And why are you so sure?"

"Because…"

"Because it's Adam? Robbie, you just said he threw you down, for no reason. Keeping him from his son is a big reason. I don't know if I want to leave you alone here."

"I'm telling you, it'll be fine. I just need to talk to him sober."

"And when will that be?"

"I have no idea."

"Robbie, this is a way bigger deal than we signed up for. We have to worry about our kids. We are not prepared to deal with this if it gets more serious."

"So, what, you think if we put TJ in child services this situation gets better?"

"Maybe for us."

The phone rang, interrupting what was feeling more and more like an argument. Robbie moved to the phone.

"Don't get that, I'm sure it's for one of the kids."

Robbie grabbed the phone anyway.

"Hello?"

"Robbie?" the voice on the other end was quiet. Soft.

"This is."

"It's…me. It's Adam."

"What's going on?"

"I need your help."

There was a vulnerability to his voice. A quaver. Had he been crying?

"Adam, are you okay?"

"Hang up the phone," Eric said sternly, but Robbie motioned him to stop.

"I need your help, Robbie. It's bad."

"What's bad?"

"Can you come over, please? I need your help. Not like any help, but you're the closest thing to a lawyer that I know."

"What do you mean?"

"I'm in trouble."

"What kind of trouble?"

"Robbie, just please can you come over? I'll tell you. I'll tell you everything."

"Tell me what."

"Please, just come. I did something, Robbie. I did something bad. Real bad."

29. JAVI

Javi was pacing around the garage. Diego was underneath the car, his old mustang, working on the engine. Javi's main role was to hand his brother whatever tools he asked for, but he had his own reasons for being here.

"Come on," Javi pleaded. "You said you would do anything for me."

"I meant like buy you beer or drive the car while you and your shitty little friends TP someone's house," Diego responded. "Not this."

"Are you saying you can't get it?"

"Why do you want it?"

Diego wheeled out from under the car.

"It's not what you think."

"Well, come on then, tell me what I think."

"I don't know."

"Javi, your girlfriend just killed herself a few months ago. You've been all withdrawn lately, and then you ask me for a gun?"

"That's the thing."

"What?"

"Bridget didn't kill herself."

"What do you mean?"

"I mean, she was pushed. She was fucking someone else, got in a fight or something, and she was pushed."

"And you know who did this?"

"Not exactly. But I'm pretty sure. And if I'm right, I want to be able to protect myself."

"Have you ever even fired a gun?"

"Not since we took Papa Miguel's rifle hunting when I was like twelve. It's not going to come to that anyway. I promise. Look, if you're that worried, then don't get me any ammo."

"Well, that's not much protection if it comes to it."

"Can you get me the gun or not?"

"Yeah.... Yeah, I can."

"Thank you."

"Javi, are you sure you're okay?"

"Not yet. But maybe once I get some answers."

30. ELI

She brushed her hair, grateful she cut it shorter. Made it a lot easier to deal with when she didn't want to deal with it. And right now, Eli didn't want to deal with anything. Danny was gone. And for all their troubles, this is not what she wanted. They were going to fix it. They were going to work through this.

Now, she was just left with so many questions. Questions that were likely to never have a satisfactory answer. She had been avoiding everyone—Dr. Gant, Harlan, her brother, Robbie, her friends. Eli wanted to wallow. And she didn't want to come clean about everything. This was a burden she was going to have to live with the rest of her life. Danny was on the road because of her. If she had been honest with him, he would still be alive. Never mind anything else. This was true.

She played her part at the funeral, and the meeting at the house afterwards. It was easy. She was sad and distraught, but she had also been lying to everyone for so long, it was just more of the same.

Work could wait. Eli didn't even call to check in the first week after it happened. When she finally did call, she took her vacation time and said she wouldn't be back until next month. One less thing to deal with. Now, she was left to wallow in this house. Alone.

She deserved this.

She couldn't even drink to wallow properly. This stupid baby she was carrying saw to that. It was a horrible thought, but Eli could at least be honest with herself. She wanted this baby, and was going to have this baby, but it wasn't always the most convenient thing. There was also the matter of the baby's father. She was all set to pretend that it was Danny, but was that still the right thing to do? She could imagine a life with Harlan, running away together and raising a kid on their own, but that wasn't really factoring in reality. He had other kids. A wife. And she had no one.

This was the problem with spending so much time in her own head. Eli was having thoughts she didn't want to be having.

The doorbell rang. Thank God. A reprieve. It was probably Eric or someone else she had been ignoring too much. She looked in the mirror to make sure she was presentable before she went to the front door. And opened the door to a complete surprise.

Donna Van Allen. She was dressed in a dark brown suit that perfectly communicated how rich and beautiful she was. Eli was rethinking the t-shirt and sweatpants she deemed acceptable enough to let someone in.

"Donna, what are you doing here?"

"Can I come in? It's starting to snow, I think."

"Of course."

Donna followed Eli in, where a number of thoughts raced through her head.

"Can I get you something to drink?"

"Scotch?"

"I might have some bourbon."

"Then I guess that'll have to do."

Eli retired to the kitchen and poured two glasses. She could fake it. She wasn't about to answer any questions as to why she wasn't drinking. Eli returned and handed the glass to Donna.

"I've never seen your place. It's very quaint."

"Well, you know, Danny was a teacher."

"Oh, I'm so sorry, dear. I didn't mean to imply anything. I'm so sorry for your loss. How are you holding up?"

"One day at a time, you know."

Eli clinked her glass against Donna's and put it to her lips, but didn't let anything pass. Donna had already turned away, so Eli didn't have to keep up the show.

"I'm sorry to barge in on you," Donna continued. "I'm sure you've been through a lot with this… tragedy. I really don't want to burden you with anything else. It's funny, I had imagined I would make a big scene at the Women's dinner. But then you had to skip that, which I suppose I should have seen coming. And what would that have accomplished anyway? It might embarrass you, sure, but it would embarrass me as well. Who needs that? But I guess I'm just old fashioned and I was yearning for a direct confrontation. But then I thought, been there done that. And with all you've been going through lately, I really am sorry for that, I didn't want to add more to your pain. Even if you are sleeping with my husband."

Eli didn't say anything but she did take a real sip of the bourbon. The baby would just have to hang in there.

"I appreciate you not denying it. It would be such a waste of time for me to convince you that I know what you've been up to. I've known for a while. I always know. And it's not a big deal. Really. I know I'm supposed to yell and scream and call you a homewrecker or demand you wear some scarlet letter branding you the whore that you are, but what does that accomplish. Harlan is the one that is deceiving me. He's the one betraying our vows. Am I supposed to tell you that you're kidding yourself, that he's not going to choose you? That this whole thing was just some fling and he would eventually find his way back to me? I could do that, I suppose. I want to do that. But what gets served? Does it matter to you that I know? Are you going to stop fucking my husband now that you know? And do I even care? Honestly, I'm not sure I know the answer to that last one. I've been trying to work that out for a while now. And frankly, it's getting exhausting have these conversations. I went through this whole thing with Andrea Donnelly just a few weeks ago."

Wait. What?

"Oh, I'm sorry. Did you think you were the only one?"

Andrea Donnelly was on the sales team. She was based out of Kansas City, but spent plenty of time in Omaha. They were friendly even. Is Donna right? Was Harlan with her too?

"I'm sorry that was rude. I expected you knew. This is not a new thing for him and you've been around long enough to hear the rumors. I mean, they're all true. Marilyn. Annette. Olivia. That woman in HR, what's her name? Carolyn?"

"Caroline?"

"Yes. That's the one. HR, can you believe it? Don't they have to take an oath or something? Anyway, I didn't want to bring up all of this. I know you've been dealing with a lot, and I just didn't want you deluding yourself that salvation was waiting for you in the arms of Harlan Van Allen. He may act like that's the case. But it's only a matter of time. Believe me."

"You know, I did tell him it was over."

"Sure, you did, dear. If that helps you. Anyway, I should get going before the snow really starts coming down out there. And believe me, there are no hard feelings. He's a charmer. You couldn't help yourself. Just be grateful you're not married to him."

Donna downed the rest of her drink.

"This was easier than I thought it would be," Donna said. "It must be getting easier with practice."

Donna handed Eli the glass, and wiggled her still gloved fingers in some form of goodbye.

"Bye, dear."

"Thanks for stopping by," Eli responded, drowned in sarcasm.

Fuck.

Eli wanted to drink the rest of the bourbon. The rest of the bottle. And she wanted to throw the glass against the wall. But she was just too tired. She poured the rest of the drink out and set it on the counter. She felt like crying, but she barely cried for Danny. Harlan wasn't about to get any of her tears.

* * * * *

Eli spent most of the day watching shitty television and trying to ignore the entirety of her life falling apart. She wasn't about to check-in to work. She wasn't even sure she was even going to go back. Maybe she could get a new job. Maybe she would just take off, on her own, and have this baby somewhere on her own. Completely start over.

There was a rustling at the door that startled Eli. She ran to the window and pulled the curtain back. Snow was falling and with the sun setting, it had the claustrophobic feeling of living in a snow globe. A figure, a man it looked like from behind was running down the street. He could've just come from her house, or maybe was only passing by. Eli grabbed a poker from the fire place and went to the front door. When she opened it, a small package fell forward at her feet.

She picked it up and saw "Eli" scrawled in black marker. She ripped open the package to see a VHS tape inside. No label. There was no note or anything else.

Eli took the tape and went to her VCR. She wasn't even sure how to work it properly. Every time they watched a movie, Danny set everything up. She pressed play, but the regular TV was still on. She pressed buttons on the remote until the screen changed and the black and white lines rolled across the screen. It was static that was settling, and eventually the word "PLAY" appeared on the screen. This must be a copy of another tape.

A moment later the split screen of the security cameras at the office appeared on the screen. It was focused on the lobby. Harlan was having an argument with… was that Bridget Kent? The girl that died? Danny's student?

Eli watched Harlan yell at her. There was no audio so she had no context for what he might be saying. But she did see him hand her a check.

The check.

Harlan had come into her office one day and asked her to deposit ten thousand dollars over to his secondary account because he "accidentally" wrote a check off the wrong account.

The check was for Bridget?

And then she noticed the date. October 30th.

Didn't she die on Halloween?

Harlan was supposed to be out of town that week. Eli remembered that Danny had a game at school that night and she was going to spend the night with Harlan, but he had to catch a flight.

And yet, here he was.

After everything Donna had told her, Eli wasn't sure what to think. It was obvious Harlan had lied to her about plenty of things. But what could this mean?

Only one way to find out.

Eli picked up the phone and dialed. Thankfully, he answered.

"Harlan, it's me. I'm home. I need to talk to you. Now."

She hung up. Not even waiting to hear him answer. He would come. She knew he would come.

She still had the poker in her hand. And she clutched it tighter as the video went to black.

31. KIRA

Jake's hand moved slowly down her side and rubbed against the side of her butt. Kira reached down and grabbed his hand pushing it back.

"Come on, Jake. My dad is going to be home soon."

"So? He's not here now."

"I think you're underestimating my father's capacity for murdering the white boy touching his baby girl."

"Point taken," Jake said, as he pulled back and sat up.

Kira giggled. She had been rubbing her hands through his hair and now the blonde strands were standing up like he'd been electrocuted. She started to pat it down.

"First sign of making out is the hair."

Jake straightened out his clothes and used his fingers as a comb to regain some semblance of normal.

"You know, speaking of murder, how's your little after school project with Abby going?"

"Oh, come on. I haven't even really talked to her."

"Does she still think Mr. Sutton is the one?"

"I don't know. I'm not so sure myself."

"You don't believe all that stuff about getting in a car wreck do you?"

"You don't?"

"Please. The dude killed himself, just like Bridget did, and they are worried people are going to start following suit like some Heathers situation."

"Who is the 'they' that is covering up everything? The police? The school?"

"I don't know. And you know, I'm sorry I even brought it up."

"It's okay. The whole thing has been bugging me lately. You ever figure out why Bridget's mom was on all those drugs?"

"I haven't really talked to her either."

She hadn't. Kira had avoided Vanessa ever since she learned about the prescription. She never told Abby about the drugs, never told anyone, because she wasn't sure if it had anything to do with Bridget's death. Maybe it suggested why Bridget wanted to run away, but Kira wasn't even sure she believed Abby's story about the journal. Kira didn't know what to do with this information so she tried to put it out of her head. It was easier to believe Mr. Sutton killed her, or that she really did jump herself.

"Hey, everything okay?" Jake asked. "You kind of zoned out there."

"Yeah, I'm fine. Besides, I think I just heard the garage door open. My dad's probably home."

"Then I better move to the other side of the couch."

"And maybe wipe my lipstick off your face."

Kira smiled, just as the phone rang. She had the cordless on the end table behind her so reached over.

“Hello?”

“Kira, it’s me…”

“Abby?”

“Is Jake there?”

“Yeah.”

“Can I please talk to him?”

There was something weird about her voice, something urgent. She handed the phone to Jake.

“It’s Abby.”

She listened as Jake answered and watched his face go from annoyance to concerned. The door from the garage opened and Randall walked in. He shouted a ‘hey’ but Kira shushed him and pointed to Jake being on the phone.

“No, it’s fine. Calm down. It’s okay. I’ll be right there.”

Jake hung up the phone and handed it back to Kira.

“Everything okay?”

“I don’t know. Abby’s freaking out about something. Says she needs my help. It’s about that after school project we were talking about.”

“What about it?”

“I’ll let you know. I know Abby and I aren’t really that close but when she needs my help I feel like I have to go. I’ll call you when I’m home.”

“Okay.”

“Be careful driving out there, Jake. The snow is starting to really come down,” Randall said, pulling his jacket off.

“Thank you, sir.”

Kira wanted to kiss Jake goodbye, or even hug him, but she always felt weird about doing that with her dad around. The more she could avoid public displays of affection, the more she could avoid a lecture.

Jake waved and walked out the front door.

"You okay, baby? What was that all about?"

"I don't know," Kira responded. "Something at home I guess."

"Well, I'm just glad you're home. It really is getting bad out there."

Kira got up and went to the front window. The snow was falling, her father was right about that. White flakes were blowing all over the place outside.

"You weren't kidding," Kira said. "Looks like it's gonna be a lot. Hopefully, that means no school tomorrow."

Across the street, Kira saw Vanessa emerge from her house. She waved but Vanessa didn't see her. She got into her car and pulled out of the driveway.

"Doesn't seem to be scaring off Vanessa. Looks like she's off somewhere."

Randall moved up behind Kira. He put his hand on her shoulder.

"You know, I think it was very sweet of you to look after Bridget's mom after…she passed, but I have to be honest, I'm glad you aren't spending so much time over there."

"Why do you say that?"

"She always seemed a little nutty to me."

"Nutty how?"

"Erratic, I guess."

"I'm sure it was nothing."

"Did Bridget ever say anything to you about her mother?"

"What do you mean?"

Kira turned to face her dad.

"It's nothing. Forget I said anything."

"No, you brought it up."

"I'm being paranoid, sweetie, don't listen to me."

"Paranoid about what?"

"I probably shouldn't say anything but I think you're old enough to know. There was an incident."

"What kind of incident?"

"Remember that camping trip, we took you kids out to Platte River State Park? You had gone off to the bathroom or something, and I was setting up the tents and Bridget was acting up about one thing or another, I didn't catch the whole thing, but when I came out of the tent I saw Vanessa practically choking Bridget. She had her arms around the girl's neck. Bridget was only twelve years old. I ran over there and pulled her off. And Vanessa started smacking me and screaming at me, and then a second later she just stopped like nothing happened and apologized, blaming the heat."

"What? Why didn't you ever tell me that?"

"I don't know. A few days later I talked to Vanessa, rationally and evenly, and she treated the whole thing like a big misunderstanding. Remember when I wouldn't let you spend the night over there?"

"That was why?"

"I told Bridget she could talk to me or could come over if she ever needed to, but she said it never happened again."

"I can't believe you never told me."

"Maybe I should have, but it's a lot to burden a kid with."

"I guess."

"I'm sorry, I shouldn't have even said anything. I never saw anything like that again. And child services cleared everything."

"You called child services?"

"Of course. I don't want that happening to a kid on my watch. But all they said was that their investigation did not indicate that it was an unsafe home environment."

"I can't believe this."

"I know, and I'm sorry to dump all of this on you. But Georgina insisted you should know. And you have to believe me that if I ever thought you were in any danger, I wouldn't have let you go anywhere near that house."

"Where is Georgina anyway?"

"Wait, she's not here?"

"No, I haven't heard from her."

Randall went to the kitchen and Kira could hear him making a phone call, but her brain was stuck on Vanessa. Her dad wasn't a liar. She was sure what happened really happened. Which meant that maybe Abby wasn't lying about the journal entry. Maybe Vanessa really was abusive. And violent. And maybe there really was something more to Bridget's death.

"Georgina's still at the office and I don't want her driving in this weather. Not as pregnant as she is."

Don't remind me, Kira thought.

"I'm going to pick her up. You okay here?"

"Of course."

"We can talk more when I'm back."

Randall put his jacket back on, and pulled a stocking hat on his head and exited through the garage.

Kira went back to the window and watched him leave. Then she ran over to the front door and pulled on her shoes. If there was something more to Vanessa and Bridget, she wasn't going to figure it out from over here. She grabbed the key, and trudged across the street.

32. BRECK

It was weird being in Scott's house when no one else was home. Breck had stopped by to have a talk with Scott, but he had run out to meet up with Javi. TJ was still at school. Robbie insisted she stay rather than drive in the bad weather. She and Eric had to run out for something important, she said, and she asked Breck to wait until Bernie came home. Scott should be back soon anyway.

She'd never been in the house when it was so quiet. There was always some noise, television, or Bernie on the phone, or Scott and TJ fighting. This was creepy.

Breck wanted to force a conversation with Scott, but she wasn't sure she could do it with his parents there. He had been acting so different lately. And they kept breaking up and getting back together so much that she wasn't even sure where they stood. She knew something was wrong with him, something more than the hospital thing, or Javi's thinking he was taking something, but Scott kept insisting everything was fine.

When she asked him about doing drugs he said he taken things a couple times but he was more concerned with TJ. Scott said TJ hid pills in Scott's stuff so he wouldn't get caught with it. Scott never trusted him, but it didn't feel like the TJ Breck knew. She didn't know much about him but they had been working on a project together and he seemed rather quiet and harmless to her.

But maybe Scott was right.

Breck felt guilty about it, but she went into the basement and walked into TJ's space in the corner of the family room. They had moved things around so that TJ had a little more of his own room. It didn't have walls or anything, but the sofa bed was arranged in a way that the back kept the rest of the room separate. There was a basket for dirty clothes, and a suitcase in one corner. There was a backpack by the couch, but it wasn't the one TJ took to school.

Breck unzipped the backpack. She knew it was wrong as she was doing it, but she couldn't stop herself. There were notebooks, some with drawings, one had song lyrics. There were other books: Catcher in the Rye, Of Mice and Men, The Great Gatsby. All stuff that was assigned reading at some point. In the middle of Catcher in the Rye, a photograph was sticking out, used as a bookmark.

Breck opened the book and was shocked to see her own face looking back at her. It was from the Halloween party. It was her and Kira and Bridget. It was one of the pictures that Scott took, and she had seen it on his wall at some point. TJ must've taken it, which was disturbing enough. But then she saw that someone had taken a marker and scratched out Bridget's face.

Breck closed the book and reached deeper into the bag but pricked her finger on something. She recoiled and pulled her hand out and saw a slice on her finger where blood started to drip. Carefully, she reached in the bag and pulled out what she had cut herself on. It was wrapped in a t-shirt, but the tip of the blade was sticking out. It was a large kitchen knife, like you would use to cut vegetables. Large vegetables. And there was something dried on the edges, and the handle that looked like blood. Dark. Spotty.

What the hell?

Breck quickly wrapped the knife back in the shirt and put the book back in. Her finger stinged so she wrapped it in the bottom of her shirt, when she was startled by a noise.

Breck turned around to see TJ standing across the room from her. There was something in his eyes that didn't look right.

"What are you doing in my stuff?" TJ asked.

33. THE STORM

THEN

"Don't you walk away from me while I'm talking at you," Vanessa shouted.

Bridget walked away, stomping down the stairs for emphasis.

"I'm not doing this mom. I have to get to the game."

"Oh, that's what it is? You think you better than me because you some cheerleader? I could've made the team in high school, but I was stuck being a mother. To You," Vanessa slurred, chasing after her.

"What are you talking about? You had me when you were twenty-seven."

"You just think you know everything."

"Take your meds, Mom. Please."

Bridget threw on her coat, and slammed the door behind her.

NOW

The garage door opened. Kira could hear it from Vanessa's room. Oh shit, she thought. Maybe she could sneak out the back door? But without making a sound? Kira bolted to the window and peered out between the curtains. The snow was falling hard, but she could still see Vanessa's car pulling into the driveway.

Shit. Shit shit shit.

Kira shut the dresser drawer she was rifling through, and tiptoed into Bridget's room across the hall. Closet? Under the bed? Kira was nervous. She could make up some lie, but what?

Kira listened as the door from the garage shut and she could hear Vanessa walking in from upstairs. She slid into the corner by Bridget's dresser, and crouched down. She tucked her knees into her chest and tried to hold her breath.

She listened as Vanessa opened the refrigerator and… was she singing? Kira couldn't make out the song, but Vanessa was definitely singing. And not softly. A deep, throaty number.

Vanessa was walking up the steps. Kira thought maybe she would just go to her bedroom and she could wait until she went to sleep, but what would her dad say? Surely, he would worry once he made it home and she wasn't there. She should've said where she was going. Told her little brother or, God, even left a note.

The door to the bedroom opened.

"She's got eyes of the bluest skies, as if they thought of rain," Vanessa sang as she walked in and sat on the bed.

Kira tried not to breathe, and hoped the massive pounding in her chest couldn't be heard. Thankfully, Vanessa hadn't turned on the lights.

Vanessa had a glass and was taking sips, in between her singing, which was trailing to a mumble.

"She's got hair reminds me of warm, place, where I'd…. pray for the thunder…"

Vanessa sat up. Was she looking right at me, Kira thought. She tried to will herself invisible.

"Baby, is that you? Why you sitting down there so quietly? Come on out."

"I'm sorry… I didn't know…"

"Bridget, honey, I can barely understand you. Come over here. I know we had a fight, but that doesn't mean you can just come and go as you please. You're supposed to call if you're gonna be late."

"I…" Kira stood up, but she didn't know what to say.

"First time you've been so quiet in I don't know how long. Now, are you gonna come over here and sit next to your mother, or am I gonna have to walk over there and pull you by that nappy ass weave?"

Vanessa's tone shifted. Kira froze.

THEN

"It's about your son. Percy," Bridget said firmly.

Harlan turned back around, while letting out a frustrated breath.

"What's he done now?" he asked.

"Um, well, it's like this. Uh," Bridget knew she just had to say it.

"Spit it out, kid. What exactly do you have to do with my son?"

"I'm pregnant. I've got the test. I can show you. Your son and I we got together at a party."

"So? You need abortion money, ask him. I'm sure he saved something from his paper route."

"He doesn't know."

"Well, he really should be your first phone call. Have a good night."

"Really? That's how you want to play this?"

"Excuse me?"

"Think hard, Mr. Van Allen. Do you really want a Christmas card with your nigger grandbaby on it?"

"You're calling me a racist? Look, girl, I have no issue with who my son chooses to… spend his time with. If he can't figure out how to put a condom on that has nothing to do with me."

"Maybe not. I guess I could go to Channel Three and talk to them about it. Didn't they do a story last month on you. I know the phrase 'pillar of the community' was thrown around an awful lot. I'm sure this town won't think anything of your white Catholic high school son having a baby with a sweet black girl who loves to talk and be on camera."

"What do you want?"

"I want out of this fucking town. I want nothing to do with your son or your family. I want some way to go someplace else. Far away. To start over."

"Blackmail. That's your game?"

"Call it what you want. I can get out of dodge without saying another word to anyone. If only I had the means."

"You've got a lot of nerve."

"Try me, Mr. Van Allen. You have no idea how much nerve I got."

NOW

Eli watched the snow falling out the window until she saw Harlan's car pull up. She took another sip of her vodka tonic. She managed to finish one waiting for him. She thought it might calm her down. But it didn't. She was still angry, though she wasn't entirely sure of how to isolate her feelings. Was it about her relationship with Harlan? Or was it that he might have had something to do with the death of that girl? And what about the baby? She shouldn't be drinking.

Everything was swirling in her brain. She couldn't figure out any connection between Harlan and that girl. And what about her husband? The girl's journal was found in his car. She was Danny's student. Eli took another swig.

Harlan knocked on her door. She opened the door but walked into the living room without saying anything. She knew he would follow her.

"It's really coming down out there," Harlan said. "How are you doing?"

"I'm managing."

"Everything okay? You sounded upset on the phone."

"Well, there's a good reason for that. Have you ever lied to me?"

"What? Of course not."

Eli smiled, and shook her head. Naturally.

"Have you ever met Bridget Kent? That young girl that died. She was in your son's class, I think. She was one of Danny's students."

"I know the name. I don't think we ever crossed paths."

Eli was staring right at Harlan. Without breaking her eye line, she pulled the remote control out of her pocket and pressed play. The TV behind her started playing the security tape.

"Want to try that one again?"

"Where did you get this?" Harlan asked as he saw the footage of him and Bridget arguing.

"Well, I think the bigger problem for you is that I have no idea. It's obviously a copy. And since we've just established that you would lie to me without a second thought, I'm almost afraid to try again. But I will.

Have you ever met Bridget Kent?"

"Yes, okay. I'm sorry. I wanted to forget the whole thing. She came to me claiming to have had some relationship with my son. And she wanted money."

"And you gave it to her? Ten thousand dollars?"

"How did you know that?"

"The money you asked me to deposit? It wasn't difficult for me to track back. I wonder how difficult it would be for the police."

"She never cashed the check."

"Because you wrote it on a Friday night. And she was dead less than twenty-four hours later."

"You don't think I had anything to do with it, do you?"

"I don't know. Have you ever lied to me?"

THEN

TJ had left home over a week ago, but since he had firmly set up camp in the bath house at Elysian Park, he wanted to collect a few more things. Someone at school had mentioned how often he wore his yellow-plaid flannel, and he needed to grab more of his clothes. He waited until his dad was out and went into the house.

His key still worked. He knew his dad wouldn't have the energy or the money to change the locks, but he thought it might be a little more difficult than it was. Nothing had changed. The house was still a mess. His room hadn't been touched. TJ grabbed a few more shirts and another pair of jeans. He went into his dad's bedroom and found the old leather jacket he kept in the back of his closet. Adam wouldn't even miss it. TJ shoved it into his backpack. It was Halloween and he needed to figure out something for a costume. He had gotten invited to a party at Elysian Park and since he was living there anyway…

Back in the kitchen, TJ grabbed any food items he could find and put them in one of the paper bags they kept by the side of the fridge.

"Get everything you need?"

TJ turned around to see that his dad had come back.

"Darndest thing, I made it all the way to Center Street before I realized I had forgotten my wallet. But you probably already cleaned that out, didn't you?"

"I didn't see your wallet."

"But you would have right? You think you can just come and go as you please and take take take without doing anything? Where are you even sleeping at night, boy?"

"Don't worry about it. I'm sure you haven't yet."

Adam darted across the room and had TJ by the throat before he could react. He lifted the boy off the ground as he gasped for air.

"I told you before, do not disrespect me like that."

Adam let TJ down. TJ started coughing.

"Settle down, you're fine."

"Why do you even act like you care? You don't want me around."

"You're right. I don't. But I don't want you to freeze to death either."

"I'm fine, you're right. Found an empty space at Elysian Park with no one around. So, you can quit worrying about me. I'm doing all right."

"Then why are you here stealing my shit?"

"Whatever. Keep your fucking food."

"If you keep talking to me like that I'm going to knock your fucking teeth in."

"Fucking do it already. Jesus."

Adam moved toward TJ, but TJ grabbed a knife from the block on the counter and held it out.

"Oh, you're a big man now? Big man with a knife?"

"I'm leaving okay? And with any luck, we'll never have to see each other again."

TJ pointed the knife at Adam while he slung his backpack over his shoulder and backed out of the house.

He left the food behind.

NOW

Eric parked the car in Adam's driveway, but kept the engine running.

"I really don't feel good about this," he said. Robbie clutched her purse tight.

"You have to let me talk to him. Alone."

"You don't know what he's capable of."

"He's not going to do anything with you out here. If I'm not out in ten minutes, then come in."

"A lot can happen in ten minutes."

"He's not going to hurt me."

"You don't know that! His kid is sitting at our house because he's afraid to go home and you think you have some 'Get Out of Jail Free' card with him?"

"He called me asking for help. Legal help. Maybe he wants to figure things out with TJ."

"Or maybe he wants you to represent him for a DUI."

"So? I did pass the bar, you know. I may not be practicing, but I can help him."

"Just be careful, okay"

"I will."

"And as soon as ten minutes pass, I'm coming in."

"Okay."

"I love you. I love that your instinct is to help people, but I'm worried."

"I'll be fine."

"Don't lock the door."

Robbie got out of the car, and tried to will herself to believe what she just said as she walked up to Adam's house.

THEN

Javi was itching his neck. He was wearing his clothes backwards for his Halloween costume (zero dollars spent), and the baseball jersey he had was tight around his Adam's apple. Bridget was off dancing or something and he was sneaking a drink from the "hidden" keg that all the underage kids knew about and were pouring into their bottles.

"Can you get me one?"

Javi turned to see who was asking the question, but he should've recognized the voice. It was Trevor.

"Hey," Javi said.

Trevor still made him uncomfortable. He didn't know how to act around him. They were friends. Kind of. They were more than that. Also, kind of. And in some ways, Javi didn't feel like he knew Trevor at all.

"I see you put as much effort into your costume as I did," Javi said, acknowledging the flannel shirt and baggie jeans with a bandana tied around one leg.

“What? This? I’m grunge.”

“You’re something all right.”

Javi handed him a beer.

“Hey, can we talk?” Trevor asked.

“I guess.” Javi looked around to see if any of his friends were around, and he motioned for Trevor to follow him outside. It was cold enough that no one was really hanging out there.

“We didn’t really need the change of scenery.”

“I just don’t need an audience, you know?”

“Afraid someone might figure out what’s going on?”

“There’s nothing going on,” Javi wasn’t mean, but he was stern. He didn’t like admitting it to himself, he couldn’t imagine verbalizing it out loud.

“I think we both know that’s not true. Or did you want me to wait for you to have another six beers like usual?”

“What do you want, Trevor?”

“I like you, Javi. I know you know that. And I know you like me, whether or not you want to admit it. And I’m not trying to push you into anything. But I don’t want to just keep messing around because you’re drunk and horny.”

“I can’t talk about this now.”

“Why not? No one is around.”

“I came here with Bridget, my girlfriend.”

“Yeah, I know who she is. And stressing she’s your girlfriend isn’t going to convince me that it means anything. Or were you saying it for your own benefit?”

“I’ve got to go.”

"You know, she's not gonna be around forever, Javi. You might need another excuse to not deal with me."

NOW

Abby tugs her coat tighter. It was stupid to do this on her own, but she couldn't go back to the police. Not unless she was sure. Her fingers clutched the stun gun that was tucked away in her pocket. She could use it if she needed to, she had no doubt.

She waited outside of the Eppley Building, one of the more boring buildings on the Creighton campus. But she had gotten Trevor's schedule from the administration office. People will believe anything if you're crying.

She watched as Trevor emerged, pulling his hood over his head when he noticed the snow falling.

"Trevor?"

He turned and after giving her a confused look at first, settled into some recognition.

"You're Javi's friend, right? Annie?"

"Abby."

"Yeah, sorry. Is everything okay? What are you doing here?"

"I need to talk to you."

"Yeah? About what?"

"Can we just go inside somewhere warm and maybe quiet?"

Trevor motioned and Abby followed him back into the building. There were other students leaving from a class that must've just let out but he walked into an empty classroom. She closed the door behind them, before realizing she might've been better off leaving it open.

"What's this about? Is Javi okay?"

"Yeah, I guess. I don't know. I don't want to talk about Javi. Not really."

"Then what?"

"I want to talk about the Halloween party at Elysian Park."

"What about it?"

"Javi's girlfriend died that night."

"I'm aware."

"And I'm aware that you were the one who called 911."

Trevor's face tightened.

"I don't know what you're talking about."

Abby pulled a small recorder out of her left-hand pocket (her right hand was still on the stun gun). She pressed play and a crudely-recorded version of the 911 call played.

"… the party. Elysian Park. One of the kids, from the party, they fell. Or jumped. I don't fucking know. I think they're dead. Oh god, they're dead. What the hell, man, you know?"

"That's you," Abby said.

"I don't know. Could be anybody."

"Cut the shit, Trevor. I know it was you. I know you were there that night. And I imagine that you weren't super happy that Javi had a girlfriend while you were crushing on him."

"Yeah, what else do you think you know?"

"Plenty. Trevor Alan Rhodes. Youngest of three kids. Mom is Jeannie, Dad is Ronald. They weren't too happy with your 'lifestyle' as they called it and you were more than happy to move into the dorms here once you graduated last year from Central Aksarben High. You were in band. Didn't play sports, but in the senior production of The Music Man you killed as Harold. No criminal past, never even detention, although juvenile records are sealed, but you're eighteen now. Should I go on?"

"Okay, so you, what, got my school file?"

"Just a yearbook actually, and then talked to someone I knew from your class."

"Why? Is this like a stalker thing? Something about Javi?"

"Be barking up the wrong tree on that one, I think."

"Yeah. So, what?"

"Tell me about the 911 call."

"I saw a body. I made a call. How'd you even get a recording."

"Don't worry about it. It's a copy. There's more. You didn't leave your name."

"I didn't want to deal with the police."

"And you didn't say it was Bridget, you said it was 'some student'."

"I couldn't be sure."

"Well, that's horse shit. Like you didn't know exactly who she was and what she was wearing?"

"Wait, did you think I had something to with her fall?"

"Did she fall? Or was she pushed? And either way, did you have something to do with it?"

Abby gripped tighter on the stun gun.

THEN

Bridget was dancing with some of the other girls and smiling back at Scott and Javi. Scott was uncomfortable. She seemed to be smiling at Javi, but he knew she was smiling at him. And he didn't like it. Not like this. Not in front of everyone. It wasn't right. He worried about Breck, but she was dancing right next to Bridget. He worried about Javi, even though he seemed oblivious.

Bridget was pregnant. She just told him outside, and now she was dancing like nothing was amiss. Scott had to think of an excuse to leave. He had to get the cash he promised to Bridget, but needed to escape without anyone noticing he was gone. And he hadn't yet figured out how to do that.

Just getting to his car would be enough. He had some pills hidden in his glove box, and he could really use some energy.

"Earth to Scott. You cool?" Javi asked. "Everything all right?"

"Yeah, just a lot going on."

"Everything cool with Breck?"

"Oh, yeah. Sorry. Look, it's nothing."

"Come on, man, I'm your best friend. You can tell me anything."

Scott wished like hell that was true.

NOW

Scott hopped the fence and made his way through the park. Snow was covering everything, which in some cases made breaking into Elysian Park a little easier. He was a little nervous about climbing up to the roof of the bathhouse. Everything was slippery, frozen in the colder months.

Javi was huddled in the corner as Scott scrambled up to the roof.

"I really don't understand why you would want to meet here," Scott said.

"Bridget died here."

"Yeah. I know. Besides that, it's colder than shit. So, I'm here. What's all this about?"

"I know about you and Bridget," Javi said as he turned to face Scott. There was a resolve in his eyes that he'd never seen before. It was like he didn't even recognize his friend.

"What do you know?"

"Come on, Scott. It's really important you don't lie to me right now. Were you fucking Bridget?"

"Javi, let's go inside somewhere and talk. It's cold."

"Answer the question."

"Yeah, we got together." Scott figured Javi already knew. There was no point in continuing to lie about it. "I'm sorry."

"Fuck off. Did you know she was pregnant?"

"Yeah. She told me. That night actually."

"Which night was that?"

"The night of the party."

"The night she died?"

"Yeah, Javi. You know that."

"Okay, then tell me something I don't know."

"What do you want? You want me to admit that I'm a terrible person. I am, okay. I know this. I've always known this. My entire life, it's like I watch my parents being these polite and gregarious people and I just… do what they do. It's like I'm play acting at being a real person. I've never felt entirely real."

"Did you push her off this building?"

"What? Of course not."

"Scott," Javi said with a quaver in his voice, as he pulled a gun from his waistband. “It’s really important you don’t lie to me right now.”

Scott took a step back and instinctively put his hands up.

THEN

TJ sat alone at the party. He watched Breck and Scott dancing to a slow song. He felt silly. Why was he even here? No one was talking to him. No one was even looking in his direction. And his costume. He thought it would be funny, but no one really laughed. A box of cereal with a knife in it. Serial killer. It was hilarious. Please. If only he didn’t have to explain it. Everyone here was too stupid to appreciate a costume with a little thought put into it.

Breck never even looked away from Scott. She kept smiling up at him. The dude was like a foot taller than her. They felt so mismatched, even with their stupid matching Star Wars costumes. She deserved so much better than that guy.

“You like her, don’t you?”

TJ saw that Bridget had sat down next to him. He didn’t like her much either. There was something off about her.

“Who?”

“It’s obvious, dude. But tuck your boner in your belt or something, because it’s never gonna happen. That bitch is hopeless.”

“Shut up. What are you even doing over here?”

“Just trying to give you some advice.”

“Well, I don’t need any of your advice. Thanks.”

“Look, no offense, but you’re kind of a creepy loser. And I know she felt sorry enough for you to invite you here, but believe me, that’s as far as it’s gonna go.”

"Why would I take offense to that? You're just being honest, right? Well, let me return the favor. I know you think being a stone-cold-super-mega-bitch to the lowest dude on the popularity totem pole is a good way to get out whatever teenage drama bullshit you got swirling around in your head. But I promise you, I don't care. I see right through you. You pretend you're such hot shit because you really can't stand yourself. I'm right there with you. You suck."

"You don't know anything about me."

"Oh well. You can leave."

"And you can fuck off."

"Be careful. I got a knife."

TJ meant it as a joke, but Bridget didn't laugh. She simply glared at him.

"Creep."

NOW

"What are you doing in my stuff?" TJ asked. Breck was standing there holding his bag. No one else was home, so what was she even doing there? And, oh shit. Did she see the picture?

Wait. Was she bleeding?

"I… um… I didn't mean… I was just."

"Are you bleeding?"

TJ started to move toward Breck but she took a step beck.

"Don't."

"Breck, come on. What's wrong?"

"Why do you have a knife? And what is on it?"

"Look, I can explain."

TJ took another step but then Breck swiftly kicked him in the nuts. He felt the pain up to his stomach and dropped to his knees. Breck grabbed the backpack, and started to move towards the door. TJ reached out and grabbed her foot. He just wanted to talk to her, but he ended up knocking her down.

"Ow."

"I'm sorry."

Breck kicked TJ's hand back and quickly got to her feet. TJ was between her and the stairs so she dashed into Scott's bedroom. TJ got up and ran after her but she made it into the bathroom and then locked the door.

TJ pounded.

"Breck, come on. Talk to me."

"Go away!"

THEN

Adam didn't know why he came to the park. TJ said he was living here, but he couldn't understand what that meant. He was calmer now. More clearheaded. He could talk to TJ. Sort this out. He had no idea there would be a party going on.

There was no security.

The sign said "CLOSED FOR PRIVATE PARTY" but he just walked right in. It was mostly kids, teenagers who probably worked at the park. And… older kids who worked at the park? Everyone was so young. He stood out, but other than a couple looks, and some hidden cups, no one really reacted to him walking around. But he wasn't here to bust them. He just wanted to talk to his son.

When Adam finally caught sight of TJ he was arguing with some black girl. He couldn't hear exactly what they were saying, he didn't want to get too close, but it looked heated. The girl scoffed at TJ and started walking away, right towards Adam.

It was an instinct, but Adam reached out and grabbed the girl's hand.

"Hey, what was that about?" he asked.

"None of your fucking business, jerk. Let go of me."

"That's my son."

"Well, that explains the creep factor."

When the girl pulled away her glove came off in Adam's hand, but she was off before he could say anything. He just looked at the small, white glove that was left in his hand. He turned back towards TJ, but he was gone. The only thing that was on the table where he was sitting was a box of cereal with a knife in it.

The same knife that TJ had pulled on Adam.

NOW

Robbie kept pacing. She didn't want to get too close to Adam. She insisted he stay seated at the kitchen table.

"I really don't think I can help you with this, Adam."

"I don't have anyone else I can call. You know me, Robbie. You know I didn't do this."

"I don't know that. Let's be clear on that. Now, tell me again."

"I told you everything. I had gotten pulled over for a DUI. They searched my car and they found this girl's glove."

"Which you had because you accidentally bumped into her?"

"Yes. I barely said two words to her."

"And they questioned you?"

"Yes. They gave me a public defender for the DUI. I have a court date, but they said I have to go in tomorrow for questioning as a 'person of interest' in the other thing."

"The other thing being murder?"

"I didn't do it."

"Then why do they think you did? This can't just be because of some glove."

"They also found my coat in her car."

"What? Why was your coat in her car?"

"I have no idea."

"What aren't you telling me here, Adam?"

Adam looked across the room. Robbie waited for him to say something. Anything. But he just sat there. Breathing through clenched jaw and squeezing his fists tighter.

"Come on. Tell me."

"I saw them arguing. It seemed like some stupid teenage thing. I don't even know why I followed him there. I wanted him to come home. But I knew he wouldn't. Something was so different about him. I'd hit him before. I'm not proud of that. But I did it. He just made me so angry sometimes. But that look in his eyes when he held that knife. I knew I lost him."

"TJ?"

"Yeah."

"What does this have to do with him?"

"I didn't know who the girl was until I saw her on the news, and the picture they showed was this sweet, smiling girl. Not the foul-mouthed, snot that was yelling at TJ."

"Adam?"

"Think about it, Robbie. TJ wasn't staying there anymore. Not after the police were swarming the place. He had my jacket. He must've left it in her car."

"Her car was stolen."

"They found it. And the plates were not for the car. They belonged to Ramona Henderson."

"Who is Ramona Henderson?"

"The sweet lady that lives across the street from me."

"You think TJ had something to do with this?"

"Yeah. I do."

THEN

Abby inhaled weakly on her cigarette and suppressed the urge to cough. Even though she didn't like her, she wanted Bridget to think she was cooler than she was. Abby wasn't a smoker, but with her pregnant nun costume, the smoking added to the whole aesthetic.

The music from the party blared in the background. Abby was happy to have escaped it, but she was surprised she ended up smoking with Bridget on the upstairs patio.

"You know, I have to say, I really fucking hate high school," Bridget huffed.

"You're a popular, beautiful cheerleader. What chance do I have?"

"Don't sell yourself short. Besides, being popular isn't all it's cracked up to be."

"Beats being lonely."

"Sometimes I wonder if popularity is its own kind of loneliness. I want to move to Los Angeles, be an actress. I think all of my friends would be surprised to hear that."

"You want to leave all this behind?" Abby said sarcastically.

"The absolute second I can, which, who knows, may be sooner than later."

"I want to go to New York. Something about the super tall buildings and people everywhere. Feels like a wonderful place to disappear."

"At least it's easy for you to disappear. I would love that. To just not have to be me for a day. When you're one of three students that look like this, people notice you. And even outside of school people notice you. How great to not have this…burden."

"Well, there's always college."

"Yeah, maybe. If I could wait that long. And if my mom could afford for me to go out of state."

"Well, trust me, reinvention isn't all it's cracked up to be either. It always follows you."

"Yeah, I guess. And if I did anything to make it keep following you, well, my bad. It wasn't personal. And I could say I'm sorry, and I am, but I don't think that would really make up for it."

"Not really, no. But it's nice to hear."

"Well, there's a party going on just a few feet from us. And for some stupid reason I want to get back to it. Not that this hasn't been real."

"Don't let me stop you."

"As if you could. But hey, this wasn't the worst part of my day."

"Don't worry, I won't let the word get out that you're not quite as big of a bitch as you might seem."

"Thanks. I do have a reputation to protect."

Bridget gave Abby a wink as she walked away. Abby felt a twinge of jealousy. Bridget had a confidence that impressed her for once. And she looked so sexy in her outfit. Except for the stupid hoop earrings.

NOW

"I swear to you I didn't have anything to do with Bridget's death," Trevor said. He seemed sincere.

"And why should I believe you?"

"Well, I don't really care if you do, but also it's the truth."

"Then why not say 'hey, cops, there's a body and it's Bridget. By the way, my name is Trevor.' That could've saved some time. Maybe they could've asked you some questions."

"Yeah, can't imagine why I didn't want the police asking me questions about finding the body of the girl that was dating the boy I like."

"Okay, that checks out. But surely you saw how much this was hurting Javi. Why not tell him?"

"If I thought he could handle it. But sometimes he gets a bit…spazzy. Doesn't quite know how to handle his feelings."

"What were you even doing at the park so late? Party shut down at midnight. I know. I was there."

"I work in concessions. And I had a little too much to drink so I was hiding out in one of the booths just trying to sober up. Must've passed out. I woke up and no one was around. I was wandering through the park when I saw her. I could tell she was dead. I didn't even get close to her. I saw the blood. And her head was all turned around. There was nothing in her eyes."

"Where did you make the call?"

"Pay phone in the parking lot. I didn't want to be here when the cops did show up."

"Did you see anyone else?"

"Yeah. Some guy."

"What? Who?"

"I don't know. He had a hood up. But he jumped in his car and bolted out of there."

"What kind of car?"

"Rich kid car. BMW, I think."

Shit. Abby felt a sinking feeling in her stomach.

"Why didn't you say anything? Even anonymously."

"I wanted to. But I didn't know how. And then Javi said some kid at the school was questioned, and it was some rich kid with a beemer so I feel like nothing I said would help."

"Which kid?"

"The Van Allen kid. I forget his name. But his dad owns like half of Omaha."

THEN

"I have misplaced my boyfriend," Breck joked. "Again."

TJ was standing off the dancefloor when Breck came up to him. He couldn't figure out why she was even talking to him, but then again, she did invite him.

"It wasn't my turn to watch him," TJ said.

"Are you having fun?"

TJ shrugged.

"Come on. Aren't you glad you came?"

"I guess."

"Where's Abby?"

"I think she went outside."

"Isn't her costume hilarious?"

"I guess."

TJ didn't know how to respond. He was starting to figure out why Breck invited him and it was to get pawned off on her friend. He couldn't figure Abby out, and he really had no interest in her. He just wanted to stand here and keep talking to Breck. There was something about the lilt in her voice, and the way she smiled through every word.

"Do you wanna dance?" TJ asked, maybe softer than he intended.

"Oh, there's Scott."

TJ turned to see Scott in his Han Solo getup coming in from the outside. Breck was already halfway to him, nearly tripping in her Leia costume. It was all so fitting. And TJ felt like a moron for even thinking she might want to dance with him. He was lucky she even talked to him.

NOW

Breck had locked the door, but she still backed away as TJ pounded on the other side.

"Leave me alone!" Breck shouted.

She was trapped. The bathroom was in the middle of the basement. No windows. Only one door with a psycho on the other side.

"I can explain. It's nothing. It's the knife from my Halloween costume. Remember?" TJ shouted from the other side of the door.

Breck couldn't remember what TJ was for Halloween off the bat.

There was a knife? Oh, right. The cereal killer. It was a silly costume. But in hindsight, it was in poor taste. Really poor taste considering that night.

"Okay, fine. It's from your costume. What's on it? Because it looks like blood."

There was no response.

"TJ?"

"I'm here. I don't want you to hate me, Breck. Please, just let me explain."

"Go ahead. But I'm not opening this door."

"I lost the knife. At the party. I left it behind somewhere. But I found it… with Bridget."

"What do you mean 'with Bridget'?"

"I was in the apartment. At the bathhouse. I was hiding out there. That night. I heard Bridget scream. Well, I heard a girl scream. I didn't know it was her right away. It woke me up. I wasn't sure what it was and I went to the window, and then I saw her. On the ground. I didn't know what I was supposed to do. But I knew I couldn't be found there. I thought she jumped but I heard someone leaving. I stayed quiet. I didn't see who it was. I just got my stuff and got out of there. When I made it down to her, she was gone. Her body was… well, it doesn't matter. I saw the knife on the ground next to her. My knife. I grabbed it and I got the hell out of there."

Breck could feel the tears coming. She didn't know if she believed him. But just thinking about Bridget lying there was enough to get her started.

"Where did you go?"

"It was so cold. I didn't know what else to do. I saw her car in the parking lot and I… it wasn't even locked. The keys were sitting in the console. I just… I got outta there."

"And you never said anything?"

"What was I supposed to say? I stayed in the car for a couple weeks but then the police found it. I wanted to get rid of the knife but I didn't want them to trace it back to me. It was from our house. I forget it was even there. I was on the street until Robbie found me. And coming back here I was just so grateful to have a place to stay. And I didn't want anything to mess that up."

Breck didn't know what to say. She could hear the despair in TJ's voice, but she couldn't be sure it wasn't all an act.

"You have to believe me," TJ said. "I didn't hurt her. I could never hurt anyone. Especially not you. I'm sorry. I didn't mean to scare you. Please believe me."

Breck didn't know how to respond. So, she didn't.

THEN

"I feel like I haven't seen you all night," Javi said as he finally got Bridget alone.

"It's been a little crazy."

"What've you been doing?"

"Dancing my butt off."

"I was watching you dance your butt off. I meant after that."

"Are you checking up on me?"

"No, I just missed you." Javi leaned for a kiss but Bridget pulled away. "Is something wrong?"

"No. Yes. I don't know. I really don't. I'm sorry. I'm a mess, Javi. But you knew that when you met me, right?"

Javi could see that something was off with Bridget but didn't know how to say that.

"You can talk to me."

"I know. It's not that. I don't want to hurt you, Javi. And I'm afraid I'm going to hurt you."

"You could never hurt me."

"How do you know that?"

"I don't know. I just do."

"You should stay away from me, Javi. Really."

"What do you mean?"

"I'm only gonna mess you up. I promise. I don't want to. But I can't help it, you know?"

"Are you breaking up with me?"

"No. Of course not. I mean, I don't know. I just don't want you to hate me. And I feel like you're gonna hate me."

"I could never hate you."

"You say that now, but you don't how messed up I am."

NOW

"Woah, woah, Javi, come on, bud, what is this?"

"It's a question, bud. And don't try to trot out some of that best friend bullshit. You haven't been a real friend to me in months. Lying about this. Lying about whatever you're using. Using me as an excuse with Breck. It's like you're some alien that has inhabited my friend's body."

"Come on. I know this is tough. But you gotta believe me. I didn't do this. I swear."

"And why should I believe you?"

Javi was pointing the gun at Scott. And Scott was moving around but Javi kept the gun on him. He had to know the truth.

"I'm going to ask you again," Javi said. "Did you kill her? And this time answer like I have a fucking gun in my hand."

"I swear to you. No."

"Does Breck know you were fucking Bridget?"

"Do you think she would still be with me if she did? Come on, man. It's really snowing and I know you don't want to kill me. I swear I will tell you everything, let's just go inside somewhere."

"I'm not going anywhere with you. If you got something to say, you can say it right here."

THEN

The party was over. Percy sat in his car, watching kids shuffle out of the park. He had parked on the street, far enough away that no one was paying any attention to him. The page said to meet on the roof, but not until 1am. He knew how to sneak in. Everyone who had ever worked there knew how to sneak in. And he had spent the summer before as a lifeguard in some lame attempt to work on his tan. It also helped him meet up with his customers.

He never wanted to be a drug dealer. He fell into it. One of his friends wanted some weed and Percy asked around about it. He found one dealer, and then found his supplier, and began to bankroll his friends. He was a sixteen-year-old sophomore when he was approached by Darian at some party. Darian lived, and dealt, in North Omaha, the predominantly black area of town. But the private schools offered more opportunity and Darian found an army of kids that could be his network in places where he wasn't able to go.

Percy never thought he would enjoy it. But people kept coming to him. And so long as Darian got his cut, he could get whatever he wanted. It made Percy feel important. It made him feel popular, which he was, though his money and status would probably have seen to that anyway.

He only saw Darian once a month. To get more stuff, and to pay him his cut. He had gotten the pager on his own and only gave it out to people he trusted, but numbers had a way of getting passed around. He knew it was Bridget that paged him that night, but he didn't know why. He assumed she might want something, but he never kept drugs on him. Not without a plan in place. He rushed over to meet her and if she did need something, he could grab it from home without even waking up his parents.

Percy waited until the parking lot was empty before getting out of his car and making his way into the park. He pulled his hood up over his head, just in case there were some stragglers still around.

NOW

Abby had enough trouble driving home in the snow, she wasn't sure she wanted to venture back out on the streets. There was a message from her mom on the answering machine. She got stuck at work late and her and some other coworkers decided to go across the street to the hotel rather than drive in the storm.

Maybe it was good she wasn't going to be home.

Abby still had Trevor's words tumbling around in her brain and she was trying to make sense of everything he said. She called her mother, to tell her she was home safe. Didn't want her to worry. Then, she dialed his number.

"We need to talk," Abby said when Percy answered. "Can you come over?"

Percy agreed. Said he would be right over. Abby knew that whatever was about to happen she didn't want to risk being alone, not if what she was worried about was true. She still had the stun gun. But that may not be enough.

She knew Jake would be at Kira's. They had been getting closer, and she wasn't sure how to feel about that, but she couldn't think about it now. She had to get Jake to come home.

Kira answered but handed the phone over to Jake.

"Jake, can you come home?" Abby asked, somewhat nervously. "I really need you to come home. Percy is on his way over… and I'm pretty sure he killed Bridget."

Jake was on his way.

THEN

Harlan was supposed to go to Chicago on business. He was meeting one of his clients for a breakfast meeting, and had scheduled a couple other check-ins while he was there, but now none of it seemed that important. He had just written a ten-thousand-dollar check to a girl simply because she said she was pregnant with Percy's child. Was it even true? He wouldn't put it past Percy. He didn't feel like he even knew his son these days, but ten-thousand dollars was nothing compared to the scandal of his son knocking up some girl—yes, some black girl.

But then what if it got out that he wrote this girl a check? He would have to figure that out later.

He was supposed to get on a plane but he didn't foresee he was going to make his flight. He didn't want to be away. That didn't mean he had to go home. He picked up his phone.

"Hello," she answered.

"Is your husband home?

NOW

"I'm not lying to you, Eli," Harlan said.

"Then do you want to tell me what's on this video?"

"I told you. It's about Percy."

"Then why didn't you just say that?"

"I don't know."

"That I believe."

"Eli, come on. Let's sit down. We can talk about this."

"No, we can't. I want nothing more to do with this. You're on your own."

"Meaning what?"

"Meaning this thing, you and I, it's over."

"What are you going to do with the tape?"

"That's your question? That's what you're worried about."

"Eli, this is my life."

"THIS IS MY LIFE," she shouted. "She was one of my husband's students. Did you know that? When the police gave back his stuff that was in the car after the wreck, there was this journal among some other books. I guess they didn't realize what they had. And her name was right there on it. There were pages missing. But the ones about her crush on her teacher. That was there. I have no idea why he had it. I have no idea what their relationship was. And I'm sitting here cursing his name and thinking awful things about him. And then I see you on this tape. Yelling at her after paying her off."

"It's not like that."

"I remember you called me that day. It was Halloween. Danny was at the store getting candy because both of us had forgotten, and you called while he was out. You told me you weren't taking your trip to Chicago that weekend. You asked what I was doing. Tried to get me to blow off Danny and sneak off with you. But I said 'no.'"

"Yeah, you did."

"So, then tell me, Harlan. After I told you 'no,' after you paid off this girl, after you yelled at her, I can only imagine threatening her, and then after getting an alibi for being out of town that weekend, what did you do?"

THEN

Vanessa woke up on the couch. The TV was still blaring, with some band she didn't recognize playing on Saturday Night Live. It must still be before midnight. She told Bridget to be home by ten, didn't she?

Vanessa got up off the couch, but kept hold of the blanket that was around her. Her hair was flattened on one side. How long was she out?

She went upstairs to Bridget's room. Bridget wasn't there. How dare she? Out past curfew? Unacceptable. Or did she have a game? Vanessa was trying to remember what their conversation was before she left. Bridget was in her cheerleading uniform, right?

Vanessa opened Bridget's closet, but her uniform wasn't hanging there. In fact, hardly anything was hanging there. It looked like someone had cleaned it out. Did Bridget have a sleepover? Vanessa was foggy. She hated being like this.

She should take her pills. Or was this because of her pills? Nothing was making sense. Was Bridget supposed to be home? Was she late? Or was she gone?

Vanessa hated not knowing what she was supposed to be worrying about.

NOW

"I said get over here, girl," Vanessa said.

Kira stood up, slowly, keeping her back against the wall.

"Vanessa… Mrs. Hudson? Are you okay?"

"Baby, call me Momma."

"It's me, Kira. I'm not Bridget."

"Why are you talking foolish?"

Vanessa stood up and moved towards Kira, but Kira darted around her and moved towards the door.

"Get back here."

"I'm right here, I'm not going anywhere. I just need to make a quick phone call," Kira said as calmly as possible. Vanessa's eyes were bouncing around looking all over the room. Kira wasn't sure what was happening but didn't want to alarm here.

The phone was sitting on Bridget's dresser, and Kira picked it up and quickly dialed home.

"Who are you calling at this hour? Hang it up."

Kira held up her hand. "This will be quick, Va… Mom."

Vanessa looked disappointed. "I said put the phone down. You never listen to me."

"Hi, Daddy," Kira said into the phone. "I'm across the street. Yes. Can you come over right now, please? I need your help."

"I said HANG IT UP!" Vanessa shouted and jumped towards Kira.

THEN

Percy made sure he wasn't seen by anyone as he made his way over to the bathhouse. He climbed the ladder up to the top. There was a lot of crap on the roof, and she didn't notice him right away. She was on the other side, staring over the edge.

"Bridget?" he called out. She turned and looked. She seemed relieved to see him, but she fell short of smiling.

"Hi."

"Okay, I'm here. What do you need?"

NOW

Percy knocked on the door, but no one answered. He let himself in. There was an urgency in Abby's voice when she called.

"Abby?" he called out, as he shut the door behind him.

"Hi," Abby said as she walked into the living room. "How were the roads?"

"They were bad, okay. What's going on?"

Abby stood across the room from him. She had her hands in her pocket. Something was off.

“Is everything okay?”

“I don’t think so,” she said. Percy started to move toward her but she held up her hand to motion him back. “Don’t.”

“What is it?”

“You need to be honest with me. About everything.”

“About what? Just talk to me, Abby.”

“I know you were there that night. In the park. With Bridget.”

Percy let out a deep breath. There was no denying it any more.

“Yeah.”

“Tell me everything.”

“What do you want to know?”

“Did you kill her?”

“Honestly? I don’t know.”

Abby took a step back, but she didn’t say anything. Her eyes just said to keep going.

“I went there. After the party. She paged me. Said to meet her up on the roof. I didn’t think it was weird. She would sometimes page me to meet her in random places.”

“Did she buy from you a lot?”

“Sometimes, but that’s not why she called me. She told me she was pregnant. And it might be mine. Wanted me to, you know, pay for it.”

“You slept with her?”

“I don’t remember that either. But yeah, there was a party we woke up together.”

“Classy.”

“I was drunk. Not that I’m trying to make excuses.”

“So, she asks for money, then what happened?”

"That's where it gets hazy. I remember waking up. But Bridget wasn't there. I was bleeding."

"Bleeding?"

"I think someone stabbed me."

Percy went to lift up his sweater, but she jumped back and pulled out the stun gun, and held it out.

"Stop."

"It's okay. I'm sorry. I was trying to show you."

She motioned for him to keep going. He pulled up his sweater on his left and turned towards her. He couldn't quite see the remnants of the gash, but the look on her face said that she did.

"I was out of it. I don't know what happened. I cleaned up my blood as best I could. Tried to hide it and then got in my car and drove home before the sun came up."

"What time was this?"

"I don't know. Like three or four? I taped up my side but I knew I needed more than that, so I called an ambulance and told them I fell and then jumped into this glass coffee table I had. I didn't think they would look too hard at the one wound if I was cut all over my body."

"It was 3:47am."

"How do you know that?"

"I heard your 911 call. Do you remember anything else? From before?"

"I was talking to her and I remember feeling the pain in my side and then a pain in my head and then… waking up later."

"Where was your car?"

"I parked on the street."

"Did anyone see you?"

"I don't think so. But I was pretty messed up. I would imagine I left blood somewhere. But I never heard anything about anyone actually finding any."

"Maybe they were saving that for when you got caught."

"But they did question me. In the hospital."

"And you lied to the police?"

"Yeah."

"Why did you lie to me?"

"Because I didn't want you to look at me the way you're looking at me right now."

"And how is that?"

"Like you're afraid of me. Like I could hurt you."

"I know you wouldn't hurt me, Percy. And I know you didn't do it."

"How do you know that?"

"Because I know who did."

"Who?"

The front door opened and Jake came rushing in.

"Abby? You okay?" Jake said as he walked into the living room. Abby moved closer to him. "Get away from her."

"Jake, Percy did it. He killed Bridget."

"What?" Percy said. He felt betrayed.

Jake lunged towards him but Percy jumped back. Abby moved toward Jake, and before Percy even realized what was happening, there was a loud buzzing sound and Jake fell to the ground. Abby was behind Jake with the stun gun out.

"What do you know? It works."

Jake was shaking on the ground, but his eyes were still fluttering. Abby reached down and shocked him again.

"What are you doing?" Percy asked.

"It was him. Jake killed Bridget. Now, help me tie him up."

"What?"

THEN

"Pregnant?" Percy asked.

"Yeah," Bridget replied.

"I'm sorry. That's rough. Are you okay?"

"I'm … fine. I just need help, you know?"

"Yeah, of course, whatever you need. You shouldn't be dealing with this all on your own. You sure you're okay."

Bridget turned away. She didn't want Percy to see her cry. Not because she was embarrassed, but because she didn't want him to realize she was lying. She wasn't prepared for him to be nice. After everyone else she's been talking to, he was the only one that showed any interest in how she was doing. But she was going to be fine. This would all be all over soon and she wouldn't have to deal with this town or anyone in it any more.

She felt Percy's hand on her shoulder, and for a moment she was comforted. But she had to keep going.

And then, everything happened all at once. There was a THUD. Percy's fingers fell away and Bridget turned around to see Percy slumped on the ground and Jake standing over him, holding a fire extinguisher. His skeleton costume was barely visibly underneath his hoodie.

"What did you do?"

"Knocked the fucker out," Jake said. "I think you and I need to talk."

Bridget took a step back. She knew Jake could be a hot head but she'd never seen him with such red in his eyes.

"Jake, I can explain. It's not what it looks like."

"Really? Because it looks like you're giving Percy the same story you gave me. And the same story I heard you give Scott. Exactly how many guys have you been fucking?"

"It's not like that. I never had sex with Percy. I just made him think we did."

"And that makes it better?"

"No. I just… I didn't know what else to do."

Bridget was really crying now. It all came rushing out of her. The lies. The build-up. All she wanted was to get out of town and the only way to do that was with money. So, she targeted the boys she knew that had money, and used them. She told herself they deserved it. She was only doing to them what they did to her, and countless others: lied to get what they want. It's just that what she wanted was different. Percy was nice, but he was a drug dealer. Scott pretended he cared about her, but he showed no remorse for screwing his best friend's girlfriend or for cheating on Breck. Jake had been a fling, her "Richie Rich," but she never felt she was anything other than an object to him. He only called her when he couldn't find anyone else.

"So, who is really the daddy here? Or is there someone else behind door number four?"

"Jake, come on. I know you're mad, but I didn't mean for this to happen."

"For what? Me to figure out you've been stringing half of Omaha along?"

"It's not like that."

"Oh shit," Jake started chuckling. "I just realized something. You're way smarter than I ever gave you credit for."

"What do you mean?"

"Hold on, I have just one question, but I think I need a little help from loverboy here."

Jake pulled up an unconscious Percy from the back of his collar. From his belt, he pulled out a large kitchen knife. And held it to Percy's throat.

"Tell me, Bridget, and if you lie to me, I'll know. Now, a few days ago, I gave you five-hundred dollars for an abortion. And then I see tonight that you have reached out to Scott and Percy here for additional funds. But I have to ask… were you even ever pregnant?"

Bridget stepped further away.

"You have to understand…" she started.

"Of course, you weren't. FUCK."

Jake let his left arm fall to his side, but he kept hold of Percy. Then he let out a disgruntled moan and jabbed the knife right into Percy's side.

Bridget gasped and held her hand to her face.

"Oh, shit. I stabbed him."

Jake dropped Percy and he fell forward with a THUMP as blood started to spill out through his clothes.

"I didn't mean to," Jake said as he stood up.

But he was still holding the knife so Bridget continued to back away from him, until she bumped into the edge of the wall.

"Help," Bridget tried to shout, but her voice only came out a little squeak.

"No no no no, shut up."

Jake ran over and put his hand over Bridget's mouth, but he wasn't paying attention and poked her with the knife. It was just a little slice, but she screamed regardless, and her arms started swinging.

She smacked Jake in the head with one hand, but cut her other hand. Jake reflexively pushed back and ended up smacking her hard enough to knock her over the edge. The knife went with her, and she screamed as she fell down to the hard ground below, staring at Jake's disbelieving eyes the whole way down.

NOW

Abby helped Percy put Jake in Percy's trunk. They had tied him up with duct tape, but he was still unconscious. Abby closed the trunk door.

"Give me your keys," she said, and Percy handed them to her.

The two ran back into Abby's house.

"We need to call the cops," Percy said.

"Not yet."

"Why not?"

"Because we need proof."

"Abby, what do you mean proof? Did he do it or not? Because this isn't the first time you were sure someone did it."

"I'm sure."

"How do you know?"

"The journal."

"Bridget's journal?"

"Yeah, she had all these stories about some rich guy she was seeing and I thought it was you, but it didn't make sense. And it didn't add up with you only sleeping with her the one time."

"So, where's the journal now?"

"I don't know. It did get stolen. Jake knew my locker combo because he had to get my homework when I was out. He must've taken it."

"That's why he sent me your suspect list. Because he didn't know you thought I was in the journal. And he knew it was himself."

"And he's left-handed, which points to the stab wound on your left side. And Trevor saw someone drive away in his BMW, but he thought it was you, but Jake drove my mom's BMW that night. He gave me a ride, but I left early. And if you were still lying unconscious when Trevor called the cops, then it had to be someone else. And I know Jake left around two-thirty."

"Who the hell is Trevor?"

"Doesn't matter."

"And how do you know when Jake left?"

"Because I think he was planning on me being his alibi."

THEN

Abby heard the door creak open. He hadn't come into her room the past couple nights, but now here he was again. She didn't turn towards him. Maybe he would think she was asleep and just leave. She could see his figure in the reflection in the window, but he didn't come towards her, instead he started messing with her clock on the nightstand.

He pulled the sheets back and slid into bed with her.

"Abby, are you awake?"

She didn't answer.

"Abby?"

Jake shook her softly and Abby relented and turned towards him.

"What are you doing?"

"I know it's late. It's like one-thirty, but I didn't want to be alone."

Jake pressed his body against hers, but then whispered softly, "we don't have to do anything. Just let me stay here until morning."

NOW

"He came into your room?"

"It wasn't the first time."

"What are you saying?"

"We don't have time to get into all that. I'll tell you everything. Later. I just need to get something."

Percy followed Abby into Jake's room. She started digging around his closet, and pulled out his video camera bag

"What's that for?"

"Easy, I'm going to get him to confess."

"What?"

"If I get his confession on camera then he's not going to weasel his way out of this."

"What makes you think he will tell you anything?"

"Because he doesn't know how to lie to me."

"What are you talking about? He's been lying to you for months."

"Well, it's not like I asked him."

Abby took a penny off of Jake's desk and unscrewed the cover off of the vent.

"What are you doing up there?"

"I know his hiding places."

Abby reached into the vent, but there was nothing in there but some bags of weed.

"Shit."

"What did you think you would find?"

"I don't know. He's not that bright. He had to leave some clue behind."

"Again, I don't think you're giving him enough credit for getting away with murder for several months."

"Son of a bitch."

Abby stormed across the hall into her room. She took the penny and undid the cover on her own vent. She reached in and pulled out several torn pages.

"That fucker."

"What?"

"Bridget's journal. I didn't put these here."

Abby reached in deeper and pulled out a large, hoop earring.

"Bridget's earring. She was wearing this that night. I think if Jake couldn't use me as an alibi, he was going to use me as a scapegoat."

"I'm sorry, Abby."

"Look, you have to call the police, but in like half an hour, and tell them… tell them everything that happened. But then tell them Jake took me."

"What? No way."

"You have to. I know I can get him to confess, but I need to get him alone. If the cops take him now, he's going to get out of it. I know it."

"What do you expect me to say? I just watched him take you away and then called once I finished watching 'Full House'?"

"Tell them he had the stun gun and knocked you out. And when you came to, we were gone."

"Come on, no one is going to believe that."

Percy turned his back to her for just a moment, but then Abby pulled out the stun gun and zapped Percy to the floor before he could react.

"Gee, I don't know. They might."

Abby knelt down next to Percy, whose eyes fluttered closed. She repositioned his head into a more comfortable position, and then gently rubbed her fingers through his hair.

"I'm sorry. I know you'll forgive me. But I have to do this."

Abby reached into Percy's back pocket and pulled out his wallet and put it in her purse. She shoved the pages and earring in as well, and slung the bag over her shoulder. She ran down the stairs and out into the cold. She hopped into Percy's car, and said a little prayer that she would be able to drive in the snow.

34. ROBBIE

The knife sat on the kitchen table, next to a bag of pills and an Altoid tin of white powder. Adam and TJ sat across the room from each other, with Eric judiciously placed in between them. Robbie leaned against the counter while Breck washed her face in the kitchen sink. Everyone was quiet.

It all happened so fast.

One moment she was confronting Adam, flabbergasted that he could think his son could hurt Bridget, let alone kill her. Robbie knew TJ. He had been living in her house for months. And that sweet young man was not capable of such an act of violence. But the next moment she called home, and the busy signal she got, sent her mind racing. She grabbed Adam and they hopped into the car Eric still had running in the driveway and raced back home, snowstorm be damned.

They found TJ banging on the bathroom door, yelling at Breck. Adam had grabbed TJ and threw him down. Robbie yelled and jumped in between them before it got worse. They coerced Breck out of the bathroom and she was holding a knife, a knife that had blood on it. Breck and

TJ were yelling back and forth and Eric found the backpack they were discussing and that's where they found the baggies of pills, and a small tin of white powder. Everyone made it to the kitchen without incident, but Robbie had no clue what to do now.

And where the hell was Scott?

"Okay," Robbie started. "I'm going to start asking questions. It's really important that no one interrupt and that no one answers any question I'm not asking. We need to figure out what happens next. Is that clear?"

Robbie met eyes with Adam, TJ and Breck and they all nodded.

"TJ," she continued. "Tell me where you got the knife."

"It's from our kitchen. At home…my dad's home. I used it for a Halloween costume. I must've left it somewhere. And… I was staying there. Above the bathhouse there's this apartment that wasn't being used and when I ran away that's where I went. And I found the knife on Bridget when she… was on the ground. And I was afraid, I don't know, that they would trace it back to our house and I didn't know what to do with it."

"Did you kill that girl?" Adam blurted out.

"Don't answer that," Robbie shouted. "Adam, you will get your turn."

"What? No. Of course not. You think I could've killed someone?"

"I was there that night. I saw you and her arguing," Adam said.

"Are you serious? What were you doing there?" TJ asked.

"I followed you. I was worried about you."

"Since when?"

"Our fight that night… I was disappointed in… how it went."

"Yeah, I wasn't thrilled about it either."

"Adam, please," Robbie interjected. "TJ, tell us what happened."

"Yeah, we fought. She treated me like crap. So what. Everyone at that school treats me like crap. Doesn't mean anything."

"That's not true," Breck said softly. "I was nice to you."

"I know. You're right. You were the only one. And when you were going through my things, I just kind of lost it. I'm sorry. I didn't mean to scare you. But I didn't do anything. I swear."

"Do you know who did?" Robbie asked.

"No. I heard her scream and then she was on the ground but I was too afraid to be seen. When I finally got up the nerve I just got out of there."

"Why didn't you say anything?" Robbie asked.

"What was I supposed to say that wouldn't make you look at me differently or kick me out of the house. Do you even believe me?"

"I do believe you," Robbie said. "But I need you to tell me everything."

TJ wasn't looking Robbie in the eye, but she did believe him. There was something in his voice, a resignation.

"I stole her car," he finally said.

"What?" Adam said, loudly, but Robbie held out her hand to keep him quiet. She didn't want him to keep TJ from continuing to share.

"I was scared. And I just wanted to get out of there. And I thought if I was walking I might get picked up. So, I took it."

"And?"

"And I broke into our neighbor's garage and stole her plates so it wouldn't be so easy to find. I parked on the other side of town, behind this church in South O, and I lived there for a couple weeks."

"Oh my god," Breck said softly.

"But I came back one day and I saw police lights and I knew that was done, so I had nowhere else to go."

"And that's why you were behind Target where I found you?" Robbie asked.

"Yes."

"Is there anything of yours in that car?"

"I don't know, I kept most of my stuff on me. I kind of figured it was going to happen sooner or later."

"There has to be something. Something that can tie the car back to your father?"

"What?" Adam said.

"Think about it," Robbie said. "You said they have something on you. The neighbor's plate isn't enough."

"His jacket," TJ muttered.

"What?"

"I took his leather jacket."

"Son of a bitch."

"Adam."

"What do you mean they have something on him?" TJ asked.

"Your father was arrested."

"Why?"

"Well, for a DUI. But after he made bail, the police asked him to come in for questioning."

"I thought you might've had something to do with it. Nothing was making sense," Adam said. "And I may not be the best father, but I was afraid of making it worse."

"I didn't have anything to do with it. I swear."

"Tell me about the drugs," Robbie said.

"They aren't mine."

"Whose are they?"

TJ looked at Breck and Robbie saw a look of recognition across her face.

"What?" Robbie asked.

"They're Scott's," TJ said.

"What? Scott doesn't do drugs," Eric said.

"What do you mean, they're Scott's? Did Scott give them to you? Were they a friend's or something?"

"I took them from him."

"How did he get them? This doesn't make sense." Robbie could feel her tone shifting. Maybe she was wrong about TJ. Maybe he was capable of lying. Certainly, Scott wasn't mixed up in all of this.

"You're not gonna say anything?" TJ said while staring down Breck.

"Do you know something about this?" Robbie asked Breck. "Did Scott get them from you?"

"What? No. I don't know. But I think Scott… I mean, it's not clear."

"What, Breck? Just tell me."

"I think… no. I know. Scott has been using."

"Using what?"

"I don't know exactly. But it's kind of becoming a problem."

"What do you mean?"

"His accident. The hospital."

"That was something with his lungs and his breathing," Robbie tried to remember what the doctor said, but Scott was the one talking, and she couldn't make the follow up appointment and Scott had assured her everything was fine.

"Scott said it was just to help him study. And maybe it was at first, but he'd gotten so moody and when I asked him about it, he got so angry and I thought I was betraying him, but Javi saw it too and I didn't know what to do…" Breck started to cry.

Robbie still couldn't believe what she was hearing. Scott? This made no sense. She looked at Eric.

"He has been moody lately," Eric said.

Moody? He's been a different person. Quick to anger. Reclusive. Every question has been an intrusion. Robbie thought it was just teenage moodiness. Hormones. Drugs? Could it be? How could she not see it?

Robbie didn't even hear the door open, but she heard the footsteps coming down the hall and when she turned she saw Scott, wet hair and shivering, with snow caked on his clothes.

"What the hell is going on here?"

* * * * *

Robbie didn't want to leave Adam and TJ, but she had to have a priority and it was Scott. Eric stayed in the kitchen with the others, while Robbie pushed Scott downstairs to his room. He was agitated and confused.

"What is happening?" Scott asked.

Robbie shut the door behind them.

"Tell me about your accident."

"What?"

"The one that landed you in the hospital? What really happened?"

"I told you. It was…nothing. I was pushing myself too hard."

"Look at me."

"What?"

Scott's eyes darted away and Robbie reached for his face but Scott smacked her hand away. It was all true. How had she missed this? She shoved Scott back against the door and grabbed his chin, forcing him to look at her. His eyes were bloodshot, and his pupils dilated.

"Oh my god. You're high right now, aren't you?"

"What? No. Why? Did Javi tell you something?"

Robbie let go and looked around the room. All the trophies and ribbons. Awards and pics. A shrine to her first born. He was always the good kid. She didn't have to look out for him. He knew better. She was so fucking stupid.

"No. Javi didn't tell me anything."

"I'm fine. I'm just tired."

"Where are they?"

"Where's what?"

"Scott, I'm not doing this with you. Where else are you hiding them?"

"Hiding what?"

"Well, we found your tin of white powder and a baggie of yellow and blue pills. What else is there?"

"Those aren't mine."

Robbie looked at Scott. She wanted to cry, but she was more angry than anything. Angry at him. But angry at herself. She let this happen.

"What else is there?" she said with a quiet tone.

"I don't know what you're talking about. I swear."

"God, when did it become so easy for you to lie to me? When you were a kid, I could tell you were lying every time. You got this crinkle in your nose. But now, it's just so easy isn't it."

"I'm not lying."

Robbie reached over and grabbed his freshman year football trophy. She threw it against the wall hard enough to break in two and the little, gold football player bounced against the bed.

"Jesus, Mom."

"Are you going to tell me?"

"Tell you what?"

"Fine, I'll find them myself."

Robbie went to the bookcase and started pulling out books, shaking them and throwing them on the floor.

"What are you doing?"

"I know there's something else here."

Every picture, every knick-knack Robbie shook and threw down. She went to his desk and started pulling out the drawers, dumping everything on the floor.

"Stop it."

"Are you going to tell me the truth?"

"I'm not lying."

Scott ran over and tried to block her but she pushed him back and continued to rummage through everything, tossing his laptop, his pencil holder, and a stack of papers on the ground. She looked around the room and then saw his giant jug of protein powder sitting on his night stand.

"No."

Robbie shoved him back when he came for her again, and she grabbed the jug and unscrewed the top. Buried in the powder was a baggie of pills. Robbie pulled it out. Now, she started to cry. She held the bag out for Scott.

"What is this?"

"It's not mine."

"Oh my god. Stop lying. Please, just stop lying."

"It's not what you think."

"What is it, Scott? Tell me."

"It's school. And football. And the play. And basketball. And gotta get a good GPA to get into college and Breck wants to do homework tonight and can you pick up your little sister from school and we need you to pick up an extra shift this week and it's everything. I'm sorry."

Robbie sat down on the bed.

"This is my fault."

"Don't do that. It's not a big deal. It's just something to help me when I need to study."

"Just don't. Okay. Don't. I thought it could wait until college. I thought you had a good head on your shoulders and you were bringing home grades and so what if you were a little short with me, aren't teenagers supposed to be moody? You didn't know."

"Know what?"

"That we aren't like other people, Scott. God, I wish we were. But it's not the hand we were dealt. My father, your grandfather, you didn't really know him but he was not a nice man. And his father was really not a nice man. And if you doubt that, I can show the scars from when he put a cigar out on my back. I thought if I didn't drink and didn't beat the shit out of you kids then the rest of it didn't matter. We're not wired like other people, my dear boy. Your father can have a beer, one beer, and he's fine. I don't get that. I can't have one beer. I can have none. Or I can have twenty. Or wine. Whiskey. It's all the same. Once it's in our system, it grabs hold and just craves… more."

"It's not like that, okay? It's just a little…"

"It's never just a little with us, Scott. I'm sorry, but it's not. And if it was, would it really have gotten this far?"

They sat in silence for a moment. Then, Robbie told him everything. When she quit. Rehab. Relapsing. How she finally quit completely when she got pregnant and hasn't had a drink since. She never got into drugs, but biologically it was probably the same for him. Once you start, it so quickly spirals.

Scott told her when he started. Thirteen years old. And how it just became easier to exist with the drugs than without. He wasn't afraid to try anything, but it was also the hiding that became addicting. He had a secret that no one knew. The pressure of maintaining his image was more important and everything was to support that. He had to be the best student. The best athlete. The best son.

Robbie blamed herself.

But she still found the energy to reach over and hug her son. In his mirror she caught a glimpse of them. Her makeup smeared from crying. His eyes watery as well. He looked like her. He always had her eyes, but something about his angst and misery, really sold the connection. This was her son.

"So, what happens now?"

Robbie sighed. She really hadn't thought that far ahead.

35. KIRA

"You okay?" Randall asked as he lightly knocked on her bedroom door.

Kira looked up and kind of shrugged. She was fine, she said. And she kind of meant it. She didn't really feel anything. There were so many things happening over the past few days that she wasn't even sure how to process anything. She was mostly numb.

"I'm here if you need anything," Randall offered. "You know that right?"

"I know, Daddy."

She didn't mean to call him that. She had moved on to just 'Dad' a while ago, but she felt so much younger these days. It felt right. He closed her door, and left her alone. He was good about not pushing. It wasn't like she was avoiding talking about it, but she really didn't know what to say.

Her best friend was murdered. She knew that for sure now. But with that news came two distressing truths.

One, she didn't know Bridget. Not really. There had been so much going on with her over the past few years that the girl she grew up with had moved beyond her a few years ago. She had this whole other life it seemed, and it didn't include Kira. That made her sad. Almost as sad as when she first learned about her death.

Bridget was planning to run away. She never believed that but after what happened with Bridget's mom, Kira could understand it. What she couldn't understand was why Bridget wouldn't tell her? Was she afraid Kira would tell someone, prevent it somehow? Bridget had always made a point of making Kira fully aware that Kira was younger. Inexperienced. Naïve. It was always a kind of joke between them. Kira liked learning things from Bridget. And she wasn't afraid of trying new things. But maybe Bridget didn't trust her. Maybe she never could. Maybe they weren't even friends. Not in the way she thought. Kira also knew she'd never get a clear answer on any of this.

The other thing, the thing that still didn't make any sense, was that Jake, this boy she had been kind of sort of dating or something, was the one that killed her. That wasn't confirmed or anything. Just rumors. But Percy had told her that he confessed, before he took off with Abby, and no one had been able to find them. It had been five days since that night, the night of the snowstorm when everything fell apart, and Kira still wasn't any closer to understanding any of it.

Jake was always nice to her. They had gone to movies and hung out at each other's houses. They could talk on the phone for hours. And they seemed to like all the same things. They watched The Simpsons on TV. She went to "The Last Boy Scout" with him and he didn't complain when she took him to "The Bodyguard." They kissed. A lot. And other stuff. He wanted to do more, he was an older boy and it didn't surprise her, but she wasn't ready and he didn't push. How could that guy have done what he did to Bridget?

Thankfully, her dad wasn't pushing Kira to go to school. Kira couldn't handle that. Not yet. Too many whispers. Too many questions. The police talked to her. More than once. They never confirmed outright that Jake was the one that did it, but she could tell by their questions, it was more than just a theory.

She cooperated. It wasn't just because Randall loomed behind her as they asked their questions, but after she heard what he did, and that he never tried to call her, tell her any different, she felt no reason to protect him or lie for him. She answered their questions, openly and honestly. Even when they got really personal.

She told them that Abby was trying to figure out who killed Bridget, but that at no point did they suspect Jake. She didn't even realize that Jake and Bridget knew each other. Not well at least. Jake always made a point to say that when she mentioned her. Kira replayed so many conversations in her head the past few days.

And what about Abby? Was she okay? They hadn't spoken much in the past few weeks. When Abby called Kira looking for Jake, Kira thought she sounded off. Did she know then? Why didn't she say anything? Or was she trying to get Jake away from Kira? She didn't know Abby well at all, but she still considered her a friend. Was Abby doomed to be another friend lost to Jake? It was hard not to take all of this personally, even though Kira knew that Jake didn't even know who she was when Bridget had died.

Kira remembered she was the one that told Jake what Abby was doing. This was her fault in that way. Maybe their whole relationship was just Jake trying to learn what Kira knew.

She didn't know anything. That was the only thing Kira knew for sure.

* * * * *

Kira walked into the kitchen. She had been sitting in her bedroom since the morning and was getting tired from wallowing. Randall had asked her to come down for dinner, but she declined. Dinner at the table meant conversation and she didn't want any of that. Hopefully, she had waited long enough to get some leftovers in peace.

She pulled out the Tupperware that held some kind of chili-hot dog combination and scooped some into a bowl. The microwave was slowly ticking down closer to freedom, but then Georgina waddled into the kitchen.

So close.

"Hey, there," Georgina said with her sweet, British accent. Her belly was sticking out so far now, a constant reminder that Kira's little half-brother or sister was only weeks away from making an appearance.

"Hey," Kira offered back, weakly.

"Your father went to get me some frozen yogurt. I know it's cold out, but the wee one wants what it wants."

Kira smiled. She didn't want to be rude, but she wasn't feeling much like talking. Georgina scooted past Kira to refill her glass of water.

"I cannot wait for a decent glass of wine again. My doctor said a little wouldn't hurt the baby, but I don't want to risk anything. And frankly, I don't know that a half a glass is going to cut it. But if I can't have wine, I will have frozen yogurt. Anyway, I hope you enjoy your dinner. I found it rather disgusting but your little brother was a fan."

Georgina smiled, and sort of shrugged and turned to walk out when Kira finally opened her mouth.

"That's it? That's how you're trying to get me to talk?"

"Kira, darling, I'm so sorry. Please forgive me if my loquaciousness has given you the wrong impression."

"I don't know what that means."

"It means I talk too much. I wasn't trying anything, I promise you. Besides you have your friends, and your father. I know I'm the last person you'd want to open up to."

"I'm sorry. I know I've been a bitch about this whole thing with you and Dad."

"Oh, please. When my mother got remarried I didn't speak to her for over a year. You're fine."

"It's not you. It's just the idea."

"Kira, I'm fine. You have had a terrible few months and I know this whole 'idea' is one more gust in the supreme shit storm that has been your life. Please, do not give me a second thought."

"You're not going to tell me how angry I should be that the guy I was just starting to like turned out to have murdered my best friend. Oh, and how dumb I was that I thought it was her mom, which really didn't matter when she tried to smack the crap out of me."

"I can't tell you how to feel, Kira. No one can. And quite frankly, you can't tell yourself how to feel. If we could legislate our feelings… well, I would have told myself not to fall in love with a man with two kids and an angry ex-wife. We all would if we could. I can only tell you that you're not alone."

"I just wish I could be done with this part, you know? I don't like feeling this way."

"Unfortunately for you, that's not how it works. When I was your age there was a boy at my school, Nicholas somethingorother. He was beautiful. Tall and skinny and hair like Mick Jagger, which meant something back then. My friend Sophie just adored him but he said he was into me. We kissed just once, but it was sweet and wonderful. I never told Sophie, and she still had a crush on him and one day he… took advantage of that, and he hurt her. Not anything like what happened to your friend, but it wasn't good. And my first thought was that she was making this up, or doing it to hurt me, because I didn't want to believe that he could do something like that. He had always been nice to me. And I felt like a horrible friend. And it took me a little while to really see him for what he was and not what I had convinced myself he was. But, like I said, different situation. And as always, my mouth moves faster than my brain sometimes."

"I just wish I knew what was real. Everything keeps playing back in my head differently and I keep feeling like I should've known something was off. I shouldn't have been such a dumb idiot."

"Well, there's one thing I know from my experience with you and that is that you are anything but a 'dumb idiot.' You're one of the smartest young women I've ever known. And one of the hardest things you're going to have to deal with in this whole mess of hard things is that you're going to have to forgive yourself. For whatever it is you are blaming yourself for. None of this is your fault."

"I know that."

"But actually feeling it is somewhat different, idn't it?"

"Yeah, I suppose."

The microwave dinged. The smell of the leftover concoction wafted out as soon Kira opened the door.

"Good luck with that," Georgina chuckled.

"Thanks, George."

The side door into the kitchen opened and Randall walked in, holding a plastic bag.

"I got you sprinkles," Randall said through his smile as he kissed George hello. "Honey," he said to Kira. "Glad to see you out of your room."

"For a moment, at least."

"How are you?"

"Okay?"

"Day by day, Honey."

"I know."

Kira noticed a subtle nod from Georgina to Randall. He handed her the yogurt, and she immediately tore off the top and plunged her plastic spoon in.

"I got you one too, if you want. Chocolate, with strawberries."

"Maybe in a little bit."

"I, uh, I got a phone call today. Mrs. Kent is back from…the, uh, hospital and asked if she could see you."

"What?"

"I told her it wouldn't happen without me being there, but either way it's entirely up to you."

* * * * *

It had been three days since her dad told her about Vanessa. It took that long for Kira to feel like she could make the trip across the street.

She saw Vanessa from the window grabbing the newspaper. She looked so normal. The last time she had seen before that was when she knocked Kira into a wall and had started to smack her. Kira held up her hands to block her but she still felt the sting of every hit. Randall had run into the room moments later and shoved Vanessa back.

Kira still remembered her eyes. There was a weird sense of confusion swirling about. But she wasn't acting like herself. Randall had called the police and waited with Vanessa until they arrived. Kira ran home only to get a phone call from Percy telling her everything else. And then everything existed in this senseless place.

Kira wore a dress. Nothing fancy. Maybe it was because she hadn't been out of the house in so long but she wanted to look nice. Randall held her hand as they walked across the street and knocked on the front door. Kira couldn't help but remember a similar walk they took after learning about Bridget's death.

"Come in," Vanessa said.

She motioned them into the living room.

"Can I get you anything? Coffee? Tea?"

"I'm fine," Kira said as she took a seat in the chair facing Vanessa on the couch.

Randall shook his head and stood back. Vanessa's hands were shaking a bit as she sipped her tea.

"First off, I wanted to tell you how sorry I am for everything that happened. I have… a condition."

"What kind of condition?" Kira asked.

"It has a lot of names, or a longer more complicated name, but you may have heard it called schizophrenia. My brain doesn't work right. And sometimes I have these episodes where I don't quite know what is real."

"And that's why you thought I was Bridget?"

"I can usually manage it with medication, but sometimes when I'm off the medication, even if I miss a couple days, I don't want to take it. It's a problem, and I'm really so, so sorry that you got caught in the middle of it."

"Did Bridget know?"

"Yes. I had had episodes with her and that's how I was able to get diagnosed in the first place. And she was really good at keeping me on my meds. She could always tell when I was off. And when she… well, I didn't have her to watch me anymore and then it got really bad."

"Did you hit her?"

"Too many times. I never meant to, not really, but one of the things with this is a violent tendency. And Bridget bore the brunt of a lot of that."

"Did you know she was planning to run away?"

Vanessa looked shocked. She took another drink. Clearly, she didn't know either.

"I shouldn't be surprised. It hadn't been… good for a while. We were fighting a lot. And being responsible for me, well I think it was getting to her. It's why it was so easy for me to believe that she could've… done something to herself. And why that would've been my fault. And without the meds when I was in this haze, well, I didn't know or didn't remember that she was gone. And that was an easier place for me to be at the time. No parent should outlive their child. And certainly not a teenager."

Kira wanted to hate her. She wanted to be mad. She wanted to blame Vanessa for everything that happened, for driving Bridget away in the first place.

But she couldn't.

She looked so small, this woman that just over a week ago was towering over her with eyes full of rage. Kira didn't see any sign of that woman.

"I'm getting help," Vanessa continued. "I need to do this on my own now that… I'm on my own. I've got really good doctors and really good medicine and a routine, routines are really important for me. I'm just…. I can't apologize enough for dragging you into this mess in the first place."

"Stop, please, it's okay. I understand. For the first time in a while, I understand something."

"You're so young, you really shouldn't have to go through any of this."

"Well, we can't really control any of that, can we?"

Vanessa smiled and reached out her hand and set it on top of Kira's. It startled her, but it was warm, comforting.

Kira couldn't think of anything to say. She wanted to cry. Her eyes were definitely watery, but maybe it was her dad being there or not wanting to appear weak in front of Vanessa. She wouldn't let herself let go. Instead, she took a deep breath and forced a smile.

"I am so sorry for your loss," Kira said.

"Thank you."

* * * * *

"And then what?" Breck asked

Kira was recounting the whole thing as she lay on Breck's bed. She had to get her homework anyway. Kira was planning to go back to school tomorrow and had a lot of work to catch up on.

"And then we talked some more. It felt like the first time I had ever met her. We talked about Bridget mostly. It had been so long since I talked about her with someone that really knew her. She had a lot of stories."

"I can't believe Bridget never said anything."

"Yeah, well, everyone keeps their secrets. Bridget didn't tell me about her mom. Didn't tell me about running away. About her thing with Scott."

It just slipped out.

"Oh my god, I'm so sorry," Kira continued. "I didn't mean to bring it up."

"No, it's fine. Scott was obviously not who I thought he was. In a lot of ways."

"How is he?"

"I don't know. He went to this program in Council Bluffs. His parents said he will probably be gone for at least a month."

"I had no idea he had gotten so bad."

"He was really good at hiding things. I know it's messed up, but I think a lot about him and Bridget. And like, I wonder if they made each other happy. I know Scott cared about me, maybe he didn't want to hurt my feelings or whatever but maybe he really cared about Bridget. And she him. Maybe they could tell each other all the things they couldn't tell us."

"Oh my god, that is fucked up," Kira said through laughter

"What do you expect? Scott always said I was too nice."

"Well, your boyfriend is a dick, but at least he's not a killer."

Breck looked starkly serious for a moment, but then Kira started to laugh so Breck joined.

"How fucked is that?" Kira asked. "I mean, he wasn't even my boyfriend. Thank god, I never did it with him."

The girls started to laugh harder until they were startled by a knock on Breck's bedroom door.

"What?" Breck shouted, rather snottily really. "I'm busy."

The door opened and both Kira and Breck sat up on the bed. Breck's mother opened the door and had a weird look on her face.

"Breck," she started.

"What, Mom?"

"It's about Abby."

36. ABBY

Abby hit record on the camera.

Jake had started to stir. Part of her was afraid, but she knew he couldn't get to her. Not anymore. The last time he came to, he was still in the trunk of the car, and she zapped him again when they had arrived. Dragging him into the cabin was the hard part, but he wasn't as heavy as she had expected.

His arms and legs were tied with duct tape to the dining room chair. She was hoping for some rope, but this was the best she could do. She didn't actually have time to really plan this out. She took off his shoes and socks, and broke every glass she could find around him, so even if managed to break free he wouldn't be in a position to run very far.

"What happened?" Jake said as he took in everything. When he realized he was bound he looked up at Abby with those soft, sympathetic eyes she now knew was part of his act. "What's going on?"

"What's the last thing you remember?"

"You were with Percy. You said he killed Bridget and then I was out."

"Yeah, that was this."

Abby demonstrated the stun gun.

"It left kind of a bruise on your side. Sorry about that. And there's another one on your shoulder. You were kind of waking up and I didn't want that. I wasn't quite ready. But now I am."

"For what?"

"For us to have a little chat."

"What the fuck is this, Abby?"

"Tell me what happened that night. With Bridget."

"What are you talking about?"

"Come on, Jake. You found my book. You found the journal. You know I was looking into it. Did you think I wouldn't figure it out?"

"Figure what out? I thought you said Percy did it."

"Yeah, that was just to distract you. But kudos to the way you jumped at him. Really sold it."

"This is all some kind of misunderstanding."

"Then tell me what happened."

"Nothing. I don't know. I wasn't there."

"Then why did you change the time on my clock?"

"What?"

"That night. I saw you."

"I don't know what you think you saw. Is this some elaborate way to get back at me or something?"

"What would I have to get back at you for?"

Jake just shook his head.

"What's the camera for?"

"Oh, I want to make sure I get your confession on camera."

"God, you're so stupid. Even if I did confess, which I'm not going to, because I didn't DO ANYTHING. It still wouldn't matter. I'm tied up and being held against my will. Have you heard of being under duress? It would be meaningless."

"Fine," Abby said, and she turned the camera off. "It's just us. Now, tell me what happened."

"Are you high? Is this part of your new look, which isn't very flattering, I must say."

Abby was so used to her dark hair and glasses, she forgot it was a relatively recent development. Jake not liking it made her appreciate it all the more.

"Jake, stop. I don't care what you think any more. I just want to know what happened."

"And then what?"

"And then I let you go."

"Yeah. I believe that. Where the hell are we, anyway?"

"The Van Allen lake house. Percy told me about it a few times. We made it to Colorado, can you believe it?"

"So, you were in on this with Percy?"

"He doesn't actually know we're here. No one does. And the nearest person is miles away at least. This is a summer place. Lake is frozen. Houses are empty. No one to hear you scream for help. I'm actually a bit worried we might not have enough gas to get back home. But that's a problem for another time."

"This is so fucked."

"There is a solution."

"Confess to a murder I didn't commit?"

"Well, I can see we're getting nowhere. I'm gonna see what passes for food in this joint. If you're ready to talk, give me a shout."

"I have to go to the bathroom."

"So? Piss yourself."

Abby walked out. As she rummaged through the cupboards, she kept an eye in the other room, watching Jake struggle to break free, without any progress.

* * * * *

Abby had another cup of coffee. She didn't want to fall asleep again and give Jake the opportunity to free himself. He had tried a couple different ways, and even managed to knock his chair over. He cut his face on the glass, and his screams woke Abby up when she dozed off in the back room. They had been going back and forth for a couple days, but he still maintained his innocence.

Abby was able to pull him back up and even wiped some of the blood off of him. But she didn't like being so close to him, even though she never approached him without the stun gun. She was wondering how long she could keep this up though. There wasn't that much food in the place, she had fed him some peanut butter to not be a total monster. But there wasn't enough to sustain her, much less both of them for more than a week or so.

Once again, Abby sat herself facing him, but across the room.

"You ready to talk?" She asked.

"Get bent."

"Lovely. I know you're running out of energy, Jake. And I know you know that no one is coming to look for us here. You're stuck here. And you're gonna die here if you don't tell me everything."

"I'm gonna die either way. Where does that leave you?"

"You're a murderer, Jake. I won't have any trouble sleeping."

"I'm not a murderer."

"I really can't figure out a motive. Was it jealousy? Did you have a thing for Bridget and get mad when you found out about Scott? Or Percy? You acted like you were friends with him at one point, but you hated him. Was it because of his money? I mean, you're not hurting for funds but your inheritance is in a trust until you're what, twenty-one? Was it because he slept with her and you didn't?"

"Please. He never slept with her. She just made him think that they had. She wasn't this saint that everyone makes her out to be now that she's dead. She was a liar and a thief."

"Is that why you killed her?"

"I didn't kill her."

"You always said you never even knew her. How do you know she was a liar? How do you know she lied about Percy?"

"She told me."

"When?"

"I don't remember. I did know her. We did mess around. She pretty much threw herself at me at a party and we would hook up every so often over the summer because her boyfriend wasn't ready to give it up."

"Did that make you feel special?"

"Oh, shut up. It was nothing. You think she's the only girl I messed around with? I've got girls giving it up to me left and right."

"Then why sleep with me?"

"What?"

"If you're laying pipe all over town why did you have to sneak into my room and force yourself on me."

"I didn't force myself on you. You never pushed me away. You never said no."

"I never said anything. Was that the turn on? I'd be perfectly still counting the polka dots on my curtains just waiting for you to finish up and leave."

"Don't turn this into something it's not. You came to me first."

"Yeah. Because I mistakenly thought you were something you weren't. The first time I tried…to kill myself… in the garage. You found me. You had just moved in. And I felt even more alone and before anything happened. I was in my mom's car listening to some stupid Madonna song and you found me. You opened the garage. Dragged me outside. Made sure I was okay. I thought you were some hero. I wanted to thank you, a hug, something, I don't know. I was fourteen, I wasn't trying to seduce you. I didn't know how to even do that. I still don't. But you took advantage of that. And you turned it into something cheap and dirty. And secret. And you were oh so happy when people started to find out. You weren't the pervert boning his stepsister. You were the big man, telling all your virgin friends what sex was like."

"You and I have very different memories of that."

"Oh, I'm sure. Because at no point did you give any thought to what I was actually thinking or feeling."

"I'm sorry, okay. I wasn't trying to hurt you. I just thought it would be fun. I just wanted to get laid. Is that what this whole thing is about? You and me?"

"No."

"Because that's what it sounds like."

"This is about Bridget."

"You don't care about Bridget."

"And you did? You killed her."

"I didn't kill her."

"Did you stab her first? I know you stabbed Percy. But it's not clear if she was stabbed. I'm sure the police know."

"I didn't kill her."

"Is it a power thing? You felt powerful sneaking into my room and you felt powerful taking Bridget's life from her. And you felt powerful lying to everyone these past few months. And you felt powerful getting away with it. Didn't you?"

"I didn't kill her."

"You watched her fall to her death or was she dead before she fell? When did the life fall away from her eyes? Was she looking at you in that moment? Did that make you feel powerful?"

"IT WAS AN ACCIDENT."

Jake shouted and Abby stood completely still. Abby's limbs felt hollow and tingly. What just happened?

"You have it all wrong," Jake said, as tears started to fall down his face. "Yes, I was mad. But I didn't want to kill her. I didn't even mean to stab Percy. I found the knife. Everything happened so fast. I didn't mean for any of it."

"So, tell me what happened."

"She was fucking everybody. Bridget. Did you know that? After we hooked up, then there was Scott, and poor Percy thought they had and who knows who else. She told me she was pregnant and needed money for an abortion. I just believed her. I mean, what can you do in that situation? If you question it, you're the asshole. And you can't suggest abortion, but when she did I was like, yeah, take my money. I can't be a dad. And then I saw her having the same conversation with Scott. And then Percy. And I lost it."

"That's how she got all that money?"

"What money?"

"She was trying to run away. At least, that's what we think."

"You gotta believe me, I didn't go up there to kill her. I was mad. I wanted to scare her. I don't know. It all went to shit so fast. I was yelling and she was lying, and Percy was there bleeding and I was already worried about figuring that out when she came at me and I didn't mean to push her back, but I had the knife, and we were so close to the edge and she just… she fell. It was all so fast. And I just got the hell out of there. I didn't mean to, I swear to fucking God, I didn't mean to."

He was practically sobbing, his voice was high, and whiney, but Abby wasn't sure if this was an act or not.

"Then why not come forward? You could've told someone. Ended this whole thing."

"You think anyone would believe me? And you think if the police started digging around in my shit that they wouldn't find other stuff? What was I supposed to do? You ever been so desperate you just start doing stuff and you know you'll figure it out later?"

"I think you know that I have."

"I didn't mean for any of this to happen."

"Why Kira?"

"I liked Kira. She's nice. But when I found out you were digging up all this stuff, I had to know what you were doing."

"Is that why you sent pages of her journal out to everyone?"

"I thought it would get everyone pointing fingers. Either that or they would see what she was really like."

"And why frame me?"

"I wasn't framing you. But if they came looking for me, I didn't want anything hidden in my room. In your room, it might just give me reasonable doubt. I don't know I wasn't thinking clearly. I was just doing things."

"And Mr. Sutton?"

"The teacher?"

"How did he end up with the journal?"

"You said he was a suspect. I just broke into his car and put the journal under the seat. If I got caught, I could throw suspicion his way. I never meant for him to find it even. But then he had the accident, and I figured maybe it would look like he sent these things. I don't know. I was just freaking out. I'm still freaking out. But that's it. That's the truth. Now, can you please let me go?"

"And then what?"

"What do you mean?"

"What happens when I let you go?"

"What do you want to happen? We go home. We forget about this whole thing and we try to get back to a normal life."

"And the police?"

"Come on, Abby, you can't expect me to tell them. There's no way they believe me. They need this to be a murder. And they need to throw the book at whoever did it. They won't care it was an accident. They won't care that I'm innocent."

"You think you're innocent?"

"I told you what happened."

"Being an accident and being innocent are two different things. Do you really think you're free of any blame here? Do you really think there's any way you just get to go back to a normal life now?"

"You said…"

"You think I know what I'm doing here? You think I can make sense of any of this? I have hated you for so long. And I care about you. I really hate admitting that, but I do. And I honestly don't know what I thought I would happen but no matter what you say I know I can and will never trust you. I never could."

"You bitch."

"Jake, I'm being serious. I don't know what to do."

"Then let me go."

Jake bucked up and down in his chair, still struggling to break free.

"I know I can't do that."

"I'm gonna fucking kill you. I'm gonna fucking kill you. I'm gonna fucking kill you."

"I thought you weren't a murderer."

Abby ran to the bathroom. She leaned against the door while Jake continued to yell from the other room. What WAS she supposed to do now?

* * * * *

Abby stirred awake. She had sat on the couch for just a minute, but didn't realize how tired she was and must have dozed off. She quickly looked behind her at the corner where she left Jake. His head was down, underneath the blanket she had thrown over him. He must've fallen asleep too.

Abby went back upstairs to the bathroom and threw water on her face. She was still stuck on what to do next. Maybe it was an accident, she could believe that, but does that really make a difference? The cover-up, the lies, the deceit. He still stabbed Percy. Was there any way out of this that made sense? What did she think coming here? Maybe she should call Percy, but the police were probably monitoring everything. As guilty as Jake was, she was now in some trouble herself. Her word against his, but this road trip was probably a mistake, even if she did get Jake to admit the truth.

She found a sweater in the master bedroom. It helped. It was colder inside than she expected and it's not like she'd packed. She'd been in the same clothes for days and was really starting to feel pretty gross. She warmed herself in the shower, the steam fogging up the glass. For some reason she drew a heart with her finger. She had no idea why. It reminded her of the cold days riding the bus to school when she was a kid and how she and Breck would draw on the windows. Things were so much easier then.

Abby got dressed in layers. Mostly in what she figured were Percy's mom's clothes. Not her particular style but she was cold. She wanted to pull her hair back into a pony tail but it was so short now she couldn't make it work.

She took a deep breath. She knew what she was going to have to do. She was going to have to make a deal with the devil. They had to go back home. That was clear. She could promise not to turn him in, but Percy had surely already told the police. Was there really any way back that wasn't fraught with issues?

Abby walked back downstairs. She could do this. She could make him see reason. If it meant letting him go, she was willing to do that. She knew the truth. That's what she wanted.

She had only made it a few stops down the stairs before the view into the dining room came into view.

And Jake wasn't there.

The chair he was in was in broken pieces on the ground. Ripped duct tape dangled from each chair limb.

Abby stopped.

"Jake?" she called out, but there was no answer.

She couldn't breathe.

Slowly, she crept down the stairs. Her back to the wall. She wasn't in the shower that long. He had to be around here somewhere. Abby looked into the living room and was grateful the open floorplan left little room for hiding places. She darted over to the couch. She thought for sure she left it here.

Then, a familiar buzzing.

Abby turned around to see Jake, standing in the doorway, not ten feet from her. He was dripping blood all over and he held the stun gun in his hand.

"Looking for this?"

"Jake, it's okay. I know I can't keep you here. It's fine. You can go."

"Don't act like you're still in charge, Abby. Now, where are my shoes?"

"In the kitchen. Underneath the sink."

Abby slowly backed up and held her hands out, as if Jake was a wild animal she had to keep at bay.

"You can't run away from me."

"Come on. You're weak and tired. And I came down to let you go.

It's over."

"Over? After this? It's not fucking over, Abby. Now, my shoes?"

Abby moved towards the kitchen. She opened the cabinet door and grabbed the shoes but moved back so he couldn't get too close to her.

"Give them to me."

Abby set them on the counter but then jumped back to stay out of reach. Jake moved closer.

"You don't have to do anything. You can just go."

"You don't have to be afraid of me, Abby. I told you I didn't mean for Bridget to die."

"You also said you wanted to kill me."

"Well, you're certainly not my favorite person right now, I must admit. But it's fine. We can be cool about this."

Jake kept one hand on the stun gun pointing at Abby, and reached to the shoes with the other.

"Catch," Abby shouted while grabbing a pot from the stove and hurling it towards Jake. He dropped the stun gun to block the pot from hitting him. Abby bolted to the back door and quickly unlocked it, but before she could open it Jake jumped toward her and knocked her head into the wall. Abby stomped onto his foot and Jake screamed and she pushed him back, flung the door open and took off running. She had no idea where she was going. She just started running.

She turned around and Jake was hobbling behind her. Not very fast. There was a limp to his movements, but he wasn't too far from her. Abby ran to the stairs at the end of the yard and jumped down and was twenty feet onto the frozen lake before she even realized what she had done.

Jake slowly stepped onto the lake behind her.

"Come on, Abby, where are you going? There's nowhere to run."

"I don't care. I'm not going anywhere with you."

"Do you hear yourself? You shocked me. You tied me up and you have the nerve to act like the victim here?"

"Just go. I'm not stopping you. And if you stay out here too much longer you're gonna get frostbite on your feet."

"And whose fault is that?"

Abby heard a cracking noise and looked down. A small vein of a crack formed from where she was standing, spreading out underneath her. She stood completely still.

"Abby, come back here. I'm not fucking around. The lake only has a small layer of ice on top. If it breaks, you will die."

Abby took a tepid step back towards Jake, trying not to shift her weight until she felt secure in the ground beneath. Jake backed up himself, moving back towards the stairs.

"Just go slowly," Jake said. "You'll be fine."

They moved slowly together in unison. Each taking steps back until Jake was on the stairs and Abby was just a few feet away. She inched closer, and could feel the ground soften beneath her, but she was almost there. She had only taken her eyes off Jake for a second when she saw him standing at the edge of the stairs with one of the large rocks that was at the edge of the stairs.

"Sorry, Abby, but you had this coming."

Using both hands Jake launched the rock forward. It only made it a few feet before smashing through the ice in front of Abby.

"NO," Abby screamed as she jumped toward the stairs.

The ice below her cracked and she fell into the water, but Abby had jumped far enough to grab Jake's pants leg, pulling him down with her. He smacked his head on one of the steps and fell into the water with her.

It was cold. So cold. Freezing water soaked into Abby instantly. Thankfully, the water wasn't very deep at this point and she pushed off the bottom of the lake towards the break in the ice.

Jake thrashed, and Abby pushed up off his chest to grab the railing of the stairs and pull herself out. She felt a hand at her ankle and she kicked him off and when his head popped above water she kicked out, almost by instinct, landing her shoe square on his nose.

She recoiled her legs and scrambled onto the stairs and turned back to see that Jake was no longer fighting to get above water.

"Jake?" Abby called out.

She moved up to the top of the stairs and called out one more time, but there was no answer. There would never be an answer. She edged toward the water and tried to see if she could see him, but she couldn't. And she was afraid to get any closer.

* * * * *

The chair was uncomfortable. No matter how many times she had sat here before, this time was particularly awkward. She couldn't help but fidget. The lights seemed brighter. The cushion was stiff.

"Do you want to talk about it?" Dr. Gant asked.

After the week she had the last thing she wanted to do was talk about it. But was that really her choice? She knew she'd be here. Back in his office. Her mom insisted. Actually, her mom had been incredibly supportive considering everything.

But she really didn't want to talk about it. First there was the police. Then her mom. Then her friends. It was exhausting. Although it did help her keep the story straight.

"I know I should," Abby said. "But I am just really tired, you know."

"Then do you want to talk about how you feel about it?"

"That's the thing. I don't really know. I guess I'm just glad it's over."

"Is it? Over?"

"Jake's not coming back," Abby said. "I know that. There's nothing left for him here. Everyone knows what he did. He's wanted. Wherever he went after he left me, he's long gone."

Abby finally made eye contact with Dr. Gant. She doesn't know why she lied. It was self-defense. He was trying to drag her into the lake with him. But with everything else going on around it—she kidnapped him, really, she tied him up, it was her stun gun—she thought it was easier for everyone if they believed the simplest version of the story.

Jake killed Bridget.

Abby found out.

Jake kidnapped her but she talked him into letting her go. She gave him all the money she had and he left at the train station in Lincoln. Abby made sure to make an ATM withdrawal when she was on her way back to Omaha. She had Jake's wallet and it wasn't hard to guess his pin. 6969. Like every teenage boy.

Abby didn't bother to clean up much of the lake house. It would probably still be a few months before the family would be there and discover the break in and by that time, it wasn't likely to get connected to her in anyway. She had removed the duct tape. Washed anything with blood out with bleach, wiped everything down that might have a fingerprint. But the broken glass, and broken chair. She left. Let someone else create a story as to why they were like that.

She dumped all the trash, including the clothes she took, in a dumpster in Ogalala. At night, when no one was around. After the ATM trip in Lincoln, she got rid of everything else that was connected to Jake. She wished she had the stun gun, but she figured that was in the lake with Jake. And by the time his body washed up, there couldn't be anything tying it to her.

Jake was gone. That last image of him screaming at her as she booted him into the lake was with her. She knew she was stuck with that. With his scream. That was her punishment. But he was gone. And her door wasn't going to creak open at night anymore and his cold body wasn't going to lay down next to her.

In Lincoln, Abby used the cash she withdrew from Jake's account to pay for a hotel. She took the longest bath of her life. Soaking in the hot water until it grew warm. In the morning, she would call her mom. Call the police. But for one night she slept on the janky hotel bed.

And it was the best night of sleep she'd had in years.

37. PERCY

It had been a few days since Abby came back, but she still had only barely talked to him. She swore she was fine and they would connect soon but there was still so much going on with the police and her mom that she was overwhelmed. Percy could spend another day staring at his ceiling, but now that it was the weekend, he was worried his parents would actually be home and want to talk to him.

He walked over to the mall. He could've driven, but for February it was unusually warm, high fifties, and it was less than two miles. He had pulled his baseball hat tight and wore his hood up from his sweatshirt. With his large jacket, he felt like he was hiding in plain sight. It's not like the attention from everyone stopped since Jake was declared the murderer. Percy was still Harlan Van Allen's son, and some people were still skeptical. There wasn't exactly concrete proof. Certainly none that was universally endorsed. The paper ran a story on the kidnapping and listed him as a main suspect, but with Jake still at large, there was no big declaration. No matter what Abby had said.

Percy didn't feel like going into any of the stores. He just wandered up and down, looking through the windows at all the displays. Nothing intrigued him enough to move in closer, but he was grateful he could go a few minutes at a time without thinking about everything. He figured once the truth came out everything would go back to normal, but far from it. None of his old friends came out of hiding to see how he was doing. His family was still mostly distant. He talked to Bailey for a while, but she was still away at school and didn't really get the whole story. And Simon was still too young to really understand the weight of any of it.

More bad news came in the mail. After missing the past week of school, he had finally amassed enough absences to make graduating out of the question. He thought about trying to crush summer school, but honestly repeating his senior year held more appeal. He could lose all the "friends" that dropped him and maybe get the chance to have somewhat of a normal year. Dances. Football games. Homework. It all sounded way more amazing than the past year.

Percy had his hands in his pockets and stared mostly at the ground, so when he bumped into the girl, he didn't think it would've been someone he knew but they were both surprised when he looked right into Kira's eyes.

"Sorry," he said, first abruptly, then – "Oh, hi."

"Hi," she said, obviously uncomfortable.

She kind of smiled at him but then seemed to hold her face back from being too friendly. Kira wasn't alone. She was with another kid, Javi, the guy that Bridget was dating when she died. Percy wasn't sure he had ever met him, but they definitely knew who each other was.

"I didn't mean to," Percy said. "I didn't see you there. How are you?"

"I'm fine, you know, I guess."

It was awkward. Percy didn't know what to say. Neither, it would seem, did Kira, as they both stood there, kind of opening their mouths to speak and no one having any words fall out.

"This is Javi."

"Hey," Javi had said. He reached out his hand and Percy shook it.

"Yeah, I know. Percy."

"Yeah."

"We're just shopping," Kira offered.

"Yeah, well, have a good one," Percy said and went to continue on his path.

"Percy, wait," Kira said. "I think I owe you an apology."

"What?" Percy said, seemingly in unison with Javi.

"I know you didn't… you know, but maybe if I had given you a fair shot, we would've gotten to the truth sooner."

"Please, don't. You have nothing to be sorry for. I didn't do anything to ever earn your trust. You had every right to be suspicious. And it's not like I was completely honest. I'm just, I'm really sorry for your loss. Both of you. I don't think I was ever able to say that."

"Thanks," Kira said.

"Well, take care."

Percy walked away and this time there was no call back. Percy was shaking. He's not sure why it was so weird talking to Kira. And why he still felt guilty, even as he knew he did nothing wrong.

He walked into the bathroom and washed his hands under the sink and then rubbed his wet fingers over his eyes. The warm water felt nice. The were no paper towels, only those blower things so he dried himself with his sleeve before turning to see Javi standing in the doorway.

"Hey," Percy said.

"I know you didn't do this. But that doesn't make you a good person. Scott is in rehab, and he almost died, all because of the drugs you sold him."

"I didn't sell him whatever landed him in the hospital, I swear. And I don't do that anymore anyway."

"Yeah, because the police were on your case. Not because you chose to stop."

"And we both know that you smoked stuff that Bridget bought off me, so why don't you tell me what you want, Javi."

"I just want you to know that everyone else may think you're some nice guy now, that because you're not a murderer that somehow makes you a good person, but I know the truth. You're still just another rich kid asshole who doesn't care about anybody but himself. And I hope you remember that and you steer clear of me and my friends from now on."

"Gladly. Can I go? You're blocking the door."

Javi stepped aside and Percy pushed his way out.

All of a sudden, he felt the urge to be far, far away. Maybe thinking next year would be different was aggressively hopeful.

* * * * *

Percy had been staring at the screen so long that it felt like his eyes were drying out. The green numbers on the monitor were so meaningless to him, between that and his rhythmic typing, he had started to zone out. It was time for a break.

Having decided to redo his senior year, Percy opted to spend the last few months of his first senior year working full time at his father's company. It only took three hours into his second full day to realize what a horrible mistake that was. He was sure he wouldn't last through spring.

He walked down the hallways, smiling at everyone. At least the women in his dad's office had stopped giving him weird looks.

When he rounded the corner into the east wing, he could see right into Eli's office. She was reaching up taking a large picture off the wall. Boxes sat on top of her desk, half full. Word of her resignation spread through the building practically as soon as she gave it, though mostly in hushed tones and side whispers. Percy figured this was public acknowledgment, and made his way to the doorway.

"I wasn't sure if I should believe the stories," he said.

Eli looked over at him and smiled.

"Yeah, well, I think approaching rumors with skepticism is healthy. But, yes, I am leaving."

"Where are you going?"

"I'm actually going to take some time. I've been working since I was a teenager, and, well, I just felt like it was time for a break. We had our issues, but my husband did just die and I don't think I've fully dealt with that."

"I can imagine."

He always thought Eli was attractive, and even now as she had clearly put on a few pounds, that didn't change his impression. He still had a hard time believing she had slept with his father, but he was really going to have to let that go.

"Can you give me a hand with something?" Eli asked as she motioned Percy in. She motioned him over the small, round conference table where there were even more boxes, and subtly managed to close the door behind him.

"What do you need?"

"I'm just curious," she asked. "Why give me the security tape?"

Percy had not told anyone about that. Not even Abby. Not yet. And he had not had a single conversation with Eli since he found out about her and his father.

"I guess we're just talking about that now."

"I can't imagine anyone else that would do it. And I could tell that you knew. You started acting…nicer, I guess. It's over, by the way, your father and I."

"None of my business."

"So, why the tape?"

"I don't know. I didn't know what to do with it. And I figured you would do the right thing. Or know what the right thing to do would be."

"Well, if I did the right thing, I wouldn't have been involved with Harlan in the first place."

"Maybe not. I'm not judging or anything, believe me. I wouldn't exactly say he and my mom have a happy marriage."

"Still…"

"Yeah."

"You know, I'm the last person to tell you how to think, especially about your father, but however wrong some of the things he did were, he did them to protect you. They were stupid things, sure. But he had good intentions."

"Yeah. He just doesn't know how to translate his intentions into actual support."

"Do you talk to him? I don't think it's lost on anyone that a lot of hurt could've been avoided if you, maybe, talked to him once in a while."

"Would you trust Harlan with all of your secrets?"

"I really wouldn't. But he's not my family."

"You have the benefit of being raised in a normal family. You might have a different experience than me."

"I don't think there is such a thing as a normal family. I think that's an unattainable myth. Like success. Or happiness. It's not this constant state of being. There are good days. And bad days. And we surround ourselves with people we think might celebrate the good, and make the bad better."

"Yeah, I think my grandma had that crocheted on a pillow."

Eli chuckled. There was something softer about her. Lighter. Maybe breaking up with Harlan was an improvement. Maybe she was really dealing with Danny's death.

"Did you think my father had something to do with Bridget's death?" Percy asked.

"Did you? Is that why the tape?"

"I honestly didn't know. I didn't find out until later about Jake, but, I can believe Harlan would lie and cheat and whatever to protect me. I couldn't believe he would kill for me."

"I couldn't believe that he wasn't capable of it. And I think that's why I ended it."

"You ended it?"

"Well, he wasn't exactly clamoring to stay together once I accused him of murder. But yeah, it was my choice. I love your father. I do. But I don't like me when I'm with him. It'd be easy just to blame him for bringing out the worst in me, to think that my bad decisions are all his fault. But I know it's me. And I don't want to be that person anymore."

"Yeah, I'm not super looking forward to being me right now either. After all the shit I went through this past year, I get to do it all over again. Senior year take two. At least I can't imagine it being any worse."

"It'll be fine. That's the thing about high school. When you're in it, you can't see how fleeting the whole thing is. I'm not saying it's not important or that you haven't gone through some shit, but it's like… it's like, you're fireflies. And you're trapped in a jar for just a little while. And you're flying, shining brightly, until you're finally free. Some people never get out of that jar. And some people forget all about it once they fly over to the trees and… I don't know. It's not a perfect analogy."

"Yeah, but I get your point."

"It's a shame we won't be working together anymore. I think we might've actually been able to be friends under radically different circumstances."

"Maybe our paths will cross again somewhere. It's a small world, you know."

"I have no doubt."

Eli leaned in for an embrace and Percy genuinely returned the sentiment.

"Did you actually need help with anything or was it just part of your ruse to get me in here?"

Eli pushed him away, laughing.

"All right, mister, you can take the rest of the stuff on the wall down."

"I think I can manage that."

* * * * *

Percy walked into the kitchen. His mom was going over homework with Simon at the kitchen table. Something about fractions. He tried to remember either parent giving him that attention when he was a kid, but they were always busy. Or is that too easy of an answer. He never needed help. He could do it on his own.

Percy started to pour himself a bowl of cereal.

"Dinner will be ready in about twenty minutes," Donna said, barely looking up from the table.

"I'm hungry now. And I'm sure I can eat both. I'm a growing boy, you know."

As he slurped his cereal he looked over. Donna was playful, but focused. Simon actually seemed to be both learning and enjoying himself. It was a weird sociological observation, as if Donna was cast as your typical Midwest housewife—prepping dinner, helping with homework—and Percy wasn't sure what to make of it. It all was a bit off.

The garage door sounded, and within a few moments, Harlan stepped inside and dropped his briefcase on the table. He gave Donna a kiss on the cheek. There was small talk—something smells great, that sort of thing—but Percy just sat there, watching it all. His father gave him a nod, asked him about his day. Percy shrugged.

There was no hint of blackmail or affairs. If Donna knew Harlan had cheated on her, she wasn't letting on. There was no dark, unsolved murder hanging in the air, no deep wounds Percy couldn't remember getting.

Maybe he wasn't the only one getting a do-over here.

* * * * *

He had been waiting for an hour, but he was early. She said to meet him at two, but he couldn't sit around anymore. It was cold out for March, so the park was mostly empty, and Percy sat on the bench she told him to. It had been so long. And her voice sounded different. But he didn't question it. He just got ready and went.

Finally, he saw Abby's car pull into the spot next to his. He couldn't help himself from smiling. He stood up and waved, and she waved back.

Her hair was still dark, he could tell by the dark curls peeking out from beneath her stocking hat. It was bright blue, and her puffy jacket was orange and white. Gone were the black colors she had been dressing in.

She sloshed through the puddles the rain had left the night before and made her way over to him.

"Hi," he said. "I'm glad you called."

"I missed you."

"Yeah, me too."

"Can we take a walk?"

"Of course."

The path was wet, and matted leaves were on the ground. They had just started growing back for spring when the rain hit. They trudged along as Abby apologized for taking so long to talk to him. He played it off like it was no big deal, but it was nice to hear.

"I don't want you to be afraid," Percy said. "You don't have to worry about Jake, he's not going to hurt you. I promise."

"I know," she said. "And I'm not afraid, because you're right. He's not going to hurt me. Or anyone else. He's not coming back."

"You sound so sure."

"I am sure."

"How can…" even as he asked it, he knew the answer.

"Jake is dead."

Percy sat with it for a moment, and then instinctively looked around to see if anyone else was in ear shot.

"Did you…"

"Not on purpose. He got free and chased me and we fought and …it was an accident. That's the short version. Longer version can wait. But when Lake Granby melts, he'll be popping up again I'm sure."

"Lake Granby?"

"Yeah, seems that when Jake ditched me he went to your cabin. You must've told him about it at some point. I hope he didn't leave it a mess," she chuckled. "Please act surprised when your father finds out."

"Abby, are you okay?"

"I'm fine. Really. This has been a lot."

"I can imagine."

"I don't think you can. But appreciate the thought."

"Why didn't you tell the police the truth?"

"I don't know, I was in the middle of so many other crimes I wasn't sure I could get out of it without charges coming to me. And I just needed the whole thing to be done. I think I washed away any presence of myself there. But I guess we'll see."

"He's really gone?"

"Yeah. I don't think anyone could hold their breath in freezing water that long."

"Did you tell anyone else?"

"I told Kira. We had a long talk. I don't think we'll ever be friends, not really, but I still didn't want her looking over her shoulder all the time. She has a lot to process."

"As do you."

"Believe me, I know. I couldn't even bring myself to tell my therapist."

"Why are you telling me?"

"Because I trust you."

"Thank you. You too."

"Look, I know we went through a lot these past few months and that kind of intensity might, you know, imply a certain connection or whatever, and if you want to just wipe the slate clean, I totally understand. We can be two kids whose parents work together and have this funny story for the Remember When section in the yearbook. I told you the truth because I want you to know that I'm sincere and you don't have to worry about me. I'm fine. I'm going to be fine. And if you want to hit reset on everything and go back to being *the* Percy Van Allen I totally understand and I won't try and talk you out of it. You deserve that. And I know I had my doubts and I didn't always believe in you and you deserve someone that will believe in you and I'm sorry I couldn't be that when you needed it, but I have my reasons. Obviously, trust is a big thing for me and I'm really not good at it which is why I want you to know that I do trust you. And I'm sorry I waited so long to talk to you but I wasn't ready and I thought if we could just stay in this limbo for just another week, another day, another minute, I could believe that you're still here and we still have this connection or whatever but I want you to know that you are free. You are not responsible for me or my safety or anything. I…"

"Abby," he said, trying to at least pause her rambling.

"Yeah?"

"Do you want to go out sometime? Like on a real date?"

"Yeah, I think I'd like that."

"I think I'd like that too."

* * * * *

He doesn't know why he suggested it. It was probably a little maudlin if he thought too hard about it, but he wanted to go back. Finally.

Elysian Park had opened again in the Spring. At first, just for the rides. The entire pool area was being remodeled. Probably to change the entire narrative around it. There was fencing surrounding it, but Percy peered in between the posts and saw the bathhouse was mostly intact. Just surrounded by scaffolding and covered in a fresh paint job. Abby rubbed his back. He wanted to say something but didn't find the words so he just pulled her along.

They had gone through the Minotaur Maze, laughing at how silly it all seemed. It was made for kids and a couple parents shot them dirty looks as they maneuvered through, giggling at the ridiculousness of it.

In Artemis' Aero Cars, they pulled the bar down and waited for the cars to spin as the started along the track. It wasn't one of the better rides, but the line was short. As the car spun they would fall into each other and Abby let out a guttural laugh that just warmed Percy. She had still been putting up a tough front, peppering every conversation with sarcasm, which admittedly he was mostly charmed by. But it was nice to get her out of her own way. To see her being a kid and not someone with the weight of the world on her.

It was the last time they would share at the park, even as they spent the entire summer together. There was just always something better to do, sure. But Percy also wanted to keep this memory for what it was: bliss. Pure, unadulterated bliss. They laughed and held hands as they bounced from ride to ride. He kissed her on the Ferris Wheel. It wasn't their first kiss. Wouldn't be their last. But it was the sweetest kiss Percy had ever had.

And for a moment there was no murder. No lying to the police. No scars of knife wounds that wouldn't go away. No redoing school years. No parents having affairs. No investigations and blackmail. No drugs and lies.

It was the perfect moment.

And the rest of it just didn't matter anymore.

ACKNOWLEDGEMENTS

Thank you first and foremost to my parents who never told me I couldn't do something even as I consistently leapt before looking. Thanks to the rest of my friends and family who have tolerated my inability to keep my thoughts to myself, even and especially the sarcastic ones.

Thanks to all who read the book in various forms before it was finished, especially Rachel and Sarah, who read chapter by chapter as it was produced and let me quiz them without telling them what my questions event meant. Also, Jen, Barndi, Natalie, my father, and anyone else I may have forgotten.

Thanks to the rest of my support system – Kecia, Bill, Michael, Erin, Jeff, David, Jill, Jason, Jean, Lydia, Ron (who gave me the best compliment of my life), Jared, Alexandra, Karen, other David, Josh, Tom, and so many others that I don't have the space for.

Thanks to Cindy for her design expertise and making an amazing cover that is so much better than what I had scribbled in sharpie as a first idea.

Thanks to my doctor for getting me medicated (and the medication itself!) which has made finishing projects an actual attainable goal.

And thanks to every teacher I've ever had. Some of you were great, some sucked, but it's a shitty job that you never got paid fairly for and you did it anyway. Respect.

Jonathan grew up in Nebraska (it's one of the ones in the middle), Omaha specifically. He graduated from the University of Nebraska at Omaha, which was a closer walk to his childhood home than his grade school.

He has spent the second half of his life in California, working as a producer on experiences for video game, TV, and movie brands. He is an award-winning marketer but has also won multiple writing accolades for his unproduced TV pilots and screenplays.

Jonathan currently co-hosts the **Legacy Cinema Club** and **Friday Afternoon Crime** podcasts. He spends his free time reading, writing, working on his house, and supporting his dog, Ripley.

www.ingramcontent.com/pod-product-compliance
Lightning Source LLC
Chambersburg PA
CBHW060606310726
48982CB00008B/1259/J
9798994742709